# THE SPIRIT KING

## A Destiny Awakens

### (Book I)

By

PAUL BRADLEY STERMAN

# A Brief Introduction

Dear reader, welcome to my brain – and into this world of spectacular adventure filled with magic, destiny, and dare I say, reality. I want to begin by sharing a little bit about myself as the author and why I decided to write this book.

I dream every night in great detail. I sometimes wake up unsure if sections of a particular vision actually happened or if alas, it was all just part of the night's dream. My dreams often take on a deeper meaning socially, environmentally, and spiritually. I have often felt in sincerity that I live two separate lives – one in reality and one in my dreams. This story takes the reader on an adventure in both the "real world" and the "dream world." *How much of our reality is only fantasy, and how much fantasy can become reality?*

When I was sixteen I had a near death experience, which may account for my wild imagination and excessive dreaming. In addition, my eyes were opened to new perceptions about life and what lies beyond, inspiring a quest for answers to philosophical and spiritual questions about destiny – some of which I have discovered in my dreams.

**Thane** (our main character), assumes an Arthurian, alter ego dream character named **Sarghon**. Like Superman and Clark Kent, their worlds collide, intersecting and influencing each other throughout their journeys of discovery.

During my life, I have had many theoretical conversations with friends who helped inspire several themes of this book, asking the questions: "What's in store for the evolution of humankind?" and "What is our true purpose here on Earth?" I believe we each take part in shaping our destiny, and like Thane and Sarghon – *our dreams inspire reality and reality inspires our dreams.*

My hope is to encourage people to think outside the box beyond individual lives, toward a more consciously evolved, environmentally friendly vision of the world and its future. ENJOY and DREAM!!

**Acknowledgements:**
Thank you to my mother, father and sister for your loyal and
continued support – to Erik, Carla, Cheryll, and David for your
enlightening conversation and inspiration – to Dark for your artistry
and talent – to Bryan for your loving support – and to Angel for your
inspired mind, your guidance, and openness to all possibilities. Thank
you as well to the Westside YMCA and to Greenpeace for continuing
to enlighten and teach people to love and respect the Earth.

**Disclaimer:**
Although this book is fictitious, there are references to real people
whose names have been changed for the purpose of this story and to
protect identity. In addition, the story represents real organizations
such as: The YMCA and Greenpeace.
Exact historical accounts attempt to be as accurate as possible with
respect to history, however some creative license has been applied for
the purpose of this story.

*"... Humans in the developed world have become tragically
disconnected from nature, which has been desacralized in both
thought and deed. Healing this rift is possible only through
a profound shift in our collective consciousness." –*
**John Halstead**

# Table of Contents

# Chapter I

## THE HALCYON

*What's happening? Where am I? It's beautiful... so beautiful.*

Staring up into the surreal distance, the watery atmosphere felt calm and silent. His body drifted deep underwater – weightless, content, and still.

*I can't move but I can breathe*, he thought. *Why can I breathe?*

Thane lay suspended in a serene trance, looking directly ahead with unblinking eyes as streaks of bright light gleamed down, penetrating him like celestial sunbeams rippling through the slow moving current. Like a giant hand with hundreds of fingers reaching down from far beyond, the light spread out like a magnificent, glistening mirror ball, cast down only at him.

*So amazing, so beautiful*, his thoughts repeated in his head like a soothing lullaby.

Suddenly the light changed and he realized he was no longer under water, but lying on a mound of mossy clover, pillowing and cupping his body as if floating on a cloud. The rays of sun became misty beams of light, cast down at him through the shadowing trees above.

He stood up and looked around. *This is a curious place*, he thought.

The vibrant, purple sky reached across the landscape toward the brilliant red-orange sun rising above the Scyllian Stone Mountains in the distance. Otherworldly birdcalls resonated, as an ethereal breeze blew pleasantly through the trees, reverberating and echoing in every direction.

Thane was dressed in a velvet green doublet over a creamy white shirt, fastened at the waist with a heavy brown leather belt. On his hip lay a hand-carved dagger sheathed in its hilt, the handle of the dagger carved in the shape of a rising phoenix. His dark pants fit loosely, his brown leather laced boots looked and felt careworn.

The surroundings felt familiar to Thane and yet foreign at the same time.

A voice came from behind.

"What do you hear, young master?"

Thane whipped his head around to see an old man with a scraggly beard, dressed in a cloak, leaning on a tree and smoking an S-shape pipe that resembled a vine branch. He exuded a fatherly, calm nature, and instantly Thane sensed that the man was a friend and teacher.

"You startled me," Thane said. "Where are we? I don't recognize this part of the forest. The sounds here are curious. Where have you taken me on this day's journey, old friend?"

The old man, who went by the name Ambroas, puffed on his pipe, keeping one eye on the boy as he tilted his head down to exhale. With a lift of an eyebrow, he answered, "Follow me. This day you will learn what it means to listen for the first time. Life, you will find, is an extraordinary thing, young Sarghon, and it is time you found out just how extraordinary indeed."

*What did he call me?* Thane thought. *Sarghon? That's an odd name; but it sounds familiar. Yes, that's what I'm called here. That's my name in this land.*

He followed Ambroas on a path through the woods across a vast meadow filled with red, orange, and fuchsia colored flowers. They arrived to find a small circle of enormous, redwood-like trees, five of which stood in a nearly perfect circle, twenty-five feet in diameter. The trees were spaced equidistant from each other, where a pentagram could be constructed in precise measurements, if desired.

"This is *The Halcyon,* a most sacred place in this land," Ambroas said intently. "Here, you will be transformed by the pure essence of the Earth and venture into the knowledge of your destiny. All in a days work! All in a days work."

Sarghon decided to play along with his teacher's little game. He recalled previous lessons with Ambroas in mathematics, star casting, map tracing and sword fighting. Sarghon also remembered naming the fish in the seas, learning the cloud patterns, and studying the natural chemicals that could be used to create smoke and blue fire.

Today, however, he didn't remember how he came to be in this part of the forest or why he was even there at all. For Sarghon, this was quite a peculiar feeling altogether. Somehow, he knew that on this day his life was going to change in a fundamental way. He could feel it in his bones, and he didn't dare ignore his intuition or fight it.

Ambroas led Sarghon to the center of the tree circle. Gesturing with his hands, he looked upward at the great tunnel created by monolithic trunks of wood and branches leading directly to the heavens. The sun, now high and bright in the sky, had turned a radiant, deep orangey-yellow.

As he stood staring up at the tops of the five giant trees, Sarghon sensed the energy that naturally focused in this sacred spot. His hair stood up on his neck and his ears rang in a high-pitched hum.

"I want you now to listen," Ambroas said in a stern tone.

"I am listening," he replied.

"No!" Ambroas snapped, putting down his pipe, as he sat down in the center of the circle. "Not with your ears, silly pup, with your spirit. Now, do as I say! Sit in the center of the circle here and place your hands upon the ground, like so."

He did as Ambroas instructed.

"The Earth is alive you know, and not just the plants and animals; I'm talking about the Earth herself. Her energy surrounds us and protects us. She continually surges with life, breathing in and out with the ocean tides, as her essence flows through rivers and streams. *She* pulses with vitality and vibrates with energy through each stone, plant, tree and crystal. Do you understand me, boy? NOW is the time of insight for what you were meant to know."

Ambroas adopted an even more sober tone. "Behold, for life is gained through sight and insight of all things, if the eyes of the soul are open. LISTEN to our Earth. She has much to share with you, lad."

*This must be a test,* Sarghon thought. *What does the old man have up his magical sleeve now?*

Sitting cross-legged facing Sarghon, Ambroas calmly placed his hands flat on the ground face down on either side of his knees. Closing his eyes, he took a deep, slow breath. "What do you hear?" Ambroas asked.

With his eyes closed, Sarghon listened to his surroundings. The sounds were foreign to him, but he tried to answer correctly. "I hear a whistling in the trees and a hum … almost like moaning."

"Good," Ambroas replied. "You are beginning to sense the *Aurora*. I want you to concentrate now. You will feel strange and marvelous."

8

With his hands still flat on the ground, Ambroas slowly whispered ancient words: *Eararath naal shara, comarath naal tara.* Instantly his hands began to glow with a soft, golden light. The radiating energy expanded out from Ambroas's hands to the edge of the trees, glowing brighter and brighter with each passing second. Sarghon felt the light-energy penetrate his skin, moving up his body, filling him with healing energy. The powerful feeling was intoxicating!

A wind of change blew through him like a zephyr of understanding, and with it came a flurry of knowledge and insight of all the nature surrounding him – as if awakening to a new acuteness of reality.

Sarghon took a deep breath, his mind swirling in a seemingly endless pool of consideration. A word came to him like a sharp slap in the face. "Life!" he shouted, "I hear the life in the air, and in the ground, and all around me! I feel the essence of every blade of grass. I can see …"

He opened his eyes. The light-energy had traveled from the ground in the center of the Halcyon into the base of the five ancient trees, reaching higher and higher up the tree trunks toward the branches. The bark illuminated brightly from within, flowing with pure energy and pulsing with colors of gold and flecks of bright green.

Transfixed by the sight, Sarghon felt elated by the wondrous feeling rushing through him. He actually felt as though his body were part of the energy he was now experiencing.

"Why don't you take a closer look at the trees?" Ambroas suggested, sitting in a composed manner with his eyes still closed and his hands still flat on the ground.

With his newfound understanding of the Earth and all the spectacular energy it possessed, Sarghon walked up to one of the trees and touched the shimmering bark. It pulsed and writhed with vibrant, green light energy, organically flowing in tiny streams, like blood flowing through veins and capillaries. The trees appeared intrinsically alive to Sarghon, as if for the first time he took off blinders he had been wearing his entire life.

"I can feel them!" he said, looking around at the grass, flowers, bushes, and trees. "How did you do that?" Sarghon asked in astonishment.

"I did not do anything, except speak to them," Ambroas stated plainly. "It seems, they too, want to speak to you. You have been granted the *Eratheen Senses*, offered only by the Earth to those considered worthy."

Sarghon placed his hand on the tree. "Eratheen Senses? You mean they can hear me? Understand me?"

"Oh, they can do more than that," Ambroas said, with a chuckle. "Ask one a question."

Somehow, this didn't seem in the least bit strange anymore. It was as if a veil had been lifted and a higher understanding enveloped his mind.

"OK, well …" Sarghon placed his hand back on the tree, "what is your feeling about humans and deforestation?"

There was no reply. Ambroas smugly glanced away with half-opened eyelids.

"Ha, hmm, yes. Well, if they understood our language then any idiot could just walk up and talk to them, don't you think?" snickered Ambroas. "You must speak in the Eratheen language, my obtuse young man. You know it as instinctively as I. You too were born with the knowledge of the sacred languages, and now that they have been awakened, you will be able to speak with them. CONCENTRATE, now!"

Sarghon shook his head trying to focus his astonished, adolescent mind. Squinting, Sarghon peered into the green, flowing light within the bark. With an open mind he concentrated on verbiage he had never before spoken. Placing his hand on the bark, he made a slow sound from the vibrations moving across his lips, cautiously speaking the words, *"Aray laraba shonashta sethonashae?"*

Nothing happened.

With more intent, still unsure of what he was doing, he raised his voice, *"Aray Laraba sho…"*

*"Gorath newtoaath! Saraesheetath kulocoth!"* the tree spoke violently, with a deep, unnerving sound that reverberated on the ground all around them.

Sarghon felt the sound vibrate from the core of the trunk. The words were not spoken aloud, but inherently understood for Sarghon alone.

*Did I just say something that made sense?* Sarghon thought. *And did he … It, just reply an answer back to me?* Yes, indeed that is exactly what happened, he realized.

"What did the tree say to you?" Ambroas asked?

"It said: *He must be stopped! Death to us is his plan.* I think it was referring to my inquiry about humans, but who is *He* and what is *His* plan?"

Ambroas reached for his S-shaped pipe from under his cloaked pocket, placing it in his mouth, before waving his hand over the bowl of herb. A puff of smoldering smoke appeared in the chamber. He took a deep inhale from the pipe, blowing out a reddish-orange swirl of smoke, "I believe I know exactly who *He* is," Ambroas said, "and soon you will as well. But, all in good time. You have done well today, young master. When the Earth made itself known to me here at The Halcyon many moons ago, it took me over an hour to speak my first Eratheen word. You're a natural, as I had imagined. My waking dreams foresaw this day, and so too, may have others. Not everyone is convinced of your foretold future, or that you even exist. There are enemies lurking in the shadows. Come, walk with me."

Sarghon picked up a stick from the ground as they walked around the perimeter of the circle of trees. Taking another long drag of smoke from his pipe, Ambroas's expression changed. His face became austere and sober again.

"Now listen to me," he said in a solemn tone. "You have a destiny, young man. You were chosen for this before you were born. You will learn the ways of the elements. You have the power within you to control them, you know. They will help you on your quest – a journey I do not envy."

He began drifting into nostalgia. "Ahh, the perilous mission that awaits you is fraught with excitement and adventure, though. The things you will see and the experiences will be breathtaking, indeed. I do wish I were younger – but alas, it is not my destiny."

Sarghon stopped walking, dropping the stick he was examining. "All right, what is all this talk about a quest and *my* destiny? What is this? Was I chosen for something I don't know about? Explain yourself! What have you been hiding from me, old man?"

The visible energy emanating from within the trees dissipated, reverting to their normal state, and the surrounding plants and grasses ceased their glow.

Ambroas sighed, his expression changing to one of compassion as he looked into Sarghon's eager blue-green eyes. He placed a long knuckled hand on his shoulder and said, "My boy, today was the first step on a long and winding path. You are special and you know that. You have always known, have you not? There are secrets in life that do not always make sense. We usually tend to find them out in times of difficulty or tragedy."

Taking another puff of smoke from his pipe, Ambroas continued. "The world that you know is changing, my boy. There are those who wish to change us, as well as destroy our land, twisting the future toward a dark purpose. If we do nothing, we will all be made to suffer. Our world is fraught with much greed and corruption and you, my young friend, are the key to saving it!"

Sarghon listened intently, his mouth slowly widening open, as Ambroas went on. "You were born with a very special and rare gift. You have within you the power to save this world, and retrieve all its goodness and riches from the darkness I speak of."

Sarghon didn't want to believe what he was hearing, wondering how he could be a savior of any kind.

"In everything you see and cannot see, there are opposites," Ambroas said. "Within universal law there are two sides, and one cannot exist without the other. You cannot have up without down, black without white, left without right, etcetera. And, as strange as it may sound, you cannot have good without evil. There is a balance to everything. When Malock, our new king was drawn toward the darkness, an opposite force of light was created. And now, the balance must be restored. Your coming was foretold ages ago."

Staring at the Earth, Sarghon tried to absorb the information into his overburdened head as Ambroas puffed away on his pipe.

"You are now old enough to hear the truth about your life, young master," Ambroas continued. "I am the elder wizard who was chosen as your teacher and guide for this very special mission. King Malock has fallen into corruption and greed. He consumes our land and its natural resources for his own malicious purpose. This was also prophesized long ago. Sit for a moment."

Sarghon did as he was asked, his mind swirling, as Ambroas stretched his arms out leaning back on a rock. "You were born at the third hour, on the third day, of the third month, at the dawn of the third millennium, under a full purple moon, I might add. These unique aspects are feared, or revered by those who can interpret them. They intuit a new beginning or … an end to everything."

Sarghon knew he felt different from all of his friends, but he had no idea just how different. The words Ambroas spoke were shocking to hear, but somehow, on this day of all others, it made perfect sense. The Earth had revealed itself to him and he felt the *Aurora* for the first time.

The trees spoke to him in a language he never knew existed, and yet, he could understand every word.

His life had certainly changed this day, never to be the same again. He didn't want to believe what Ambroas was saying, yet he knew intrinsically that the words he spoke were absolute truth. Sarghon was fast becoming a man, but not how he had ever imagined or intended.

"Does that mean when the balance I am meant to restore has been set straight, and darkness is turned to light, that a new force of evil will then challenge me?"

"A wise suggestion," Ambroas answered, "but it never works out so evenly. Good may prevail for many years to come. Or you may fail, and we will all succumb to Malock's tyranny until another comes along to challenge the unbalance. In any case, both forces will always exist, as I have explained. Do you understand your purpose now?"

Sarghon followed Ambroas across a vast meadow of purple flowers, back to the path they took through the forest. Sarghon now viewed his surroundings in an entirely different light. The air smelled as if it were grown from the plants – fresh, new, and sweet. The grass sparkled with glimmers of life he had never observed before – and the trees! The trees were alive in a way he could only have imagined in a dream.

As he walked by, their branches bowed and beckoned him in waves of gratitude. He wondered if they knew his purpose and could read his mind, guiding him with safe passage. The leaves sang in the enchanting breeze, with a whispering, rhythmic melody. He now truly knew the meaning of an *enchanted* forest.

"Tell me more about this *Aurora*," Sarghon asked, "this incredible connection I feel to all the life around me."

"Ahh, incredible indeed," Ambroas said, with a twisted grin. "When someone is open and unfettered enough to feel, as you are, a conduit exists that connects emotionally and vitally from your inner core to the energy that surrounds us. Scientific, invisible, and metaphysical it may be, the energy of nature is indeed quite strong. We call this connection between us and the Earth, the *Aurora*. It's quite magnificent. It can come in many forms, but usually invokes emotion and passion. Some quixotic idealists even compare it to the true feelings of love, but you will feel it for yourself when the time arises."

Already having tasted the sweet, infectious feeling, Sarghon was completely intrigued. Along their path he became keenly aware of insects and woodland creatures that he had never taken notice of before. He instantaneously knew the name and species of each, as his mind raced with this newly acquired knowledge.

"Try it out then," Ambroas suggested, with a flamboyant gesture of his bony hand. "Tell me what you perceive within the nature all around you."

Sarghon glanced at everything in sight: "Dragon Beetle, Blue Harumpa Moth, Diaphones Wood Crickets, Striped Sapphire Caterpillars," he said out loud, as they walked by, "and, a Black Tail Winged Squirrel! I never knew what that thing was called before today. Marvelous!"

The names just leapt into his consciousness the moment he observed anything moving. Even the grasses and ground shrubs came into complete understanding as soon as his eyes gazed upon them: Loof Moss; growing in bubbling, pale green mounds – Bayaba Berry Brush; the red tipped, thorny canker sore of the forest – Mura Flowers; large, opalescent bouquets of floral magnificence veining up the trees in delicate sweeping vines. And Oedin Budding Root, a pale blue root that slithered like a snake in every direction with orange buds on protruding branches that never open.

It was an encyclopedia of earthen knowledge laid out before him like a blank canvas, slowly being covered with every color of the rainbow. The instant he observed a new life form he knew its name, recognized the medicinal or poisonous properties of each, and understood which plants could be combined to make tinctures for sleep, killing pain, soothing a wound, or even instant death.

Sarghon's eyes were wide with fascination, as he absorbed the cornucopia of knowledge. *What a miraculous gift this was!* he thought.

Ambroas stopped in his tracks, gesturing sharply to Sarghon. "Do not move," Ambroas said, in a tense whisper. "Someone, or something is observing us. Can you sense it?"

Sarghon reached out with his mind and body, testing his new senses, and indeed, he could feel someone or something peculiar beholding them.

Both gingerly turned around. From behind a large loof moss covered stump, waddled a very short, stout creature of a man. Certainly not human, he was dressed in what Sarghon would have pictured a leprechaun might wear: large black leather boots (for his small size), a reddish-brown jacket with large, gnarled wood-carved buttons, an organically wrapped leather belt that continued over his shoulder, down his back, and then around his waist again, and a heavy cloth knit cap that trailed behind his head almost to the ground.

He possessed lopsided ears: asymmetrical globular tips sticking out from under his cap, pointing up toward the orange sky. His strikingly bright green eyes were very large for his head – poignant, yet wise. His nose and mouth spread widely across his spongy, wrinkled face.

He carried with him a large, gnarled burl-wood walking stick that reached above his head. *"Gooood day Divine Spirits,"* he said.

Ambroas looked as if he was staring at a ghost. Bowing to the creature with dignity, he said, "Good tidings to you as well, Divine Spirit. We are indeed fortunate for your generous audience. I am Ambroas and this is …"

*"Sarghon, yeees, I know,"* the little creature-man interrupted, dismissively.

"Of course you do, your eminence. Forgive my imprudence," Ambroas respectfully replied. "I have never actually met a *Tarpin* before. You have caught us off-guard. How may we be of service to you?"

*"Yooos can not,"* he answered, *"oweever, heee* (gesturing his walking stick toward Sarghon) *maybee can."*

His accent was obscure and strange to Sarghon. Never before had he imagined such an odd, little creature as this Tarpin. Ambroas spoke to him with more respect than Sarghon had ever seen him do with anyone in the past.

*Something must be very powerful or important about the creature to grant such behavior from Ambroas*, Sarghon thought.

He decided to speak to it. "Mr. Tarpin sir, what can *I* do?"

*"Zzeee Earth has giveen meee a geeft for yous. Weee welcomes yous,"* he said, in his strange dialect.

The Tarpin placed his walking stick directly in front of Sarghon's feet. He then pounded it once against the ground sharply, before stepping away. The staff stood on its own, as the ground began to rumble from beneath.

Piercing up from the Earth, sinuous, intertwining vines began rapidly growing along the staff, bursting with leaves and small-multicolored flowers. The vines grew up to engulf the entire staff, until there was no wood left showing. The top abruptly bloomed into a spectacular, radiant white flower.

In the center of the flower sat a perfect diamond-like crystal, the size of a man's eyeball. It sparkled with brilliant, multifaceted chromatic life. This was magic at its finest! Sarghon wondered if this exceptional gift was being procured in his honor.

*"Take eet,"* said the Tarpin. *"The Eratheen Creestal possssess great power. Her eenergy can be harnesssed and focussed with eet. Place eet in thee hilt of yous sword. Focus yous mind cleeerly in time of neeed, and yous be giveen zee geefts of zee Earth.*

*"Beeware, yous must bee. Shee is most precareeious, shee is. Power beyond yous, shee has. Use wiselee! Produce nature, can create mountains, shee can; or eeasily crumble them beneeath yous feet."*

Ambroas appreciated that this magic could only be created with the influence of a Tarpin, in combination with the essential powers of the Earth.

The Tarpin then held his hand out and spoke the words, *"shuatze-shawantanzee."* The vines and flowers disappeared back into the Earth, as the walking stick flew back into the Tarpin's hand.

Turning away, he waddled a few steps from the two of them, and with one last look back, he said, *"Divine Spireets bee with yous!"* And then, as fast as he appeared, he vanished into a small puff of light blue mist that swirled around for a moment, then was absorbed into the ground.

"Well now, just when I thought the day wasn't unusual enough for me," Sarghon said, holding the crystalline gem up to the light. "That was awesome! Who, and WHAT was that Tarpin fellow?"

"That, my fine, feathered friend, was an actual Tarpin," Ambroas said, still in a state of disbelief himself, "the rarest magical creature ever known! I did not believe they actually existed until just now. They are mythical beings that are said to live in the dimension between light and dark – between what is seen and what is in shadow. One has not been sighted in hundreds of years. It's considered an exceedingly fortunate omen to be visited by a Tarpin. They are solitary immortals that choose not to be seen by anyone but the earthen creatures of the forest... or so it has been foretold. And he has validated my faith in you, boy!

"Sarghon, what you hold in your hand is extraordinary, beyond belief. Do as he instructed. I will help you as much as I can, but you heard him plainly, *you* are the one he spoke to and *you* are the one granted the stone. We must find a sword suitable for its magic, and then you will learn to control its energy, as instructed. As you now are beginning to understand, dear boy, our future depends on it."

As they walked back toward the direction of home, Sarghon held the glittering stone in his hand, staring at it, wondering about all the power it possessed and how he would actually be able to manipulate material using concentrated energy of the Earth.

*This is all happening so fast*, he thought, *what wonders might I be able to compose!*

"Shall we try it out?" he shouted to Ambroas, who was twenty-five paces ahead of him. "I want to see if this thing ..."

"Not today," Ambroas replied in haste, without turning around. "We have seen enough for this day, indeed. I do not feel like rescuing you from a falling tree or a cascade of tumbling boulders, should you use the stone's powers incorrectly."

Several long moments passed as they continued their long walk home, before Sarghon stopped in his tracks. "Why me?" he asked. "Why was I the one chosen for this perilous mission, whatever it is? Why was this stone given to me and what am I meant to do, anyway? Slay a dragon? Fight a three-headed beast? Topple mountains? It must be dangerous, or a Tarpin would never have shown himself to *me*. Ambroas, please, what am I meant to do!?"

Ambroas placed his hand on Sarghon's shoulder, and said calmly, "You were chosen because you have bravery within you, my boy. Some are born with it, some learn it over time, and some have none at all. But bravery indeed, is in your blood. It's a presence of strength within you that you don't know you already have.

"But you will learn all of this in due time, son... in due time. Come, you must meditate in the Crystal Pool."

Sarghon's mind spun in a constant flurry of images and possibility as they walked along a winding, pebbled pathway in silence. The breeze sang through Sarghon's ears like an enchanting, whispering lullaby as the sky changed from deep yellow to an orange-red. Lucent clouds floated above, like powered sugar drifting through the atmosphere.

"Here we are. Ahh yes, one of my favorite places in all our glorious land," Ambroas said, with a knowing smile.

The Crystal Pool was located in a serene, picturesque setting, as if taken right from the mind of a poet or dreamer. Wildflowers bloomed along its bank in shades of purple, pink and yellow.

Ambroas led Sarghon to the edge of the water. With his hand

once again on Sarghon's shoulder, Ambroas said, "You must go in alone. Empty your mind of all peripheral thought, and try to relax. The water has magical qualities. Do not fight them, or try to hold your breath. Do you understand me?"

After the day's mystical experiences, Sarghon understood that many more things were possible in the world that he had not believed possible before.

*Another test?* he thought, taking off his clothes and entering the crystal blue water. It was warmer than he imagined it would be and it felt completely marvelous.

"Lay back and let the water guide you to the quietude within your mind," Ambroas said. "Keep your eyes closed until you feel compelled to open them."

Sarghon floated on his back with his eyes closed, breathing in and out in steady breaths. After several long moments, his body began to sink. He felt as though he were being pulled underwater, sinking further and further, imagining the surface moving away into the distance. At first he was scared, wanting to swim back to the surface for fear he would drown, but then he remembered that Ambroas told him the Crystal Pool had magical qualities. He let his body sink slowly deeper and deeper, like a decent into an abyss, allowing the water to control him and guide him.

Still holding his breath, he began to tremble. Ambroas's words came into his head, *"Do not fight them, or try to hold your breath. Do you understand me?"* He had to trust. This was the test.

Letting out all the air from his lungs, he breathed in the water. It was an odd sensation at first, and after several labored, liquid breaths, he could breathe underwater. Once he surrendered himself to the acceptance of the magic, he felt unusually calm, opening his eyes.

Celestial beams of light pierced through the water from above. Once again, they reached toward him like a giant godly hand, cradling him in the deep, silent water. What he saw and felt were stunningly beautiful and his body and mind became filled with elation. Something about it felt familiar.

Paralyzed by the mesmerizing glory of it all, he began drifting slowly toward the light, wondering if anyone else in the world had ever experienced such contentment and beauty at the same time.

This was a new feeling – a new understanding of something intensely profound and important. Like a drug, he wanted more! He wanted to hold onto this feeling as long as possible – to stay in this perfect moment, this exquisite solitude – peaceful, so perfectly peaceful.

*Is this the Aurora?* he wondered. *Is this God? Is this heaven? It's so incredibly beautiful. Can I stay in this moment forever? Am I...*

# Chapter II

## REALITY

Thane squinted, slowly opening his eyes to the brightness. His hand quickly blocked the glaring morning sunlight as it pierced through the lacy curtain. He had been dreaming.

"Wow, that was really intense," he mumbled out loud, blinking his weary eyes open and shut several times. The details had been incredible: the colors, the textures, the smells. The fantasy of it all was nearly overwhelming.

Colors? *Did I just dream in color?* he pondered. This was the first time Thane could remember such vibrant color in a dream.

*How wonderfully insane that was,* he thought, *and they were calling me Sarghon. What kind of a name is that? What the hell did I eat for dinner last night?*

Once his vision finally focused, he took in a deep breath and sat up in bed. It was 6:59am, one minute before his alarm was set to go off. Reaching for the "off" switch, the radio alarm beat him to it. The Eurhythmics, *"Sweet Dreams"* played for a moment before he turned it off with a smack from the back of his hand. "Well, that figures," he muttered.

Thane was back in his body, and the year was 1983.

He stared at the dizzying, paisley wallpaper for a long moment before cracking his neck on both sides and finally slipping out of bed. Wandering across the room stretching his arms, he took off his white tank top and boxer shorts, tossed them in the laundry hamper, and stumbled into the shower.

Thane Winstrom, currently a sophomore in high school, lived an average middle-class life in West Los Angeles, California. He was sixteen and three-quarters years old, five feet eleven and one-half inches tall with light brown hair and blue-green, charismatic eyes.

A normal, ordinary teenager, as far as most people could tell from the outside, Thane possessed one unique quality: an extremely vivid imagination. Thane excelled at sports, was creatively minded for his age, and his long eyelashes gave him a look of mysterious, quiet beauty.

He was at that specific, magical age when everything in life presented a flurry of awakenings. Philosophical thoughts of possibility, both imagined and real, washed over him like waves of discovery, constantly crashing ashore in his turbulent mind. He navigated a sea of hormones and emotions that could become chaotic without trying, and stimulated without knowing why. What a time to be frivolous, boundless, and young.

Thane entered the kitchen and made himself a bowl of *Special-K* cereal. He sat at the off-white, tiled counter, slowly crunching each bite, his bizarre dream still fresh in his mind. As he swirled his spoon in the floating flakes Thane's mother, Susan, hummed a Carpenter's song as she brewed a pot of coffee.

"Hmmm… hmmm…*We've only just begun to live…*"

Thane's sister brusquely entered the kitchen. "Mom, have you seen my *Breakfast in America* tape? I've looked all over for it," she said, agitated. "Thane, did you borrow it again?"

Lara, Thanes older sister, was being her normal, dismissive self, embodying all the self-obsessions that a girl of eighteen has to offer. A senior in high school, Lara was haughtily determined to know everything there was to know about everything. A consummate tomboy with a mullet that actually looked good, Lara was one of those girls that other girls loved to hate, and boys hated to love.

"Well, good morning to you, too," Thane replied.

She looked at Thane. "I'm just saying … usually when I can't find something, it ends up in your room."

Susan poured her children glasses of orange juice and gave them some allowance for the weekend. "Now, you guys be nice to each other. Lara, are you giving your brother a ride to school?"

Thane jumped to his feet. "No Mom," he said in a huff. "I'm going to the movies after school with Aaron. I'll take my bike today. May twenty-fifth! Don't you remember what day it is?"

"Oh yes, the new Star Track movie."

"It's Star TREK and no, mom, it's the new Star WARS movie!"

Thane brushed his teeth and collected his books for school, systematically shoving them into his already over-stuffed school backpack. The book that was last to be maneuvered into the pack was the newest – a four hundred pager on Latin for English class. Thane had begun memorizing early English and Latin root words, as well as a variety of words he never believed he would ever use in a sentence. As he memorized the anomalous words, they often swirled around in his head like a cryptic inner conversation. He possessed a keen knack for linguistics. Shakespeare actually came easily to him, when other students viewed it as a foreign language. Even so, as he headed for the front door, he rolled his eyes, wondering how he would ever learn all the Latin root words needed before the English class final.

2:30pm, one-half hour before the end of biology class, Thane was unable to keep any semblance of focus or concentration on his class subjects. His mind was still engulfed in a wondrous fog from last night's excitement.

He sat staring out the window lost in thought, watching the trees wave slowly in the wind. The muffled voices of classmates, the teacher, and chalk writing on the chalkboard played like a distant echo in the back of his mind. His teacher, Mr. McBraggen, began explaining the theory of evolution.

"According to human skulls found in Ethiopia, man is carbon dated to be close to two million years old; however the 'missing links' are still missing, and unfortunately the field of paleoanthropology has been riddled with fraudulent claims of finding the missing link between humans and primates. We *do* know, however, that all living things change, adapt, and in essence, evolve. Life on Earth is quite unique and special, Human Beings in particular. We are infinite!"

Thane popped out of his daze and began to listen.

"We all came from space dust – molecules that originated trillions of miles out in space. Each of you came from somewhere, right? Where do you think the matter in your body came from? You are each a very special combination of elements that came together in just the right recipe to create YOU. And if we take just a moment to *really* think about that, it's pretty incredible, isn't it? Our planet evolved from galactic matter that was radiated and energized by the Sun, our nearest star. And as we know, organic matter began to grow in all kinds of primordial ways, and then – whim, bam, boom! – Life on the planet began."

Sharla, Thane's boisterous best girl-pal, raised her hand while blurting out... "But how did life *actually* begin?"

"Well Sharla, the best scientific hypothesis is that life began approximately three-point-five billion years ago as the result of a complex sequence of chemical reactions that took place spontaneously in Earth's atmosphere as bacteria, and precipitated to the Earth. The bacteria probably consumed amino acids, sugars, and other organic minerals and compounds that were also forming at the time. Then something really cool happened: they changed, they mutated and *evolved*." Mr. McBraggen stressed the word in a fun, whimsical way. "And then you and Thane crawled up out of the ocean onto the land. Viola!"

He snapped his fingers, winking his eye at Sharla. "But to be honest, we'll never truly understand its complexity completely. It happened some three-point-five billion years ago. We know that the miracle of life has evolved us into the exact pattern that we are today, as modern human beings, BUT the question I want you all to ponder today is... Can we predict the NEXT stage of human evolution?"

Thane considered the question for a moment. *What will humanity become*? he wondered.

"If we've been modern human beings for hundreds of thousands of years," Mr. McBraggen continued, "maybe we're finally ready for our next phase of evolution. Our technology has evolved and grown exponentially to become an essential part of our lives and well-being. The last one hundred years alone brought us the industrial age, the modern scientific age, and the computer age – just to name a few! And in the animal world, it's pretty apparent. Creatures such as dogs, fish, and farm animals have been bred to be extremely different in shape, size, and even intellect! Think about a Chihuahua and a Great Dane. They all evolved, bred, changed shape, color, characteristics and size from a basic wolf, or dog-like wolf. Man must have evolved from a *man-like* ancestor. As you know, chimpanzees have the closest DNA to humans, but we have examples of this in Cro-Magnon and Neanderthal man. They had smaller brains, larger sculls, and looked like Mike."

The class chuckled as Mike, a stocky kid from the football team, embarrassingly sat up in his chair against the back wall of the classroom.

The last school bell of the day rang.

"Before you all go, your final will be a five-page essay about *YOUR* personal version of evolution as *you* see it. Be creative!" he stressed.

As the students exited the classroom, Thane sat in his chair looking out the window at the tree still waving gracefully in the lulling breeze. Everyone exited the room but Aaron, his best friend.

"Come on," Aaron said, "let's get outta here! We don't want to be at the end of the line!"

Thane got up, grabbed his backpack, threw it over his right shoulder and headed toward the door.

"Have a good weekend guys. Enjoy the movie," said Mr. McBraggen, knowing where these two were headed after class.

"Oh, we will!" replied Aaron, with a big smile.

"You too. Have a good weekend," Thane added, as they trotted out.

Walking along the front lawn of the school, before sliding sidesaddle down the last staircase handrail, Thane and Aaron knew the weekend was now upon them.

"Hey dude, we're actually, finally, really going to see it tonight! What has it been – like three years since *Empire*?" Aaron asked excitedly as he grabbed a bag of sunflower seeds from his backpack, opened it and cracked one into his mouth.

"Yeah, I wish they would have kept the name *Revenge of the Jedi*, though. I like how that sounds better. But, would a Jedi take revenge?"

"Who cares? I just wanna see the fracking movie! There better be a really cool light saber dual though. *The circle is now complete, when I left you, I was but the learner, now I am the master.*"

"*Only the master of evil, Darth.*"

Both Thane and Aaron knew most of the dialogue from the previous *Star Wars* films. They made light saber sounds, as they pretended to have a light saber dual portraying Obi Wan Kenobi and Darth Vader, before running down to where their bicycles were chained. Unlocking the bikes, they hopped on for the fifteen-block ride home. Both knew they were *Star Wars* geeks, and although they were getting older, there remained a universal mystique about these films that captured the young Jedi in everyone, young and old.

Just as Thane was about to step down on his bike pedal, a hummingbird flew directly in front of him, hovering in the air two feet from his face. Fascinated by the vibrating sound of the wings flapping at over one hundred and fifty times per second, he studied its little, black, steady eyes, completely stationary curved beak, and iridescent glints of green, red, and purple light reflecting off its body.

Thane tilted his head to the right without knowing it. Time appeared to move in slow motion as he noticed a faint glowing aura around the bird that seemed to pulsate in slow, constant measures of energy.

Completely mesmerized by the curious beauty of it all, Thane felt an identifiable connection between him and the small hovering bird. In that same surreal moment, he recalled the intense feeling of peace and serenity from his dream the night before.

After what seemed to be an infinite eight seconds, the hummingbird flew away, up and out of sight. "Did you see that? He was just sitting there, floating inches from my face and I was like …"

Thane tried to explain, but it sounded too weird. "It was just … amazing! And he kind of … glowed." Thane changed the subject, "Hey Aaron, have you ever heard of a Tarpin before? Does that ring any bells?"

"A Tarpin what? Where did you hear that?"

"In my dream last night," Thane answered, with a crooked expression. "It was this little creature-guy who gave me a magic crystal and told me to save the world, or something. It was really wild, totally voofed up, man!"

Aaron knew exactly what *voofed up* meant. He chuckled to himself before answering frankly, "Well, if you have any more, let me know, and I'll call a psychiatrist for you."

"If I have many more like the one last night, you just may have to!"

They rode home to drop off their backpacks and grab their jackets for the night.


Aaron and Thane both ran to get in line. *Return of the Jedi* opened the week before, and the lines had been too long to attempt. They tried not to listen to all the gossip chatter in school about the characters and what other students and friends had to say about the story. Both had caught mumbled conversations with mixed feelings about new characters called *Ewoks*, and a cool battle at the end with Luke and Vader. They had been successful in covering their ears and starting other conversations in order *not* to find out what happened to their favorite characters *ever* in a movie.

"Shit man, this line is totally constrafiafed!" Aaron stated in agitation.

"This movie better voof the spoofin off the roofin," Thane replied excitedly.

The two of them had grown up together since early childhood, creating a kind of lingo of their own over the years. Most people thought they were from another country or galaxy, or just fell off their skateboards a bit too often, but Thane and Aaron understood the odd words when others couldn't. It was a kind of childhood secret code to them that lasted into their teen years.

"Well, I can't wait to see how they bring it all together. *Empire Strikes Back* is a hard act to follow," said Aaron.

During the movie, *The Force* once again intrigued Thane. Luke Skywalker had been born with these special abilities that just needed honing – a hidden power within him that could be trained and mastered.

Thane pondered certain questions: *Why was he born with these powers? Was he chosen?* The film never really answered that question, but it made him think about humans and their fascination with telepathic ability and psychic phenomenon, and how a human may evolve to possess such abilities. While the epic movie played, he thought about Sarghon's destiny from his dream, wondering, like every other person in the theatre, what it would be like to wield such powers? He was suddenly reminded of the upcoming biology final.

"Oh my God!" Thane shouted in a whisper.

"What is it?" Aaron asked.

"I just figured out what my *"Concept of evolution"* biology final will be about."

"Star Wars?"

"Tell ya later," he said with a smile.


On the walk home, Thane and Aaron discussed every detail of the movie. They still couldn't figure out why the *Ewoks* were part of the film. They thought it may have been all about merchandising toward kids, but both still liked the third installment of the *Star Wars* trilogy, in any case.

"Hey," Aaron exclaimed. "Ewok is the reverse of Wookiee!"

"Ahh, you're right. You may have something there," Thane replied.

"What do you think Lyeana would look like in Princess Leia's slave girl outfit from Jabba's Palace? I bet she could fill out that costume with the boobs she has!"

Thane thought for a moment about Lyeana, his crush from volleyball class, dressed in the slave costume from the movie. "Damn straight! She'd look amazing in Leia's costume," he replied with a raised brow. "And I can be Han Solo!"

Aaron was one of the few friends that he had confided in about his feelings for Lyeana. Her popularity and natural beauty caught many an eye at school. Thane daydreamed about going out with her – having Lyeana for a girlfriend would boost his popularity and confidence by a thousand-fold but knew that it was only a pipe dream.

In the past, he had been told by girls that his long eyelashes and blue-green eyes were the nicest in the school, but at sixteen, Thane still didn't know how to use them very well to flirt. He wasn't the book linguist in front of girls as he was in his own head. As it stood, he was a quiet kid with a vast imagination, and only spoke out when he felt passionate about something.

Thane couldn't help thinking about how the evolution of humanity may be destined to follow similarly in the footsteps of *The Force*. He considered how people might evolve to the point of levitating objects and influencing others with a thought, alone.

"Hey, you could just wave your hand in front of Lyeana and say... *You will now go out with me*," Aaron suggested, waving his hand across Thane's face, eyes wide open.

"Yeah, I just might try that out if she turns me down."

On their walk home, they both approached random people, saying things like: "*You don't want to go into that grocery store*", and "*You will now will me all of your money*", and "*You do not like to eat veal.*"

Laughing the rest of the way home, they thought about all the tricks they could play on Thane's sister Lara if they had the influential powers of *The Force*.

That night at the dinner table, Thane couldn't stop talking about the movie. After she had had enough talk about other galaxies far, far away, Lara excused herself to her room to gab on the phone in private.

When his mother, Susan had also been subjected to enough intergalactic space talk, she interrupted saying, "Thane, are you excited about Camp Whittle this summer? You and Sharla are camp counselors at the Y this year, aren't you?"

"Yes, we are," Thane answered, snapping out of Star Wars mode. "I'm really looking forward to it. We'll both be junior counselors together, which will be awesome. Sharla and I have some serious conversations ahead."

Sharla and Thane had met when they were campers together at the Westside YMCA summer day camp. They had become fast friends early on, discussing just about every subject under the sun.

With light-mocha skin, and a versatile Afro that seemed to change shape and style every week, Sharla glowed with charisma. She was one of those girls that you could confide in as much as the boys. Kinetic energy seemed to follow her wherever she went. She was calm and collected in one moment and geniusly intuitive in the next.

Sharla could also be completely oblivious at times. She would be discussing significant ways to end world hunger over lunch, while adding three too many sugars to her iced tea and dipping her sleeve over and over in the thousand island dressing meant for her fries. Humorous as well as endearing, there was never a dull moment when Sharla was around.

No sexual tension arose between Sharla and Thane, which made for a strong friendship. Both were a bevy of philosophical ideology, a quality that strengthened their friendship. Each could toss ideas of the universe and how it all worked at each other, constantly coming up with new and exciting possibilities.

Conversations would often go on for hours, frequently losing track of time. At the end of a camp beach day, it wasn't unusual for one of the counselors to find them together in the sand, kicking their feet in the water, talking and laughing, when the entire bus was loaded and ready to go. It was almost an expected response: *"Well, big surprise! Thane and Sharla late again? Where were they this time, up a tree?"*

Camp Whittle was a one-week mountain camp during summer, when kids could get out of town, far away from it all in the local San Bernardino Mountains. Both the campers, as well as the counselors, looked forward to escaping the hustle and bustle of the city to really explore, adventure, and grow without parents anywhere near.

Sharla and Thane were to be first time *"junior"* counselors, each with an older, *"regular"* counselor per cabin. They knew this would be an excellent week, filled with amazing experiences. They had been campers at Camp Whittle years before and were ready to approach it now from a new, mature perspective.

Thane had a curious feeling about this particular summer. He felt something was going to happen that would alter his life.

"It'll be nice to have the house to ourselves for a week," stated Thane's father, Reece, who realized both of his children would be gone for a full week. "Your sister wants to spend the week with her friend Isabelle, so your mom and I will just have to figure out something for us to do while you're both away. Poor us." He made an over-extended droopy smile.

"Dad, you and mom do whatever you like. I give you permission to have fun without us. Just don't come anywhere near our camp site, or Sharla and I will make you sing and dance and watch all our campers while we go swimming and hiking."

"It's a deal!" Reece replied with a snap of his fingers.


One of Thane's favorite games was called *Tangos.* It consisted of two sets of five shapes (black and red) that when put together correctly, made a perfect square. Cards with different shapes were chosen and whoever made the correct shape with the five pieces first, wins the round.

This was a game using skills of perception, deductive logic, and spatial acuity. The shape being made usually seemed impossible to create using only the five different shaped pieces, and yet, Thane was a master.

"Hey mom, how about another go at Tangos?" Thane called up the stairs, after finishing his math homework. "You almost tied me last time. Of course, it was because I was falling asleep and memorizing volleyball plays and Latin root words in my head at the time … but, how about it?"

"Ok, sweetie," she replied, twirling a curl from her recent "perm" hairstyle. "I'll use my blue eye to win."

Susan had one blue eye and one green eye, yet you would need to look closely to notice.

They played six rounds. During the seventh round, Thane held up his triangular playing piece to the light, asking, "Mom, do you remember this one time when I was three years old? I was sitting in the living room, watching reflections from the stained glass window on our old, orange shag carpet. I used to try to move the colored shadows with my fingers, but I never could. The light would move like liquid on the carpet. Do you remember?"

"I do," she said, putting down her game pieces, listening more closely.

"Well, one morning I was sitting there playing with the shadows, and I began to cry. It was weird. I remember asking you a strange question. Does this sound familiar at all?"

She offered a gentle, loving smile. "Honey, I remember you playing on the carpet a lot, but I don't recall any odd question. What do you think you asked me?"

Thane paused for a moment, clinching his eyebrows together, taking a deep breath before speaking. "Now mom, I know this would sound really strange coming from a three year old, but I think I told you, that I was afraid of dying before I fulfilled my destiny."

"What!?" she exclaimed, her eyebrows shooting straight in the air.

"I know, I know," Thane responded, taking her hand. "I don't think I used those exact words, but I did say something to that effect. I recall being upset about a really important mission I was meant to accomplish ... some journey or destiny to fulfill. I remember feeling very upset that I may not succeed in time – in my lifetime."

"How on Earth do you remember something as abstract as that from when you were three?" she said, tapping her index finger with one of the game pieces. "Darling, I think you've been watching too many of your Star Wars films. You've always been a sensitive kid with a keen intuition, but three year olds don't usually think those kinds of thoughts."

"No", he whispered, "not usually."

Thane won the last round of the game by making the shape of a sailboat from his five pieces. Before he retired to his room, his mother changed the mood, "Well, peace and go forward."

She was trying to pose her fingers into Star Trek's famous Vulcan V-shape, but she just looked as if she were having a mild stroke. "I believe it's *Live long, and prosper,* darling," Reece said, entering the room with a smirk.

"Right!" she shouted. "Well, at least I'm trying."


Thane headed off to bed. He hadn't thought of that particular childhood memory in years, wondering why it had chosen to surface on this night. His mind swam in a tank of emotions, with a thousand more questions than answers.

*What an odd memory to recall,* he thought. *What did that memory have to do with my life now, or my future? Was it connected to the dream?*

Thane stared into his twenty-five gallon fish tank. It was filled with six neon tetras, three swordtails, two large blue gouramis, five fantailed cobra guppies, one black sail-fin molly, two angelfish, and one spotted algae eater. The oscillating, fanning motions of the angelfish fins were mesmerizing, as he stood transfixed by the hypnotic, fluidic movement. He wondered if the fish knew they were being watched – specimens of human delight and fascination.

After brushing his teeth, Thane watched the end of *The Bionic Woman* on television before writing in his book of poetry. This was a very personal collection of his writings that he kept by his nightstand, but took with him when he traveled far away from home.

Thane's mind was a bevy of passion and intrigue. He would often write down his thoughts in poetry when he was filled with emotion, love, sadness, or philosophical consideration. *Tonight was special,* he thought – enough to warrant a poem. Filled with contemplative inspiration, the words seemed to flow from his mind directly on to the paper:

### When?

*When is it time to stretch out and fly,*

*How long must I wait as each day goes by,*

*I picture so clearly everything inside,*

*I'll never live up to 'sorry, I tried'.*

*When will the dreams finally come true,*

*I won't be content until I break through,*

*My new wings are ready to test in the sky,*

*It seems a never-ending struggle between me, myself, and I.*

*But when will it be, and how long must I wait,*

*When can I walk through that great, golden gate,*

*The time will come,*

*I must be patient inside,*

*I will bend with the wind,*

*And roll with the tide.*

*By Thane Winstrom*

He set the poetry book back inside his nightstand and turned out the light. Taking in a deep yawn, Thane cracked his knuckles and stretched his body out fully on his bed before quickly falling asleep.

Yes, tonight had been special, indeed. His mind was awakening to a new perspective. His thoughts while awake, took him to the past as well as the future – to galaxies far, far away, and to introspective corners of his psyche. But it was in his subconscious where his dreams would take him even further away, back to an alluring parallel life in another world – A world that continued an extraordinary adventure…

# GLADANTEUS

"Sarghon, Sarghon!" Ambroas called, echoing from within a cave .

Sarghon awoke from a light sleep. He had drifted off, standing against a large loof moss covered rock. Preternatural light streaked through the trees in refractive striations of mist, as the wind whistled across the mountains.

"Snap to it!" Ambroas said, his cloak billowing in the wind like a rising spinnaker sail, catching a sporadic gust. "No time to daydream or somnambulate! The winds are calling, and you must learn to fly. But first things first! Meet me at the Esplanade at sundown. You need a sword worthy of the *Eratheen Crystal*. It certainly cannot stay in your pocket much longer. Then, I will show you the *Diaglyphen Prophesy*, and you will understand everything more clearly."

Sarghon sluggishly stood up and yawned.

"Come now, boy!" Ambroas shouted, "What were you off

dreaming about, anyway? Some fantasy world, I assume. You do not have the luxury of indolence."

Sarghon wasn't certain where the Esplanade was, but within moments things began to come back to him. He soon recognizing his surroundings, recalling where he was and what Ambroas was talking about.

"The sword… right, I must find a sword and learn of my destiny. But where am I to …" Sarghon looked up, but Ambroas was gone. "Just as tricky and steadfast as ever, I see. You move spryly for an old man!" Sarghon yelled into the openness, hoping Ambroas would hear him in the distance.

Walking back to the path he recognized through the forest, the trees and plants were as vibrant as ever. The magic crystal in his pocked vibrated with a very soft hum. It felt warm to the touch. His sagacity was still heightened ever since he received the *Eratheen senses*, once again recognizing every minute detail about the nature all around him.

Along the path he was drawn to a large tree covered at the base with mura flower vines reaching up the trunk. He touched the twisted, rough textured bark with the tips of his fingers, his hand contouring with the curvature of the wood, as he peered into the glowing veins of sap running through the bark like blood. Like an amplified sound wave reverberating through his hands, he could feel its energy.

Just then, the tree spoke to him, *"Shoron varouth kanatal, zzebbie-taranashhhta."* (Save us from the taker of life, prophesy-chosen one.)

Sarghon understood the words. When he went to reply, the earthen language flowed easily from his lips, *"Dareeoth tarasta cantoneth, shaarenteth fareen karteneestath."* (I will do all I can do, but I will need your strength and wisdom.)

The tree replied, *"Jsho valenoth car soooth valenoth, bayamera bes a zhaashh"* (Your protection is our protection, stand firm and bend with the wind.)

Sarghon bowed his head in respect and acknowledgement. He now knew the trees were a much more significant part of the landscape than he had first imagined, or ever known before. They were sentient and wise creatures of the Earth that spoke to each other through the ground, as well as the wind. He felt their life force when he was near them, and knew they were on his side, no matter what. It gave him some equanimity to know that the Earth was his ally, having the flora of the land to guide and serve him in his quest, wherever it may lead.

Sarghon followed the wandering path alone for some time, before coming upon a fork in the road. He couldn't recall which path led to the Esplanade.

*I should know this,* he thought, *but everything seems to be changing with every moment, and I'm having trouble keeping up.*

He looked from one path to the next for a few moments, when he noticed one side began to appear more detailed and highly focused. It emanated a slight pale yellow glow, like energy radiating from beneath the dirt and grass, barely lighting the path.

Sarghon felt compelled to go in that direction, inherently knowing it was the correct way toward the Esplanade. Sensing that the Earth was helping him, the willing desire alone was enough to allow him to connect with the Earth, influencing his desired direction.

*It seemed logical,* he thought, fascinating as it was.

Walking on, the orange sky melted into a brilliant fuchsia, forming an expansive violet-indigo sunset. Two moons appeared above the horizon; one, a very large and pale crescent shape with many craters, the other, an azure colored crescent, further out in its orbit.

As sunset turned to dusk, the stars began to appear in multi-colored glints, dazzling the sky like floating glitter. Sarghon looked up, just as three shooting stars shot across the sparkling night horizon all in a row. It was a magical time.

An impressive lake soon came into view, reflecting the deep purple sky, making it appear larger as he crested a hill, arriving upon a small waterfront village. He spotted the Esplanade, a substantial open dirt street where wooden buildings stood back-to-back along a semi-circular marketplace on the lakefront. The winding street curved around for several hundred paces where people sold their wares during the daytime hours. At this time, however, the shops had closed for the day and the street was deserted.

Sargon noticed a single window frame lit from behind a woven tapestry, picturing a giant beast being slain in the heart by a warrior with a long broadsword. He heard voices from within the small shop.

Approaching with caution, Sarghon tiptoed softly up to the front door. When he got close, the tapestry blew violently open with a huge gust of air, revealing Ambroas and Kron, the blacksmith.

Kron was a large muscular man in his forties, with a stern disposition. His hands and arms wore the stains and calluses of ironwork, yet, his deep, hazel eyes appeared sorrowful and kind. "Come in Sargon,

I believe we have found what we are looking for," Ambroas said, in a brusque tone.

The rustic dwelling was illuminated with three oil lanterns: two along the far wall, and one larger round iron chandelier hanging in the middle of the vaulted ceiling. On the table in the middle of the workshop lay three exquisitely handcrafted swords, each a truly fine work of art.

The first was a beauty of shimmering steel, with a diamond formed tip and an s-shaped cross guard. A serpent was fashioned into the hilt. An artfully crafted bronze lotus flower had been carved into the pommel, housing a light blue crystal.

The second had a dragon-carved cross guard and grip, its mouth closing onto a round, black onyx stone at the pommel, with a single grooved "blood run" fuller fashioned into the blade. Gold wire and embossed leather adorned the handle, which ran down the dragon's back, allowing for extra grip.

The third embodied an ornate, golden, twisted tree trunk design. Fashioned from bronze, the grip curved organically into a cross guard that umbrella-ed out in branches, which protected the fingers and wrist. The pommel opened into a setting that held a large red ruby at its base. The blade, a double fuller with intricate gold filigree engraved into both sides. All were true visions to behold; metalwork at its finest!

"This is the one!" Sargon insisted. It was the third, with the organic wood features and ruby.

"My thoughts exactly," Ambroas added. "I would have agreed with whichever one you chose, but I was hoping you would pick this one. The *Eratheen* Stone will fit nicely where the ruby now sits. Please hand it to me," Ambroas asked.

Sarghon reached into his pocket, handing the magnificent, glittering crystal to Ambroas. Holding the chosen sword in one hand with the hilt upright, Ambroas placed the crystal in his other hand, equidistant from the ruby, before speaking the words, *"Sharateth aronaal."*

The two stones began to vibrate and ripple at the same time. For a moment, they appeared to share the colors of each other. As they vibrated, the stones morphed into one another, the magic perfectly placing the *Eratheen* Stone in the sword's pommel, and the ruby into Ambroas's hand.

"Kron, I believe this belongs to you," Ambroas said, handing Kron the ruby. "You have fashioned a sword fit for a king, and now it has the power only a king should wield. Rest assured, it will be used in the name of truth and victory, as the *Diaglyphen Prophesy* states."

Kron bowed his head to Ambroas, before turning to Sarghon. "Young master, when I found out that I was to construct a sword for the defender of the land, I was truly honored. These swords are of my finest work. May your choice protect and defend you in battle."

Bowing his head to Sarghon, he said, "One more thing, sir, before I forget! You must have a scabbard suited for such a sword and the sword will need a name."

Kron's eyes gleamed over his master achievement in its new owner's hands. Turning toward another table behind Sarghon, Kron returned with a gold and bronze gilded leather sword scabbard. Garnished with intertwining leather braids, delicately tied into decorative knots, and embossed with intricate filigree patterns of trees and roots, even the sheath was a sight to behold.

"I will do what I must. Thank you for your fine craftsmanship. It is exquisite," Sarghon said, sheathing the sword, holding it in his eyes for a moment, as Ambroas thanked Kron, setting a velvet bag filled with gold on the table as payment.

Ambroas and Sarghon left the workshop, walking across the Esplanade toward the waterfront. Reaching into a sack he had been carrying under his cloak, Ambroas presented Sarghon with a leather belt, complete with sword hanging straps and "frog," to hold the hilt in place. He wrapped it around Sarghon's waist, placing the sword and scabbard in its proper position.

Stepping back, Ambroas viewed his handiwork. "That will do nicely, I think," Ambroas said, twisting his beard back and forth several times between his thumb and index finger. "Now all you need to do is learn how to use it!"

Sarghon felt like a new man. The sword around his waist gave him a new sense of purpose. He felt the soft molded metal under his fingers, caressing the handle, as he measured the weight and sensation of wearing and walking with the new appendage.

"Kron said we must name it. What name would suite such a prize?" Sarghon asked, eagerly.

"You must name it. I can only guide your path. You must be the one to walk it," Ambroas replied. "Come, you can name it at the Phrontistery. We are not far.

An extraordinary, magical place for thinking and meditation, The

Phrontistery was where Ambroas spent hours meditating over spells, oracles, history or magical books. It was also a place where he found solitude and solace. No one knew how to find the Phrontistery except Ambroas, and possibly few other magically inclined friends, due to the fact that it was hidden by magic.

As they walked along the water for a while longer, their path turned toward a hillside lit by fireflies. Sarghon caressed the jewel on the handle of the majestic sword that lay against his waist. As he walked, he felt its weight on his hip, balancing out his stride. He pondered how he would use it in all its glory – this beautiful new addition to his life.

As the two approached the peak of a solitary hill, the grass became tall, reaching above their heads, as the tiny lights twinkled in the soft evening light. The fireflies were now all around them, pulsating in fluid, organic waves.

Ambroas stopped, "When we enter this place, young master, you will learn of your destiny," he said, speaking to Sarghon in an intimate tone. "Be not afraid of what is written there; your coming has been foreseen for many years. Inside, you will contemplate on what is, what is not, and what is yet to come. This is a place of magical knowledge. It is written that one will come along who will learn how to harness the elemental powers. Tonight, I will teach you to focus what you already hold within you, your inner *spirit* energy. It's time you learned your birthright!"

Sarghon was at a loss for words. He looked at Ambroas with his large blue-green eyes, then back at the fireflies glittering like tiny candles being lit, extinguished, and then lit again.

"Focus your mind here in front of us and tell me what you see," Ambroas asked. "Do not allow any distraction from beyond. See only what is in plain sight. Do not look for what is *not* there, rather focus on what *is*.

Sarghon tried to focus on the sights around him. "I see tall grass and fireflies," Sarghon said.

"Good, what else?" Ambroas asked quickly.

"Um, … I'm not sure?"

Ambroas stood behind Sarghon, assisting him by lifting one of Sarghon's arms and holding it outstretched in front of them. "Open your hand to the energy – feel what is around you. There is more here than you think," Ambroas said with a slight laugh. "Concentrate on *all* that is before you. *See* it and *feel* it as one.

Concentrating on the emptiness in front of him, Sarghon stood with his arm outstretched, palm open and fingers extended, as Ambroas pulled out his s-shaped pipe from within his robes, lighting it with a magical gesture. Inhaling a large puff, he blew out the smoke in front of Sarghon.

The smoke appeared to bounce off a flat surface, then dissipate. Sarghon noticed the outline of what looked like a threshold on the ground. Reaching his arm across the line and squinting his eyes with more concentration, he watched the fireflies make a pattern around what looked like a door. The rectangular space in front of him emptied itself of fireflies and a vacant area appeared.

"I see it!" Sarghon said excitedly. "Did I do that? Did I open the door?"

"I believe you did," Ambroas said, with a grin. "Why don't we go inside?"

Ambroas ushered Sarghon into the newly formed doorway shaped by fireflies. The tiny glowing creatures parted, forming an arched entrance.

As Sarghon stepped through the doorway, the world they had just been in disappeared from view, as they emerged into a magnificent, colorful garden. The light changed to a brilliant deep blue, with yellow and orange cloud-like vapors swirling above their heads in a slow, circular vortex. Multi-colored flowers and plants bloomed in every size and shape, some hanging in mid-air, like a floating floral bouquet. Beautiful beyond his wildest belief, Sarghon stood in dreamlike astonishment.

He felt protected in this magical Shangri-La called The Phrontistery. It was as though time was unable to touch this wondrous place. He sensed the mysterious consciousness that exuded from everything around him.

Walking forward into the center of the garden courtyard, they became surrounded by topiary statues of animals bordering a large stone monolith circled by five stone benches. "Everything you see here, except possibly for the stone in the center, was created by magic," Ambroas said with pride. "Many of the flowers are of my own creation. I like to take a pinch of this, and mix it with a patch of that. It keeps things more interesting, don't you think?"

Sarghon was riveted by the spectacle of it all. The flowers were a mixture of colors, in multi-dimensional layers, with shapes never before imagined.

"You know you can do many of these things now, yourself. I am not the only one who has the knowledge. You opened the door, did you not?"

Sarghon sat on one of the five benches. "You must believe in yourself, my boy," Ambroas stated plainly. "That's the first step. You must always hold on to your inner strength. No one can take that from you!"

Ambroas sat down on the bench next to Sarghon. "This Phrontistery is where we keep the *Diaglyphen Prophesy*, there before you." They faced a massive, smooth stone tablet carved with strange writing. "It was etched on that stone long before our time. I come from an ancestry of spellweavers that dates back over a millennia, preordained to teach and protect the *Spirit King*."

"The Spirit King?" Sarghon replied, with concern.

"Well, any run-of-the-mill soothsayer can predict the future, as we know; and there are many prophecies and predictions throughout our time depicting wars, plagues, earthquakes, domination and such; but, this one ... this special prediction, the *Diaglyphen Prophesy*, tells us of something GOOD! Ninety-nine out of one hundred prophetic predictions are of some horrible, disastrous future ending in peril and despair. This one is different! It speaks of an uprising of a great, dark and evil power being challenged and defeated by one man – a *Savior of Earth*. The dark power, as we know, is already here. King Malock resides in a fortress far to the north. All the land surrounding it for leagues has been sucked of its natural life energy. Trees, animals, grasslands, anything that grows is being destroyed and decimated as we speak. The energy he absorbs from every bit of life is somehow making him stronger every day. The time of prophesy is upon us. Let us read now, shall we?"

Ambroas directed his attention to the carved etchings in the large stone facing them. Small hieroglyphs of battles surrounded the edges of the monolith, with writing in the center.

"It is written in the ancient *Earatheen* language, which you now should be able to read," Ambroas said, with pride.

Sarghon stared at the strange, ancient language carved into the monolith. It was completely foreign to him, yet felt familiar at the same time. Squinting at the writing, he concentrated on its interpretation. At first the task seemed futile, but as he spoke, the words slowly formed in his mouth:

*"Behold, for it is written that under a full moon, on the third day,*
*Of the third month, at the dawn of the third millennium,*
*Shall be born a child granted thine elemental powers.*
*All must be willed to stand in battle,*
*Flowing together, as in life.*

*Darkness shall fall upon thee, hard and severe,*
*From force of greed will then appear,*
*A Lord of death to ravage thy land,*
*And suck all life from Earth and sand.*

*3-3-3 of decent and decree,*
*Cometh as savior to all,*
*Elemental gifts shall bestow,*
*To the one whose spirit shall know,*
*From Fire and Water, to Earth and Air,*
*The warrior's soul shall have to bare.*

*When death dost returneth to life,*
*A King of Spirit shall rule in peace,*
*One as brave and strong to be,*
*A savior of Earth, Air, Land and Sea."*

Sarghon sat staring at the stone for a long moment, before finally saying, "And, you think this is referring to me?"

"I know it is," Ambroas replied, "and so do you."

A few moments of silence passed before Ambroas placed his hand on Sarghon's shoulder and spoke again. "Every once in a long while someone comes along with a special gift. I was one, born with gifts of insight and magical talents … not like yours, of course, but with some abilities beyond others. You are a very special person, no different on the outside, but born with gifts exceeding the imagination. *You* are what legends were written about! *One* among many, who has the ability to save the world."

Something about the words made some fraction of sense to Sarghon. Ever since he could remember, he had felt different from others. Never did he believe, however, that he was written about in prophecies over a thousand years ago – but different, yes. His perceptions had always been keen, he was athletic, had good balance, and usually learned new things without too much difficulty; but not until this day had he ever believed the scale of his identity or destiny.

Sarghon touched the ancient writing etched into the monolith. It was true, he had been born on the exact date stated in front of him in stone.

"You will be faced with the challenges written here," said Ambroas. "You will be *granted thine elemental powers*, and thus, you have already been given the *Earatheen* Stone by one of its most sacred creatures. The powers of our Mother Earth will be yours to use at will. How you find the other elementals, I do not know, but I am certain you will grow to find them and master their gifts. It may take years for this to happen, who knows? You are young."

Reading the stone's contents once again in silence, Sarghon sat rigid and calm. Then, as if injected with a dose of courage, he stood up, raised the sword above his head waving it in a circular motion, and with a heaving grunt of determination, pierced it straight down into the ground.

The rock and Earth around the blade cracked open with fractures and electricity. The trembling ground began to rise up from beneath with quaking ferocity, forming a stone mound, twisting and growing under his feet. He rode the rising wave of rock and Earth more than twenty feet high, hanging on to the grip of the sword for balance.

When it finally stopped rising, the mound instantaneously grew moss, vines and multi-colored flowers, spurting out in all directions with magical magnificence. Next to Sarghon's foot sprouted a single root that grew quickly into a trunk that burst forth branches and leaves, forming a gleaming, fresh, full-grown tree at the top of the newly formed miniature mountain. The tree continued to shoot up past Sarghon, writhing as it grew, bursting with cobalt blue and fluorescent pink flowers. Ambroas stood in paternal delight as he witnessed the spectacle.

The thundering movement abruptly stopped, becoming silent, as the dust settled all around. Pulling the sword from the Earth, Sarghon held the blade before him, "I think I shall call her *Gladanteus,*" he stated,

"Sword of the Earth."

Sheathing the magical sword back into its scabbard, Sarghon looked down from the mountainous addition to the **Phrontistery** directly into Ambroas's eyes and said stoically, "I believe you now, my teacher. For the first time, I actually believe you!"

Thane awoke with the dream playing in his mind. Pictures, colors, even smells were still present in great detail. Realizing he was back in his room, he stared at the curtain as though it were a movie screen with fading images, trying to hold on to each feeling.

He could sense the weight of his sword, Gladanteus, and see the magical garden in his mind's eye so clearly. The details were incredible. Sarghon's frustrations were also still present, as he sensed feelings of impending pressure, as well as an uncertain future. Living the multifarious life of his alter ego felt inspiring and magnificent in this magical world that his mind once again created.

Delighted to have returned to his dream world, Thane realized he had experienced a reoccurring dream. He had forgotten the details about the first one until this second dream began. He wondered if these unique dreams might be sparked by the worries and excitement in his own life, bringing them to light in a fantastical way.

*What's in store for this guy,* he thought. *I must know what happens in the world of Sarghon, the apprentice with a vital destiny ... MY destiny?*

# Chapter III

## THE ODYSSEY

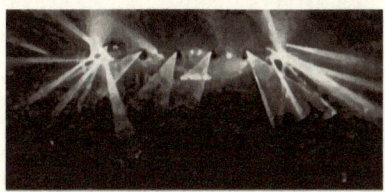

The completion of Thane's high school sophomore year ended with the eagerness of summer, as it does for every sixteen year old. The anticipation was over and now he and his friends were ready for some real fun.

It was now the summer of 1983 in Los Angeles and at the age of sixteen, going on seventeen, life was innocently decadent – all about the style, the music, and trying to get into the hippest nightclubs with your most recent fake I.D.

Thane, Aaron, and Sharla decided to kick off their vacation by hitting the most progressive eighteen-and-over nightclub in LA, *The Odyssey*. Like most teenagers, they felt the call of the night and searched for the magical, kinetic energy of the Los Angeles city nightlife.

*Billy Idol, Duran Duran* and *Cindy Lauper* were among some of their favorite music artists, along with *Tears for Fears* and *Depeche Mode*. The "New Wave" style of European music brought with it some very colorful fashion trends.

Aaron wore a double wrapped, leather-studded belt with a zippered *"Members Only"* jacket and acid-washed jeans, his hair feathered in a stylish mullet.

Sharla teased her hair on one side to the point of looking like a wind-blown palm tree, while sporting a dress with puffed sleeves, complimented by a lacy black bottom trim that stopped at her knees. Her arms were covered with silver bangle bracelets, an accessory that was a must for a night out on the town.

Deciding to be low-key, Thane wore eyeliner under only one eye, and spiked his hair up on one side. He wore his "cool" midnight-blue parachute pants – the only ones he would dance in, as well as a sleeveless black and red shirt with a single zipper off the shoulder, printed with a Chinese symbol for "strength" in the center.

Their parents weren't always exactly aware of what happened when their teenagers went out together at night, but Thane, Aaron, and Sharla earned the break and were trusted not to get into too much trouble.

The first to get a drivers license, Sharla was usually the designated driver. She parked her red Nissan Sentra behind the gas station on the corner of Beverly and La Cienega, half a block from the club.

While walking around the corner toward the club, a smarmy man in his mid-fifties unexpectedly brushed Thane's shoulder as he walked by. "Oops, sorry, I didn't see ..." the man said, looking up at them.

As the man turned around, he looked at Sharla with a debasing gaze, before glancing over to Thane, who was holding her hand. "Uhmph," he grunted, with a disgusted look in his eyes.

"Whatever!" Sharla scoffed, grabbing Thane's arm and trudging on. "Some people are really damaged!" she yelled back at the bigot.

When they got to the front door of the club, a muscular security guard with highlighted shoulder-length hair and tight faux-leather pants greeted the threesome. He looked as if he belonged in a metal rock band.

"Hey bro, what's up? Three of us tonight," Thane said, approaching him. "Cool wristbands, man. Where did you get 'em?"

"Dunno," he replied, glancing at their I.D.s, then to his wristband. "Probably Melrose, I guess. OK, go on in."

Shuffling through the door, they paid the five-dollar cover. "That was easy," Sharla remarked.

"Don't look suspicious, you two. Keep walking," Aaron snapped.

"It's all about the finesse. I had him more concerned about his rocker wrist-bands than our real ages," Thane whispered to Sharla, as they entered the main room.

Although Club Odyssey was eighteen-and-over, it catered to a vast variety of LA's nightlife sub-culture. Whimsical and flamboyant, the club encompassed a cacophony of eclecticism. Once inside, one never knew what demonstration of fervent behavior would first catch one's attention. Tasteful, it wasn't, but no other Los Angeles eighteen-and-over club was as electrifying, and everyone always left The Odyssey with a story to tell.

Aaron went straight for the bar, as Thane and Sharla visited the indoor/outdoor patio with a long brick wall and multiple gas fire pits, flaming through black lava stones. Being the preferred chatting and smoking spot, Sharla lit up a *Djarum* clove cigarette.

Casually leaning back on the wall with one arm extended, she blew the sweet, pungent smoke into the air above like an Indian princess. "Here darling, share this with me," she said, fanning her fingers across her breast with the cigarette in a smooth gesture, before handing it to Thane.

"Ya know," he said, taking a drag, "I really just like to people-watch here. I'm totally freaked out just to ask a cute girl to dance. I don't even like the way I look when I dance. I was dancing in front of the mirror the other night to Billy Idol's, *'Dancing with Myself,'* and I looked nothing like him when he dances with himself."

Acquiring the cigarette back from Thane, Sharla took another long drag, feeling the head rush and squinting her eyes. "Well, you just need to have rhythm like me, Thaney boy. It's all in the soul," she said, pushing away from the brick wall, swaying her hips. "You're either born with it, or without it, ya know? You gotta feel it from DEEP inside."

She began to dance, waving her hands from side to side in the air, making large sweeping movements above her head. "I know 'I' was born with it," she said, her eyes loose and floating with her clove cigarette head-rush. "I got the grooves and the moves!" she shouted.

Suddenly, one of Sharla's flailing hands smacked a girl straight in the face, while walking by. It was like a scene from *Dynasty*, when Alexis slaps Krystle Carrington across the face in slow motion.

The Tom Collins drink the girl had been holding went flying into her male friend's face and chest, drenching him all the way down the front of his shirt and into his pants.

"Oh, God!" Sharla exclaimed, "Did I do that?"

The girl fumed with anger, her face slowly transforming into what looked like one of the ugly, wicked stepsisters from Cinderella. "You total bitch!" the girl yelled. "You almost broke my nose! Look what you made me do!!"

Standing up, Thane tried to apologize to the girl and her friend, whose make-up and eyeliner was running down the side of his face. "She didn't do it on purpose," he said. "She was just ... OK, let me buy you and your boyfriend a drink."

"How old are you two anyway?" the girl snapped. "You don't even look old enough to buy ME a drink!"

She was right. Thane suddenly felt caught, like a dear in the headlights. He had to think quickly for fear of getting kicked out of the club in front of his peers, humiliated to the maximum degree a sixteen-year-old could. He had to do something fast.

Pushing Sharla aside, Thane grabbed the pack of clove cigarettes from her purse. "Here, have these," he said, shoving them at the disgruntled girl.

She was too dumbstruck to respond, mouth gaping wide open, watching the makeup drip down the drenched face of her male friend. His foundation and eyeliner had melted down one side of his face, making him look like a Salvador Dali painting.

"I don't think that's her boyfriend," Sharla mumbled, as Thane quickly dragged her onto the dance floor and away from the scene. They could hear the panicked screaming of the 'boyfriend' in the distance, as he grasped his predicament, realizing how he must now appear.

"Dang, man, that was close! I think that girl truly wants to kill me," Sharla said, while laughing and snorting in-between laughs. "Did you see that guy? Pancake all dripping down his face!" She laughed again with a bigger snort. "I think half of it melted onto that tacky, acid-washed *Guess* jacket. I can still hear him screaming. Heeee, ooooeee!"

Sharla was still laughing loudly, trying to catch her breath while snorting, "Ooooeeee, well, that girl deserved to be slapped in her face. She was the bitch!"

They moved to the center of the dance floor, where the crowd would conceal them. *Rock the Casbah* was the song playing, as they danced in the traditional eighties style, head swaying from side to side, while snapping fingers and kicking a foot out.

"Have you seen Aaron? I have GOT to tell him what just happened!" Sharla said, with one last chuckle.

"Last I saw, he was trying to chat up Tina," Thane replied, "you know, the girl that keeps giving him poppers? He's had a thing for her all year, but I think she's just leading him on."

They danced for another minute before Thane leaned into Sharla's ear and said, "You know what you said about having something inside you ... unique feelings, being born with it and all? Well, I've been seriously wondering about some things lately. It goes all the way back to when I was a little kid."

Sharla was feeling the music and singing along. "*By order of the prophet... degenerate the faithful...* Yeah, I totally hear ya, baby! I feel like I'm completely connected to this song right now – like I'm one with it, or something. Oh yeah, yeah!"

"Well, that's not exactly what I mean, but we can talk in more detail later!" he shouted, over the final lyric of the song, realizing it wasn't the ideal time to begin a philosophical conversation.

Glancing toward the bar, he saw Aaron talking to Tina and … could it be … Lyeana? Yes, his school crush was across the room talking with Aaron and Tina.

Leaving Sharla on the dance floor in her flurry of rocking the *Casbah*, Thane headed over to Aaron, Tina, and Lyeana.

"Dude! This stuff is really crazy! You gotta try it," Aaron said, with a huge grin and bulging eyes, referring to the small bottle of poppers in his hand.

"Hi Lyeana, how're you tonight?" Thane said to Lyeana, ignoring Aaron.

"I'm pretty good. This club is really cool," she said, smiling at him.

"Yeah, guess so. I've never seen you here before. Are you with friends?"

"Just my cousin Tina, here," she replied.

Leaning into his ear, she whispered, "I think your friend, Aaron is into her." Thane felt a tingle run down his spine. Lyeana had never whispered in his ear before.

"I didn't know Tina was your cousin. Aaron's had a thing for her for a while. I guess good looks run in your family."

Thane suddenly turned red. He wasn't expecting to compliment her outright like that. It just came out of his mouth. Unexpectedly, a wave of courage overcame him. "Do you want to dance?" he asked in a hurried manner.

"OK," she answered, "I kinda feel like a third wheel with these two anyway. Oh, I love this song!" She grabbed Thane's hand, pulling him onto the dance floor. *The Safety Dance*, from the band *Men Without Hats*, was playing. It was one of those songs that anyone could dance to and not look ridiculous doing so.

Sharla was busy creating her own *Safety Dance* moves on the dance floor, when she noticed Thane and Lyeana dancing together. As she shot Thane a wink he smiled back at her, shrugging his shoulders with a puppy-like, indicative head tilt.

Thane was enamored with Lyeana. He watched her every move, appreciating every inch of her body. Trying to look as cool as he could on the dance floor, he emulated some of her movements and gestures. Still feeling unworthy and awkward, Thane fell completely under her mystifying spell. In his mind, she could do no wrong.

*What is it about this girl?* Thane thought. *I've never felt anything like this before.*

She grabbed his hands and they began to dance together more intimately. Thane was nervous, but too excited to let his fear overcome him. Dropping his guard, Thane danced to the music, letting it penetrate and flow within his body. He felt fearless and intrepid, testing out a new sense of daring and self-control, as an overpowering wave of bravery washed over him, like a suit of armor.

As he swayed to the beat of the music, for the first time in his life, Thane felt completely in tune with his body, actually enjoying himself dancing on a dance floor at a nightclub. When his eyes met Lyeana's, the music seemed to take control, as he slowly moved in closer. Maybe it was her infectious smile, or possibly the magnetic energy in the air – but he couldn't help himself as he lurched forward and planted a kiss on her lips.

For what seemed like infinity, his lips were connected with hers.

Taken by surprise, she retracted, opening her eyes largely. "Thane, wow ... I wasn't expecting that. I ... well, I'm actually seeing someone at the moment. He lives in Redondo Beach."

Thane's momentum came to a screeching halt! "I didn't mean to lead you on," she said, "I thought we were just having some fun."

"I'm sorry, I couldn't help myself. I thought maybe you ..."

Thane was mortified. He immediately lost his cool, as well as his words. He froze, standing in a complete void for several seconds, which felt like an eternity. "It's OK, Thane. I like you. We can be friends, right?" she finally said.

"Oh, wow, yeah ..." he mumbled, snapping out of his romantic spell as if a bucket of water had just been poured over his head. "Sure, that's cool, no worries. Let's grab a drink."

They exited the dance floor and went back to the bar where Thane ordered two Cokes. After a few more awkward minutes standing at the bar waiting for the drinks, Thane said, "That was fun dancing together, thanks. You're really hot on the floor ... I mean, good ... you know what I'm saying." He was fumbling again.

"You too," she replied.

Thane excused himself with an uncomfortable exit, returning to the patio, where he found Sharla posing lavishly against the half-brick wall, smoking another clove cigarette. "Where did you get that?" he asked.

"I bummed it from another girl," she replied, haughtily, "since you gave away my whole pack to that skank! So, you were dancing with Lyeana, huh? I knew you could do it."

"It's not exactly what you think," he confessed. "I tried to kiss her. Well, I did kiss her. I somehow found the courage. With the music, and the right moment, I thought maybe ... then she told me she's dating some guy from Redondo! What shitty luck, huh? And just when I finally found the guts to make a move. It was really strange though, I felt the impulse to just go for it, ya know? Something came over me – like an extra boost of confidence or something."

Sharla pursed her lips, tapping her fingers on the brick wall near one of the fire-pits as she leaned into Thane. "Something looks different about you, Mr." She took a drag from her clove and blew it out, pointing at him with the two fingers holding her cigarette. "You have a sparkle in your eye, and you're kinda flush."

Backlit by the flickering fire pit, she leaned back on one arm again, silhouetting into her dramatic pose on the brick wall. "I'm proud of you for making a move, though. It's about friggin' time."

The night went on without any additional disasters and by 1:00 am they were ready to go home. Nudging Aaron toward the front door, Thane found Sharla digging in her purse for her car keys. "Dude, this was sure a different night, alright," Thane said to Aaron. "I don't think I've ever felt so incredibly good and so insanely bad all in the same night."

"Well, at least Tina and I have a coffee date," Aaron said with a smile.

"You don't even drink coffee," Thane replied mockingly.

"Well, I guess I'll learn to like it!"

The three drove home singing Billy Idol's, *White Wedding* for the entire ride. After dropping Aaron off at his house, Sharla slyly looked over to Thane. "You know, this is just the beginning of love for us," she said. "We've got a long way to go, honey. Just wait until camp. You'll have female junior counselors all over you."

"I just wish it didn't hurt, though," Thane replied. "Why does love, or whatever this is, have to feel so shitty? Why do I even have the desire to be around Lyeana? What is that? This really sucks, ya know? Girls suck!"

Thane leaned his head on the passenger window peering out into the night like a lonesome puppy.

"Well, not tonight, apparently!" Sharla blurted out, before letting out a high-pitched, hysterical laughing moan followed by a snort. Thane caught the innuendo, as well as her infectious laughter and joining in as they laughed continuously for the next two minutes.

Finally saying goodnight with a hug, they parted.


The next week, Sharla invited Thane and Aaron down to her great aunt Angelica's house for the 4th of July. Angelica's home was just outside of San Diego in the picturesque coastal town of La Jolla. With perfect weather for the occasion, firework shows could be viewed all the way down the coast.

The threesome arrived in La Jolla on the evening of July third. Sharla's great aunt lived walking distance from the famed beachfront cliffs. After dinner, with a small bottle of vodka in tow, they decided to take a walk out to the edge of the cliffs.

A light ocean breeze blew across the clear, night sky. The nearly full moon was framed by wispy clouds stretching out across the sky, reaching toward the horizon in multiple stratospheric levels. The stars were incredibly clear, as the ocean waves thundered in the distance, crashing on the shore hundreds of feet below.

"I love this place," Sharla said. "It makes me realize how small we really are. Just look out there at all the stars, the sky, and the ocean below – forever crashing its waves on the shore, carving the landscape. It's majestic in every sense of the word."

"Are you drunk or something?" Aaron interrupted with a chuckle. "You sound like some after school special on how the Earth was made."

"She just has a bigger brain than you do," Thane replied, taking a swig from the vodka bottle. "Her intellect is ... *more powerful than you can possibly imagine.*"

Thane was quoting the famous line from Star Wars that Aaron knew so well.

"Hey, come out here! Out to the edge!" Sharla yelled, beckoning them to the edge of the cliffs.

"That's a long way down," Aaron pointed out.

"Damn straight," Thane replied, "don't get any ideas that you can fly, either. I wouldn't want to follow you off this cliff!"

"Hey, let's all try something," Sharla suggested. "Lay down on your back, like this."

All three followed her lead, rolling over on their backs, with their heads hanging off the edge, seeing the panoramic horizon in reverse.

The transformation of the landscape was fascinating. The moon's light appeared to be reflecting on the ocean horizon upside-down, shimmering slowly upward into the distance, creating the illusion of an alien landscape.

"Oh, my God," Thane exclaimed, his head dizzy from the vodka. "Do you guys see what I'm seeing? The clouds look like the water, and the waves are crashing upward into the sky. It's like the ocean *is* the sky! That's fucking incredible! It's like seeing an exact opposite version of our world."

"Look," Sharla pointed out, "the moon and stars are all part of the land, like lights in houses. And look how the clouds are like mountains; it actually makes sense in some backward, upside-down way. It's freaking me out!"

Aaron was basically speechless just saying, "Whoa, whoa, whoa," over and over.

"What if everything on the planet were in reverse?" Thane suggested. "When people used to believe the Earth was flat, maybe they thought the people on the other side lived upside-down?"

Aaron began to laugh at the thought of that. "They would have really big heads," he said.

The three of them laughed together until they had to roll back over, for fear of accidentally falling off.

"That was really trippy. You'd think we all had one of my aunt's special brownies," Sharla said with a loud chuckle and a snort.

"I wonder what life would be like if up were down, and down were up?" Thane replied.

"You guys are nuts," Aaron said, taking another swig from the little bottle.

"Well, we just try to think outside the box, unlike your hollow head!" Sharla said with a laugh, along with one last loud snort.

They finally stood up and finished off the vodka while taking in the view one last time. After a few deep breaths of fresh ocean air, the three said goodbye to the cliffs before heading back to the house for the night.


The next evening was filled with a jubilant sense of freedom. 4th of July had always been a time of barbecues, fireworks, and family. This year, however, Thane was with his friends in a new place. Away from home, removed from his typical circumstances, it seemed easier for Thane to see the details of his life.

Thane was becoming a man, feeling new passions within him that were frustrating, as well as sensual. He was seeing things more clearly, and feeling things more deeply, questioning ordinary circumstances and issues he hadn't found of interest in the past. In Thane's enigmatic mind, the questions and concerns of today were crucially more important than they had been yesterday – and tomorrow, in turn, would offer more questions that begged even more profound answers.

Thane sat hypnotized by the exploding colors and patterns as they emerged from loud bursts that became glittering streaks across the sky, dissolving into hundreds of white smoky trails. He pondered how the diverse, explosive material would need to be packed in order to ignite at a specific time to create the desired dispersal pattern, size, and color. In addition, he wondered if he would follow in his father's footsteps, becoming a scientist of some kind – possibly an astronomer or astrophysicist.

Reaching down to pick up two handfuls of sand, Thane felt the texture of the granules in his hands sifting through his fingers and falling to the ground. He contemplated how many millennia it took to mold and shape each grain of sand and how many trillions of single pieces surrounded him where he sat.

He imagined how the Earth and ocean must work together to form the vast beaches of soft, silky sand, and how each tiny little stone or shell had come to land exactly in its place, ending up at this very moment in his hands.

These were not things he had considered in the past. He had never taken much time to dwell on anything long enough to matter this much, but now Thane seemed to be curiously lost in a trance of never-ending questions.

"Thane! Are you gonna play in the sand all night over there by yourself?" Aaron said, appearing behind him. "Sharla's aunt has a bunch of fireworks for us to light. Here, start with this," he said, handing Thane a glittering green sparkler, encouraging him back to where Sharla and Angelica were.

"Well, there you are. It's time to light the cool ones," Sharla said, handing Thane a fountain cone firework named, *The Golden Dragon*.

Looking down into the large box filled with an assortment of 'safe and sane' fireworks, he saw: *Violet & Crimson Showering Waterfall*, *Jumbo Carnival Cone*, an assortment of *Spinning Flowers* and *Ground Bloomers*, *Showering Wheel Spinners*, *Multi-colored Sparklers* and *Black Snakes*. Just the names and pictures on the packaging was enough to make him want to light one.

Aaron was busy dancing in the sand around a large shower of sparks from a fountain cone, kicking sand in the air, singing what sounded like *Yankee Doodle Dandy*, but making up his own lyrics: "I'm a Yankee Doodle stud-man, a Yankee Doodle studley guy…"

Sharla pulled Thane aside. "So, ya having fun, babes? It's like one big beach party down here, huh? Ya know, I'm really looking forward to Camp Whittle. We're gonna have a blast! It'll be different having responsibilities, though. I hope Aaron can keep up. We'll each have our own cabin of kids to be in charge of, so I hope it's more fun than work. And, we better make some time to take a few long walks together. Remember that time we got lost? It was like two hours before we found our way back to the mess hall!"

"It'll be different," Thane pointed out. "Everything's going to be different," he said, looking out at the exploding fireworks, reflecting on the water up the coast toward Laguna Beach.

"How do you mean?" Sharla asked, with concerned intrigue.

"I don't know," Thane said closing his eyes, "I don't really know how to explain it. It just will. We're approaching a magical age, where the world is ours to create as we see it – as we dream it.

# Chapter IV

## MOUNTAIN CAMP

The week of mountain camp had finally arrived. Both Sharla and Thane were ecstatic that Aaron had been able to twist his mother's arm into allowing him to join as a junior counselor as well. Aaron's mother was a single mom who was overly protective of her only son, and thus, domineering about everything he did that took place out of her sight. After enduring Aaron's pleading and begging every night for the last month, she finally caved.

The bus ride up to the San Bernadino Mountains was long and winding, filled with many camp songs and laughter. Thane was the junior counselor for cabin #3, filled with eight boys, age ten and eleven. The older counselor in his cabin was named Brad, a friend from years at YMCA day camp.

Aaron had cabin #6, with eight boys, age nine, and Sharla was in cabin #14, in charge of seven, eleven-year-old girls.

The boys were mostly interested in the camp's sporting events, such as Capture the Flag and Archery, where the girls were usually excited about arts and crafts, nature walks and hanging out at the swimming pool. There was never a dull moment with all the activities Camp Whittle had scheduled for this year's campers.

The YMCA (*Young Men's Christian Association*) was originally an all male boys organization, but eventually developed an openness that included all men, women, and children regardless of race, religion, or nationality.

The week had a set schedule of activities. At 8:00am the cabins gathered at their designated cabin lines at the flagpole for role call, before being excused for morning *Chapel*.

*Chapel* was a time to wake up, listen to the birds, feel the morning dew, smell the morning mountain scents, and gather together before the day's activities. It was also a time to set an intention for each day, sing a song or two, and just sit together in a common place with purpose. Of course, Thane and Aaron had been used to sleeping in later due to the summer schedule and on the first morning of *Chapel*, they were barely awake.

As Thane walked sleepily toward the outdoor seating area, his senses seemed heightened, taking notice of things he hadn't previously observed when he was a camper. After a deep breath of brisk morning air, the city seemed a world away, as he became keenly aware of the diverse bird songs all around, vanilla scent coming from the surrounding sugar pine tree bark, and the ethereal colors of the morning sky.

After *Chapel*, everyone walked over to the mess hall for breakfast before the day's activities began in an excited rush.

Sharla's first activity was Archery, while Thane was stationed in the Arts and Crafts Lodge. Aaron had a slightly younger group, so he was busy teaching field sports and hiking for most of the day. The three had no time on their first day to see each other, except momentarily at dinner and Campfire that evening.

The second day was different, however. There were two activities when Cabin #3 and #14 were in the same place at the same designated time. First was the swimming pool and second, horseback riding. Aaron had been scheduled at the pool all morning teaching younger campers how to dive off the diving board. For an entire hour Thane, Sharla, and Aaron could finally hang out together.

When Aaron was done with his last student, the threesome sat together along the edge of the pool with their feet dangling into the cool water. "How are your girls?" Thane asked Sharla.

"Well, you know girls, they're all about their hair, their lip gloss, and which boys they think are cute. Shauna likes one of the boys in your cabin – I think his name is Joey. She just giggles and says his name a lot. I really don't have anything in common with most of these little brats! OK, just kidding, a few of them are sweet, I guess. How are you guys do'n?"

"My boys are cool," Thane said, splashing his feet in the water at one of his cabin-mates. "Joey's a troublemaker though. He wanted to collect frogs from the meadow and put them in the sleeping bags of cabin eleven. If Brad hadn't overheard them plotting, we would've had a slimy situation."

"I'm having a blast!" Aaron interjected. "Hey, when are we going hiking together? Remember that awesome rock face at the other end of the meadow? I'm leading a climb there soon. Let's try to climb together. When do you have a free period?"

The boys in the pool splashed back at Thane.

"Ohh, this water's cold!" Thane said, leaning back from the pool's edge. "I need to check my schedule and get back to you on the rock climbing, but that sounds like fun. Sharla and I need to take some time to discuss our *rag* ceremony as well. We're both getting red ones together this year. The ceremony's in two more days."

"Yeah, and it's an evening ceremony," Sharla said excitedly, "with all the stars that come out up here in the mountains, it's gonna be awesome! I can't wait. It'll be amazing up at Raggers Point at night. I've never been there at night before."

Closing her eyes toward the sun, Sharla arched her back, leaning on the concrete with both arms extended. Aaron stood up, pretending to gesture to a camper on the diving board, inconspicuously positioning himself behind Sharla. Creeping up quietly behind her, he shoved her in the pool.

Sharla let out a blood-curdling shriek as she toppled spastically into the pool with a huge splash, nearly kicking one of her campers in the back of the head.

That morning Sharla had teased her Afro out to its full length, tying it in two neat ponytail-like puffs that sat on either shoulder. When she surfaced from underwater, her hair looked like two wet rats hanging from her head on both sides. She emerged from the water infuriated, with a flabbergasted expression on her face, yelling at Aaron. "You bast… you … aarg, I'm gonna …"

She couldn't yell out what she wanted to say with all the campers and other counselors around. "Aaron, I'm gonna get you for that!"

Sharla wasn't one to be duped without retaliation. She would certainly plan on something worthy of her merit and Aaron had better be on the look out! Thane stayed out of this one for the time being, giving Aaron a wink for his brave trickery.


Taking advantage of his next free period, Thane relaxed at the cabin with one of his favorite young campers named Lucas, teaching him how to make a colored lanyard before sweeping out the dirt and pine needles from the cabin.

Thane wore his *gold rag,* a regular sized, gold colored bandana, loosely tied around his neck in a square knot. "Next year I'll get my Blue

Rag, right? What'll it be like?" Lucas asked, intrigued.

Putting down the broom, Thane smiled, leading Lucas outside to sit on the front porch of their cabin. He thought the boy was ready to hear the whole story. "Well Lucas, the YMCA Raggers program is a series of challenges for individuals wishing for growth personally and spiritually. Once each year, a good friend or counselor who has already received that color rag, can be chosen to tie your rag, like the one I'm wearing."

Thane gestured to the golden bandana around his neck. "The square knot represents strength and commitment. As you may know, the 'rag ceremony' takes place at *Ragger's Point*, a very special place where we can always go to reflect upon the challenges and goals we set for ourselves. At *Raggers Point*, there are rocks placed on the ground in the shape of a circle, then inside the circle the rocks shape a square, and inside the square is a triangle. At the center of the triangle, lies a cross. Here, look on my rag."

Thane took off the *gold rag* from around his neck, presenting it to Lucas, who studied the four shapes. "Now, there are seven different colored rags you can get each year if you decide to. Each color corresponds to a different set of challenges. Blue, Silver, Brown, Gold, Red, Purple and White. Each rag stands as an outward sign of an inward goal."

*Wow, I like that description*, Thane thought, proud of himself for remembering the meaning.

"Why are they called *rags*?" Lucas asked, curiously.

"Well, I guess 'bandana' was already taken," he chuckled, "I believe they're called *rags* to show they're really not worth anything physical like money or jewelry, but worth something of inner value to each person who wears one."

Thane pointed to the square inside the circle. "See the square here? The four points represent balance. They're the *Social, Mental, Physical & Spiritual* parts of life. We strive to balance them out equally, but it can be difficult because life is always changing and often unstable."

Thane stopped talking for a moment, reflecting on what he just said. His words seemed to be coming from an outside mature voice or self – an authentic self. Many friends and mentors had spoken these same words to Thane, but he was keenly aware of how "grown-up" he sounded.

Lucas had a quizzical look on his face.

"I know, I know," Thane said, reassuringly, "this is all a bit too much information for you at this stage, but I thought you were ready to hear it now, so you'll be prepared for some of your own challenges next year."

"OK, that's cool. Will you tie my Blue Rag next year?" Lucas asked.

A large smile grew across Thane's face. "Well, Lucas, I would be honored. Thank you for asking me, it would be my pleasure."

Putting his hand on Lucas's shoulder, Thane hugged him with one arm. "You know, you remind me of myself at your age."

And with that, they walked toward the mess hall for lunch.


That afternoon, both Thane and Sharla's cabins went horseback riding together. The campers had been looking forward to it all day, since they only had one opportunity to ride all week.

The horses were a bit ragged looking and tired from all of the different riders, but that didn't matter to the group. Thane had ridden horses before with his family, as well as when he was a camper himself, but Sharla had always been a bit skeptical about getting on a horse after having been thrown two years earlier.

"This dusty thing better not kick me off!" she scoffed to the trail guide, as he helped her into the stirrups and onto the saddle. "I could break my back, or hit my head on a tree, or twist my ..."

"Stop all your nagg'in, girl! You're gonna give your horse ideas," Thane shouted.

Once the campers were all mounted on their designated horses and lined up behind the trail guide, they were ready for their ride. Last in line, Thane held up the rear with his horse, Pasha, keeping an eye on anyone who may veer off the trail or have trouble keeping up.

After a short time, Thane and his horse fell back several horse lengths, lingering a bit on purpose, wanting to take some quiet time to himself away from the laughter and constant banter from his boys and other campers.

Waddling back and forth on the hard saddle, Thane walked his horse in a steady pace along the well-memorized trail. Thane's mind drifted back to the trees from his dream. *Do they know we're here?* he thought. *Can they sense us, hear us, feel us? Can they talk?*

Recalling his ability to communicate with trees from his

fantastical dream, Thane saw them in a new light – with admiration and respect. Whenever he saw one fallen or chopped down along the horse trail, he felt a sense of sadness he hadn't felt before.

Along the trail, other forest life also became noticeably more vivid to Thane. The maidenhair and mountain ferns, as well as the colorful wildflowers, seemed more alive than he ever observed before. The intricate patterns and shapes of leaves popped out at him, as if trying to convey some secret environmental message. With each breath, Thane felt more and more connected to the forest.

Captivated by the nature all around, he fell into a trance-like state. With his body drifting from side to side with the lulling momentum of his horse, his mind slowly slipped into a kind of euphoric rapture – eyelids drooping with each lulling stride.

The colors all around were spectacular! *Is it the lack of oxygen at this altitude?* he thought? *Is it the fresh mountain air that's playing tricks with my vision?* Feeling high and light-headed, he gazed around at the forest splendor, as sunbeams cast through the tall pines.

Then, something unusual grabbed his focus. Off to one side of the trail, he noticed that the plants seemed to glow in the afternoon mountain light. One after another, the flora lit up with a soft, glowing aura, demanding his attention. Like the breadcrumbs left behind by Hansel and Gretel in the fabled story, he was being lead to something … but what?

A glint caught Thane's attention, reflecting brightly through the wildflowers. The object reflected three distinct colors. Both he and his horse seemed lured toward it. *What was this compelling treasure? It must be a message of some kind*, he thought.

"What on Earth?" he said out loud with anticipation, approaching the glittering object. Squinting determinately, he focused on the sparkling, shinning, metallic shapes of … three bent soda cans.

"Huh?" he grunted, tilting his head far to one side.

In his still bemused state, Thane leaned too far over to the right side of his saddle, nearly falling off his horse. As she caught her hoof on a rock, he sat up rigidly, snapping out of his disorientation. "That's it?" Thane moaned, with disappointment. "Just some trash left behind by careless, littering jerks? What the hell?"

Having fallen too far behind, Thane kicked his horse into a light trot to catch up with the pack. After another fifteen minutes of trail, the group came back around toward the front of the stables.

It seemed curious to Thane how fast the ride went, or maybe he had been in his euphoric, *"connected state"* for longer than he thought? He decided the beauty of the mountain foliage, as well as the altitude, had overwhelmed him – at least that's what he told himself.

He went back to his cabin to write down his experience in his poetry journal. Today was indeed worthy of a poem.

### How high will I climb?

*"So many things have passed through my eyes,*

*Absorbing, thinking, experiencing the time,*

*Wondering now, as I look to the skies,*

*How far have I come,*

*How high will I climb?*

*The emotion will be there, remembering so clear,*

*Through laughter, excitement, amazement and fear,*

*There's so much to see, so much to take in,*

*A whole new perspective, a journey to begin,*

*I'm seeing so clearly, new visions and life,*

*I'm feeling the rapture, the pain and the strife,*

*What are these sensations, these tricks of the mind,*

*Where am I going, and what will I find?"*

By Thane Winstrom

The rest of the day consisted of an afternoon game of *Capture the Flag,* in the large central meadow.

The object of the game is for players to make their way into the opposing team's territory, grab their flag, and return to one's own territory, without being tagged. If you make it into the safe zone, you can make an attempt to return to your territory with the flag. If you get tagged, you go to jail. The game is won when a player returns across the center line to his or her own territory with the enemy's flag.

The male counselors and female campers were on one team, against the female counselors and male campers on the other. The afternoon game went into overtime with a tie, and after an hour and a half of nearly constant running in the twilight, the team of female counselors and male campers finally won the game.

The day's activities had taken a toll, and after dinner and an evening of skits, stories, and songs from the nightly jubilation around the campfire, Thane felt completely exhausted. Once in his sleeping bag, nestled snugly in bed, Thane fell directly asleep. The chattering of whispers from his cabin of boys didn't disturb him like it had during past nights, becoming only background white noise. The muttering of exterior sounds and night crickets only added to the mystery, as he drifted into a deep slumber – back to the dream adventures in a world of magic, destiny, and orange colored skies.

# Chapter V

## AIR

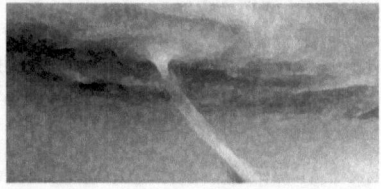

The tall mountain pine trees billowed with the premonition of a storm. The breeze whistled through the treetops of the Scyllian Stone Mountains, echoing like a desperate cry of help from distant faeries.

Sarghon awoke on a rocky hillside at the entrance of a large cave carved into the side of a granite mountain. His eyes blurred at first from the gusting wind, but after focusing on his surroundings, everything slowly became clear.

He wore a doublet of green velvet and leather with a dark brown half-cloak and hanging hood. Looking down at his hip, protected in the intricately decorated sheath, there she was at his side... *Gladanteus,* Sword of the Earth.

"What are you doing out there, when I have procured us some tantalizing rabbit stew in here," Ambroas called from inside the cave, before stepping into view. "Ahh, yes, hmm," he said, rubbing his fingers in the air, surveying the approaching weather. "The wind is talking to us. There's a storm brewing, and not the kind that will pass merely with the weather. Come inside Sarghon, you look famished. Been dosing on your watch, I see. You look as if you've been asleep for years. We have much to discuss, lad. And you must eat some of my stew!"

Sarghon followed Ambroas inside the cave, where they sat on the ground around a stone slab table. Candles hung in crevices in the walls, lighting the room with dancing shadows that flickered with curiosity. In the cave dwelling, furs lay along one side of the room, where they had apparently been sleeping. The opposite wall was filled with an assortment of weapons of varied size and shape, where they had apparently been training.

After finishing his stew, Ambroas sat up squarely. "Malock is becoming stronger," he said. "He leads his brainless hoards in the North, across the Melting Plains to infect the good people in all its surrounding villages."

A look of disgust came over Ambroas's face. "He must be stopped!" he said loudly, in an aggressive whisper. "His power grows daily as he sucks the land of her delicate life force. I can hear the trees cry out. Sarghon, can you sense the sorrow and death from beyond? If not now, you soon will; mark my word."

"Malock is the *other* you spoke of, isn't he. He is my brother, then?"

"NO!" Ambroas snapped, "He is no brother of yours. He is your nemesis, your destiny to conquer. He must be destroyed!"

Getting up from the table, Ambroas wandered awkwardly in a semi-circle, before placing one of his long boney hands on the wall of the cave. He leaned his weight against the wall, exhaling deeply as he looked back sorely at Sarghon. "I am sorry, my boy, that this task has been laid before you," he said. "But look at you, you are no longer a boy now. The years have been good to you, young Master. Yes, a strong warrior you are becoming, especially if you eat more of my stew!"

He chuckled as he stirred the stew pot. "The time has come for you to seek flight. The elemental of *air* will soon be yours to command at will. Legend has it, the clouds hold the secrets of the skies. I, myself, have never been able to find as much – they just look like pretty, fluffy, useless things to me. I have never found the magic to control the weather, but you may have better luck. You must! And then of course you will need to locate *The Keeper of Fire,* and the Water Elemental. Ahh, but I am jealous. The wonders that await you."

Ambroas stood up, looking toward the cave entrance. "Now, I must leave you for a time; there is much changing in the land," he said, gathering his belongings throughout the cave, packing up provisions here and there. "A dark cloud surrounds the Northern Territory around the Kingdom, stretching farther out each day. The insects and animals are deserting miles of forest, causing the vacated land to become infertile. Malock has poisoned thousands of acres and that number continues to grow with each passing moment. We must make every attempt we can to stop this atrocity and you must become the man you were meant to be, my boy."

He smiled at Sarghon. "And now I will never call you that again. You are ready for the next step in your training, alas, the next leap toward your life's path. My help is needed in the east to rally troops to our cause.

"So many people are blind to what is coming. They sit and pray to the heavens for answers, hoping that their gods will save them. But, someone needs to warn them and open their eyes to the real demons. Knowledge is power, after all. I must inform them of the impending danger that approaches and mount an army of those willing to defend their land. You on the other hand, my prophetic friend, will learn the secrets of the remaining elements on your own. When the time comes, I will be there. Do you trust me? Do you trust yourself?"

Sarghon paused for a brief moment. "Yes, I do," he said, before standing up and walking toward the stash of carved metal and leather. "We've been training with all these weapons, I see. If I recall, I am quite proficient with a bow and arrow."

Sarghon picked up his bow, pulling back the string, testing the tension. "Bow and arrow can come in handy, but your enchanted blade will be your weapon of choice. Remember to concentrate when using it. It's not just for growing trees in a pretty garden!" Ambroas said, raising an eyebrow. "You will be on your own for now. There are other inhabitants among the forests and plains that will be allies. Befriend who you must, but remember to follow your instincts and trust in yourself for each task at hand. When you can, meditate and search your senses, as you have been trained … for your *path* is your destiny. It will be the one you are predominantly drawn to."

Ambroas gesticulated his hand, fluttering it in the air, "But you know all of this already; there is no need to speak in repetition. Just do as you have been taught, and you will be guided by your forward momentive energy. When the time is right, I will send a sign as to my arrival."

Ambroas then raised his satchel over his shoulder and set off down the mountain.


It was all becoming clear to Sarghon once again. He had been training with Ambroas for years toward his preordained mission to save the land from the tyrant ruler Malock, the mysterious Dark Lord with a perfidious plan.

Yes, this was his destiny, the prophesized battle foretold by the *Diaglyphen Prophesy*. To ignore this instinct, would be akin to trying to live without food. It compelled him now, with every fiber of his body. He must trust entirely in himself and his innate ability.

Once Ambroas disappeared toward the Eastern Hills, Sarghon began a climb up to the highest peak in the Scyllian Stone Mountains.

They had been named for their shape, forming a long mountain range that resembled a giant, winding serpent. Ambroas had found the cave in these ever-twisting mountains many years ago when searching for *Postemp Fruit*, whose juice calms the mind and soothes the skin.

Sarghon climbed higher and higher up the steep, razor sharp rocks, gauging each step with precision, for fear of slicing his skin to shreds. His agility and dexterity grew exponentially since his first days of training, and his balance and confidence impressed even him.

When he reached the top of the mountain peak, he was breathing deeply, as he surveyed the extraordinary landscape. To the east, he viewed the stretch of winding evergreen hills Ambroas was traversing. To the west, he barely made out the shoreline of the Udanax Sea in the distance, with its misty marine layer of fog that hugged the coast like a giant down comforter. To the south, lay the multi-colored farming plains of the villages where he grew up, and further on, the vast, empty red sand desserts – a desolate place he never desired to visit.

It was the north however, that forced his attention. There, beyond the immense Gallandrean Forest, he saw darkness in the distant skies. Sarghon sensed an evil within the darkness, as well intrinsic sadness radiating from within it. Even from this vast distance, he felt life being taken and altered in unspeakable ways.

"You were right old friend, I feel sadness and death in the distance," he said under his breath. *Who must this Malock be, to have such disregard for life?* Sarghon thought. *And what must I do to stop him?*

Taking another deep breath and looking up to the clouds, he stood steadfastly with his legs together and palms open to the sky. This was a meditative lesson Ambroas had taught him. Outstretching his mind and senses, Sarghon could connect with many things at one time, both near and distant. This time, Sarghon focused his energy toward the clouds, ready for whatever may happen next.

With the wind billowing through his cloak, he spoke to the open skies with purpose and determination. "I am Sarghon, bearer of the Diaglyphen Prophesy! Hear my words. I beseech your audience and ask that you reveal unto me the elemental of *Air*!"

Nothing happened.

Concentrating his focus with added command toward the skies above, he intensified his resolve, speaking again, "I request an audience with the spirits of the wind, – no, I demand your audience! I cannot continue my quest without your assistance. Hear my words!"

The wind began to grow stronger, singing in multi-tonal whistles, stinging his eyes, as he maintained his gaze upon the sky. The clouds changed, drifting together and apart again, flowing with wispy gracefulness, intertwining and merging like wet paint on a canvas. Sarghon appeared to have gained the wind's attention.

"In the name of life, and all that is good, grant me the sacred knowledge of the wind and air!" he continued, not knowing exactly what it was that he should ask the vast emptiness of the sky.

Until now, Sarghon didn't believe anyone could actually receive an answer when shouting at the sky, but on this day the skies were indeed communicating with him. The clouds swirled around into shapes of symbols which at first looked odd, other than their symmetry, but after studying them, Sarghon was able to translate the shapes into an ancient form of writing he never knew he could read. The clouds were testing him, spelling out a phrase only he should know how to read – if indeed he was the foretold prophesier.

Sarghon decided to take a gander: "See ... no, wait." He stopped, concentrating on the shapes before speaking again. "Behold, for life is gained through sight and insight of all things, if the eyes of the soul are open."

After speaking the final word, a funnel of wind surrounded Sarghon, lifting him off the ground, raising him fifty feet up into the air. He wasn't spinning, but standing straight up, able to see clearly through the cyclone of wind that held him in place.

He felt gusts of air lifting him from under his feet and shoulders, as his mind rushed with fantastic imagery. The information came from a consciousness beyond the wind, sharing knowledge of how to control and manipulate all forms of air and wind power. He learned the dynamics of speed, airflow, pressure, velocity, and more, as an anthology of information flashed before his eyes. Absorbing the information willingly, Sarghon gained complete understanding of exactly how to wield the element of Air, all while floating effortlessly in the air stream.

The Elemental taught him that air was controlled using clear mental focus and acceptance known as: *the lightness of the mind,* a magical technique of complete clarity without distraction of any kind.

Images of countless flying creatures flashed across his eyes, as words whispered in his ears: *As a bird flies without wondering if it will fall, or a dragonfly floats over a pond not worrying if it will drift falsely into the water and drown, you must allow yourself to mentally trust, accept, and affirm absolutely in your conviction when wielding the Air element.*

Finishing the lesson, the funnel of air gently returned him back down to the Earth, before dissipating into a light breeze. The clouds swirled around in graceful, whirling wisps before settling back into a natural formation, as if nothing had occurred at all.

Energized and exhilarated by the experience, Sarghon felt the strength of the wind tingling throughout his body, knowing that the power and knowledge of the air element was now at his fingertips to use as he willed.

A thought flashed through his mind, imagining the devastation and havoc he could now generate, if he so desired. This kind of power in the hands of an evil warlord such as Malock, gave him pause.

He decided to try out his new gift.

Lifting his right hand, aiming his palm outward, he focused his energy toward the trees below, but nothing happened.

Recalling what the air element needed to work, *lightness of the mind*, he cleared his head completely while taking in a deep, calming breath and focusing on the forest below. Raising his arm once again, with no other thought present but the task of creating wind, he focused his energy while gesturing his hand outward. A gust of air blew out from his hand, rustling a grove of trees, as several disturbed birds flew from the treetops.

"Let's see what I'm really packing," he said under his breath, feeling a bit more daring. Raising his arm above his head while pursing his lips, he looked up to the sky and concentrated.

A funnel of wind began to form in the palm of his hand, growing larger with each second. With focused thought, the mini-tornado grew bigger and faster, while he controlled its shape and flow. It continued to grow, on and on, larger and larger, gaining more strength, until it reached the size of a tempest cyclone swirling in the clouds above him hundreds of feet high.

The trees below bent in the whirlwind, as dust and dirt were swept up into the funnel. "That's what I am talking about!" Sarghon shouted with exuberance. It was incredible fun!

Astonished, he began to laugh. It teetered back and forth in the sky above, when he realized it was starting to move on its own, circling around back toward the hillside where his cave dwelling lay. Sarghon had to think quickly.

Calming his mind, concentrating only on the wind, he used his other hand to create a second cyclone. Waving both hands in opposite directions, the second cyclone grew, blowing against the first one.

His tactic seemed to be slowing the first funnel, filtering air in the opposite direction, as the second funnel of air began to merge with the first one. The wind blew back at his face with great force, blinding him.

Sarghon couldn't maintain control. He was blown backward in a huge gust, shooting his entire body off the ground and across the gravel onto his backside. Retracting his hands into fists, the wind instantly stopped.

"Wow, what a rush! That will definitely come in handy," he said out loud, grinning a cunning smile toward the sky. "I had no idea how invigorating it would be! You were right to feel jealous old man!"

He scaled down the mountain, back to the cave to gather his leather bag, bow and arrow, lambskin gloves and provisions for his journey northward. "Know thy enemy as thyself," he said to himself, while stuffing bread and dried sticks of cured, smoked meat into his leather satchel. "Wise advice indeed, old friend."

Ambroas had always quoted proverbs and maxims to him while puttering around a dwelling or while cooking his famous rabbit stew: *Follow the truth, but not too closely*, or, *Think as other's may not, where others do not*. Some sayings were in jest, but Sarghon often took heed applying what he had been taught. *Know thy enemy as thyself,* topped his list.

He felt compelled to understand what drove his enemy toward the darkness, learning as much as possible about Malock's deathly agenda. Although Sarghon was still short two out of four elemental powers, he felt the risk was worthy of some reconnaissance.

Setting down a rocky path toward the forest below the Scyllian Stone Mountains, Sarghon found he could move discretely through the lush underbrush without being detected easily by rivals or spies.

With his newfound power and determination, Sarghon felt a renewed sense of purpose. The youthful doubts from before had vanished, being replaced with daring and courage. Every tree he touched gave him a sense of gratitude. With each step, Sarghon felt hopeful energy from the trees and plants, as well as from the woodland animals and insects. As if reading their thoughts, he felt each living creature he encountered offer encouragement for his venture.

After several miles, he stopped to rest by a large Maroobi Pine, placing his bag and bow on the ground. Unsheathing Gladanteus, he held the magnificent sword before him with both hands. Sarghon then closed his eyes, lowering the tip of the blade to the ground next to the giant pine. When it touched the grassy Earth, a slither of vines grew out and up, twisting, maturing, and blossoming into the succulent Vinum Berry plant, with its purple, ripe fruit the size of quail eggs.

Placing Gladanteus back in her sheath, he sat on the grass against the tree, picking ripe berries off the newly formed vines that arched over his shoulder at his elbow.

He devoured at least a dozen thirst quenching berries, when from behind his head he heard a ticking noise. Sitting up on one arm, he turned to see what was making the odd sounds behind him. There, on the tree above his shoulder, was a *Turquoise Spider*, one of the largest and most rare spiders in the land.

Mesmerized by the sight, Sarghon watched the spiraling, changing turquoise patterns on its large, glassy back. It stood nine inches long and when provoked, it would raise its back to hypnotize its prey with an entrancing motion.

Sarghon recognized the legendary creature immediately, for the Turquoise Spider possessed venom of *nepenthe,* a very unique property, indeed.

He moved back to assess the spider's nature, when the Maroobi pine tree spoke to Sarghon, *"Shantana souath-tara. Whishastoren Turquana nepenthaas estas shey shey shey, eeshoranath whofarra."* (Welcome chosen one. I have not observed a Nepenthe-Arachnus in 333 years. It is a sign. Take it as such.)

Sarghon knew that if a tree chose to speak first, it would be for a reason of great importance. Replying in the earthen language, Sarghon answered, *"Sarathonaasta whey shenoreth, vey tarasareth a whoosholar."* (Thank you great wise one for your wisdom and guidance)

Sarghon directly considered the particular number the tree just shared with him. 333 was the number mentioned on the stone tablet as his date of birth. It could not be a coincidence. This added to the importance of the moment.

Turning cautiously to the spider, Sarghon knew he needed to extract the rare, magical *nepenthe* venom. He recalled that when ingested as a tincture, *nepenthe* became a strong potion, capable of erasing memory of all sorrow, pain and grief. One drop could ease the suffering of an illness, or make one forget why he suffered in the first place. This single spider alone held enough *nepenthe* for a small army.

Contemplating exactly how he would get the precious venom from its fangs, Sarghon recalled that it must be willingly injected by the spider, for if it was forcibly taken, the magic of the *nepenthe* would only poison and kill.

*But how to extract it, and where to put it?* Sarghon thought quickly, as he looked around. "Think as other's may not, right Ambroas?" he said to himself, peering down the blade of Gladanteus, as he caressed the magical jewel embedded in her handle.

Sarghon had a brilliant idea. His water sack was too large and bulky to store the precarious venom, and he had no potion vile on his person. Reaching for the sword, he held the crystal pommel in one hand, placing the other hand on the ground, concentrating very precisely on the task at hand. Focusing his thoughts on the Earth and its molecular structures beneath his hand, Sarghon imagined the shape of his intention while working the earthen magic. The ground moved under his fingers as a solid, clear crystal stone rose up from the Earth into his hand.

Blowing the excess dirt and dust from the magically formed crystal, he held it up to the sunlight. "This will do," he said under his breath, keeping a keen eye on the spider from the corner of his eye.

Focusing his thoughts on the stone and clasping it tight in his hand, while still holding Gladanteus in the other, the crystal glowed with blue light, shaping into a perfect crystal-clear sphere.

Holding the orb in one hand, while hovering his other hand above with a hint more concentration, he worked a bit of his own magic, making it perfectly hollow. It now resembled a large, hollow glass marble.

"Now, Ambroas, if you are listening to me or watching me through a gazing ball at this very moment, you will be proud of this little trick," he snickered to himself. It was the *pièce de résistance* of his plan. He placed the clear crystal orb in front of the spider, waving his hand over it with an eccentric, magical gesture.

The orb instantly glammered into a small, wounded sparrow. Flickering his index finger, Sarghon made the sparrow hop and flutter its wounded wing, like a puppet. Slowly the Turquoise Spider took notice, crawling down the root of the ancient Maroobi tree toward its meal. It crawled up in strike position behind the wounded, dancing sparrow, with its front legs poised for attack.

The spider raised its rear turquoise abdomen, dazzling its prey with swirling translucent blue colors.

Then, with lightning sharp speed, the large spider lurched forward with astonishing agility for its size, clutching the helpless bird, as it sank its fangs into the tender breast.

Sarghon stopped twitching his finger, allowing the spider to inject its venom of pure *nepenthe* into the heart of the helpless bird. Normally, the Turquoise Spider instantly pleasures its victims into a relaxed seduction with the magical venom, while it devours the prey alive and whole. It is said: *to be bitten by one is extraordinarily good luck, if you survive.*

Once the regal creature retracted his fangs, he was ready to feast.

"Oh no, my beautiful, magical beast," Sarghon said, raising his finger once again as he spoke, "I'm afraid YOU are the one who has been seduced today."

Making a gesture with his hand, the magical sparrow became the crystal orb once again, now filled with a glistening, milky liquid of cherished pure *nepenthe*.

Sarghon bowed his head, thanking the rare spider for its valued gift, as it scurried back up the tree trunk without its meal. He picked several more Vinum Berries for the road, sheathed Gladanteus, and hooked his bag over his shoulder for the rest of his day's journey.

Heading due North, Sarghon decided only to stop for short rests. With the element of Air at his command, he would soon need to test out his ability of flight, but wanted to stay concealed by the forest while he had protective use of its cover. Once in the lower foothills, he would find a large expanse to practice controlling the winds in his favor for flight.

Continuing his day's journey northbound through the forest, Sarghon allowed his intuitive senses to guide him once again. It had become easier to determine a desired direction or path. All he needed to do was focus on a place within his mind and the path toward that place would reveal itself. Whether it be a slightly illuminated shrub, or just an inner sense to move left or right, Sarghon felt his way with a knowing ease.

If he accidentally took an incorrect step away from his intended destination, or wandered into danger, he sensed a tingling sensation warning him that he was headed in the wrong direction.

He often spoke a kind gesture to the older, more regal trees as he passed them. "Shorentara" (Good day), he would say, or "Saranoth boren tatharasa" (What sturdy roots you possess, friend).

*"Whishastoren, taranashhhta"*(Welcome, chosen one), they would reply, or *"Earathe benosta uraay"* (Earth be with you). Sarghon felt a sense of peace and protection knowing that all the trees of the land were on his side.

His connection to the Earth was fast becoming second nature. This was his inherent intuition at work and he knew he would soon be one of the most powerful beings in the land.


# KARA


Sarghon walked on for several hours, as the afternoon light saturated the deep, orange sky. As he entered a clearing between the trees, he saw a figure moving toward him in the distant sky. *That's a large bird,* he thought, watching it fly directly toward him.

Standing ready to blow it out of the sky with a forceful burst of wind should it attack, Sarghon realized it wasn't a bird at all. It was a person with giant wings. Moreover, it was a woman – a woman with wings.

As she approached, Sarghon admired her majestic, white wings; her long, flowing blond hair; and her shimmering, silver battle gear.

Floating down with grace, she landed imposingly near Sarghon. "I am Kara, daughter of Freja, Queen of the Valkyrie," The Female creature said, bowing to him with one hand on the pommel of her sword, "I was sent to aid you on your quest in whatever way I may be of most assistance. It is an honor to meet you, sire."

"The pleasure is mine," he said, admiring her striking beauty and amethyst colored eyes. "I am no one's sire, however I do hold the name, Sarghon."

"Are you not the *Spirit King*, from the legendary prophecy?"

"Of the prophecy part, you appear to be quite correct; nevertheless, I have not yet been crowned king in any land that I can recall," Sarghon said with a slight smile.

"Oh,"… she hesitated, "then I shall think on you as a prince. You *are* quite a bit younger than I had imagined. My mother did not know exactly what you would look like. Ambroas described you as a warrior, but you do not look as much," she said, folding her wings, tucking them neatly against her back.

"You know Ambroas? Did he send you to spy on me? Tricky old devil."

"No, I was sent by my mother. I have only met Ambroas once, but my mother is our queen and they are in contact often. She is fond of him," Kara said, as her eyes sparkled with iridescent glimmers of sunlight.

Sarghon was taken with her beauty and inherent authority. Muscular, yet graceful, she possessed a strength and poise that befit royalty. Her movements appeared unusually non-human, yet extraordinarily refined.

Sarghon stood curiously enchanted by Kara, Princess of the Valkyrie.

"Our lands have been infiltrated by King Malock's death curse. The Eastern Hills are black and dead as the Odinian Desert. Neither plant nor animal lives on them anymore. Ambroas warned us of the impending danger that is now upon us, so the queen sent me to assist you."

"How did you find me?" Sarghon asked, knowing he was the only one who knew his current plan of action.

"I have been following you for the last three hours. I can read the wind. I see we are headed north. Are you planning your attack on the Dark Lord so soon?"

Her matter-of-factness and intuition intrigued Sarghon. He decided to be honest with her as well.

"No, just doing some reconnaissance. I desire to see this Malock up close – maybe determine a weakness. I want to find out anything I can about him before I form a concrete plan of action."

"Both a wise and foolish choice," she said, piercing him with her dazzling amethyst colored eyes. "Many have tried to attack him where he lives, but none have returned. They all become converted into his mindless followers. He wields a powerful magic. There is much speculation about him and his army. The black cloud surrounding his fortress is toxic to us. We cannot fly close enough to see through it. Our wings lose all flexibility and our feathers shrivel in the black air and break off."

"That's unfortunate. Well, when we get close, we will just have to enter on foot. The closer I am to the Earth, the better," he said, gripping the handle of his sword, thankful that Gladanteus was near.

"Can you fly?" she asked simply.

Sarghon was embarrassed that he had not yet attempted flight. While standing next to this beautiful, enchanted being with giant, shimmering wings, he suddenly felt inadequate. It was clear she was superior in the sky. He knew this would be the time to sink or swim … or soar.

"I can … well, I know I can fly, I just have not yet done so of my own choosing, that is." He squinted his brow in frustration, as she gave him a very confused look .

"Well, it seems there is no better time than this moment. Shall we?"

Unfolding her impressive, brilliant white wings, Kara stroked them with steady gusts as she rose up backward, still watching Sarghon on the ground.

*I will need both my hands controlling the air for balance,* he thought, securing his shoulder bag, bow, arrows and sword belt, poising himself for lift off.

"OK, here I come!" he shouted up at Kara, positioning his hands facing toward the ground.

*Steady* … he thought to himself. *Not too much power … NOW!*

Pushing air down toward the ground, he began rising up five feet, seven feet, ten feet …

The air under his hands became unsteady. The slightest arm bend caused his direction to change uncontrollably. "Whoa," he said, bending his left arm too far, causing his other arm to react impulsively.

He spun cartwheels in the air, tumbling toward the ground before crashing down, head-over-heels in a clumsy, awkward landing.

"Well that was graceful," Kara mocked. "All the poise of a falcon."

Sargon shot her a snide, yet embarrassed glare.

*Wait,* he thought, *maybe I should direct the air to rise under my arms in order to keep my hands free. Yes!*

Making another attempt, Sarghon concentrated on positioning pockets of air under each arm to lift him evenly. The wind tickled his underarms as the air rushed forcefully under both armpits. He concentrated specifically on the empty space under his arms, in order to keep himself evenly balanced. It was working – he slowly rose up into the air.

*This is a very odd sensation, indeed*, he thought, as the invisible force lifted him into the vast sky, rising higher and higher. *I will NOT fall this time,* he willed himself. For a moment he thought he may fall, but soon he got the gist of it and was able to control his speed and angle of flight.

He found that he could gain maneuverability and control by expanding the air under his arms, spreading it out along his body, positioning the wind under his outstretched limbs. Feeling euphoric and exhilarated, he was flying!

*I am one with the sky!* he thought, feeling free. The open expanse before him was an awesome thing of beauty, and it made Sarghon feel as though anything were possible.

He followed Kara northbound but after some time, his muscles, especially in his arms, became fatigued from holding his constant weight against the wind. "Do you have any advice for resting while in flight?" he called to Kara.

"Are you tired already? Pity one so powerful has such limits," she said tersely. "I suppose wings have their advantages when flying long distances. If I want to rest my wings, I spread them out to their full length and catch the air currents. Can you not just sit back on the air you control?"

Sarghon hadn't thought of that. *Of course,* he realized, *I could just direct the wind to lift me, as if it were a lounging chair,* he thought. "Kara, fly in circles while I attend to my fatigue. Remember O' mighty flightress, I am still new at this!"

Sarghon came to a halt in the air, directing the wind to cushion his back and underside, as he carefully leaned back in a lounging position. Releasing the air under his arms so he could rest the weary muscles never before utilized in this manner, Sarghon realized he would need to strengthen these specific muscles in order to fly with more proficiency.

"Flying is more work than I had imagined," he muttered to himself, as he concentrated on shifting the airflow. It appeared to be working, as he sat motionless in mid-air, catching his breath and resting his limbs.

"Sarghon, the orange sun will be setting soon," Kara called down. "We should not fly in the darkness. Follow me; I will lead us to a safe location on the ground."

Sarghon thought it best to follow her lead, for she knew these lands much better than he.

"Lead on!" he shouted back, as he took a flying position once again.

They continued on for another twenty minutes, before landing in a clearing on the edge of the Northaxion foothills. There they could survey the dark northern landscape from a clear vantage point, while still being camouflaged by the foliage of the hills.

"This is where we will camp for the night," Kara said authoritatively.

"I will not disagree with you, Princess of the Valkyrie. I haven't provisions for the both of us, however, I can grow some if you like?"

Kara looked intrigued, as Sarghon smiled at her obtuse expression.

"You are welcome to share my blanket, if you wish" he said, unclasping his shoulder bag and pulling out the small woven blanket he carried with him on which to sleep.

Reaching into his satchel, Sarghon scooped up some berries. "Here try one of these," he said, tossing Kara a Vinum berry. "You must be thirsty, no?"

Kara caught the fruit in one hand with lightning speed, never once taking her gaze from Sarghon's eye. "Have you acquired the element of fire yet or must we procure heat between us the normal way?" she asked plainly.

Sarghon was now the one wearing the obtuse expression, as he struggled to grasp her meaning. "No ... well, I have yet to receive the *fire* element. Which way is the, um ... *normal* way of staying warm, in which you speak?"

He was clearly fumbling for words.

"I said nothing of staying warm. The heat of which I speak is to cook the meat I mean to hunt for our supper."

Sarghon suddenly felt foolish.

"I see," he said, blushing, "Well, let's begin with some food from the Earth."

Unsheathing Gladanteus, he held the sword in both hands.

"A mighty blade, you posses. Does she have a name?" Kara asked softly, seeing her reflection in the mirror-like blade.

"Gladanteus, Sword of the Earth – and mighty she is, indeed,"

Sarghon replied, gripping the sword decisively with both hands and bringing the tip to the ground with a firm strike.

All around the area where the blade tip pierced into the ground, stalks of bright green began to grow, budding into branches and leaves that extended out, bearing yellow oblong fruit. Vines grew from beside the newly formed tree, sprouting Spiral Sweet Peas and Zarcana Berries, larger and plumper than Kara had ever seen.

Next grew a vegetable vine flowering in enormous pink flowers bearing the Jantu Squash, striped green and white, with reddish speckles.

A small bush burst from beside the tree, where Shangala Nuts instantly appeared on the tips of thin, winding branches. It was a virtual banquet of tasty vegetarian treats.

"Please, take your fill," Sarghon said, gesturing his open hand to Kara.

"I am impressed with your earthly abilities, young prince. I hope Gladanteus serves as well in battle."

"I am no prince," he said plainly.

"You may as well be," she replied.

Sarghon accepted the comment, unsure if he wanted or even deserved the adoration, considering what it would truly mean to be a ruler.

Kara paused, looking at the fruit. "Is this a Begodel?" she asked, picking one of the hanging yellow fruits from the tree. "These only grow in the tropical sands along the southern-most point of the Udanax Sea. I happen to like these very much. Did you know that? I rarely fly that far south."

She appeared to be complimenting Sarghon, for her expression became soft and seductive. "This fruit is an aphrodisiac, you know," she said, picking several of the plump, ripe, yellow fruits from the new tree. "We Valkyrie are more susceptible to indulgences of the flesh than you humans. Time was, when Valkyrie served only kings and magical creatures. We do, however, have the instinct to locate heroism when we choose. That is how I found you."

Sarghon was stunned by her audacious and frank nature. She possessed an attractive boldness he had never seen before in a female and she was unknowingly flirtatious.

He watched her eat the Begodle fruit with exactingly clean accuracy, not letting a drop of juice fall from her lips. Her eyes sparkled with each bite, and as she sunk her teeth into the succulent flesh of the fruit, her expression was evocative and she became flush.

"I didn't know those things about the Valkyrie," he said, trying not to watch her every enticing movement. "And you think me heroic, do you? Well, that is yet to be determined."

"For the sake of our land, you will need to be," she said, swallowing her food.

Leaning against the Begodel tree, looking off into the distance, his tone changed. "I never chose this path. I was born into it without any knowledge of my foretold destiny. I fear I may not be the 'hero' you think me to be. I never desired to be a king, or prince, or anything out of the ordinary. These powers I possess may end up being a curse. What if I can't control them or hurt someone I don't mean to? And then there's the Dark King! If I cannot defeat Malock, the death of our land will fall on my shoulders, don't you see? It will be my fault!"

Sarghon turned around, gazing broodingly out at the northern landscape, feeling wounded.

"No one asks for their destiny," Kara retorted, with sincerity. "We all act on instinct. If we are taught righteousness, rectitude, and morality, then we should grow up as such. But that is not always the case."

She stretched out her wings with closed eyes, then brought them back in again, settling them softly behind her back. "I believe we are born with our own conscience," she said softly. "Instinct tempered by mind and heart, becomes consciousness. Those who stay in the *individual consciousness* are ruled by the *ego,* and those who choose to lead a tyrannical, despotic path such as Malock, will pay the price within their soul as well as in the flesh."

He listened, trying not to look her in the eyes. "You are part of the *universal consciousness*," she said with sincerity, "connected to a greater understanding of all things seen and unseen. You are greater than the darkness, for you can see the light – something that Malock cannot. What you lack is confidence. And that is something I can help you with. Draw your sword!" she demanded, unyieldingly.

Sarghon was taken aback. He wasn't expecting a duel.

"I said draw your sword, or be cut down by my first blow!!"

She came at him full force, as he released Gladanteus just in time to counter her cutting strike. "You have a unique way of encouraging my imperfections," Sarghon said, as he countered two more potent blows.

She was lightning fast and stronger than Sarghon. Her movements were precise and controlled with inexorable force. Sarghon had to use all his skill to keep from being dashed to pieces.

"Are you sure *you* are not being ruled by your ego at this moment? Sarghon groaned, as he held back her weight, the blade of her sword leaning ever closer into his neck.

"I am part of the *collective consciousness*," she replied, as sparks flew across her chest from Gladanteus, "a wisdom and creativity harnessed for the common good, with the ability to intuitively sense ..."

She moaned as Sargon pressed into her, "and understand the interactions between energy fields, physically, emotionally, mentally, and ..."

Her breath panted upon Sarghon's lips, as her sparkling amethyst eyes penetrated his. "... spiritually!" she said, with a final breath – her face less than an inch from his.

Sweat began dripping from Sarghon's brow, as Kara's eyes grew in size and intensity. Both of their lips quivered, their muscular bodies pressing firmly against each other with strength and anticipation.

In less than a heartbeat, Kara released her wings, shooting into the air above Sarghon, her sword raised to the sky as if summoning the Gods.

Lightning struck her blade from above, electrifying the entire sword. She pointed the lightning filled weapon at Sarghon's feet, releasing electricity down the blade with imposing power.

As the energy exploded inches from his right foot, Sarghon was blown backward.

Landing gracefully in front of him, Kara was silent as he sat staring at her in astonishment, stunned by her display of power and further amazed with this magnificent creature of a woman.

"I am impressed by *your* heavenly abilities, winged Princess," Sarghon said with a witty smile.

"As you can see, perception is subjective. Things are not always what they appear to be. You should remember this when facing the power of the Dark Lord. It may be your way to victory or escape.


From the fire left over from Kara's lightning strike, they roasted some vegetables, and ate their fill of fruit.

Sarghon gently laid his blanket down under the Begodel tree, hoping that Kara may eventually join him, when he sensed danger!

A feeling of immediate concern grabbed his body, like jagged ice being scraped down his back. Kara hadn't noticed anything, but he shouted to her in a harsh whisper. "Don't move! Something is in the woods behind you."

Kara froze in a battle stance, her wings slowly opening, ready for action, eyes surveying the forest all around her in the dusky light. A rustle was heard from behind a bush.

With his sword drawn, Sarghon walked several paces from their campfire around hedges of brush, looking in the direction of the sound, when from behind a large tree walked a giant Qilin. It was a truly impressive and unusual, magical beast of the forest, resembling a stripped stag, with a single great horned antler and wispy, long tail.

It walked across the ground almost floating, without a sound, not bending one blade of grass as it moved. Its eyes glowed orange as it snarled its lip several times, showing its large fang-like teeth.

"These are peaceful creatures of the mountain forests," Kara said under her breath, "however, this one seems different."

"With my new senses, I can connect with any living creature, but I do not sense this beast at all," Sarghon responded with concern, "It is as if its mind is completely blank."

The beast grunted, lunging toward Sarghon with its horned antler, using it like a blade and spear together.

Sarghon leapt out of the way, rolling to the ground with a graceful recovery. The Qilin flared its nostrils, puffing out smoke, as it kicked the ground with its front hoof.

"I have never seen a Qilin with orange, glowing eyes," Kara said, "Nor have I ever seen one attack another mammal. They are spiritual, docile creatures with magical attributes. They do not attack people. This one is under some kind of spell."

The Qilin darted toward Kara, with its horned antler poised to strike. It was fast and agile.

The sharp horn caught Kara's silver shoulder plate, as she flew into the air, flipping forward, landing on the other side of the beast. Raising her sword, ready to strike, Sarghon yelled out, "No, we cannot hurt this creature. It's clearly being manipulated to do someone else's bidding. If we must kill to save our lands so be it, but we must at least try not to harm the innocent who know not of what they do."

"Agreed," Kara said, somewhat reluctantly, with a calculating sneer. "How do you intend to subdue it?"

The beast came around for another attack. Using their swords against the creature's massive horned antler, Kara and Sarghon tried not to cut into its skin. The Qilin was unusually fast and dexterous for its size, and the horn was as strong as their blades, showing no damage at all after each attack and counter attack.

After several more strikes, Kara was becoming impatient. "We are not going to sleep tonight unless this beast is unconscious!"

Raising her sword to the sky, she summoned lightening to her blade. When it was filled with electricity, she released it toward the creature. The Qilin saw the attack and lowered its head, directing its horn toward the oncoming strike of lightening.

Next, something miraculous happened. The electricity was absorbed by the Qilin, who took the energy into its horned antler, glowing bright white. Then, the Qilin shot the electricity directly back at both Kara and Sarghon, who tried to block the blasts with their swords. Both were blown backward, hitting the ground in a cloud of smoke.

"I forgot that Qilin can manipulate light energy. I've never had to attack one after all," she said, irritated.

"I have an idea," Sarghon pronounced as he stood up, brushing the dust off.

Walking up to the fuming beast, Sarghon held Gladanteus before him, as the Qilin dug its hoofs into the ground ready to charge again. Before it could gain ground, Sarghon brought the blade down onto its horn and held it there. Concentrating on the glowing Earatheen Crystal, he made the horn grow.

The beast tried to back away, but Sarghon lurched forward keeping Gladanteus connected with the horned antler as it grew larger and heavier.

Soon the Qilin's neck began to bow forward. When the horn was as large as the beast's entire body, Sarghon released the blade and stepped back. The Qilin's head fell to the ground along with its body. It was now incapacitated and unable to lift its head.

"Ingenious," Kara said, tilting her head to one side, staring the creature directly in its glowing, orange eyes. It kicked and snorted, letting out a frustrating whine.

"My plan is not over. We cannot leave the thing to die here in the forest."

Placing his sword to the Earth and focusing his mind once again, Sarghon brought forth a bush from the ground. Twisting and writhing up, the trunk sprouted branches and leaves which burst into flowers that quickly matured into a round, red fruit.

"This should do the trick. The Silpnas apple; a single bite and one will be asleep for hours. Amazing the things that are swimming through my mind. Strange, I've never seen this fruit before, and yet, I know everything about it: where it grows, how it reacts with each creature, that it's used as a sleeping tincture or remedy for anxiety and hysteria, but in very small doses."

Sarghon was rambling. "A full apple should do. And, they are so pleasing to the eye, are they not?"

Sarghon shoved one into the creature's mouth, noticing how delectable and enchantingly delicious the fruit looked. "Your resourcefulness is intriguing," Kara said, with a tinge of approval.

Sarghon picked another Silpnas apple. He held it in his hand, staring at its alluring beauty, as the teeth of the Qilin clicked together in rhythm chewing the apple in its mouth. Then something odd happened – Sarghon took a bite.

He had been enchanted by his own magic. Kara had not noticed at first and, as he chewed the sweet flesh of the fruit, time began to slow. The odd clicking noise from the Qilin's teeth continued from behind the bushes in the darkness. It persisted, then stopped, then started again becoming louder and louder as it echoed off the trees.

Kara turned toward Sarghon, realizing what he had done, but it was too late. Sarghon's eyes swam with fog as he became dizzy and lightheaded.

He fell to the ground, passing out cold.

# Chapter VI

## INTUITION

Thane woke up to the sound of a blue-crested mountain woodpecker banging his beak against a pine tree just outside the open window. The cabins had no doors or windows during the summer and all the woodland sounds resonated any time of the day or night. Thane was the first one up, and without waking Brad or his campers, Thane put on his fuzzy slippers and thick bathrobe creeping softly outside to watch the sun rise.

Mountain dawn: that awe-inspiring time of the morning when the dew still sparkled like tiny crystals on the grasses and pine needles, and the air felt intensely crisp and clean. The birds sang their morning songs, as a grey squirrel scurried by with his breakfast acorn in his mouth.

Thane walked out to the edge of the mountain meadow, found a tree stump, and sat. As the sun approached in the east, his view encompassed the glistening cattails and long grasses of the open meadow.

He sat silently reflecting on the fascinating and inspiring dream he had just awoken from, still raw with detailed magical pictures and feelings running through his mind and body.

With a large smile across his entire face, Thane felt overjoyed that his dream had returned once again, continuing on its destined course, aware of how unusual a progressive dream like this was.

As he peered across the beautiful mountain scenery, Thane couldn't help but sense the natural energy all around. He inhaled a deep breath of fresh vanilla pine and morning dew, appreciating the life all around.

Closing his eyes, listening to the forest sounds, he recalled Sarghon's walk through the mystical forest, Kara's awesome strength and beauty, and his intense connection with the wilderness from his dream. He also remembered the horseback ride from yesterday. The interconnectedness between his dreams and his current reality weren't overlooked. The comparison excited him.

As the sunlight breached the horizon, golden rays of light cast through the trees onto Thane's face. While squinting his half-closed eyes from the light, a green and purple-breasted hummingbird flew directly in front of him only a few feet from his face. The wings moved in a slow-motion blur, as the bird hovered for several moments, staring eye to eye. The intensity of colors on its body reminded Thane of the colors from Ambroas's magical garden.

The hummingbird flew away as fast as it had arrived. Thane felt an uncontrollable shiver ripple throughout his body, as he experienced a state of awe. He was connected, and unable to put his feeling into words, so he just smiled. Indeed, his appreciation for the immaculate life around him was heightened. Thane felt an inherent connection to it all: every tree, every blade of grass, and every rock. With each breath of crisp, morning mountain air came admiration for Earth's grand and beautiful design.

He walked back to the cabin feeling refreshed, eager to share his feelings with Sharla. She would understand. She wouldn't judge him for these strange new feelings and incredible dreams he was experiencing. The two had planned a walk today for their official ragger's talk, and he certainly had much to discuss.

Thane knew the situations he created in his dreams were the duality of his conscious and subconscious mind. Something was beginning to make sense – to break through, but he needed to talk it all out with someone.

At morning Chapel, Thane once again felt immersed in the tranquil beauty of his surroundings. At breakfast when he overheard a kid making fun of another boy from across the table, instead of reacting as he usually would by scolding the troublemaker or stopping the encounter, Thane sat trancelike, pondering silently to himself: *That was mean spirited, but he'll grow up one day, and learn from life's errors,* he thought, *All is meant to be as it is.*

Shaking his head, Thane snapped out of his Zen-like euphoria as a string of pancake syrup dripped from his chin down the front of his shirt.

"Ahh, shit! – I mean *shoot*. I said shoot!" he shouted, shaking his head again, looking around the table of boys. They had all stopped eating and were staring at Thane. "Wow, what the … I'm OK, just a bit of syrup, is all," he said, trying to cover, wiping the syrup from his shirt with some ice from his water glass. *I'm trip'n out. This is definitely something to discuss with Sharla today,* he thought, considering his mental state.

      After breakfast, Thane headed to his first activity period. Archery had always been one of his favorite mountain camp sports. He didn't feel like wasting his time babysitting campers, so whenever he had the chance, he grabbed a bow and arrow, practicing his aim and precision.

      The archery area included three haystack targets, each painted with a bull's eye in the center. Thane pretended he was Sarghon, practicing for his great, foretold battle. He imagined his engraved armor glistening off his shoulders as he slowly pulled back the tension of the bowstring.

      With one eye closed and the other gauging the distance, Thane released an arrow, hurling it into the center of the target. "Bull's eye!" he shouted. "Take that Malock!"

      "Will you let us have a turn, Mr. Windstrom? Please," begged a short ten-year-old boy at his side. During his fantasy distraction, Thane hadn't realized the small line forming behind him and his target.

      "Oh yes, of course," he answered, returning to *counselor reality.* "Wow, where did you come from, you little forest beasts? If you need any help, just let me know. That's why I'm here, right?"

      Thane also enjoyed his second period at the craft lodge. He was an artist at heart and loved using his hands and mind to create anything out of anything. A craft teacher worked in the lodge with the campers, but Thane never played creatively by the rules, deciding to make something for himself while the other campers followed the guidance of the teacher.

      Thane had picked up a perfect walking stick on the way, and holding the thicker side in his hand, he selected a carving knife and began carving a handle on it. After whittling off the sides and sanding it to a smooth finish, he rounded off the bottom while considering the handgrip. *What to place on top?* he thought, recalling the odd Tarpin creature and magical stone from his dream.

      The craft lodge was filled with granite rocks, agate, and crystal geodes for use in craft projects. He located a round, crystal geode that sparkled with purple and clear white crystals. The top of his stick had enough room for an object to sit nestled in the handle if he carved it out a bit.

After carving the right depth in the top of the stick, Thane wrapped the handle with a thin strip of leather, crisscrossing the geode stone in the notch. He then wrapped the remaining leather strip around the handle, making a grip by fastening it tightly with a small flush knot.

Thane completed his creation by attaching a striped owl feather along the base of the handle, dangling several inches below. When finished, it was a uniquely practical piece of art. Happy with his efforts by the end of the period, Thane headed to the campfire pit where he would meet Sharla for their two-hour ragger talk.


"Wow! Cool walking stick. Did you make that?" Sharla said, lounging leisurely on one of the large logs surrounding the group campfire area.

"Just now, in the craft lodge. It's the perfect shape, right? And there's a story behind it. Let's follow the trail up past the chapel. I heard there's a stream back in the woods up there."

With the next two hours all to themselves, they made their way through the camp, past the chapel area, to a beautiful, winding fern-banked trail in the lush wilderness.

"So, what the heck's been going on with you?" Sharla asked, "I know something's up, even if Aaron doesn't see it. You've been somewhere else lately. Am I right, or what?"

Sharla knew him intuitively. "Yes you are insightful, indeed."

"Indeed, I am," she said, with a cunning grin.

"Well, I'll try to explain it," Thane said, after a silent moment. "I've been having these crazy dreams lately. Floating underwater, peering at celestial light beams, walking through magical forests, talking to trees, and a Tarpin. I have this incredible sword with a magical crystal that harnesses the powers of the Earth. And there's this teacher-guy named Ambroas, who calls me Sarghon and ..."

"What's a Tarpin? And what do you mean he calls you Sarghon? What the hell, dude? You mean you have another name in your dreams?"

"Exactly! And even wilder, I have this profound connection with the Earth. It's really intense. And here in real life, I'm beginning to sense a total connection to nature, like in the dream."

Thane touched one of the trees with his walking stick. "It's mind blowing! Like, on the horse trail yesterday, I drifted off into a trance or something. I was drawn to this area where the plants were glowing and it felt like something told me to go in that direction, and … well, shit. It's kinda crazy – like everything exploded in extreme detail."

Sharla appeared dumfounded. "Wow, so I'm beginning to see why you keep drifting out into the ozone, like you're high or something. I thought maybe you slipped some weed into your duffle bag," she said with a laugh, finished by a little snort.

"No, I haven't been getting high, although I can see why you'd think that. It's really strange, though. It's got me thinking – I mean … like, who are we really? Where did we even come from? If we really are made from space dust, then how can we think like we do, and feel like we do, and love? Why are we the only species on the planet that feels so deeply, and then contemplates WHY we feel so deeply?"

Thane began to pace, getting more riled up as he continued, "I mean, what the hell is *love,* anyway? Where does THAT come from? It feels so good to love someone or something, but it causes so much hurt and pain when it's taken away or broken. Why do I care so much about Lyeana, and what she thinks of me? Why should I even give a shit? What causes those feelings? I mean really!"

"Whoa, slow down there, Mr. Universe! Simmer down now, simmer down! One thing at a time." She picked up his walking stick, examining the purple geode crystal on top of the handle. "I think there's a reason for everything we experience. The Universe is infinite to us, which means there are infinite possibilities, yeah? We have free choice because we're human. We can choose to love, and laugh and even talk to trees if we damn want to!"

She sat down on a fallen log near the trail, studying the walking stick's handle. "It's like this crystal here; it sparkles everywhere. There's so many facets, angles and details. Every thought is unique, and that's what makes us unique!"

"I know, but I just wonder where *love* comes from," Thane said, in frustration. "Is it in our DNA, our instincts, our chemical make up? Can we live without it?"

"Who the hell knows? I thought I was in love with you when we first met," Sharla replied, as Thane chuckled, "and just look at us. I'm a beautiful, black, divine creature, while you're a white, insightful, creative being – and we're friends. Some people, and even whole groups of people, still have problems with that too. Where's all this coming from, anyway, Thaney boy?"

"I don't know? My head's just spinning all over the place. I seem to be contemplating everything I see. I mean look at this tree, for instance," Thane said, walking up to a mountain sugar pine, closing his eyes and leaning in to smell the vanilla scented bark. "This detail, and the shapes in the bark, the smell, the texture – it's all alive, beautiful, and inimitable. I feel like there's more to it all – like there's some deeper meaning we're meant to understand or discover somehow."

Sharla sat poking Thane's walking stick at a rock in the dirt, pushing it closer to a row of red ants that scurried methodically in front of her, as Thane went on.

"In my dreams, the trees, plants, and ALL of nature, hold secrets. They have a higher consciousness. American Indians seemed to have it right. They respected the land and the animals, right? They used all the parts of the animals they killed, and chose spirit guides from nature around them. Trees and animals were sacred, not just used for their needs and pleasures, like so many other cultures do. And when they moved their camps, they picked up after themselves! The other day on our horseback ride, I saw soda cans left in the forest. I felt so peaceful until then. When I saw that, it made me angry, snapping me out of my relaxed mental state. I almost fell off my horse, for Christ sake!"

"Maybe you did fall, and you hit your head. That would explain a lot!" she said, with a single laughing snort.

"Things seem unbalanced," Thane said, still disturbed. "I feel like humanity is heading toward a crossroads – like, we'll need to make huge choices in the near future."

They walked on along the forest path for several minutes in silence, before coming to a small stream with a fallen-log crossing. Thane went first. "OK, so here's a thought – if I fall off this log into the stream and break my leg, was it my destiny to do so, or would it be just fate? How much control in life do we really have after all? Is there some great plan set out for us from the moment we're born?"

"I think we make our own choices in life," Sharla answered. "I know I choose what I like to do, what I like to eat and wear. But it's a good question, babes. At some point we all have to let ourselves surrender to a higher power, consciousness, or whatever you want to call it. We can't control everything."

Sharla followed Thane across the log bridge with her arms stretched out to each side. "I'm balancing on this tree," she said, stopping in the middle, lifting one foot. "What happens if I fall?"

"You'll end up on your ass," he said with a chuckle.

"I know, but like the Raggers Handbook states, we need to find balance in our lives: social, spiritual, physical and mental – or, like I prefer to say, emotional. If I fall, I may be hurt for a bit, but I can always get back up! I can *choose* to."

"Always the optimist," Thane said, rolling his eyes.

"OK, nature man, what are your challenges for the Red Rag?" Sharla asked, "I really want to hear this now."

Thane sat on the fallen tree trunk at the edge of the stream, poking his walking stick in the running water. "I know something's changing inside me," he said. "It's actually pretty cool, and beautiful, and confusing all at the same time – like my will is being directed by feelings of intuition and energy."

"That's deep, mister."

"There's a higher consciousness out there somewhere, allowing us to see connections to everything – I know it. Like, when I look at the trees, I don't just see wood, and bark, and pine needles; I see *life* in its immaculate and perfect form. Am I sounding like a nut job?"

"I think you sound really amazing. You know what you're getting at though, don't you? God," she said unequivocally.

Just then, Sharla's face went blank, as she stared into the sky. "Whoa! That's wild!" she shouted, "I'm having a total deja vu just now. I … we've been here before, in this very moment, I'm sure of it!

She stood up, turning around in circles, looking all around. "That was really freaky-cool!"

"OK, so now, what was that?" Thane said excitedly. "What is a deja vu, actually? Why do we feel like we've been in this moment before, like time is repeating itself or overlapping? Sharla, that's exactly what I'm talking about! I think it happened just now for a reason – maybe to prove my point about how energy is connected, or maybe even listening to us. Do you think that's God's way of communicating?"

Sharla made the Twilight Zone song sounds, "Do, do, do, do … do, do, do, do."

"Stop it," he said, teasing. "I want to write. It's something I've really been thinking about. I want to write music and poetry. You know I've been writing poems since I was a kid, and now, I want to write songs and learn how to sing – but something passionate and meaningful! I feel a calling to connect with the inspiration all around me, and turn it into significant art – something evocative.

Thane raised his eyebrows. "There ya go! My social, spiritual and emotional challenges in a nutshell. I just need to bring my work into the physical – all four corners balancing together!"

"I like it," Sharla said.

"Ya know, what if this inspiring energy I'm feeling is actually tangible, something we can tap into at will?" he said, looking around at the beautiful forest surroundings. "I want to understand our true relationship with the Earth on a conscious level, if possible. We have the opportunity, the ability and the duty to tell her stories – like the American Indians did. All it takes is appreciation, right?"

He paused, with a sigh, "That's what I've been trying to understand," Thane said, with a touch of clarity. "The connection. We were born here on this planet. We're intimately connected to it. If we left, we would die."

"What exactly are you saying, Mr. Philosophical? Do you think it's as simple as appreciating nature to understand our connection to it? Or are you talking about a spiritual connection?"

"The trees, the light, the smells, the hummingbird, the soda cans … I'm starting to appreciate how miraculous we are and why we all need to work together for us to survive. American Indian's understood. If that's my higher self talking, then I want to shout: It won't work for mankind to POLLUTE the Earth, or HATE each other, or FIGHT in wars for years and years. Chaos is our enemy, and a direct road to destruction! It's like a fast flowing river, or speeding freeway of cars. Everything is fine until you dam up the water and it floods, or cause a crash with a deadly pileup. When the flow is stopped, chaos ensues."

Sharla sat silently, in awe, feeling as though they were growing up too fast. Thane looked up at the tall pine trees casting beams of filtered sunlight down to the forest floor. "Am I totally losing it, man?" he said, holding his head in his hands.

"It's love," Sharla said, peered into Thane's piercing blue-green eyes, wondering why he appeared so philosophical and creatively abstract on this day. She felt hesitant to question him further on these subjects, and thought it best to talk about herself instead. "It sounds really cool and, kinda 'out there' to me, but baby, that's why I love you. I'm afraid to ask too many more questions, for fear that your head may explode, so let's talk about me for a while."

"Yes, that's probably best."

Sharla grabbed Thane's hand, pulling him back on the path

leading along the stream. "OK," she said, as they walked through a grove of mountain ferns, "so I've been thinking a lot about the *Raggers Creed,* and what it means to me. The first phrase: *I would be friend to all the foe, the friendless.* I like that one. What it means for me, is reaching beyond people's boundaries, ethnic and otherwise, trying to see the true person inside. We all have fears, right? So, if I can make people feel comfortable around *me,* then maybe I can help make people forget about their fearful personal issues and teach them to see the love without the judgment. Then everyone'll like me!"

"Everyone already likes you."

"Well, I guess my challenge is trying to like them all back," She said, leaning against a tree with one hand on her hip. "How can they resist," she said, with a wink.

"But didn't you just say…"

"It's a vicious circle, isn't it," she went on, cutting him off. "And, *I would look up and laugh and love and lift.* I like that last phrase of The Creed. My personal challenge to myself is to attempt to always stay positive, no matter how dire the situation or circumstance, and just laugh as much as I can. Laughter *is* the best medicine, ya know."

"You and I don't seem to have any problem with that. We usually can't *stop* laughing most of the time."

"Laughter is love too," Sharla said, "I think we all have the capacity to love from the deepest part of our heart, and transfer that love to others. God is love, yes? Love is the only thing that can lift a heart out of darkness."

She began singing: "*Love lifts us up where we belong…*" They giggled for a moment, before Sharla's expression changed. "It's not meant to hurt," she said softly. "I think the hurt we experience from love isn't the love at all, but something totally different. Maybe it's an opposite byproduct – like polar magnetic energy. It pushes and pulls at us at the same time. You can't have love without the hate, pain, or whatever the opposite of love is. And unless you're a Zen Master, I'm not sure if there's a way to make love without the negative of love somewhere in the mix. If we could bottle that, we'd be millionaires! So, let's just paint our world in bright colors, look up instead of down, and search for love more often than the hate."

"And horses would fly and flower children would rule the Earth!" Thane shouted, before jumping on to a fallen tree trunk. "Ya know, speaking of love, I really love these talks we have. And there's no better atmosphere than being out here with you in this amazing nature and clean air. I want this moment to last forever."

Thane leapt off the tree trunk into the air, spinning around with his walking stick spiraling above his head like an acrobat with a large baton weapon.

"Impressive, young master! Sharla shouted, clapping for his aerial dismount. "Now, there's one other thing that's been swimming around in my head from the Ragger's Creed," she said. *"I would be brave, for there is much to dare.* I know I can be brave when I really need to be, but for some strange reason, I think that line refers more to you than me, at the moment. Don't ask me why."

"Well, if you spent one night in my dream world, you'd totally understand."

"Oh, my God! What time is it?" Sharla exclaimed, in a panic, "I think we missed lunch."

Thane looked at Sharla for a split-second before raising his shoulders. "It was worth it," he said with a grin.


Back at camp, their lead counselors Brad and Karen were upset with the two of them for being incognito for most of the afternoon. They had missed lunch and were both late for their next period assignments.

Thane and Sharla had rarely been in trouble before, and when Brad approached, fuming, he didn't cut them any slack.

"What the hell were you guys thinking?" Brad shouted, "You know better than to run off in the woods somewhere getting lost and leaving me cover you at tether ball without knowing where you were! You show up thirty minutes late, and then tell me you were on some silly nature walk? What the hell were you thinking, Thane?"

Sharla lowered her head, staring at the ground. Thane saw the look in her eye, so he leaned over and whispered in her ear, "Look up, and laugh and love and lift, babe." It was the last line of the Ragger's Creed.

Thane then turned to Brad in rebuttal. "We're sorry Brad, but it's not like *you've* never lost track of time before. There's no reason to get so upset with us. We've never broken any rules before, never missed a meal, never stepped out of line ONCE, and you have the nerve to get upset over this? You know we're both getting our Red Rags tomorrow, and we were on an important, meaningful ragger's talk, which was more than I can say for you. You're just pissed you missed out on flirting with Lifeguard Suzie from the pool. I know that was your next period and I

92

saw you making moves on her yesterday. This isn't about *us* being late at all; it's about *you* missing extra time with the lifeguard!"

Sharla went bug-eyed, her mouth gaping open. She'd never heard Thane defend himself like that before. It was like listening to a completely different person.

Sharla's lead counselor, Karen, stood listening, her eyebrows in a high arch. When Thane finished speaking, Karen broke out in a guttural laugh, "Ha, ha, ha, ha! I didn't think anyone else had noticed. Brad, you can't argue with him there." She turned back to Thane and Sharla. "But you two know better than to show up so late. You still have responsibilities." She looked at Sharla and added, "Both of you."

"We're really are sorry," Sharla interjected sincerely. "We really did totally lose track of time. It was the only alone-time we've had to discuss our rag challenges and everything. We'll never be late again, promise! Right, Thane?"

"Right," Thane said, softly.

"You better not be late again, or there's gonna be big trouble!" Brad said, nostrils flaring, breathing heavily through his nose. Pursing his lips, Brad stomped off in a huff kicking a pinecone or two.

"Well, I hope he can keep his weenie in his shorts at the pool, or there's gonna be even bigger trouble," Karen said, with a smirk. "I know how much this means to you guys. You're the only two receiving your Red Rags in the entire camp this year and I'll be there tying yours, Thane. Just make sure your challenges include being on time as well."

"You got it! Thanks Karen, see you tomorrow," he said, giving her a hug. "Sorry I lost my temper. I haven't yelled at anyone like that in a while. It's been an interesting day since I woke up this morning. I'll try to keep my emotions in check. We really are looking forward to the ceremony."

"Me too," Karen said sincerely, before heading toward the Craft Lodge.

Thane stood with his head tilted downward, looking up over his arched eyebrows at Sharla. With a clever little smile, he said, "I don't know what came over me. I just felt like we didn't deserve to be berated like that. Neither of us! We're examples of perfect counselors, right?"

"Well, sorta. We have a reputation for being a bit late." Sharla said coyly. "Nobody's perfect. Besides, I would have done it all over again."

"Me to."

# Chapter VII

## RAGGERS POINT

The evening of the Rag ceremony had arrived. The sun fell below the horizon, creating the glowing mountain dusk, as the moon appeared full in the sky. At seventy-four degrees Fahrenheit, the temperature was perfect for an evening ceremony.

Sharla and Thane had been anticipating this night for weeks and their talk in the woods the previous day had filled their minds with myriad philosophies and inspiration. They were teenagers quickly approaching adulthood. Thrilled to be participating in this unique ceremony together, they were both ready to face each challenge with honesty, integrity, and excitement. There was nothing they couldn't share with each other and this was indeed a very special night.

Karen was to tie Thanes rag and Rob, another counselor and friend of Sharla's, would be tying hers. The ceremony was led by one of the camp directors, named Al.

After dinner, while the rest of the camp was at the evening campfire, the group walked quietly up the rustic mountain trail, winding past large rocks and giant redwoods toward Raggers Point.

Placing her arm around Thanes shoulder, Karen gave him a warm smile in silence, before coming to a halt.

"If we can stop here for a moment, please," Al said, beginning the ceremony. "We are here to celebrate the challenges set forth by the Red Rag for Thane and Sharla on this beautiful summer evening. The reason this is an evening ceremony rather than a morning one, like most of the others, is because this transformation is a completion of aptitudes, and like the setting of the sun at the end of the day, we too move along a cycle into the darkness of our future unable to see what comes next. We must trust in ourselves to guide us through our life and aspirations toward a higher goal. You will now be blindfolded."

Rob and Karen each blindfolded the candidates, keeping one

hand on each of their shoulders, as Al continued, "You are now leaving behind all frivolity. You have nothing to fear. The blindfold is to remind you to trust yourself completely and to keep out all distracting sights allowing you to concentrate on your own path. Pay close attention to all that is said to you, but speak only when you are spoken to. Karen, whom do you bring into our Realm of Ideals and Sacrifice?"

"I bring Thane," she replied.

"And Rob, whom do you bring into our Realm of Ideals and Sacrifice?"

"I bring Sharla," he replied.

Blindfolded, Thane and Sharla were led by Rob and Karen up the path toward the ceremonial point. It was Rob's turn to read: "Sharla, Ragger who represents Ideals, I am bringing to our Realm one who desires to share in our purposes and fellowship. In our Realm of Ideals, our trust is placed in that which is greater than we. Sharla, whom have you chosen as your ideal, whose spirit and attitude toward God and life you wish to emulate?"

"My great aunt, Angelica Lucinda Johnson," Sharla said, "a spiritual teacher and life path advisor."

"It is well, you may proceed."

Karen read, "Ragger who represents Sacrifice of Time, I am bringing Thane, who has chosen an ideal and wishes to dwell in our Realm. The need for leaders who are followers of the highest ideals is great. Wherever and whenever in the history of mankind there have been needs, God has raised up noble men and women to fill the need. As you become a wearer of the Red Rag, the call comes to you to prepare yourself that whatever need for leadership may present itself to you throughout your life, you will find yourself ready to devote time and talent in the service of others. Isaiah tells us: *And I heard the voice of the Lord saying, 'Whom shall I send and who will go for us?' Then I said, 'Here am I, Lord. Send me.'*"

Thane began tearing up under his blindfold. The words seemed to penetrate through his soul, speaking directly to him on a deeply personal and emotional level. He heard an owl cooing behind him, branches rustling, and a twig break under his foot as his senses heightened to include all that was happening around them. He felt the air blow softly across his cheek, continuing up into the rustling trees, as his nose filled with essence of pine and wild flowers from the meadow in the distance.

"As a representative of the Sacrifice of Time," Al continued, "I must ask you this question: Are you willing to answer the call with the words, *Here am I, Lord. Send me?* If so, please repeat them as a personal commitment."

Both Thane and Sharla repeated the words, "Here am I, Lord. Send me."

"You may proceed."

They were finally led up to Raggers Point, a beautiful landing overlooking the mountain wilderness valley below. Sheltered along one side, Raggers Point sat by a large granite rock formation standing forty feet high, acting as a monolithic backdrop.

The Point was inherently a sacred place and whenever Thane had been there before, he always felt the same beautiful, spiritual energy as he now did, even blindfolded.

On the ground, stones were placed in the shape of a large circle with a square inside, and a triangle inside the square. Within the triangle was a stone cross.

"Whom do you bring into the Court of the Red Rag?" Al continued.

"Thane and Sharla," Karen and Rob answered in unison.

"By the spirit you have shown, we believe that you are ready for the experience of the Red Rag. We also believe that you will uphold the tenets of the Red Rag: a willingness to sacrifice time, talents, and will for the benefit of those about you. I would urge you at this moment to completely clear your mind of everything except thoughts of the vows you are about to take. Kneel on your right knee."

They did as instructed, and Al continued, "You are now in the position of resolution. By kneeling thus, do you firmly resolve here before Spirit, and in the presence of your friends, to keep the creed of the Red Rag uppermost in your mind and to live an upright life after the pattern of your ideal? If so, please answer *I do.*"

"I do," they both answered.

"Kneel now upon both knees," Al said.

Thane and Sharla did as instructed. "You are now in the attitude of prayer. Remember that prayer is communion with your God. Raise your head toward heaven as a symbol of pride for your religion or spiritual belief and as a sign of acceptance of ideals and challenges of the Red Rag.

Al, Rob, and Karen read together:

*"God be in your head and in your understanding.*
*God be in your eyes and in your looking.*
*God be in your mouth and in your speaking.*
*God be in your heart and in your thinking.*
*God be in your end and at your departing."*

With Thane and Sharla both kneeling, Karen knelt down next to Thane, and Rob next to Sharla, as they tied the fresh new red bandanas around their necks with the traditional square knot.

"You are special, my dear friend," Rob said, leaning into Sharla's ear. "You know you have a unique flare and a special way with people. You're a natural with music and I think you have a mind that can teach. Your charisma is infectious and it will take you far in life. Never lose that shining light within you. Shar, I wish you all the best on your journey toward your goals and I know you will find a way to make the world a happier place."

Sharla's warm tears began soaking into the blindfold.

With her hand on Thane's shoulder, Karen leaned in to his ear. "You're an extraordinary guy, Thane," she whispered, "I've watched you grow to become an amazing young man. You have a beautiful mysteriousness to you that sets you apart from others. It's a true gift. Use your talents like magic, to inspire and lead others. Some people are chosen by destiny to a higher understanding and purpose of life. Don't shy away from *your* destiny, my friend. I believe you are meant for greatness."

A shiver ran down Thane's back. *Did she just say like magic to inspire and lead others, as if chosen by destiny?* he thought.

Breathing deeply, Thane placed his head on Karen's shoulder, experiencing a slight head rush. Rob then knelt next to Thane while Karen knelt next to Sharla, sharing more encouraging words with the initiates. Once finished, Al said, "You may now remove your blindfolds."

With their eyesight slowly coming into focus, Thane and Sharla realized they were kneeling inside the square made of rocks, but outside the triangle with the cross in the center. Candles surrounded the outside rock circle, lighting up the ceremonial stage with a sacred and wondrous ambiance.

Karen, Rob, and Al sat equidistant from one another, outside the circle, each holding a candle, as Al completed the ceremony. "As you become a Red Ragger, you pass from a simple life of service to a life of dedication, leadership, and sacrifice. With your acceptance of these new challenges, you place your life on the altar of dedication to those principles which have just been made clear to you. Remember that your Rag is not an honor, but an indication to those about you that you have passed into the Realm of High Ideals, offering as your sacrifice your Time, Talents, and Will.

"You see before you the Emblem of the Ragger. The circle stands for the circle of friendship. The square represents the foursquare life of a true Ragger: physical, social, spiritual, and mental. The triangle stands for strength because it is the strongest geometric figure known to man. Because of this strength, we have named the three points, Body, Mind, and Spirit, to remind you to keep the challenge that you have accepted for yourself. And at the center of our emblem and at the center of our hearts, lies the cross. It appears so that we never forget the wonderful lessons that Jesus and other prophetic leaders teach."

Al placed his candle on the ground in front of him, "On a personal note, I would like to add that we learn best in life by the 'feelings' we intuitively have that move and flow inside us, like an internal spirit guide who is always with us standing by our side. The blind hone their other senses by default, allowing them to hear and visualize more deeply things we take for granted or do not chose to see. We, however, have the ability to connect with a higher power, using that wisdom to guide us through our lives in a direction that is best for us – It is within us all to do so if we choose."

Thane soaked up every one of Al's words, his mind swimming with cognizant perspicuity, taking in all that was happening and being said – when he suddenly became dizzy. Thane's knees gave way beneath him and he slumped to the ground, landing on the side of his rump.

"Thane, are you alright?" Sharla said fearfully, jumping to his side.

"Ohh, sorry, I'm just light-headed. I lost myself there for a moment."

Al rushed in, "Thane, is everything OK? I have some water if you like."

He sat with Thane on the ground for a few moments as Rob handed Thane the bottle of water from Al's satchel. "Sometimes these experiences are – well, overwhelming to say the least. It's OK, now. Just take a few deep breaths and some sips of water."

Sitting back up and sipping the water, Thane blinked his eyes several times, coming to. "Thank you, I'm alright now," he said, "Sorry for that. I'm not sure what just happened, but I'm feeling much better now, thank you."

"OK, now that we're all back to ourselves," Al said, "let's sing the Raggers Creed together; then you two can stay up here for a while to reflect or meditate on your experience. Shall we then?"

They all sang together:

*I would be true, for there are those who trust me;*

*I would be pure, for there are those who care;*

*I would be strong, for there is much to suffer;*

*I would be brave, for there is much to dare.*


*I would be friend to all – the foe, the friendless;*

*I would be giving, and forget the gift;*

*I would be humble, for I know my weakness;*

*I would look up, and laugh, and love, and lift.*


After saying their goodbyes, Al, Rob, and Karen left Sharla and Thane sitting within the square made of stones. Sitting in silence for some time staring at the stone cross in front of them, Sharla finally spoke. "How do you feel?"

"I feel incredible. It's so amazing up here right now. I'm nearly out of my body at this very moment, just trying to take it all in."

"Should we chant or something?" she said with a giggle.

"Can you believe what Al said about our internal spirit guide who's always with us, and then about an ability to connect with our higher power and all that? It's exactly what I was thinking when he was saying it, almost like he was reading my mind and interpreting it into cohesive thought. And what about the connection to my dreams! This is so wild! Karen said something that freaked me out too. I guess it took me by surprise so intensely that I became light headed and just collapsed. It felt like the kind of energy Al was describing! And I just felt paralyzed. I couldn't feel my body for a few moments."

"Wow, freak'in wow."

Sharla paused, as the candles flickered in the light breeze casting dancing shadows on the large granite rock face. "I have to tell you something too," she said very quietly.

"OK," Thane said, listening intently.

"I had a dream last night," she said in a somber tone. "We were here, just like we are now, up here at Raggers Point having our ceremony and, well, it was ... odd."

"Odd, how? Wait a sec." Thane blew out the five surrounding candles. The full moon and stars above were now the only source of light as they sat overlooking the silvery meadow landscape below.

"I was sitting right here, inside the square of rocks," she said, looking deeply into Thane's eyes, recalling her dream with an intensity he'd never seen in her before. "In the middle, where the cross should be, was a bright, white glow. I didn't know what it was or why it was glowing. It wasn't fire; it was just this bright light filled with ... love or truth, or something. But, it was radiating energy. I reached out to it, trying to touch it."

Reenacting her dream, Sharla's eyes became wild and intense, extending wide open with concentrated focus, as she reached her arm out toward the center of the triangle where the cross lay.

"What do you think was in the triangle? What was making it glow?" Thane asked, trying to calm her while studying her peculiar behavior.

Her eyebrows clinched together with consternation as she sat rigidly with her arm fully extended toward to cross, fingers trembling. She reached even further, going through the motions of the dream, when her mouth slowly opened into a gape and her eyes bulged out toward the vision she was re-witnessing. She tried to speak, straining to make sense of it verbally, but nothing came out. Then in a slow, eerie whisper, she gasped the word, "God."

What happened next was baffling on all accounts. Sharla whipped her head around looking directly at the dark rock face, before letting out a blood-curdling scream that pierced the night with terrorizing intensity – as well as Thane's eardrums. She didn't stop until every bit of air from her lungs was completely exhausted.

Breathing heavily, trembling with fear, she pointed toward a crack in the rock behind them. "Sharla, Sharla!" Thane said, grabbing her by the shoulders. "What is it? What's wrong? There's no one there." She was sobbing with one hand over her mouth and the other clinched tightly to Thane's arm.

"Oh my God, oh my God!" she repeated over and over.

"OK, Sharla, take a breath. It's all OK. We're safe. Did you see a wild animal or something? Did you see someone behind us?"

"No, not an animal. I, I saw …" Her terrified eyes filled with tears. "There, in that little cave in those rocks," she said, pointing to a triangular crevice that stood about two feet tall, and ten inches wide at the base. It resembled a miniature cave, completely dark inside. It was impossible to gauge how deep into the rock it reached.

Thane was completely bewildered. He had never seen Sharla react like this over anything before. *Could someone be playing a trick on them?* he thought. "Is anyone out there!" he shouted, "Boo! Go Away!"

"No," Sharla said softly, "it's not a person – well, not really. But, there was something in there, in that crack."

"What was it? What did you see?"

She started to whisper, but her lips just quivered anxiously. With tears running down her face, she trembled as she pointed into the crevice and said, "Jesus was in the rock."

"Huh?"

"His face was illuminating right there! I saw it -- his expression, his eyes – glowing at me. And then he vanished! Holy shit, man. What the hell's happening here?"

Thane looked at Sharla as if she was playing a practical joke on him. He walked over to the crack in the rock and inspected it. "I don't see anything inside, but it's too dark to see. Let me just reach around in here and …" Thane reached into the crevice, when Sharla stopped him. "No! No, don't do that! Who knows what's in there."

It was too late. Thane had reached his hand nearly two feet into the darkness, feeling something hard. It was a rod-like shape standing straight up, and it was warm!

"What the …" Thane exclaimed, pulling out a white candlestick melted into a metal, antique-style candlestick holder with a rounded handle. The wax was still hot on top and the wick was burning with a puff of smoke.

Sharla trembled again in a combination of wonderment and panic. "How could this be smoking? And how could it have been lit?" Thane said, completely bemused. "The others left over twenty minutes ago. There's no way this candle was lit in that dark crack by Al, Rob or

101

Karen. They couldn't have even known it was there! How can this be warm and smoking? How can this be at all?"

"I feel like we're in the twilight zone again or something," Sharla said. "I knew tonight was going to be an experience to remember, but I wasn't expecting this!"

Sitting back down, Thane placed the newly found candle in the center of the triangle next to the cross. It didn't match any of the candles used in the ceremony. They just sat together staring at it. Finally Thane broke the silence. "Did you really see Jesus in that rock, or are you just screwing with me?"

Sharla put her hands on either side of her face, with her elbows on her knees. "Honey, there are a whole lotta things I would make a joke about – you know that more than anyone, but this – this is some crazy whoo-ha, here. I don't know what to make of it? Jesus scared the b-Jesus outta me! It would make a good joke though: 'Guess what campers – I just saw the face of Jesus in a dark crack! How was your day?'"

They both laughed for several minutes until tears ran down their faces. Once they caught their breath, they sat for the next ten minutes in silence looking over the moonlit mountain landscape. There was no need to attempt to ascertain what had transpired in the previous moments, for no words could accurately explain it.

The two decided to climb up the short path of the granite rock formation behind them, to a large rock slab overlooking the point. It was the perfect size for two people to sit together in meditation. The mesmerizing stars reached out over the mountain horizon like thousands of sparkling pinholes of light. A sense of perfect quietude permeated the setting, as they absorbed the serene landscape trying to clear their minds in silence.

Not completely silent, they heard the wind rustling through the trees, night birds hooting and chirping, distant frogs and crickets from the meadow, as well as their own breathing. Wispy cirrus clouds floated across the backlit moon's silvery, reflective lining, perfectly manicured, making it look like a scene from a Dracula movie.

After fifteen minutes, Sharla said, "We'll never forget this night, ya know."

"You can say that again."

Thane helped Sharla stand as they gathered the remaining candles from the ceremony and placed them into the satchel left behind by Al, containing two water bottles and a single flashlight. "Next time, I should look for the flashlight *before* reaching my arm into a dark crack in the rocks," Thane said, arching his eyebrows high. "I think we should put this one back where it belongs, yes?" he said, removing the candle from the center cross and examining it one last time.

With a nod of acknowledgment, Sharla watched cautiously as Thane reached back into the crack in the rock placing the candlestick back exactly where he had found it. "It must have been meant for those who seek it," he said, taking Sharla's hand.

"I didn't know that's what I was seeking in my dream?" she said, sincerely.

"And I thought MY dreams were unusual!" Thane said, raising another eyebrow. He turned on the flashlight, grabbed the bag, and joined Sharla as they walked arm in arm down the trail and back to the camp.

## THE ROCK

The next day, both Thane and Sharla floated in a euphoric, blissful daze for most of the morning and throughout the afternoon. Everyone kept asking about their Rag Ceremony, commenting on the new colored bandanas they wore tied around their necks.

Thane told people that it was, "an experience he would never forget," and Sharla just told those who asked, that…"it was really amazing," or used words like, "life changing," and "spiritual." Neither discussed the ceremony too deeply or even touched on what happened afterward. For the time being, that experience was meant only for the two of them. They didn't want to alarm anyone or attempt to explain the unexplainable.

After lunch Thane arranged to meet Aaron at the large rock formation at the far end of the meadow, where Aaron was scheduled to teach select campers who wanted to learn basic rock climbing techniques.

Aaron and Thane hadn't spent much time together over the last two days due to the camp activity schedule, as well as Thane's time spent discussing rag challenges with Sharla and Karen. Aaron met another counselor named Julie who had occupied much of his free time, but now it was Thane and Aaron's time to catch up.

Walking alone across the meadow, trying not to step on any frogs sitting in the meadow pathway, the tall grass brushed against Thane's calves and elbows as he made his way toward the large rock mound.

Still distracted by the previous night's events, Thane tried not to let his wandering mind consume his entire day. Eager to talk about the strange experience at Raggers Point with Aaron, Thane hoped they would find an appropriate time for that discussion when not surrounded by loud, excitable campers.

"Hey Thaney! How goes it, man? " Aaron shouted, waving from the top of the large rock formation. "I'm on the top of the world! Come on up, the air's fine up here!"

Wearing a climbing harness, Aaron attached a long rope to the top bolt with a carabiner. A small group of campers looked up from below, as Julie harnessed up one camper at a time to climb the rock face.

Free-climbing up the first twenty feet or so, Thane got stuck on a steep ledge. "Hey, is there an easier way up around the back side?" he shouted up to Aaron.

"Yeah, just go to your right and you'll find the free climb to the top!"

Thane located the path and climbed another fifteen feet, before rounding another large, granite slab and arriving at the top of the rock mound with Aaron.

"Wow," Thane said, "you can see all the way across the meadow and almost over to the next valley from up here. Cool!"

"Yeah," Aaron said. "This is one of the best spots in the whole camp. Before the kids showed up, Julie was up here with me and we kissed."

"Well, at least one of us is getting some action," Thane said, spanking Aaron on the butt. "I've had some action myself, but not the kind you'd think."

Aaron yelled down to the next climber. "OK, climb on! Look for finger holds and cracks in the rock to help you. Remember to use your legs!" he shouted, pulling up slack in the rope through the carabiner latched onto his waist harness, as each climber made his or her way to the top.

"So, how are things with you and Sharla? Cool new rag there. I like the color," Aaron said, as he continued to communicate with each climber, "That's it! You're half way there! Just focus on the rock and your next move!

"Tell me about the ceremony and all," Aaron said, keeping an eye on the climber.

"I think I'll have to tell you the details another time. It was really incredible though, and there's a lot to talk about, but we need to be alone and ... undistracted. Believe me, you don't want to be holding any ropes with kids on the end when we do."

A young boy climbed over the top lip of the rock, throwing his hands in the air like Rocky Balboa. "I made it, Yeah!" he shouted.

"Right on, kid. OK, now go down the back way. It's the easy way down, but be careful, alright?" Aaron said, coiling the rope for the next climber. "Rope!" he yelled down, as he threw it off the rock face.

"So, you and Julie, huh," asked Thane. "She's pretty cute; well, in a nerdy-cute kinda way."

"And did you see her tits? Climb on!" he yelled down to the next climber to start.

"They're nearly perfect, right? She said she'd come meet us down at the beach sometime at our spot, lifeguard station number eighteen. And she's a body surfer too!"

"Nice. In that case, I'll invite Lyeana."

Aaron gave Thane a wink and a smile of acknowledgement.

After another seven more climbers made it to the top, with two others who made it only half way before needing to be lowered down, Aaron and Thane were alone at last. Julie waved a suggestive goodbye before leading several girls back to her cabin.

Unhooking himself from the rope, Aaron sat with Thane. "Ya know, I think I want to go to Hawaii," Aaron said, as they looked over the majestic landscape. "We always talked about going to Hawaii together, right? I love Catalina and being on a boat, hiking and snorkeling and all, but the water's so cold most of the time. I want a tropical sunset every night and crystal clear, warm water. Like Fantasy Island! Wouldn't that be cool?"

"Yeah, I bet it would. I like the mountains up here, too. Wouldn't it be great to have a cabin up here somewhere and in the winter we could ski."

"OK, I'll have a place in Hawaii and you'll have place in the mountains. Then we'll have the best of both worlds."

"That works for me," Thane said, standing up to gaze further out over the mountain landscape.

The afternoon breeze rustled through the trees, as the mountain air filled with scents of pine and wildflowers. Thane reached his arms out to either side with his palms extended, closing his eyes and breathing deep. "I could stay up here for days. I feel so relaxed and refreshed in these mountains, away from the city. It's like we can escape reality for awhile and connect with nature and ourselves and ... God, or whatever God is. Not some old, white-bearded man in the clouds, but that divine energy that surrounds us."

"Ohh, OK," Aaron sighed, standing up to look around at the trees. "Yeah, I guess I know what you mean. I never went to church, so as you know, I don't really have a religion to speak of, but I get it. Like when we used to have *Martian Time;* we sat on the roof looking for Martians – Remember? We knew they were out there somewhere, but had no way of proving it."

"Well, sorta – yeah, I guess."

Looking over the side of the rock, Thane noticed two campers kissing. "Hey I see Joey, one of my campers, kissing ... I think it's Monica from Sharla's cabin."

"Let me take a look!" Aaron said, leaning over the edge to see for himself. "Yup, that's a make-out fest down there, alright. Should we surprise 'em? Let's toss a pinecone down and see what they do," he said, with a sly little laugh.

"I don't see a pinecone anywhere up here. Be careful Aaron, that's a long way down."

Aaron was just inches from the edge of the rock, trying to get a better look at the young couple. Moving close to the edge, Thane motioned Aaron to come back.

"Maybe we shouldn't disturb them. They're probably having their first kiss. It would suck to be interrupted by a flying pinecone on your first kiss, right? Aaron, you're getting really close to the edge!"

"Yeah, I remember my first kiss. Her name was ..."

Just then, the dirt underneath Aaron's foot gave way and he stumbled. Thane stepped in, attempting to grab him, but was a foot too far away. Aaron wavered back and forth for a second, before recovering his balance. "That was close," Aaron said, stepping toward Thane and then balancing on one foot.

"Dude! That's not funny. It's a long way down," Thane said, angrily."

"Well, it's not like I've never balanced on one foot before when hanging off a rope and tying a ..."

Suddenly, the dirt beneath Aaron's foot shifted again and as he stepped backward onto his free leg, Thane reached for him, but was only able to grab his shirt. "Aaron!" Thane yelled, trying to pull him back by the shirtsleeve.

The inertia from trying to catch Aaron pulled Thane toward Aaron and they both went sliding off the edge, down the steep rock face.

They were free falling.

For what seemed like minutes of slow motion, Thane witnessed the terrorized look in Aaron's face as he flew by and out of visual range. Images and colors blurred together, like paint swirling in a puddle of water, floating past his face at very close range: pine tree branches, mountains in the distance, the meadow, the rock – all moving like a measured, deliberate hallucination. His mind documented the fall in surreal frame-like pictures, as if a camera lens shutter was going off continually in blurry slow motion.

Then with a sharp, jolting bump, Thane's head hit a rock half way down, tossing him in a flip and sending him head-over-heals toward the ground. Still seeing a kaleidoscope of images, Thane impacted the Earth with a hard, muffled thump. His shoulder hit first with a crack and immediately following, his left hip and head.

Then, only silence…


*"Where am I?"* Thane thought. *"What's happening? It's so peaceful; and that light is magnificent. I have no body."*

Thane was unconscious – at least his body was. His mind raced wide-awake, entirely conscious, in another state of being.

In front of him a soft light glowed in the distance, not emanating from any light source he'd ever seen before, but glowing nonetheless. He felt completely at peace, secure and protected here in this curious place.

In his tranquil state, he could almost *hear* the silence.

*It's so beautiful. OK, so, I have no body"*, he thought, floating ever closer to the light in a steady pace. *"I have ho head, no eyes, and yet, I can feel utter bliss, and see the light ahead. It's so calm, peaceful, and perfect. What is this place? Where am I? I don't care. Why don't I care? It doesn't matter. It's so wonderful and I feel … love, pure love."*

Drifting slowly toward the enticing, glowing orb as if moving through a tunnel of empty space, Thane's consciousness felt only complete joy.

*So beautiful, so peaceful, so…*

Suddenly Thane's eyes popped open! He was back in his body. *What's that shrieking noise?*

The trees above moved like a wavy mirage as they slowly came into focus. His head hummed and he didn't know where he was, or how he got there. Bewildered by what he was seeing and hearing, Thane still couldn't feel his body, as he arduously tried to sit up.

"Uhhaaa," he grunted, attempting to lean up on one elbow, but failing. Settling his torso back down on the grass immobilized, Thane laid face up looking into the blurry, terrified expressions of Joey and Monica.

Monica screamed incessantly, gasping for air in-between shrieks, tugging on the back of Joey's shirt while Joey mumbled, "Oh my God, Oh my God," over and over.

*"Am I at the bottom of the rock?"* Thane thought.

The feeling in his body began to slowly return with his vision. It wasn't a welcome feeling, and as the nerves throughout his body re-sparked, the result was utter and absolute pain.

A stabbing jolt shot through his left arm and shoulder, as stinging needles worked their way from his neck to his wrist, which was bent sideways, swelling up and turning purple. His left leg was bent improperly to one side, throbbing and immobile. The back of his head began swelling with a softball-sized bump that dripped with blood, growing larger and more excruciatingly painful. Scraped by the rough granite, his elbow looked like raw hamburger, along with bruises and bloody scratches across his body.

*"We fell!"* Thane suddenly realized. *"We fell from the top of the rock!"*

Panic began to sink in.

"I sent for help," Joey said, leaning down on his knees, placing his hand on Thane's shoulder. "I don't think you should try to get up. You fell a long way and I think you may have some broken bones. It's Joey. Thane, it's Joey … from your cabin. Do you know who I am? I'll stay here with you. You don't have to talk."

Thane was silent for several moments, staring up through the tree branches into the sky, recalling the last thing he remembered before they fell. *They* fell…

"Aaron!" he shouted through a rough gasp. "Aaron, where are you?"

"Joey, where's Aaron? Thane pleaded, looking at Joey with an expression of dread. "He was with me when we fell! Aaron!"

Mournfully staring into Thanes eyes for a terrified moment, Joey gestured behind him.

Thane painfully twisted his bruised torso around. He saw Aaron's body lying on the dirt fifteen feet away in an unnatural position. From the tears beginning to run down Joey's shocked face, he knew the answer.

"No! No!! Thane shouted, breathing faster in short panicked bursts. "Aaron, no!"

"Go see to him," he said, grabbing Joey's arm, "See if he's breathing! Help him, damn it!"

With tears in his eyes, Joey trembled, placing his face in his hands, attempting to speak, "We did. W' … we found him f'first. His n'neck. Oh God, oh God."

"It's OK, Joey," Thane said, beginning to cry. "It wasn't your fault. It wasn't your fault."

They held each other while they cried, wanting to turn back the clock for only a few moments. Thane wondered how this could have happened, wanting to wake up from this nightmare.

# Chapter VIII

## SOMEWHERE BEYOND THE BLUE

Thane woke up in a white room at the Big Bear Lake Municipal Hospital, eight miles from the campground. Sitting at his side, Sharla held a wad of tissue in her hand. Her eyes were puffy and red from tears and her face long with grief. She didn't see Thane open his eyes.

"You're here," he mumbled quietly, blinking several times trying to focus.

"Oh, thank God you're OK," she replied, looking up. "You're finally awake. They had you hopped up on painkillers while they set your broken bones and patched you up, and now you're here, and I'm here, and you're OK, dammit! That's all that matters. Thank God, you're OK!"

She sat up closer to him. "We're at the hospital near the lake. Al and Karen are out in the waiting room, but I didn't want you to wake up not knowing where you were. I've been here the whole time since they brought you back from surgery. They say nothing's damaged too badly internally, but you broke your knee, your left elbow, and your left wrist – but the rest of you is fine! Oh, and there's a really big bump on your head too."

Reaching over the hospital bed, Sharla gingerly embraced Thane.

"I feel like shit," he said, "but I think I'll live." Thane froze. "Oh, God ... Aaron. We fell ... and Aaron landed on ..."

With a terrified glance at Sharla, the tears in her eyes told the story. For the first time in her life, she was at a loss for words. She just held Thane's good hand, letting the tears stream down her cheeks and onto her shirt.

Thane looked out the window at Big Bear Lake in silence. He knew Aaron hadn't survived their fall. He didn't need to ask. He just stared at the serene view for a long moment. "How could this have happened?" he finally said in a slow, quiet measure. "One moment we were on the top of the rock and the next … how in God's name could this have happened?"

He took in a long, labored breath and exhaled with a heavy sigh, before looking back at her with a perplexed expression. "Sharla, there's … something else. Something else happened to me. Something very strange."

"What do you mean?" she said, looking up at him through teary eyes.

Thane had remembered the entire experience of his vision toward the light with complete accuracy. He recalled the euphoric feelings and the profound sensations of peace, serenity and near bliss. He remembered it all with absolute certainty and authenticity. There wasn't a doubt in his mind that he had ventured out of his body to another plain of existence. Thane wasn't sure how to explain it to Sharla without sounding as if he was high on drugs, but he tried.

"I went somewhere. I went to the light. You know, like you see in the movies. I was there, I'm sure of it. I know it sounds absolutely crazy, but I was there – without my body – just drifting toward this amazing, beautiful light. And it was so wonderful, so peaceful and serene. I think I was … dead."

Staring intently into Thanes eyes, Sharla sat without blinking while listening to every word, trying to picture and comprehend what he was telling her.

"Maybe the drugs they gave you are playing tricks with your mind. Do you know what you're saying? Maybe you had another crazy dream? You were out for awhile and you could have …"

"No!" he snapped, "It was no dream. I know I have insanely tripped out dreams, but this was NOT a dream! I was there. I was in this *other* place. I can't accurately describe it with words. I had no body, no head even. I mean … I was still me, but I didn't care about my life, or my skin, or anything at all. I was just a floating consciousness, moving toward a brilliant light in this … endless, beautiful space. I could have stayed there forever."

Taking another labored breath, he peered back into Sharla's eyes with complete honesty. "And then I just snapped back into my body and woke up on the ground next to the rock.

"Well, you fell a really long way. And you hit your head really hard. Do you realize what you're saying though, Thane?"

Nodding his head, he gently laid back down on his pillow,

staring up at the ceiling. "Yes, I do. I know exactly what I'm saying."

Sharla squeezed his hand, tightening her shoulders at the same time. "I can't help feeling that our experience at Raggers Point was a premonition of some kind," she said, "like a warning." Her shoulders relaxed, as she looked back into Thane's saddened eyes. "Maybe it was a message to keep you off the rocks or something?"

"I don't know. I don't know anything right now. I don't know what's real or what's a dream. I just want to wake up from this life and be someone else in another world."


Thane reached his arm out toward the distant beams of light, as he fell slowly deeper underwater toward the unknown. Once again, he felt surrounded by silence – that same silence that had a sound of its own. The feeling was peaceful and calm, like being in an impressionistic watercolor painting comprised of brush strokes of rich, dark colors, all moving and melding around him in slow motion.

The beams of light extended from a central point, casting down at him and all around. In the distance he saw the shadow of a body that was backlit, dark, and lifeless.

"I need your help," Thane called out. "I need you! Ambroas!"

The figure slowly waved its arms in the rolling current, as if beckoning for Thane to come.

Anxiously, Thane tried to breathe the water. This had never been a problem until now. His heart raced as he struggled, sinking deeper and deeper away from the beckoning specter. He was drowning. Trying to swim, his arms and legs were slow to react, like being stuck in molasses. Writhing in a panic, he yelled out, "No! I can't help you! I'm trying to come to you. Ambroas! Kara! ... Aaron!!"


Thane sat up violently in bed, opening his eyes in a blur of waving shadows. The curtains of his bedroom window cast shadows once again, as streaks of sunlight danced across his face.

His pain meds were in full effect, as he realized he had had another dream. This time it was reminiscent of his experience during the accident, mixed with his longing for the Sargonian dream world.

The feeling was similar – peaceful and beautiful, yet eerie and dark, most likely induced by his medication, but still just a dream in the end. He wanted this one to go on for much longer. He wanted to join his friends again. It was the first time he felt at peace in so very long, until the violent ending.

*"Maybe I'd be better off if I were dead,"* he thought.

He lay staring at the ceiling, not wanting to get out of bed, as a single tear ran down his cheek. Thane was a different man and he knew it. He considered the idea that his dreams may be a link to the "other side" – a fine veil that allowed a brief glimpse into the place that awaits. He also realized the notion of that would open up a whole new can of worms with his family and friends.

During the following week, Thane's life was reduced to a miscellany of extreme reactions to any number of normal every day occurrences. He was in physical pain as well as emotional pain and the slightest thought, image, or sound would trigger him into a fit of uncontrollable crying.

Everything seemed to remind him of Aaron: school, sports, even his Rubik's Cube. A glance at the Star Wars poster on his wall sent him into turmoil, storming out of his room.

Feeling distant and unsympathetic about nearly everything since he returned from camp, it seemed nothing was in its proper place to Thane. In just one week, he had experienced the highest elation of his life, along with the deepest sadness, both at extreme polar opposites. His mind swirled with emotions and images of Aaron, white lights, and hummingbirds, yet he was as numb as an ice cube.

He shut himself up in his room for three days not speaking to anyone, only coming out from time to time to eat a bowl of cereal, leftover slices of pizza, or other monotonous snack food items. And, of course, the bathroom. His family desperately tried to understand and empathize with his grief, allowing him space to cope as best as they could, but only time could heal these wounds.


Aaron's memorial service happened two weeks after Thane returned home from the hospital. It was late summer in Los Angeles, the day was a warm eighty-eight degrees, with scattered clouds in a light, dry breeze.

Thane recognized each of the classmates he hadn't seen all summer. They looked odd all dressed up in suits and dark colored dresses in the middle of a warm summer day, their expressions mostly blank, confused, and sad. It felt like a surreal high school reunion to Thane, with the kids more grown up looking than usual – like a film set for *Prom of the Dead.*

People whispered and mumbled behind cupped hands, making the atmosphere even more bizarre. He knew everyone there, but they all seemed like strangers to him.

Aaron's mother asked Thane to speak at the service, and although Thane still felt too fragile to speak candidly about Aaron and their friendship, he had written two poems about his best friend for the occasion.

Everyone finally sat down and the service began. As family and friends spoke about Aaron and his life, Thane couldn't help realizing that none of the people there really knew Aaron the way he had. Their words were sincere and beautiful, but somehow unrealistic and empty to Thane. Aaron had been all of those things, but he was so much more to Thane, and there were attributes and personalities about him that no one, other than Thane, would really know.

He missed Aaron's joking and laughter. It seemed somehow that none of it was real, that Aaron would sneak up behind him and say that this was all just an elaborate hoax and he was really alive and well.

At Thane's side, Sharla held his unbandaged hand in hers. She was crying into a tissue with her other hand, silent for the most part, still in a state of shock. "I never got the chance to get him back after he shoved me in the pool," she said awkwardly, with a slight chuckle.

This day made it all too real, and seeing a casket surrounded with flowers and photographs of Aaron alongside, made it feel eerily impossible.

When the time came for Thane to share his poem, Aaron's mother introduced him. For a moment, Thane sat rigidly in his seat with a vacant expression, wondering if he could really do this. He stood up, grabbed his crutches and painstakingly made his way past Aaron's coffin and up to the podium.

The room fell ruthlessly silent as Thane took a long, difficult breath. With tears welling up in his eyes, he recited his two poems.

### *"Somewhere Beyond the Blue"*

*"What would you say if all the clouds just blew away,*
*And all the leaves fell from the trees down to the ground?*

And what would you do if I were sent away from you?
Would you send your heart in a broken-glass jar,
Or make a wish on a long lost star?
Would you remember that I will always be there?
And what can I say that would take the pain away,
And make the story come to a better end?
How could I know about all the things that come and go?
Should I have read the minds of the prophets of fate,
Or looked between the lines before it's too late,
Forever searching, somewhere beyond the blue?
I'll find my way back home, drifting straight into the light,
No turning back, no need to fight, forever searching,
And maybe I'll find a better way, somewhere beyond the blue."


### "Until I am Whole"

"Let me soar above all troubles,
Let them drift far away,
Let my mind go blank with nothing to say,
The clouds can be beautiful with color and shade,
As all worries soon start to fade.
I am only one person, Why do I ask so much?
Why do things happen as they do?
A feeling, a pleasure, a whisper, a touch,
A yearning for something brand new.
The boundaries of question seem endless,

*The mind finds its answers in time.*

*But where and when appear hopeless,*

*A useless riddle and rhyme.*

*Be strong, I will try, to counter the pain,*

*Whenever it comes again and again,*

*And soar, I will, whatever it takes*

*To hold on to the life I was given.*

*Answer my cries, guide my soul,*

*I weep through closed eyes until I am whole ".*

When finished, Thane looked up to see the guests reacting with varied stages of tears and emotions from his words. Slowly gathering his poems, he reluctantly left the podium to sit back down with Sharla. After tucking his crutches along side his seat, she placed her hand around his shoulder, leaning in to his ear, "That was one of the most beautiful things I've ever heard you say, babe. I know Aaron was listening."

"Thank you. I have so much more I want to tell him. I just …" Thane began to cry.

"Just talk to him whenever you want to," she said. "He'll hear you. I know he will."

They held each other close until the service ended. Before Thane stood up, he looked into Sharla's eyes with sincerity well beyond his years, "I want my life to have purpose," he said, "I want to do something meaningful. I need to make a difference on this Earth, ya know? I don't know how, or when, or what it will be, but I need to do more than just exist."

After Aaron's funeral Thane went numb, blocking his emotions and senses externally, as well as internally. He had been shaken to the core by his near-death accident and the death of his best friend. The result had closed him off socially and emotionally to his other friends, and the rest of the year seemed to fly by in a subtle, maudlin blur.

He turned seventeen in the fall, without a birthday party. Still isolating himself for weeks at a time, Thane focused only on his homework and whatever task was at hand in order to get through each day.

One morning, he came to an unusual realization. It had taken several months for him to connect the dots, but he had been dreaming every night since his accident. Not a recurring dream, but random dreams of unusual intensity and detail. He felt his excessive dreaming was a result of the accident, even though he couldn't prove it to anyone. A new dream came every night without fail. One night he may be flying through his neighborhood, the next, swimming from a shipwreck or sinking underwater. There always seemed to be water in his dreams, and always fine detail.

Sometimes he wrote them down, trying to ascertain a higher meaning, but they would fade with each passing minute, losing pieces and essence along the way. He found this frustrating and often wished he could have a night of uncomplicated sleep, without another wild, esoteric story playing through his head.

The adventurous trials and tribulations of Sarghon and Ambroas seemed far from his current state of mind. Or were they? If he dreamed every night, then surely they should return. He hoped they would.

# Chapter IX

## A Letter to GREENPEACE

"Thane, I don't understand why you want to go traipsing off to the Pacific Ocean with a bunch of strangers?" Thane's mother, Susan said from the kitchen while tossing a Caesar salad. "It really isn't the right time for you to go anywhere. You have two more years of college left."

"Mom, we've gone over this before. I've been accepted to join a *very* special group of people doing *very* important work. The United States isn't the only technologically advanced nation conducting nuclear weapons tests, ya know. The French are the current culprits testing their nuclear bombs in Tahiti. Greenpeace is the only organized international group that's protesting with any significant action and I want to be a part of that!"

Thane had grown up quickly in the years after high school. Friends and family saw him as an idealistic and sensitive young man filled with determination and curiosity, but his wide blue-green eyes had also matured into the eyes of a young man who saw a future of purpose and discovery.

Three years after the accident, he did his best to move on toward the next chapter of his life, attempting to keep painful memories blocked somewhere safe behind a sturdy wall of new beginnings, philosophies, and questions about the meaning of life. His curiosity urgently needed answers.

Thane often wondered what had actually happened during his accident. Was it God he witnessed in the tunnel of light? Was it a conduit to Heaven? Or could it have been the beginning phase of the *after-life* that he experienced? These questions and more often wandered in and out of Thane's psyche, pulling him toward a higher cause.

Thane spent one year at UCSD (University of California, San Diego), studying toward a degree in English Literature, with a minor in

Environmental Science. This is where he first learned about the radical, environmental protection organization called *Greenpeace*.

At nineteen, one month before his twentieth birthday, his thirst for adventure and his drive to help the Earth finally connected to a greater plan! He felt a passionate desire to reach out to the needs of the planet, even if in some small way. Thane wanted to be part of a movement that helped people open their eyes to man-made disasters in an attempt to decrease our ever-growing carbon footprint.

When Thane's acceptance letter from Greenpeace arrived, he felt both excited and a little nervous. He knew he was making an impulsive and exotic request of himself, something he hadn't expected to do at this point in his life. But once he was accepted and invited to become a team member for the summer on an environmental expedition supporting the Mururoa Atoll nuclear testing ban in Tahiti, his decision was made.

His parents weren't completely on-board with his idealistic choice to leave the university to follow his heart around the world before finishing college. They invited him and his sister, Lara, for Father's Day dinner to discuss it more seriously.

"Well happy Father's Day to both of you too," Reece, Thane's father said with a touch of sarcasm. "I hope tonight doesn't turn into a war zone in our dining room. It's supposed to be all about me, isn't it?"

"Dad, did you know they're now estimating that the radiation from the Chernobyl disaster is one hundred times more powerful than the bombs dropped on Hiroshima and Nagasaki? Can you even believe that?"

The recent environmental disaster caused by a meltdown at a nuclear power plant near Chernobyl, Ukraine had occurred only a few short weeks prior. The world was holding its collective breath after April 25th, with the colossal catastrophe that dramatically changing the world's opinion about using nuclear energy for power.

"It's a tragedy; a horrible one. We're not disputing that," Reece said, before sitting at the head of the table. "We just want what's best for you. Sometimes you get so passionate about something, you don't think clearly. We want you to really consider this decision before you commit to something so grandiose."

Susan entered with a large Caesar salad. "Lara, dinner!" she shouted upstairs to Thane's sister. "You know, darling, I nearly joined the Peace Corps," she said, turning to Thane. "I wanted to help end the Vietnam War and bring that horrible thing to an end peacefully. We all did. I understand your desire to want to make the world a better place, I really do. But we want you to finish school."

Lara entered the dining room and put an arm around Thane's shoulder. "Boy, you've got guts, I'll give you that," she said. "My adventures happen underwater with a scuba tank in a world beneath the surface, or in the microcosm of a droplet of seawater under a microscope. I give you props for going it alone and following your heart. Rock on, bro."

"Lara, you're not helping," Reece said.

"Well, in addition to war and nuclear threats," Lara said with the flare of a biology master's student, "scientists are becoming aware of something they call *The Greenhouse Effect,* an increase in global temperature, causing sea levels to rise due to melting and retreating glaciers. They say the effects include increases in extreme weather events and species extinctions."

"I think that's all due to how we're polluting the Earth," Thane said, speaking with his mouth half full of garlic bread. "The Gulf War last year sparked all kinds of propaganda about the Persian Gulf and the United State's government securing its position over foreign oil, land control, and socioeconomic status in the Middle East. Ya know, people are just beginning to connect fossil fuel burning and deforestation to the increased greenhouse gas concentrations. As far as the oil companies are concerned, it's just a few paranoid scientists making up figures in a laboratory. Oil corporations don't want to see a connection to consumption, pollution, and human behavior for the melting of our ice caps."

"It's true, Dad, many scientific answers are supplied to the powerful oil moguls," Lara agreed, "but not enough to make them accept alternative sources of energy in return for a smaller paycheck."

"It's much easier for them to stick their heads in the ground, ignoring the problem all together!" Thane said doggedly.

"You two sound like you've been watching too much CNN," Reece said.

"Darling, tell me about that girl you were dating in San Diego," Susan said, trying to change the subject as she brought a plate of roast beef to the table. "She looked very pretty from the pictures you sent."

Thane dated several girls while in college, falling helplessly in love on each first date and fumbling each relationship as he went. Hormones heightened his emotions, which only made communicating dramatically more complicated. No one seemed to be the "right" one. The girl his mother was referring to was the only girl that stayed around for more than a few weeks.

"Girls are only a distraction from his inexplicable mind, Mom," Lara said, teasing. "He's not ready to settle down with anyone yet. His wanting to travel with a group of environmental mercenaries proves my point."

"They're not mercenaries," Thane interjected. "They're heroes helping to protect the Earth. We don't make money doing this!"

"And there's the rub," Reece said while chewing a piece of roast beef. "You certainly won't be covering the full cost of the trip yourself, I can guarantee that."

"Ya know what is certain," Thane said as he stood up and raised his voice, "the fact that human impact is dramatically altering the environment faster each year in shorter periods of time! I'm not completely insane," he said, sitting back down and calming his temper. "I just feel like this is something I need to do *now*. I'm not planning on leaving college forever, ya know. Just one semester, maybe two. Then it's back to school – promise."

After dinner, Thane gave his father a watch with two time zone options on it for Father's Day. "See Dad," Thane said, "you guys will always know what time it is in Tahiti while I'm there. You can look up at the moon at night and know I'm looking at the same moon even if it's daytime where I am."

He gave his father a long hug.

"Thane, I read the letter you wrote for your application to Greenpeace," Reece said, his voice gentler than at dinner. "It was really good, kiddo. I'm not kidding; if I were recruiting for them, I'd want to hire you. I'm proud of you, son. I don't always understand what's going on in that crazy head of yours, but I'm proud of you for making the effort." He gave Thane a hug in return.

# ANGELICA

While still grieving the loss of his best friend, as well as attending his first year at college, Thane never lost his desire for answers. He remained compelled to ask theoretical and emotional questions about life, love, and spirituality, knowing that answers lingered somewhere in the distance.

He yearned for the dream world of his alter ego, Sarghon to return, as well as for those friends he knew only inside his head. Although Thane still dreamed every night, what he called The *Sargonian Dreams* were the only dreams he now welcomed.

During Thane's time in San Diego, he only saw Sharla on occasion, but they spoke on the phone often. He had developed a lasting friendship with Sharla's great aunt Angelica, who lived very close to his campus along the Southern California coast in La Jolla. He visited her home near the cliffs often, sharing a love of mind-expanding concepts and conversations. As their friendship evolved, Angelica became like an aunt to Thane as well.


In early summer, Thane took a final weekend trip down to La Jolla to visit Angelica before leaving for the South Pacific. She hadn't been feeling well and they wanted to spend a bit of quality time together before Thane left for Tahiti. Angelica had a uniquely open mind about philosophies of life and the universe, something he truly appreciated about her. Thane needed her company and advice one more time before embarking on his environmental-activist adventure.

Thane arrived late morning in good spirits at Angelica's house near the beautiful beachfront cliffs. "Hello? Yoo-hoo, I'm here," Thane shouted as he knocked on the open screen door.

Angelica always left her door open with only the screen door shut, feeling audaciously confident that she could handle any situation that may happen to wander in unwanted. There was no answer at first, but Thane knew she often muttered around the house changing the energy and *Feng Shui* of each room by rearranging the furniture or redecorating according to her current state of mind.

As well as a spiritual advisor, Angelica was one of the only knowledgeable non-Asian women on the West Coast who studied and practiced *Feng Shui*, the Chinese philosophy and art form of how energy flows through a space. She had studied with a Chinese master who taught her the intricacies of the ancient art form.

Thane found her in the *blue room,* positioning a sofa-chair along the southwest wall. "I'm in here, Thane. Come on in! Coffee's on the stove. Go ahead and pour me a cup too. You know how I like it, extra milk and honey, no sugar!"

"Got it!" Thane shouted, placing his overnight bag on the floor near the hallway, before proceeding toward the kitchen.

Angelica's house was filled with a captivating assortment of treasures from around the world. She had visited every continent in her lifetime and was an avid collector of unique and unusual items, statues, paintings, and artifacts – usually spiritual or historical in nature. The eclecticism of her home decor seemed to work in tandem with her personality – fascinating and sporadic, yet harmonious and intriguing.

She wore a flowing, light green shirt and black skirt, with a blue scarf batiked with Chinese symbols that she had tied around her waist. Her hair sat in a curly, organized mop atop her head, which usually held her finger-smudged reading glasses. A solid gold necklace in the shape of a dragon adorned her neck and sparkly bracelets dangled from her thin, boney wrists.

Thane entered the living room with two cups of fresh coffee. "Wow, I like what you've done with the place! You moved the coffee table out from the wall, I see. And the sofa looks good there. Are you feeling any better?"

"Will you put that coffee down already and help me with this chair!" she shouted, trying to drag a flowery patterned sofa chair across the room by herself. "My back is killing me and unless you like to watch an old lady struggle, I could use some help here."

Thane gripped the back of the large chair and they positioned it exactly as she was envisioning it. "OK, see how if I put the chair facing east, there's no secret arrows shooting out at me and it opens up the space to walk all the way around without feeling trapped in the corner – much better flow. Also, now I can face whoever walks in my front door. No one getting behind me and taking advantage, capiche?"

"I get it. As usual, you've solved the metaphysical problems of your house yet again. At least for today, that is."

"Except now, I have no idea where to put this plant," she said, leaning over a large potted plant, attempting to drag the ten-gallon palm tree back across the room where the chair had been.

"Angelica, go sit in your newly positioned chair," Thane pointed, as he escorted her toward the gaudy, overstuffed piece of furniture. "Let me move this thing before you pull something. I think it would look good behind the chair in the corner," Thane said, heaving the huge pot where he mentioned. "See, now that looks good right there."

"Well, alright, if *you* say so, my dear," Angelica said with a smirk. "How are you now, child? And when do you leave to go off to that little sand dune in the middle of the ocean on your environmental quest and all? I should've known you'd end up somewhere like Tahiti. You have several *grand water trines* in your chart, after all."

She pointed to a strange object hanging on the wall. "Oh, see that colorful blow-gun up there? I picked that thing up in Tahiti when I was there in `79," she said, as if having a Tahitian blowgun was as normal as having a wall clock. "You know I'll miss you now, don't you?"

"I leave in a week," he said. "I'm really excited. You know how much I want to fight for environmental awareness. And since Chernobyl a few months ago, everyone's really up in arms. But I'll be going somewhere out near the Mururoa Atoll in Tahiti. It's supposed to be a beautiful place. I don't think I can pick you up another blowgun there, though. Not much living above the ground un-radiated after the test bombs detonated."

He took a sip from his coffee mug. "Hey, did you know the French secret service blew up a Greenpeace ship last year in New Zealand before it could make it out of the harbor?" he said. "It was called the *Rainbow Warrior*. That crew was totally dedicated, man. They're all heroes. Some of them will even be my guides. I'm gonna be on a ship named *The Greenpeace*."

Thane seemed to be getting a quick coffee-buzz on, speaking slightly faster as he continued. "Some people are really insane, ya know. I don't get why anyone needs to keep testing nuclear bombs. We know what they do, right? They kill everything in sight and cause deadly radiation fallout for years afterward – Period! What possible positive use are they at this point? We know what happens! Duh? Didn't we already learn from Hiroshima and Nagasaki?"

"Well some people use power as a tool for control," Angelica answered. "They aren't part of the *cosmic* consciousness. They live and operate in a mindset of *tribal* consciousness, fearing the outside world, taking what they need from others or from the Earth without consequence. That's why we have war, my dear. Each group, religion, culture, society, or what have you – believe that they're right and others are wrong. It's as simple as that." She took a long sip of coffee, and continued, "You see, the lowest plane of consciousness is on the same plane as the highest."

"What? What do you mean?" Thane asked, with an utterly confused look on his face.

"Listen now, there's no distinction of high and low consciousness in the whole scheme of things. It just *is*. There either *is* consciousness or there *isn't*. There's no real right or wrong, no up or down, left or right, etcetera. It's all determined by one's point of view."

She picked up a small Egyptian statue of a pyramid and turned it upside down. "You see, if I were in China, my *up* would be the opposite from yours – that is, if up really is *up*. Direction can only be determined by each person's point of view as they're positioned on the ground by gravity."

Returning the statue to the coffee table, she tapped her finger on her golden dragon necklace before continuing her explanation. "Or, simply, if I was Muslim and you were Jewish, your right would differ from mine, and so on, because *right* is determined by what you believe or what you were taught to believe."

She turned the statue back over, "Is this cobra image etched here representing protection, strength, Lower Egypt, or demon god of the underworld? Again, all depends on who you talk to and what you believe. Which side of this pyramid is most holy? Which side is more important? Which side is facing east? It all depends on where you're standing on the Earth, and what you believe inside your individual head. Is this even a pyramid at all? It could be a beacon to the gods, a tomb, a holy shrine, or just a pile of rocks. It's all of these things and none of these things, depending on who's looking at it, yes? It's all just an individual's perspective based on societal upbringing and teaching," she said, as if Thane should instinctively know her exact meaning. "But really it's all just an illusion."

"Why is that?"

"Good question. If you were taught to hate someone and chose not to ask why, then it's *your* ignorance that's in question, don't you think? Your *tribal* consciousness is then at work guiding you like a moth to a flame. Without questioning actions, one often flies blindly into the fire – or in some cases, is forced to."

She opened her eyes wide and walked like a zombie with her arms and fingers outstretched in front of her. "Tribal instinct is good for protecting a society or for keeping others out, but it causes narrow mindedness. *That's* the ignorance of organized religions around the world. It's their way or the highway, baby. They're egotistically flawed. Can be the nicest people in the world too! Just blind to certain realities," she said with a pleasant little smile. "It's like, when you're in a theater filled with people and someone coughs – then other people join in! Have you ever thought about why that happens?"

She jumped up to her feet. "Oh, I almost forgot! My brownies are in the oven. Are you hungry?" Angelica awkwardly sat up from her overstuffed chair and waddled over to the kitchen. The smell was overwhelmingly pungent – chocolate mixed with an unambiguous, sweet herbal fragrance.

"I must warn you though, these brownies come with a punch," she said with a wily grin. She had whipped up a batch of what she called, her *Lovely* brownies: dark chocolate with walnuts and a finely ground mixture of *Maui Wowie* marijuana.

"I haven't done these in a while, so I thought since you were off to tropical Timbuktu, we ought to start you off on your trip the right way," she said with a sly little smile.

About an hour after they both ate a large *Lovely* brownie, Thane asked, "How can our government and the governments of the world allow for the Earth to be raped and used like some big toxic experiment? I mean, we're already creating enough pollution to wipe out hundreds of plant and animal species each week. How much nuclear, radioactive waste do we really need anyway? Why is it so damn important to blow things up?!"

Thane found that words were fluttering out of his mouth with complete conviction and intensity. The world around him was more fluid and he felt pleasantly lightheaded.

"It makes me sad, really," Angelica replied, "It's a new world out there with all this new technology. Computers are only getting smarter and humanity seems to only be getting more and more arrogant. Could be from all that technology we found from the aliens. Everything happens in cycles, always has and always will. Twelve hundred years ago, we were in the dark ages. People slaughtered and burned each other for thinking differently. Emperor Charlemagne the Great beheaded people for not converting to Christianity. He killed anyone who burned their dead or practiced pagan beliefs. He conquered all of Europe and created the Holy Roman Empire in the name of the church, slaughtering thousands in the process. Slightly misguided if you ask me."

"I would say egomaniacal, at least. Wait, did you say aliens? Ya think that's where we got all the computer technology?"

"Sure, all that *Area 51* stuff. Some say it's where Velcro came from too. Super-charged our leap into the computer age, that's for sure!"

"Well, I wish greedy people would stop sucking the Earth for all she's got, like a cancer, killing everything in its wake."

"That's why I like grass, my dear. It distracts me from thinking about all the ugly in the world that happens each day. It rounds out the edges of life."

"I've never agreed with you more," Thane said with a big smile. "That's a perfect description. You should register that in some big book of cool sayings."

"I don't think I made that one up, but you never know. It just came outta my mouth. A lot of stuff does," she said with a light chuckle.

"You'd think if we all just mellowed out and got along, things would be better."

"Yes, the hippy mentality," she said. "Ahh, the *hippy* consciousness! I need to add that one to the list for sure. Now those were the days, honey! During the Vietnam War, something amazing happened in human behavior. There was an opposition to war like never before that was fueled by love. *Flower Power*, we called it. There was such an uprising for peace, it influenced our attitude, music, our hair styles, our clothing, everything! It brought forward a whole new movement of higher awareness; something we could use more of today.

"You see, 'every action has an equal and opposite re-action.' Now, I certainly didn't make that one up – it's science fact. So when violence, fear, and death were created by the war, there was an equal amount of love and peace flowing in energy waves around the Earth. It works like the ocean tides."

She began waving her hands and rippling her fingers around her head in a wave-like motion. "When one side of the Earth is being pulled by the moon, the opposite side of the Earth is being pushed, creating low and high tides, right? It's how *all* energy works, even spiritual energy. The more concentration of thought, emotion, love, or what have you, that condense in one place at one time – the more people are aware of it. They're called energy vortexes. Sedona, Arizona is chock full of 'em. It can all be scientifically measured, I tell you!"

Angelica continued her fluttering arm movements, wiggling her fingers in the air and spinning around. She finally sat down. "What happens next is anybody's guess. But we do often tend to come together as humanity in times of great loss. The problem is, frightened people and governments with large militaries usually come together with tanks, bombs, and guns, whereas the rest of us try to use peace, love, and diplomacy as our resolve."

She held her fingers up to her eyes, making cylinders, as if looking through binoculars. "I don't see the world or think like anyone else, and neither do you," she said. "But free thinkers, philosophers, and creative minds don't seem to have the instinct to want to blow things up. The other mindset sees the world as a place to conquer and absorb for themselves."

She looked Thane deeply in his eyes. "You vibrate on a higher consciousness, my friend, seeing the world as a place of natural beauty. That's a gift! If you think something is one way, then for you it *is*. Like the pyramid. It's unfortunate and confusing, but you'd be surprised by how many people see more darkness than light in the world. Now hand me another bite of lovely."

Thane felt relaxed as they nibbled on more of her *lovely* brownies. "In my dream, there's a beautiful warrior princess with wings," Thane said. "She talked about being part of a *collective* consciousness. She said it was, *'a wisdom and creativity harnessed for the common good, with the ability to intuitively sense energy fields, physically, emotionally, mentally and spiritually.'"*

"She sounds like a keeper!" Angelica said, slapping her hands together, brushing off the excess brownie. "Your mind was certainly picking up on some good woo-woo. Seems like she was talking about a collective *wisdom*, which is different than tribal or collective consciousness. Maybe she's a reflection of yourself, manifest in your dream? She's also an *intuitive sensor*, someone or something that helps hone your own intuition and inspiration. I like her."


For the rest of the afternoon and evening, Thane and Angelica continued their talks of universal energy and global politics while they moved furniture around the house until it seemed the appropriate fit for the time being.

After the sun set on the La Jolla beach horizon, Thane surprised Angelica with one of his pasta creations. He prided himself on being able to look through anyone's cupboard and whip up a gourmet meal with whatever was on hand. Most people had no idea that their kitchen held the ingredients needed to create such delectable dishes, and Thane had a knack! Inspired by her brownies, he went through each cupboard pulling out different pastas, canned vegetables, sauces and spices. He found an onion and some garlic in the fridge, and frozen chicken and artichoke hearts in the freezer. In the back garden, he picked some fresh rosemary to chop up and sauté with the garlic and onion. When all was said and done, he had created a chicken and artichoke linguini with a creamy red tomato, garlic and onion sauce with fresh roasted rosemary. With every bite, Angelica closed her eyes and moaned with pleasure.

"I don't know how you do it, honey. I had no idea this was in my kitchen! You could be a gourmet chef, you know that? When you're done healing the world from radiation and bombs, you should come home and cook for me!"

"I'll keep that option open," he said with a warm smile. "I'm pretty stoned too. I don't really remember exactly what I threw in the mix, but it's good, right! Hey, there's something else I wanted to talk to you about."

Thane's mood changed as he picked up his coffee cup and stared into the creamy, brown liquid halfway down the mug. "I've been thinking a lot about Aaron recently, as well as my experience floating toward the light after I fell. It's hard to talk about it with just anyone, but I know you'll understand. It's not something most 'normally minded' people can accept. When I've brought it up in the past to my parents or friends – even Sharla, they just give me this bizarre look, like I've lost my mind or something. But I know what I felt and I know what I saw. I can sense it now, as real as if it just happened yesterday. I went out of my body to somewhere wonderful. In the midst of my physical pain and horror, my consciousness was taken to a very pleasant place where fear and pain didn't exist."

Thane sighed, as he tried to convey his feelings. "OK, so *feng shui* is all about the energy that flows all around us all the time, right? Well, once in a while I have this weird interconnectedness with nature. I think that's why I'm drawn to Greenpeace and the desire to help stop the bombings."

"Interconnectedness, huh? That's a good word. Go on."

"Well, how do I say this? It's kinda like I can sometimes *feel* the energy that vibrates in and around living things, as if they have an aura. I know this is pretty *woo-woo*, but sometimes I actually feel the energy throughout my body, or see light glowing from a tree or a patch of grass, or something in nature. I think it's all connected to my accident somehow. I wonder sometimes if it isn't just my mind or my vast imagination playing tricks on me. I get emotionally touched by all this stuff in a fundamental way – sometimes I'm even drawn to tears. I can't deny the reality of it. It can be overwhelming. I think it may somehow be connected to … *love*."

Thane got that wondering look on his face. "Is this what people experience when they feel touched by Jesus or God in church? Or, maybe those whack-jobs that go up to get slapped in the forehead by a fundamentalist preacher and then end up convulsing and drooling all over the floor. I think my brain got fucked up when I fell off that rock. I've wondered about that quite a bit. I could be brain damaged. Is that totally crazy or what? Am I a freak?"

"Honey, you aren't a freak at all. You're special. You have a gift. The world would be a better place if more people were as sensitive as you. It may sometimes feel like a curse, but it's not. I'm an artist, a free thinker, and different from most – different from everyone else, in fact." She rolled her eyes back, smiling a crooked smile. "I often feel as though I were meant to give people a message of some kind or another. I still to this day don't know what that message is honey, but when I figure it out, you and Sharla will be the first ones to know."

Angelica took a sip from her coffee cup, before gesturing with it, "You see, the universe has immutable laws; they're undeniable. You're wanting to break free from the *tribal* and *collective* consciousness into individuation. You're evolving, my boy!" She took another nibble from her brownie, chewing as she talked, "Once you evolve, you can't go back to ignorance. You can't un-evolve! Breaking free from the ordinary isn't easy. Individuation is a lonely place, believe me. It's wonderful and challenging at the same time, but you can feel like an outcast. Until you connect with others to create a new *collective* consciousness, you'll feel isolated."

Angelica sat back in her chair, as Thane pondered all she was saying. "But in the end, every perception is just a lie," she said. "The sun rises and sets. We all believe that, but it's not true. We just believe it to be true."

She looked Thane right in the eye and laughed. "Ha! Or maybe I could just be bat-shit crazy! Usually I am. But I think y*ou're* in the process of discovery. You're breaking away from the tribe into the *super* consciousness, or *spiritual* consciousness. You must release the belief that you have *control*, because that's also a perception. The universe is the only thing in total control. Once you do that, you're free to raise your awareness to what is really happening – as it seems you've been doing from time to time. That's what all that stuff with the trees, auras, and nature is all about. You're just opening your energy to a higher vibration! Not everyone has experienced the heightened level of consciousness that you have from time to time, but every human being is certainly capable of it. Where else would all the religions come from, right? Ancient man worshiped the sun, the moon, spirit animals, Earth Goddesses, and volcanoes, just to name a few. Prophets such as Moses, Mohamed, Jesus, Buddha, even Joseph Smith all had spiritual experiences that were incredibly unique and powerful. They created religions because of them. They needed answers for all the unanswered and fantastical questions that came from their personal experiences. Science was too young, so they came to their own conclusions or made stuff up that seemed logical at the time."

Angelica tapped the arm of her chair. "We're a questioning race for sure, my dear, but *answers* – those are harder to come by. No one would judge you too harshly if you said that God, Jesus, or Buddha touched your heart and connected you to the other side or to the energy you felt."

She paused, looking up to the ceiling with a solicitous expression. "To me, they're just symbols of the higher energy vibration that's always around us, permeating throughout the universe. In special moments we feel it – some more than others. You see, everyone creates their own answers for unexplained personal spiritual experiences, no matter how bizarre. And each answer is no less valid or real than the next." She smiled genuinely. "You should celebrate your uniqueness, not fear it!"

"I knew I could count on someone as odd as me to understand," Thane said with a lighthearted chuckle before giving her a hug.

Angelica suddenly stood erect, then wandered in a small semi-circle, seemingly coming to an epiphany. "Here's an interesting thought, sweetie. Now this may be the brownies talking, but go with me for a second. What if it's all part of the master plan of human evolution? I mean, we have pretty fancy technology with computers and all, advancing our way of life exponentially with each decade, yes? By the end of the century, our idea of the future: space shuttles, techno-science, and such, will be completely realized. We're almost there now! But as humans, we haven't changed very much in thousands of years. The ancient Egyptians were as clever, complex, and complicated with their way of life as we are today. So…"

An expression of excitement came over her face as she clapped her hands several times and continued, "what if all the things you and others like you are experiencing, are the first signs of ..."

"Our next step in evolution! Exactly! I've been thinking the exact same thing for years! I even tried to write a paper about it for my high school biology final. Is that what you were going to say?" Thane's eyes were the size of salad plates.

"It was. It's not so farfetched! You certainly aren't the only one who's sensed the other side, and the 'interconnectedness' you speak of.

"It could be like a fifth element that we're just beginning to tap into!" Thane said.

"We all have the capacity to be psychic, you know," she said, knowingly. "Maybe we're beginning to rise up in our evolutionary process to the next level, like ascension. What do you think?"

Thane sat with an enthusiastic look on his face. The words she was saying seemed to make complete sense to him. "Actually, that feels completely plausible to me. Ha! Aaron and I always wanted to use *The Force* growing up. It could be something like that. What an awesome thought."

With the fresh, wondrous ideas now flowing through his mind and still feeling the effects from the brownie, Thane's eyes widened. "It's true though, when I experience that interconnected feeling, all the things I thought were so important don't even compare to the larger picture that comes into focus. It's a wonderful feeling. Even my soul feels free." He let out a silly laugh. "I think I was meant to be a hippy. I was just born too late."

He smiled at Angelica with a very stoned look on his face, eyelids heavy and grinning. Then his expression became poignant. "Maybe the small-minded people pulling strings in governments around the world just haven't felt the effects yet. If they did, they would understand how they're hurting our Earth and our future much more than they realize."

"Ain't that the truth," Angelica agreed. "Think about it this way – there are enlightened folks in the world and unenlightened folks. Which do you think are gonna evolve quicker?"

"It just doesn't seem so farfetched an idea to want to live in a world where there's more love than hate."

Thane walked over to a window and looked out at the tall grass blowing across the sandy dunes. Angelica didn't need to say a word. She understood as well as anyone what Thane was talking about. Her days as a flower child allowed her opportunities into the inner psyche and everywhere else the mind can go when enhanced with hallucinogens like LSD, peyote, and magic mushrooms. Thane hadn't yet experimented with those drugs. He felt his mind and his dreams allotted him enough fantasy and adventure already, without need for added enhancements.

The next morning, Thane walked along the famous beachfront La Jolla cliffs for a several hours, pondering all that he and Angelica had discussed the night before.

It was a hot, sunny day and the next activity on his weekend agenda was a long swim and some body surfing. The waves were perfect for the occasion; not too small to catch a nice curl and not too big that he would get tousled like a rag doll in a giant washing machine.

After forty-five minutes, Thane caught a final, perfect wave that he rode all the way in to the sand. It was time to eat. He had packed a nice lunch for himself in a brown paper bag: A turkey sandwich, a banana, a chocolate chip cookie, and a can of 7-up. The combination of fatigue from the morning activities mixed with the tryptophan from the turkey and banana would make for a lovely nap in the sand.

Making a cozy area under a short date palm with one of his island print beach blankets, Thane laid his head down on his backpack in the pleasant patch of shade.

Within moments, he was out like a light. He soon drifted away somewhere in the deepest part of his brain.

Thane had maintained his diverse and fantastical dreams, but his adventures had not included Ambroas, Kara, or the Arthurian magical world from his sixteenth year. Now that he was embarking on a real adventure of his own, something finally shifted in his mind. While images and specifics from his Sargonian dream quest were often muddled in his waking state, Thane had kept them locked up somewhere in the ethers of his subconscious, hiding the details of his dream alter ego… until now.

# Chapter X

## THE BASAI

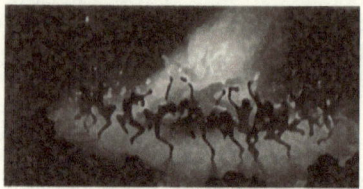

"Hurry up! You are lagging behind. Must you always daydream while we're on the ground? One would think the grass you are staring at is more important than saving all our lands," Kara said in a loud whisper, as they moved onward through the tall grass along the forest's edge. Raising his head, Sarghon realized that indeed his mind had been wandering; where it had wandered, he could not recall.

"Why are we on the ground again?" he asked, looking up at the stars. Should we not just fly over the forest as we have done before?"

"I told you, it is not safe to fly at night while there are Wyverns under Malock's control. Their sight is much keener than ours at night and they could detect us leagues before we would see them. We would be picked out of the sky like bats in the daytime before we even knew they were upon us. But I've told you all of this already. Do you always forget so easily, or were you off in your daydreams as well during our last tactical discussion?"

"Right, I remember now. We're on our way to find ..."

"Stop! Listen," she said sharply.

Sarghon froze in his tracks. They heard sounds of drums and singing in the distance. To Sarghon's knowledge, no one lived this deep in the forest secluded from the rest of the population, where the trees grew to be monolithic in size – more than twice as large as the biggest tree in his part of the Gallandrean Forest. Whoever they were, they meant to keep themselves hidden and were most likely reluctant to see foreigners.

"Who do you suppose would be this deep into the forest?" Sarghon said, leaning closely into Kara's ear.

"I do not know. But our path led us here. The trees bent with the wind in this direction for a reason. They serve you now, so I suppose we should follow their wise lead. Can you not just ask them?" she said bluntly.

"I suppose I *just* could," he retorted, sarcastically.

Sarghon walked over to the nearest tree and placed his hand on its trunk before speaking in the ancient, Earatheen language. "*Warath verahune sarangeth shonathta?*"

He waited a moment, sensing the inner thoughts of the young tree, wondering if it was old enough to communicate with him, when an answer came, "*Sharenth comera bensethuash Profenata Diaglyfinashta.*"

"Indeed, we are meant to be here," Sarghon said. "This young sapling believes we should proceed in …"

Just then, a burst of wind swept past their knees, parting the leaves at their feet and creating a footpath toward the singing and music, "…this direction," Sarghon responded with a lift of his eyebrow.

Following the path onward toward the sounds, they came to find the beating drums and voices of tribal song sung in a language that neither Kara nor Sarghon recognized. Torches lit the perimeter of an elaborate campsite gathering, with a large fire pit in the center. The atmosphere was celebratory, with dancers and chant-like singing.

Sarghon and Kara approached with caution, not wanting to frighten the remote people. They were pale skinned and the dancer's faces and arms were painted with elaborate tattoo-like tribal designs. They wore free flowing clothes made from animal skins and natural hand-woven fabrics.

As the drum circle pounded out the trance-like music, both women and men danced around the fire tossing small sacks of multi-colored, flammable material into the flames. As each sack hit the fire, it exploded into colorful sparks that shot streams of glowing embers high into the air.

When Sarghon and Kara stepped out from the brush into the light, the drumming stopped. The singing and dancing also stopped as the scene came to a deadly silence. Extending her wings out from behind her shoulders and metallic chest-plate, Kara showed herself to the people. Gasps exploded from all around the campsite.

Stoically, Sarghon stepped forward grasping the handle of his sword, Gladanteus as he spoke, "We mean you no harm. We were led this way and need your guidance through this part of the forest. I am Sarghon, of the *Diaglyphen Prophesy*. This is Kara, Princess of the Valkyrie."

The people stood in silence, wide-eyed and awestruck, but not in the least bit scared by what they saw and heard. A mysterious woman approached, covered with a large cape made from dyed animal skin and beaded with intricate flame-like patterns. The palms of her hands were dyed red and she wore a headdress of bright orange and yellow feathers. Her white hair hung straight to her waist, outlining an aged face that once was strikingly beautiful. She appeared to be their leader.

Walking up to Sarghon without a word, the woman eyed him up and down, as Kara stood ready to pounce like a feral cat. "Di-gly-feen-pro-fassy?" the woman said. "Yes, I see. I see you. You speak the truth!"

Her accent was slight, but foreign to Sarghon and Kara. Turning to her people, she shouted, *"Halvor! Halvor!"*

The fire people all repeated her chant in unison over and over, *"Halvor! Halvor!"*

The drum circle started back up with intense enthusiasm, as the dancers and singers began a new song, dancing around the large center fire-pit. Two perfectly muscular young men with nearly white, pale blue eyes ushered Sarghon and Kara to follow their leader into her dwelling on the far side of the fire. As they passed the celebration, some people tossed offerings of dried flowers and crystallized dust at their feet, while others bowed their heads, muttering what seemed like a prayer.

Once inside, the two beautiful young men gestured for Sarghon and Kara to sit next to a small fire pit in the center of the room, before pouring juice in hand-carved stone mugs for them to drink. With her shrewd eyes on the two, the elder female leader walked with beautiful grace, her long flowing white hair trailing behind her in long wisps as she moved. She possessed a regal quality, yet mystical and wraithlike. Her eyes were kind and deeply set, reflecting silvery, pale blue glints of light from the fire.

She sat down in a sling-back chair held together by large, carved wooden branches that spiraled in all directions. It was obvious that these people worshipped fire. It wasn't by chance that Sarghon was led here and he knew it.

"Fortune has smiled upon us," the old woman said. "We have been dancing and singing for your arrival. The gods have been watching over us and they have listened. We welcome you Halvor; and you, Princess of the Valkyrie. Our fire is your fire."

"I have not heard of your kind," Kara said, curtly. "The Valkyrie have flown over this forest for many years and not once have we encountered people here. Only in our ancient text is there mention of *fire people* and, even then, it is thought to be only legend."

"We are but a small number of what we once were," she replied, "I am Elda, leader of the Basai. Our people used to live throughout the forest in underground sanctuaries. We numbered in the thousands. Our kind lived in secrecy, coming above ground only when we needed to. But we are disappearing. Now, our tribe is all that's left. We come up from underground on the night of the full moon to sing to our Gods. Tonight, is one such night."

"Do you know *The Keeper of Fire*?" Sarghon asked bluntly. "My name is Sarghon, not Halvor. I am in search of the fire element. If I am to gain sufficient power to stop the encroaching darkness, I must attain it. If you indeed worship the element of fire, you must know how to summon it forth, and thus, our reason for being led to you."

Elda began to laugh. "You are bold, young warrior, I must give you that. You will need audacity if you are to stop the atrocities that plague this land. Halvor means 'savior' in our ancient language. When we pray and dance for a cause, a savior or 'Halvor' has always arrived to help. Let me tell you the story of our Gods. Maybe that will help you in your quest."

Reaching into a stone bowl, she pulled out an incense bundle, lit it on fire, and waved it around cleansing the room with its smoke. "As I mentioned, we live deep underground and only come up to the surface for hunting, collecting, and ceremonial times. It is said that our Gods, Kegan and Tana were once like us, living among our kind as we do now. They were lovers, often frolicking through the forest like free spirits do, filled with curiosity for what lay on the surface beyond our forest. No one had ever been beyond the forest's edge, you see.

"One day, Tana ventured off by herself. Drawn by her curiosity, she followed a bird and got lost. Kegan was heartbroken, having searched everywhere on the ground that he knew of. He built fires to lure her back, with no avail. He finally decided to find Aedus, one of the rare fire horses, to aid him in his search for Tana. Aedus was a majestic and magical horse that could fly. Kegan set off to tame the beast and ride him high in the sky where he would be able to see much further into the distance. Once Kegan found Aedus, he begged the horse to allow him to ride on his back across the sky to search for his one and only love, Tana. Sensing Kegan's broken heart, Aedus allowed him this favor. They flew into the sky, higher and higher, but Tana was nowhere to be found. Even higher they flew, in a fiery ball of light across the sky. Around and around they flew, day after day, vowing to find Tana out of pure love."

"Did he ever find her?" Kara asked with interest.

"The ball of light circles still. Kegan and Aedus bring us the day. And when they are on the other side of the world, we light our fires in the night and sing his songs so that he will find his way home again."

"What does all this have to do with us?" Sarghon asked.

"Ahh, yes. I was getting to that," Elda said with a gracious smile. "Aedus has a sister, Atasha."

Picking up the incense bundle again, she waved it above her head in an obscure gesture. "Kegan and Tana may be a fantastic legend, but Atasha is real; very rare, but also very real. She lived in our forests until recently. She was captured by the mindless followers of Malock and has not been seen since. We are the only people she would allow to approach her – the only ones she trusted. You see, we share the fire bond with her. She is our guardian. Only a god can ride her in the sky though, or that extremely rare individual who possesses fire magic. If you are able to ride Atasha and not get burned, then you are truly *Halvor*. She carries within her the pure element of fire. She is 'The Keeper.' It is what allows her to fly."

Sarghon was excited as much as he was confused. "I am not anyone's *Halvor*. I am Sarghon, from a small village somewhere in …" he pointed randomly over his shoulder, "…that direction. I am not here to be worshiped or chanted upon. I need to find the elementals and stop Malock before he destroys all the lands!"

"Then you will have to dance," Elda retorted.

"What?" Sarghon responded, dumbfounded.

"It is what will allow you to ride her. You must find your passion. Our dances are based on ancient riding techniques passed down from generations of when our people rode the *fire* beasts on land. The dance teaches how to mount and ride. It's not like riding a mere domestic horse, you see. There are very specific movements that allow one to slide up her torso and hold the fire mane while balancing on her back. Also, there is a motion that you must make."

Sarghon listened with great intent and curiosity.

"Before you mount, you must carefully place your hand over her eyes until you gain her trust. She will sense your purpose and decide whether you are worthy. None have been in my lifetime."

"And you think Atasha will find me worthy?"

"*You* must think it, young *Halvor*."

"Please, don't call me that."

Turning his head away, Sarghon pondered the idea of riding a horse that burst into flames when it ran too fast.

"And in order to feel the fire energy within you, there must be passion present at all times," Elda said. "This ardor can manifest itself within you in many ways. It can be created through anger, love, or intense fervency aimed toward your goal. Fire is made from extreme friction, you see – excitement and turbulence come together to create the pure, ideal, and divine element of *fire*. We learn these principles through our dance. Come, Aidan will show you how it is done."

Elda gestured for the muscular, young man to lead them out to the fire pit. "You will need to learn the *Dance of Atasha*."

Outside, the music, drums, chanting, and dancing continued, as Sarghon and Kara were led back to the grouping of people gathered around the large fire. Everyone seemed to be in a trance-like state, pulsating with the musical rhythm. A select group of men and women danced in graceful, choreographed motion around the fire. They stepped in unison, beautifully fluidic in their movements, repeating the dance over and over.

"You must follow the dance as they do," Aidan explained to Sarghon. "Begin with your arm outstretched like this."

Aidan showed Sarghon the beginning movement, reaching forward with his arm, extending it out in front of his body. The movement ended with a gesture that looked like fingers wrapping around a rope.

*That must be the movement for grabbing onto the mane,* Sarghon thought.

The next set of movements consisted of a double quickstep into a barrel leap high into the air. After several jumps, the arms switched position; one stretching out far in front with the palm facing down, the other balancing behind with the palm facing up. Then the torso bent forward, the knees spread and the dancers shifted their weight from their heels to their toes. This whole movement repeated in the dance over and over with great passion and beauty.

Watching the dance in silence, Kara turned to Sarghon. "They are more graceful than you in the air."

"Thank you for your vote of confidence," he responded.

"At least you may soon be able to keep up with me in the sky – that is, if this fire horse, Atasha really exists."

Lifting her chin in the air, Kara glanced alluringly over to Aidan and his muscular companion. Her eyes danced along his shimmering, sweaty body. Sarghon noticed her dubious advance, becoming intrigued by her expression.

Kara was a fantastic mystery to Sarghon and he became physically excited knowing he would soon be dancing and sweating in front of her, determined for her to look upon him in the same way she was now looking at Aidan.

For some reason, she appeared more attractive than before, standing stoically in the firelight, watching the dancers. *It's as if I have been asleep for years,* he thought. *I knew she was intriguing, but something has changed.*

Indeed, something had changed. Sarghon was now a man, with all the desires a young, adult male feels within him. Watching Kara's eyes follow Aidan's nearly naked body, sparked a new desire.

As he began the first set of movements, Sarghon emulated what he was taught. At first it felt strange, but after the repetition of movement, his body naturally seemed to pick it up. He moved through the air, following each motion as if he were floating.

Glancing over to Kara, her gaze shifted in his direction. He pulled off his shoulder cloak and tunic, tossing them aside, before posturing with more confidence. He was now bare-chested like the other male dancers.

As he danced harder, he focused on the repetition of movements, falling into the trance-like state of the dance. Gliding through the actions with precision and elegance, the crowd couldn't help noticing how quickly and instinctually he picked up the motions of the dance. Moving faster and faster, Sarghon flew through the series of movements until he was barely touching the ground.

One by one, the other dancers stopped dancing and moved out of his way. He danced around the fire so quickly that most of his movements looked like a beautiful blur in a perfect circle. Trying to impress Kara, Sarghon became caught in the emotion of the fire dance, connecting him directly to the fire itself.

The fire in the middle illuminated his glistening body, as it started to funnel along with his circular movement, acting like a central beacon or pillar reaching up toward the sky and synchronizing with the dance. As the drums beat faster, it looked as if Sarghon were melding with the fire itself – his body twirling through the air at lightening speed. All eyes were fixed on him, when suddenly he stopped.

Out of breath, Sarghon peered around at the stunned audience, his body dripping with sweat, his head dizzy and disorientated. The other dancers sank to their knees, placing their hands on the ground. Kara stood wide-eyed, riveted by what she had just witnessed, her wings pulsating with each breath she took, her eyes glued to Sarghon's bare, shimmering torso.

"What just happened?" he said in bewilderment, as he looked around at a stupefied audience, unsure why he was standing alone at the fire pit. "Why was I the only one dancing? Was I doing it incorrectly? Please rise, I am not to be worshipped like this!"

The dancers slowly stood, keeping their heads bowed and their eyes down. Kara approached him, placing her hand in his. "Your skills are indeed impressive," Kara said in a deep whisper. "Do you recall what just transpired? The dance?"

Catching his breath, Sarghon held her hand while glancing around at the people. "I was … dancing?" he said, looking back into Kara's eyes.

"You were doing more than that. I have never seen anyone move like that before. Whatever it was you were doing, you were born to do it. It was astonishing," she said with sincerity as she watched beads of sweat drip down his smooth, athletic shoulders and chest.

"Are you sure you are not one of us?" Aidan said, stepping forward and approaching Sarghon. "No one has ever learned our dance as quickly or impressively as you have just done. Whatever your quest, I am here to serve you. I offer whatever I may have to give."

Elda stepped forward, speaking only a single word, "Santeen!"

The crowd repeated her. "Santeen!"

"It means *Champion*," Aidan said.

"Well, I guess I can accept that over *Halvor*," he said, reluctantly.

"And you were the finest of all the dancers," Kara said, as a surreptitious smile crept up her face. "I believe you are now worthy of the fire element."

"We are with you!" Elda shouted. "Bring our people back to us,

Santeen. Our future may depend on you. Aidan will show you our secret paths through the forest and any other assistance he can offer. He is the strongest and fasted of our kind. And if you need fire, he can provide it. At least until you find Atasha," she said, with a slight bow.

"Rest and feast with us tonight. It would be our honor to have you dine with us before going into battle. You need to replenish your energy after the dance. It is our duty to offer you our hospitality. To refuse us, would be bad luck, so come!"

They were led into another dwelling made of stretched animal skins and carved wooden posts, set against a large painted stone slab wall. The paintings and carvings all depicted ornate flame designs. One showed flames coming from the hands of a person – possibly one of the gods he heard about in the story.

"Do these carvings represent real occurrences, or legend?" Sarghon inquired to Aidan.

"Ahh, you refer to: the *Hands of Fire*. There are those of us selected and taught the secrets of our kind. Some are chosen at birth to receive the gifts. I am one who was given the *Hands of Fire*. It's not magical, but based in science and herbology.

Deep in our caves exist a rare plant root that when combined with the crystalline sand phosfrolite, found only in our forest, can create fire. I was specially instructed in the technique. The root tincture was given to me as a small child in a toxic drink we call *wook*. It is poisonous to all but a few. Many have died attempting its gift. It is now in my blood. With proper friction, along with a gesture of with my fingers, I can create fire with just the sand from the Earth. The movement, like certain dances, is taught only to a chosen, worthy few."

"Fascinating," Sarghon said. "So your culture combines ceremony, spirituality, and legend with passion, science, and practicality. I am intrigued."

"As we are of you," Aidan replied, turning to Kara. "And, it is an honor to have the company of a Valkyrian warrior such as yourself. We have indeed been blessed this evening. Let me share with you another of our customs, one that includes a diverse forest palate."

Aidan led Sarghon and Kara to a table in the center of the room. Laid out before them was a bountiful selection of cooked meats and vegetables from the region. Thane recognized roasted Black Tip Deer, Carrow Boar and Linzar, a wild large rabbit-like creature that hopped long distances as well as climbed trees.

Large wooden bowls filled with long, wild Babok Mushrooms and Oedin Budding Root garnished the main dishes, as well as a strange, curved squash called Kreb, that Sarghon recognized only in the moment, due to his new senses.

An assortment of wild berries garnished each place setting. It was a virtual banquet of forest flavors and smells. Both Sarghon and Kara were impressed as well as instantly hungry.

Elda, along with other leading tribe members entered the room and stood behind large, ornately carved chairs set at the grand table. Elda gestured for Sarghon and Kara to sit first.

"This is more than we could have imagined for our evening's meal," Kara said. "We are most grateful for your generosity."

"The forest guided us to you," Sarghon said, "and we truly appreciate your kindness, however, after this abundant meal, we must be on our way to find Atasha and King Malock. Your feast will certainly aid us with nourishment and a full belly.

"Then sit and eat!" Elda ordered. "This is the least we can do for such esteemed guests."

The others were instructed to sit once Sarghon and Kara were seated. Elda sat on one side of Sarghon, with Kara on the other.

As they ate, a new sense of camaraderie and purpose grew in Sarghon, knowing that he may be able to help these people and others like them. Until now, he had not spoken with anyone who had been directly affected by the Dark King's take over, and the gratitude he witnessed in the eyes of the Basai made Sarghon feel truly needed.

As they finished their meal, Elda leaned in to Sarghon's ear, "I hope it was to your liking, Sarghon Santeen. I am a mother and, as such, it is my sworn duty to feed my children well. I only wish we had the flavorsome allspice herb, Carnassion. It would go so well with the roast deer and linzar, but it only grows near the East Ocean – such a shame. Now, on to a more important subject."

Her expression changed, becoming somber. "Aidan, my youngest and strongest son will guide you through our hidden trails to the edge of the forest where you will find the road leading into the darkness and toward Malock's fortress. I must warn you, it is a despondent place of sorrow and death."

As she looked out at the night forest, her aged eyebrows winced together. "When our people disappeared, I followed their tracks to the edge of the darkness where all life ceased to exist. To look upon it can cause instant misery. You must be strong, young Santeen. You must find the spirit within you, the inner strength and passion you were born with – else, you will fall prey to the sadness and despair."

Sarghon contemplated her words in silence. Kara's keen hearing had picked up every word Elda said as well, as she sat in silent, strategic thought.

"I will do my best to stop the evil that has plagued our land," Sargon said. "I was lead here for a reason. You and your people have shown me that I must trust in my instincts, allowing myself to let go – to dance with fearlessness."

"Yes, yes, that's how you find inner strength," Elda said with enthusiasm. "Never forget that lesson." She gave him a warm, motherly smile. "Now, you must be on your way, as you have insisted. We will sing and dance for your courage, your … *santeen*. We will burn fires every night, praying for victory."

Kara and Sarghon were led outside where Aidan joined them. They said their farewells to the Basai people, before gathering their few things.

Elda walked them to the edge of their village, when Sarghon released Gladanteus from her sheath, holding the majestic sword in his grip. "Dear Elda, leader of the Basai, we thank you and wish you well."

"Dance with fearlessness, friend," she replied with a warm nod. "May the fire protect you."

Placing the tip of the sword to the ground, he gave Elda a wink. Instantly a plant sprouted from the Earth, growing, twisting, and maturing into deep green vines that burst by the dozens into vibrant, orange flowers that bloomed in every direction. It was the carnassion allspice plant. Elda smiled from ear to ear, bowing her head in gratitude, knowing that her meat would now be more flavorful than ever!


Aidan walked Kara and Sarghon through the trees along a path leading due north toward the edge of the forest. The path was not marked, or even tread upon, as it wound past ancient pine trees, over trickling streams, and across moss covered rocks.

Aidan moved like a sleek, large cat, gliding from rock to rock effortlessly, with ease and grace. Sarghon and Kara had a hard time keeping up with him. Kara was as strong as a giant elk, but her speed and agility was in the air, not on the ground. Sarghon kept pace, but often stumbled along the dark and uneven path, needing to stop from time to time to catch his breath or drink from a stream.

"Aidan, if you would be so kind," Sarghon said, with a deep exhale, "may we stop for a moment? I am curious – how many people of the Basai have been abducted into Malock's service?"

When they stopped, Kara was also glad for the respite. Aidan was as calm as if he had been standing still for the entire journey.

"For the last ten moon cycles our people have been taken while gathering and hunting food and provisions above ground," Aidan answered with melancholy in his eyes. "We spend most of our time below ground in deep caverns, tunnels, and caves, as you have been told, but we must come up to the forest often. At night we are safe, but during the day the King's patrols are sent throughout the forest in search of anyone they can capture. We don't know why no one has returned. We pray they are alive somewhere. We are not a warrior tribe and do not have an army to fight back. So, you can see why we are so grateful that you have come. We are only a small few who have been affected by the Dark Lord's influence on this land, but our numbers are dwindling and soon we will be no more."

"Ambroas, my teacher, told me of similar stories where people have been taken from villages, never to return. What do you suppose Malock has done with all the people?" Sarghon asked. "If he is just killing people, there are more thorough ways to do so. He must have some use for them."

"I agree with Sarghon," Kara said, "but we must keep moving if we are to reach the edge of the forest before dawn. We have not slept and we will need sleep if we are to be of any use to anyone during the daylight. And I must rest before I take flight again."

They continued on, following Aidan as best they could, not stopping as often as before to rest. After another hour of trekking over, under, and through the lush forest, Aidan stopped. "We approach the edge of the forest," he said calmly. "Beyond the trees ahead lie the dead-land, where life has been taken from the ground and nothing will grow."

"Then for the rest of the night we will camp here and sleep as much as we can," Sarghon said, catching his breath. "How do you prefer to sleep, on the ground or upon soft grass?"

Aidan thought it a strange question at first, but then he remembered with whom he was speaking. "We sleep on animal fur blankets on the ground or rock," he answered.

"Then this is for Kara and myself."

Releasing Gladanteus from his belt, Sarghon once again placed the tip of the sword to the ground. Light green grass began sprouting in a patch where the sword touched. It grew and swirled in soft tufts, until a perfectly clean patch had developed.

Kara noticed it was large enough for only two, as a small smile crept up the side of her face.

Fascinated by the magical, earthen powers Sarghon possessed, Aidan wondered what else he was capable of, knowing how quickly he picked up their sacred dance. "Wondrous, indeed!" Aidan said, wide eyed. "I will make us a fire to keep us warm while we sleep."

Looking around, Aidan found several adequate pieces of wood and placed them in a pile near the newly grown grass pad. He reached into a leather pouch from his waist and pulled out a small handful of dark crystalline sand, arranging it in his palm very particularly, patting it as he whispered. He then rubbed his second and third fingers with his thumb. With a lightning fast flick of his wrist, fire exploded from his hands onto the wood in a brilliant flash of light. The fire lit over the entire pile of wood with no smoke – just clean, warm fire.

"I see why you possess the name you do," Sarghon said, staring into the flames. "Quite wondrous as well, and if I may say, beautiful to watch. You are a fervent, disciplined people. Let us rest now. Our day is sure to be challenging."

The heat of the fire kept them warm as they each found a comfortable spot to lay. Due to her wings, Kara had to sleep on her side. She covered one of Sarghon's legs with her wings, and although she was facing the opposite direction, he could tell she did it on purpose.

As he lay, Sarghon was unable to sleep. Staring up at the dark treetops rustling lightly in the night breeze, he tried to clear his mind for what lay ahead. Stars poked out beyond the tall, pointy shadows, as he listened to the sounds of the night. The crackle of the fire reminded him of his task ahead. *I must find Fire,* he thought.

The mesmerizing flames from the campfire danced with yellow and orange swirls. No two flames were exactly alike. Each had its own brief, dazzling life, flickering up, before being instantly replaced with another uniquely alluring wisp of flame. Sarghon wondered what it would be like to control such a powerful and destructive element: Would he burn, or be immune to the extreme high temperature? Does Atasha really exist, or is she a fantasy born of the Basai? Will he actually be able to mount and ride her? How powerful is Malock?

All these questions and more continued to flow through

Sarghon's mind, as he lay watching the enigmatic flames flicker before his eyes.

Several hours passed, as he lay in trance-like meditation, trying to answer questions that existed only in the future. He envisioned himself riding the legendary fire horse while wielding great elemental powers. It was all fantastically overwhelming, as he tried to relax his body and mind as much as possible – but he could not sleep.

Sitting up quickly, Sarghon sensed something approaching. Grabbing his sword with beguiling intrigue rather than fear, he witnessed a ghostly shape forming before him. The ghost manifested into the figure of an indistinguishable man wearing plain clothes, hidden in the darkness. The male figure walked slowly toward him out from the shadow.

Something familiar resonated from deep within Sarghons being, as the man's face appeared. *Could it be,* he thought, ... *no... how is it possible that* ... "Aaron?"

As he stepped into the light, the landscape and surroundings became blurred. The only thing now in complete focus was the form of Aaron. The rest of the world seemed to move in very slow motion. The trees swayed, as if time were slowing to a stop, as a falling leaf sat in mid-air, rotating very slowly as it floated in slow motion toward the Earth.

Aaron took a step forward past the floating leaf. "Is it you?" Sarghon said, bewildered. "Aaron, I am Sarg ... wait, no it's Thane." *That's right, my real name is Thane,* he thought. "I'm dreaming, aren't I? And you – WE fell, and you're ... "

In that instant, he realized he was having a lucid conversation with his friend, communicating with him from another plain of existence. "You look pretty good to me for a dead guy," Thane said, intrigued.

Aaron was dressed in clean clothes, casual and nondescript. The colors were muted, but he was definitely in color. He looked very healthy and happy, with a smart grin on his face.

"Yes, it's really me," Aaron said, placing his hand on Thanes shoulder as he spoke, "and you *are* really dreaming at this moment. I wanted to see you too – to tell you how much I love and miss you."

Thane's heart swelled with emotion as he felt Aaron's energy. It was beautiful, yet focused and very real. He felt completely aware of all that was happening, no matter how unbelievable.

"I miss you too," Thane said, "More than you know. There's so many things I want to say to you. Things happening I can't even explain."

"I know. You feel overwhelmed and full of energy that doesn't always make sense. You're seeing things in a new light, with new eyes and ears. It's only the beginning, my friend. Your life will change. I was worried about you, and wanted to make sure you were OK."

Thane was speechless, trying to absorb what he was hearing and feeling with every ounce of his being.

"I also wanted to show you that I'm fine where I am and all is well," Aaron continued, "You don't have to worry about me at all, OK? I came to you to let you know that what you're feeling now is *real*. The energy we share right now, at this very moment, is real energy that you're tapping into. Love, passion, emotion, empathy – those are the parts of us that make us human, allowing us to move forward – to evolve. It's also the conduit that gives us power."

"Aaron, I'm not sure I understand what you're saying. You're starting to sound like Yoda, you know that?" Aaron chuckled.

"You will. I know you've felt it. You tried to tell me before, but I wasn't ready. I didn't understand then. Continue to search within your heart and mind – they are one. You're on a glorious path, Thane."

The slow-motion leaf began coming back into focus, floating down slightly faster, but still in slow motion. "I don't want you to go!" Thane yelled. "I want to tell you about something special that happened with me and Sharla… and so much more. I miss you so much."

Aaron stepped forward and they embraced. Thane held on tight.

"I need to go now," Aaron said, reluctantly. "It's all good, dude. Remember what I said. It's *real*, our connection, our consciousness, our future. Don't be afraid to feel, Thane. See you around, buddy."

Aaron stepped back, fading into the colorless forest. The look on his face was one of truth and love. Then he was gone. The surroundings came back into view, but not as they were before. There was less detail as the trees sped up to normal speed in the wind and the falling leaf drifted in real-time, landing at his foot. *His* foot.

*I'm Thane,* he thought. *I'm dreaming and I'm about to wake up.*

He looked back at the campsite, trying to stay in the moment, holding on to the forest landscape. For a few long seconds he rode the line between his dream world and reality, knowing that his experience and feelings in the dream had been as potent as any in the real world.

The campsite faded into the landscape and the landscape faded into nothingness. And then it was gone. The dream was over.

Thane lay almost comatose on the sand as he slowly opened his eyes. Tears were running down his face, as the sun and shadow from the branches of the palm tree blurred his vision. He was smiling, euphoric and elated, shedding tears of immense joy. He was filled with heightened emotion and empathy – the same emotive energy that Aaron spoke of. In this special moment, Thane was certain of at least that much.

Still unable to move, feeling slowly crept back into his entire body. He felt as if he were surrounded in a cocoon of light and love, embracing him from all sides, filling him to the brim with sensations of indescribable beauty.

*Wait!* Thane thought. *It's the same. This is the same feeling I had when I was floating toward the light – when I went out of my body during the accident! It's the same sensation of complete peace, harmony, serenity, and ... LOVE.*

"Aaron. It really *was* you, wasn't it," Thane said aloud.

He wasn't asking a question, but rather a affirming a statement. "It was real," he spoke out loud again.

Tears continued down his face as he gradually sat up in the warm, soft sand. Reaching for his 7-up, his hand trembled as he took a sip, trying to recall what Aaron said about higher consciousness and energy.

Once Aaron had entered his dream, Thane knew without a doubt that it was actually Aaron he was communicating with and not a figment of his imagination. The intense feeling, the lucidity, the color, the connection; there was no uncertainty at all. *It was Aaron,* he reaffirmed to himself several times. He had just connected to the other side – he had spoken with Aaron and he knew this to be absolute truth.

*What about the dream?* he thought, *Sarghon and Kara had just become friends with the Basai while on a daring, adventurous task. They're back. My dreams are back!*

Thane was thrilled to have his friends return, now more than ever, wanting to know where the adventure would lead. It had been three years and, once again, Thane had forgotten most of the details from these Sargonian dreams until he had awakened back in the dream as Sarghon, continuing the quest to save their land.

His mind kept on without pause. He recalled his conversation

149

with Angelica about Kara's words: ... *'the ability to intuitively sense energy fields, physically, emotionally, mentally and spiritually.' Could that be what Aaron was talking about?* he thought, *He mentioned that love and passion gave us power. Could they be talking about the same thing?*

It was his near-death experience that allowed him to connect with Aaron in his dream, and he knew it. The blissful feeling was exactly the same, something that confirmed the profundity of the lucid visit.

*Could this be why I feel so emotional in my dreams?* he thought. *Are my worlds colliding?* "I think I'm losing it! I'm really losing it," he said out loud, grabbing his forehead in both hands.

Thane took a well-deserved breath, trying to clear his head, feeling the weight of another world on his shoulders. He yawned, stretching out his body as far as he could from fingertips to toes, before packing up his things from the sand, folding the blanket and putting them in his backpack.

He walked out to the surf, standing with his feet in the cool ocean water. Peering out onto the shimmering, infinite liquid horizon, Thane wondered why his dreams decided to come back on this day.

He knew he was dreaming the instant he recognized Aaron's face. Aaron actually validated the fact plainly in the dream. It was the first time he was able to say exactly what he wanted within a dream. It was incredible.

Smiling, as he looked out over the glistening water, Thane felt at peace. A weight had been lifted from his shoulders. He now knew Aaron was OK. Aaron had taken the sadness away – sadness that Thane had held on to for so very long.

"Thank you, my friend," he whispered, gazing toward the clouds along the horizon.

*What now?* Thane thought. *What now?*

# Chapter XI

## THE BLACK PIG

A week had passed since his visit to see Angelica and Thane was leaving on a flight to Tahiti the next morning. With his suitcase fully packed, he was eager to set out on his exotic, environmental adventure. As he looked around his room, it reminded him of the boy that he used to be.

He picked up the going away card on his bed from his sister, reading it for a second time: *"Dear Thane, wherever you go, I encourage you to keep your eyes open to all that the world has to offer. There's a lot out there to discover, just be safe, have fun, and take risks rationally. One day I'll join you and we can make the world a better place together. Bon voyage, 'lil bro."*

Feeling rejuvenated with a new sense of purpose, Thane acknowledged there was something significant about this particular time in his life. His decision to work with Greenpeace gave him a place to focus his energy and desire. It had been a long time since he felt this way and it seemed these feelings were somehow related to the return of his fantastical dreams – although the mystery was yet to be completely understood.

Thane's parents planned a going-away dinner for him at their house the evening before his big trip. He didn't know exactly how long he would be gone, so Thane was happy to be with them for one last night.

"Thane, come sit down! I'm putting dinner on the table. Your father's getting restless," Susan called from the kitchen. "We have a surprise for you!"

"Coming Mom," he answered, trotting down the stairs. "I was just making sure I had enough sunscreen and ... Sharla!"

"Surprise!" Susan, Reece, and Sharla shouted.

"Now how could you leave without a real goodbye from me?" Sharla said with an inquisitive smirk.

Thane gave Sharla a long hug before sitting down beside her at the dinner table. "How've you been, miss thing? You know I just saw Angelica last week. We had a nice visit. I can't wait to tell you all the crazy stuff we talked about. But first, how are you? It's been way too long. How is UC Santa Cruz? Are you digg'in it up there?"

"Well, " she said with raised eyebrows, "I took a job working part time in a rad surf shop. The guys up there are super sexy. But now it's summer break, so I took a little time off. When your mom called, I told her we should make it a surprise. And well – here I am!"

"It's really great to see you," Thane said, hugging her again. "I'll write when I can. I'm looking forward to sending you letters with all the craziness I get into."

"So, you're really going off to do this thing?" Susan said, with motherly concern. "It's so far away. Your father and I won't be able to sleep thinking about the danger you could be in."

"Oh, let the boy live a little," Reece said. "He's old enough to make his own decisions and learn from his own mistakes. How else is he gonna grow up? Besides, if I were his age I'd probably be doing the same thing. I'm kinda jealous, if the truth be known. And hang on a sec, I have a present for you."

Reece handed his son a black bag. "Before you open it, pass me the green beans and butter."

"Thanks dad," Thane said, opening the bag to find a thirty-five millimeter Cannon camera, zoom lens attachment, and carrying case.

"Wow, I'll use this for sure. This is really great, dad. Thanks!"

"Now you can document everything you do, so your mom can sleep at night," Reece said, winking to Susan.

"So, what are they gonna make you do?" Sharla asked. "Throw stink bombs at the French ships like they do with the Japanese whaling ships? Or paint guns! Are they teaching you how to shoot paint guns? That would be cool."

She stuffed a large bite of chicken into her mouth, talking on without hesitating. "Isn't it totally radiated there from all the bombing – three-headed fish and all? Will you have to wear a special suit or something? I don't want you com'in home all glowing and setting off the airport security alarms."

She waved her arms in the air as she enacted a scenario, "Beep, beep, beep!" She laughed loudly at her own joke, snorting her notorious *Sharla snort*, nearly choking on the chicken in her mouth.

Then, with one large cough, a piece of unswallowed chicken shot through her teeth, landing like bird poop on Reece's shoulder.

"You know, you should swallow your food before trying to be a comedian my dear," Reece said with a chuckle. Susan put her hands over her mouth to stop from laughing, but it came out the other end in a short, loud fart.

Sharla, having just taken a sip of water, shot it straight out of her nose and all over her food.

Thane and Reece couldn't help themselves any longer. Both burst out in uncontrollable laughter as Susan said, "Oopsy daisy." The table erupted into a group laugh that only happens once in a blue moon such as this. It took several minutes before they were able to catch their breath and return to sanity.

"I'm gonna miss you all," Thane said sincerely. "If anything, I'll come back with a good tan. And hopefully not glowing. I don't know exactly what I'll be doing out there, but I know it's something I want to do ... Something I *have* to do."

"Can I just talk seriously with you for a minute, Thane," Reece asked.

Thane's father was an understanding man who liked to laugh and was usually the life of any party, but he was as rational as they come and when he asked to speak seriously with Thane, it was for a reason.

"Everything seemed so important and serious when I was your age," Reece said, looking into Thane's blue-green eyes. "I wanted to change the world too. But you'll find that it's the experiences along the way that make you who you are, son. Look at me – I used to be a conservative, coming of age in the 1950's as a staunch right-wing Republican before I met your mom. But then I dove head first into the 1960's *free love*, *hippy* movement, changed my affiliation to Democrat and married the cute, sexy girl I met at a San Francisco non-verbal party during the *Summer of Love*. I became a dichotomy to my own nature. I both love and resent the free spirited mindset. It's a trip, ya know? You're part of me, so I understand your desire to search for meaning, truth, and answers out there in the world. Just be aware of the journey. You may not find exactly what you expect to find."

Thane didn't know anything *exactly*, but he wasn't expecting that sentiment from his father. "I don't know what I'll find out there, dad," Thane said honesty. "I just know it's where I belong at the moment."

"I envy you. If I were in a different place in my life and if I weren't so damn busy keeping this family afloat, I just may have joined you on this crazy escapade. Hey," he said with a glint in his eye, "save an island out there for me, will ya?"

Reece then leaned over and hugged his son.

The flight to Tahiti was long and Thane dozed off to sleep most of the way as he crossed time zone after time zone. When Thane arrived in Papeete; Tahiti, Christian, a twenty-five year old biologist and member of Greenpeace, greeted Thane at the airport. Christian had been sent to pick Thane up and deliver him to the ship with the same name: The *MV Greenpeace*.

As they drove toward the harbor, Thane peered out the car window marveling at all the coconut palms and brightly colored, tropical foliage along the roadside. The air was thick and humid, with a fresh scent of ocean and sweet tropical flowers.

Excited beyond measure, Thane started to ramble, asking questions about the people and the work that awaited him. "I know we're headed out to the atoll, but what else will we be doing?" Thane blurted. "You guys are all so amazing, dedicating your lives to helping the Earth. I wish there were more of you … us, I mean." Thane's eyes bulged with excitement. "How frigg'in cool is this place! I really want to help. When do we head out, by the way? Are we boarding the ship today? I hope I brought all the right stuff. Oh, I have this new camera. It's awesome! I gotta show you."

"Which one of those would you like me to answer first?" Christian said with a knowing grin, understanding Thane's exuberance.

"I'm sorry, I'm a bit of an eager-beaver, I guess. I'm just excited to be here. It's so incredibly beautiful. Why would anyone want to blow up paradise?"

"Your guess is as good as mine," Christian said with a sardonic expression, "but I would put my bet on at least three things: control, fear, and ego. I'm sure there's more to it than that, but it seems to me that anger and fear just feed more anger and fear. The less of it we have in the world, the better we'll all be. And it usually comes with a large dose of ego."

"I hear ya!" Thane agreed.

"As for your other questions, we leave tomorrow morning bright and early. You're the last recruit and the team's already on board. We're headed for the new *MV Greenpeace* now. It's composed of most of the old crew from the *Rainbow Warrior*. They're a great group of folks – kind of hippy throwbacks at times, but all good people. You'll have your own opinions soon enough," Christian said with another grin. "How old are you anyway? I don't think we've ever had someone so young on board."

"Nineteen," Thane shrugged, "but I'll be twenty pretty soon. I know I probably seem like a kid to you, but I have an old soul."

"To be dedicated to a cause like ours at your age, you must have something special about you, mister. I look forward to getting to know you better. And by the way, I used to be one of the youngest aboard. I'm twenty-five.

"As for what else we'll be doing – well hold your horses, boy; you'll be seeing action soon enough. Better it be a surprise to you. I feel that if I have an expectation of how something is or should be, it never turns out that way in the end."

They arrived at the ship and boarded across a narrow plank walkway with rope handrails. Before going to his cabin, Christian gave Thane a brief tour of the ship so he could get his bearings aboard the expedition vessel.

The ship was mostly black, equipped with four other small inflatable outboard boats known as dinghies, as well as a helicopter-landing pad at the stern. The side was painted with rainbow stripes – a tribute, Thane imagined, to the former Rainbow Warrior. The MV Greenpeace was fifty-eight meters long, able to be out at sea for several months on its own. It housed an array of radar, spouting from its main tower and looked more like a research vessel than an environmental protesting ship. All in all, it was quite impressive to Thane.

After the tour, Thane was led to his quarters, a snug cabin that he would be sharing with the ship's cook, Chef Davey. After surveying the cabin, Thane decided the accommodations were very small, but clean and adequate for the adventure. He unpacked a few items of clothing and toiletries into an inset dresser cabinet that closed with magnets. Sitting on his humble bed, Thane closed his eyes and tried to picture what the days ahead would bring; however, his mind was a flurry of images: nuclear bombs detonating over the ocean, boats racing around each other, crossing wakes and shouting words of protest, bull horns, paint guns, and stink bombs.

He had only read about Greenpeace and seen highlights of their activities on television. He could only imagine what it was truly about. When he signed up to join the team, the enthusiasm was infectious and welcoming, but exactly what they did was still a bit of a mystery. They had asked Thane to keep an open mind, as well as a positive attitude. He knew not everything they did was legal; in fact, most of what they did broke the rules of one sovereign nations treaty, or another. But the way they looked at it, these nations had crossed the sovereign treaty of the Earth, polluting and destroying without cause or need.

A knock sounded on Thane's door and Christian poked his head in. "Hey bro. The Captain's about to start orientation and everybody on board needs to be in attendance. Meet up in the mess hall in ten. You remember – it's out your door to the right, up the stairs, and down the corridor on your left. See ya in a few."

"Right, sure thing," Thane replied, as Christian shut the door.

He sat for another moment, soaking in the reality that he was about to take a giant leap for mankind through a brand-spanking new door! *Am I supposed to bring a pad of paper and a pen to take notes?* he thought. *No, don't want to be* that *guy. Better to just be open and present,* he decided. With that settled, he headed to the crew orientation meeting with a hop in his step.


Thane met up with his roommate, Chef Davey, as well as fourteen other crewmembers that came from a variety of countries including: Holland, Germany, Italy, Canada, Spain, and Australia.

Thane sat next to Maggie, a curly haired, mousey Australian woman with big brown eyes, who wore a very colorful tie-dyed shirt with a peace symbol in the center.

"Welcome my friends, new and old," the Captain said, addressing the group. "I'm Captain Parker Granger, your humble and loud-mouthed Captain. You can call me Captain Parker or Park, for short – Captain, or just Cap, or even Super Stud if you want, but don't ever call me Mr. Granger. Now, I can't tell you enough how proud I am of each and every one of you for just being a part of our new 'Black Pig' crew."

He winked at a group of veterans on his right as he continued. "For those of you who don't know already, we call our ship the 'MV' or the 'Black Pig'. We have an exciting voyage planned and I hope to make history on this one! Let me fill the newcomers in on some of our recent history and remind everyone why what we do is so important.

"Last year, as most of you know, French commandos blew up our flagship, the Rainbow Warrior. We have a lawsuit in the works, by the way. We lost much more than a boat, our pride, and valuable information. The Rainbow Warrior was sunk just before midnight on July tenth, nineteen eighty-five, by two explosive devices attached to the hull by operatives of French intelligence – D.G.S.E. Of the twelve people on board, our photographer Fernando Pereira was drowned when he attempted to retrieve his equipment. Fernando will live on forever in our hearts and in history."

Thane knew some of the details, but hearing them from the lips of the Captain was inspiring. He listened with intense curiosity as Captain Parker continued his address.

"France's nuclear testing in the South Pacific, especially on the atolls of Mururoa and Fangataufa, has inflicted long-term environmental damage to the geographical structuring of the Tahitian atolls. Jacques Cousteau's courageous team has already uncovered proof that radiation has seeped into the fissures of the Mururoa Atoll. A French map from nineteen eighty shows us very clearly that years of nuclear testing have cracked the coral foundation at its very core. All this nuclear testing has caused serious fissuring, destroying the coral and even altering the land plates. The radioactive material trapped under the atolls could eventually escape and contaminate the surrounding ocean. As we know, excessive amounts of toxins such as iodine 131, cause thyroid disease and cancer – among other horrible things.

"This kind of nuclear testing is in *complete* contradiction to France, as the 'Cradle of Democracy and Human Rights.' French Polynesia is economically dependent on France, therefore helpless in resisting nuclear tests. We believe that it's our solemn duty and our obligation to do everything we can to stop these continued tests! They pollute and destroy one of the most beautiful parts of OUR Earth, creating more political tension and fear among all the countries involved. Greenpeace has always been there and we won't stop now. Especially not after what they did to us last year."

"Here, here!" shouted Franz, one of the former Rainbow Warrior crewmembers.

There was a burst of applause with several more random cheers that followed.

"The exact effects of the French nuclear tests won't be known for years," Captain Parker continued, "The French government is very secretive about releasing information concerning environmental hazards associated with nuclear testing. There's grave lack of statistical research to assess the risks to the environment and the people in the South Pacific. Due to pressure from the European Union and the scientific community, France was urged to conduct several tests to assess the health and environmental risks associated with their nuclear tests. Now here is the clincher! Let me read to you the latest news about all this stuff."

He presented a copy of newsprint. "According to a French science team (most likely provided by the government), their conclusion reads as follows:

'There will be NO radiation health effects which could be either medically diagnosed in an individual or epidemiologically discerned in a group of people, and which would be attributable to the estimated radiation doses which are being received or which would be received in the future by people as a result of the residual radioactive material at Mururoa and Fangataufa. Overall, the expected radiation dose rates and mode of exposure are such that no effects on biota population groups could arise,'

"Are you fucking kidding me? Wait, there's more ... 'although occasionally individual members of species MIGHT be harmed, but not to the extent of endangering the whole species or creating imbalances between species. Similarly, NO further environmental monitoring at Mururoa and Fangataufa Atolls is needed for purposes of radiological protection.'

"Of course not! Everything's just honky dory, right? I can't believe they think the world is so ignorant to believe that: '...no effects on biota population groups could arise?' Basically they're saying that all the nuclear testing they've done over the years has had NO affect on anything! Well, we know better and we're going to prove things otherwise. President Chirac can't ignore the strength of international opinion against a resumption of testing at the atoll. So, I have a little plan scheduled for us all that will be sneaky, risky, clever, and fun! Who's in?"

The inspired and encouraged audience roared with enthusiasm. Thane felt the infectious camaraderie, knowing he was in the right place at the right time.

"They say 'chivalry is dead'! The dictionary describes chivalry as: *The combination of qualities expected of the ideal medieval knight, especially courage, honor, loyalty, and consideration of others.* I can't think of better words to describe this crew. You're all knights of the round Earth, sworn to protect her at all cost. I commend each and every one of you for your bravery and service. You've chosen a gallant path, or rather – your path has chosen you! If it weren't for people like us, no one would be there to question any political agenda that rapes the Earth of her natural resources and doesn't care at all about the devastation that's left in the wake. Humanity is slowly absorbing the life essence from the Earth and her oceans, contaminating them with sewage, radiation, pollution, and disease."

The Captain looked around at his devoted audience. "You don't have to be a tree hugger to love the Earth, but with an excess of power, comes excessive responsibility! Greenpeace is the result of one side pushing the boundaries *too* far. If we don't at least try to show them reason, we're just as guilty for idly standing by while intelligent animals are butchered into extinction, atomic bombs run rampant as a common past time, and the human race is expedited into extinction. Any questions?"

His enlivened audience was glued to his every word. The captain then gestured in Thane's direction. "Now, we have our newest and youngest member that just came aboard." Captain Parker looked directly at Thane. "Mr. Winstrom, I presume? We have a very special mission for you and Christian."

Thane's heart thumped hard in his chest with adrenalin-filled excitement.

"I had Christian pick you up and show you around, so we could assess your legitimacy and passion for our work. You passed the test so far and I believe you may be perfect for the task at hand."

He pulled out a folded piece of paper from his pocket. "We look for dedication; we look for sacrifice, and we look for the desire to make a difference. But what we love to find is *unique* passion. You wrote something quite interesting in your application letter that I liked."

He opened the piece of paper and began to read from Thane's letter:

*"I feel intimately connected to the Earth. I want to feel her unburdened heartbeat and learn from her myriad secrets. We are her children, not her executioner. We need to learn from her, to see her more honestly and deeply, and to find our own tender way to touch her soul.*

*Only then will our eyes be open to the reality, abundance, and potential that we will one day achieve."*

The room fell silent. Thane's cheeks began to turn a deep red as the captain looked at him squarely and said, "We have a real poet on board. And passion enough to want you on our team. After all, we're a family, and we work with a common goal in mind."

Thane sat rigidly in his seat, stupefied that he had been singled out, but excited beyond belief that the Captain chose him for a special task.

# MURUROA

"Now, if you're up for it," he continued, "we want you and Christian to take a skiff out to Mururoa and secretly camp there for one week, collecting as much data and samples as you can. We want to conduct *our own* sample tests, uncovering the *real* truth. You'll be learning on the job. Christian is our biology master and he'll be your teacher."

Thane was on the edge of his seat, speechless and wide-eyed with flashing images of being on the atoll with the tropical white sand beneath his feet. "Yes, um … sure! Sounds like a blast. I mean …" Thane caught himself, "I would be honored to conduct such a mission, sir."

"Great! Then it's settled," the Captain replied. "We set sail in one hour. It'll take us a few days to get there in stealth position. In these next few days, you'll be learning all about taking samples and nuclear level readings with Christian. The rest of us will be planning our biggest convoy ever!"

Franz stood up. "You did it? Are we really going through with it zees time?" he said eagerly, in his Austrian accent. "Who else is in wiss us?" he asked.

"While Christian and Thane are camped out on Mururoa, we'll sail to an undisclosed location where we'll meet up with eighteen other ships coming in from all over the place. New Zealand is our largest supporter and they've been incredibly helpful in making this happen with us very quietly. Only the captains of each ship know the heading coordinates. We'll need our crew to lead the flotilla convoy into French waters and into the atoll lagoon, culminating around the oilrig near the east end. It'll be the largest international convoy ever mounted against nuclear bomb testing… and we're the flagship!"

He raised his glass of Champagne high above his head. "To the Warrior and the Pig!!"

The crew roared with excitement and enthusiasm. Franz stood up on one of the tables, dancing an exuberant, little jig.

Christian walked over to Thane and sat in the empty chair next to him. "Hey partner, looks like we're gonna be camping buddies. It'll be your first adventure with us, man," Christian said with a wink. "Most newbies are put on deckhand help and cleaning duties when they first arrive. You're lucky to be working with me. We can make it our own little camping trip."

"Awesome," Thane replied. "I knew this would be an incredible experience for me, but I had no idea something like this would happen. I can't wait. Thank you for anything you may have said to the Captain about me. I can't thank you enough, Christian. Really, I'm totally stoked."

"Alright then," Christian said, placing a hand on Thane's shoulder, "let's start your spy training protocol ASAP. After dark, we set sail quietly so no one follows us. Then I'll come get you and we can go over the sample testing materials and procedures. Welcome aboard, man."

Thane smiled from ear to ear.


For the next two days, Christian gave Thane a crash course as his lab assistant for radioactive material testing. He learned about each sample taking device and how to use each piece of radiation detecting equipment.

Christian taught him about the most commonly used Thief samplers: the Kemmerer sampler and Van Dorn sampler, as well as the isokinetic depth-integrating sampler and nonisokinetic open-mouth sampler. In addition, he was instructed in the use several radiation-taking devices: a spectroscopic personal radiation detector (SPRD), Geiger counter (to detect the ionizing radiation levels of each sample), and a hand-held radiation detector for measuring localized radiation at extremely low levels of the order of 1 CPM (counts per minute).

Thane felt as if he were back in biology class, using glass vials of colored chemicals and wearing protective gloves and goggles. He was having a ball!

"Where did you learn all this stuff, Christian?" Thane asked, while shaking a tube of yellow chemical liquid.

"I graduated with a bio-chemistry degree from Berkeley. Didn't really gel with the offers I got after I graduated, so I took a different approach. I wanted to make a difference with all the crap I was taught. This just seemed the logical place for me. I don't always fit in here like a perfect puzzle piece, but I like what we stand for and I love the group. It's a chance for me to utilize my knowledge at a time and place that makes me feel good about the work and the messages we send."

"Nice. Kinda like a calling, I guess."

"Yeah, you could certainly say that."

"I feel the same way," Thane said, staring at all the equipment. "I just don't know what my expertise is yet. I sometimes have trouble putting my thoughts and feelings into words."

"Well, your letter said it all pretty well to me, and we should have plenty of time together on Mururoa to discuss anything you want. Hey, do you like Frisbee? Football? I'll bring them with us for the beach!"

"Sure, love both," Thane said with a smile, knowing they would become fast friends. "Sounds like fun."

The team arrived at their location off the coast of Mururoa in the late afternoon. The Tahitian sky glowed with wispy clouds spanning across a beautiful, orange and pink horizon. It looked like a classic tequila sunrise cocktail. The air smelled warm and fresh, with a hint of the salty ocean.

The atoll of Mururoa appeared to be a normal island, as the MV Greenpeace approached land. Coconut palms, white sandy beaches, and scattered vegetation covered a wide, flat land surface. In the far distance, various buildings poked up from the foliage, appearing uninhabited. There were no other ships in sight.

"Be on alert everyone," Captain Parker announced quietly over the speaker system. "The French scout ships can pop up at any moment from any direction. We'll keep a distance of two miles, but we're already breaking the law by being inside the French Polynesian atoll zone perimeter, so everyone be on your toes. Anyone who spots a vessel of any kind, come directly to the bridge."

Captain Parker met with Christian and Thane in the captain's quarters to discuss the mission plan. They were to take the smallest of their launch vessels to shore and camp there for a week, taking as many readings and samples as they could carry back to the Black Pig without being detected.

The skiff had been fitted with a special quiet motor, engineered by their head mechanic, Wolfgang. They packed a portable tent, backpacks with clothes, sunscreen, and food for more than a week. Christian also made sure to pack some of the leisure items as well.

"You two keep a low profile now, will ya," Captain Parker said. "Collect as much data as you can and we'll return at the rendezvous point seven days from tomorrow at twelve hundred hours, got it? The convoy will be in tow, so be prepared to make a fast exit. I'm sure eighteen international ships parading across the no-sail zone will make quite an uproar with the French authorities, but they won't be able to do a damn thing. Remember, be ready next Tuesday at twelve-hundred hours, sharp! We'll be the lead ship."

"Aye, aye, Capitan," Thane said with an eager grin.

The Captain gave Thane a wink before tipping his hat at them both. "Make us proud, boys!"


The next morning at 3am Thane, Christian, and their bags were loaded onto the skiff as they set off for land. Still two miles from the shore, hardly a breeze was felt across the quiet waterscape, as they secretively putted across the water in the black, rubber dinghy.

Filled with adrenalin, Thane's fingers wouldn't stay still as he gripped tightly to the side of the rubber boat. They chose a calendar day when the moon had waned into its new, dark phase, with the brilliant stars of the Milky Way guiding them across the serenity of the water. The outline of the atoll was clearly visible on the night horizon.

Looking down at the water splashing alongside the boat, Thane noticed it was glowing with bioluminescence. He placed his hand in the wake, allowing the water to flow through his fingers, glistening with intense, light green luminosity.

"Wow!" Thane said in an excited whisper. "Do you see that? It's fucking amazing. The water is radioactive or something."

Christian laughed quietly. "If I weren't a biologist, I might have thought the same thing," he said, leaning over to examine the dazzling phenomenon. "It's beautiful, isn't it? It's alive, you know."

Thane quickly removed his hand from the water. "They're tiny bioluminescent organisms that generate emission of light when they're disturbed," Christian said, before Thane's eyebrows shot up. "Pretty cool, huh?"

"Damn straight. That's incredible. Never seen anything like it. Well, maybe in my dreams," he said, with a slight cock of his head. "You sure they're not glowing like that 'cause they're radioactive?"

"They may be slightly radioactive, but that's not why they're glowing," Christian answered, with a witty grin. "We're approaching the beach. I'm gonna shoot us straight onto the sand so we don't get wet. You jump out with the rope and pull us up, cool?"

Thane did as instructed, jumping out and pulling the boat onto the beach. They dragged their humble craft up to a sandy area near a patch of coconut trees and ground brush.

After unpacking the boat, they covered it with shrub branches and dried coconut palm fronds. Several hundred yards from the outer beach lay a secluded patch of sand across the sandbar, facing the inner atoll lagoon pool. It was a perfect place to make camp, protecting them from both the wind, as well as detection from outside patrol ships.

They quickly set up the tent and covered it like an African bush dwelling, with branches from bushes and coconut palm fronds. The opening was a small, triangular slit that Christian made from mangrove branches. Only one person could crawl through at a time. After securing all the gear, they crawled into their sleeping bags.

"Here's to us," Christian said, pulling out two beers from the cooler and handing one to Thane. "May this be a camping trip we never forget."

"Damn straight," Thane replied, cracking open the can and toasting with Christian.

Thane felt comfortable with Christian, respecting his attitude and demeanor. He appreciated Christian's ability as a teacher, as well as his unique way of making Thane feel included and useful – whether it be for work or play. This adventure was definitely a variety of both.

Dimly lit with a shirt-covered flashlight, the tent had a faint glow as they finished off another beer. "We can't be detected by anyone while we're here," Christian said, "so tomorrow, I'll be the look out in the morning when I go on my daily wake-up jog, and you'll be the lookout while I'm working with the instruments. Remember to keep everything camouflaged and covered with brush."

"Since we're here for a full week, will it be cool to swim in the lagoon, or will we be radiated and glow like those organisms we saw earlier?" Thane asked, almost seriously.

"If you start glowing, we can save the batteries in our flashlight," Christian chuckled. "But seriously, I think it should be safe for us to be here for this short period of time. But there are still dangers around every corner. Don't eat anything from here. If we fish, I would suggest we do it from the ocean side, not the lagoon side where radiation residue may be leaking. We test everything we ingest. Got it?"

"We can't light a fire at all, right?" Thane asked for certainty.

"Nope, we would be giving off a smoke signal to our location. But if you see a campfire anywhere, that means others are here. We need to be aware of any-and-all signs of human activity. Patrols are periodically sent to keep an eye on this place, but they never stay too long. I think they may also be afraid of coming away with a green glow."

Christian opened another beer, before handing it to Thane. "So, do you have a girlfriend somewhere? Or a boyfriend?"

Christian was being familiar. "Oh, nope, not now," Thane replied. "It's been a while since I let anyone into my heart. I had a girlfriend briefly last year, but it didn't last. How 'bout you?"

"I've had girlfriends, guyfriends… but no one at the moment. I had a girlfriend on the last Greenpeace mission trip, but it fizzled. We're just friends now."

"So are you straight then?" Thane asked, carefully.

"I have more of a European attitude toward relations, sex, and mutual communication. I hate labels. Who says I have to be one thing or another. I go with the flow and let my true feelings decide for me. It seems the most logical and natural way to go about it, don't ya think? Why should I leave it up to someone else to determine what I'm supposed to feel or not feel?"

"You shouldn't."

"Hey, can I be totally honest with you?" Christian went on, feeling more relaxed and familiar with Thane, partly due to the beer. "I don't know if you follow any particular religion or whatever, but I don't believe my feelings for another human being should be dictated by organized religions. Hellfire and brimstone are human creations. It's none of their f-ing business who I choose to love, right?"

Christian took a long chug from his beer.

"No, it should be up to you. I agree," Thane replied.

"There are so many religions making up different rules based on antiquated biblical and religious texts that have been bastardized and twisted throughout the ages. Don't get me wrong, there are great lessons to be learned from the Bible and all, but the rules and regulations are just interpretations of each opinionated misinterpretation. I say follow Jesus' true messages: *'Love and let love,' 'Love thy neighbor as thyself,'* oh, and how 'bout this one, *'Blessed are the peacemakers, for they shall be called son's of God.'*"

"Yeah, what the hell happened to, *'Peace be with you?'*" Thane interjected. "Now it's, *'If you don't do as we say, bombs be with you!'*"

"In essence, that's why we're here, my friend. The world has always been a tumultuous place and we hope to have some small impact by helping people realize more of our humanity. There doesn't need to be so much anger, judgment, and hate."

"Hey," Thane said, "remember what Yoda said in Empire Strikes Back, *'Fear is the path of the dark side. Fear leads to anger. Anger leads to hate. Hate leads to suffering.'*"

Christian nodded his head. "I'm liking you more and more, man. Yoda's the bomb! The Earth is a sacred place that needs protection. We're higher beings with the capacity for love, compassion, culture, incredible works of art, and the intuition to know better! We just need to evolve to a place of understanding."

Thane got excited. "That's what I've been saying. We have it within us to evolve past our differences and integrate with the universal energy that connects us all."

"Exactly. Right on!" Christian said with enthusiasm.

"I bet it's like a fifth element, or some energy wave that surrounds the Earth. I think we can actually tap into it," Thane said, eyebrows raised. "I've seen it and felt it! We just need to like ... tune in."

Thane sat wide-eyed, staring at Christian with a manic expression. "Wow, man, you do have a lot going on in that complex head of yours," Christian said, taken slightly off guard. "I just want people to wake up and smell the coffee, but if you can see a whole new existence of humanity, then I say go for it. Or maybe we're just drunk and talking out our asses."

Christian and Thane looked seriously at each other for a silent moment, then broke out into hysterical laughter, slumping over onto their backs trying to catch their breath.

"I guess I'm not really explaining it right," Thane said, rolling back over. "Sometimes it feels like there's an energy that's always there – something natural and substantial, but hidden behind a thin veil just out of reach. It must be a higher energy or spiritual energy of some kind." Thane clinched his fists. "Is this sounding too weird to you?"

"No, no, I think I know what you mean, man," Christian said softly. "I've had brief moments of complete understanding of certain things, or some sixth-sense feelings over the years. How cool that you're so open to possibility and uninhibited by feelings at such a young age. I'm jealous. So many people choose to see things as right or wrong, black or white, good or bad – but there are so many more colors out there. Free thought and love is a God given right to us all. I'm glad you're one of the colorful ones, Thane."

Christian turned off the flashlight. "And with that, my friend, I will bid you good night."

Thane laid back, looking up at the faint shadows of the branches cast on the outside of their tent, back-lit from the starry night sky. He thought about where he was: this exotic, radioactive atoll of an island, out in the middle of tropical paradise, surrounded by a world of water. It was a place he never dreamed of being and yet, he felt completely comfortable and secure. He was exactly where he was meant to be at this moment in time – with a new friend, serving a higher purpose for the sake of the planet.

His eyes fluttered shut as his body relaxed completely to the sounds of the lulling surf, while his mind drifted far, far away.

# Chapter XII

## ATASHA

Dawn was breaking on the misty morning horizon, as shadows of purple and orange streaked through the pine trees. The smells were a mixture of maroobie pine, vinum berry, and something else – something peculiar.

*Where am I again?* Sarghon thought. *Oh yes, I'm with Kara and Aidan and we're at the edge of the forest searching for Malock's fortress.* It was all coming back to him like a memorable smell from childhood, or the melody of a familiar song that had been forgotten.

Sarghon walked quietly alone toward the edge of the living forest. *The Basai,* he thought, *the Fire People, the dance, Atasha – I must acquire the fire element.*

Still in a trancelike state, he recalled Elda's warning, unsure of what he would see. He visualized rotten plants and shriveled vegetation as he mentally prepared himself for the sight of Malock's destruction. He had become tremendously connected to the Earth, her balance, and all the majestic wonder that she was. Seeing her land raped and destroyed would be heart wrenching.

As he approached the forest's edge, the trees whispered, *Bareth sharatonath, bareth sharatonath.* (Save our kind, save our kind).

The foliage ended at a very defined line and as Sarghon stepped past the last tree, he stood looking out over a completely barren landscape. With his mouth gaping open, his heart sank as he peered out as far as the eye could see over dead Earth. Not a blade of grass survived. The trees were shriveled into lifeless, waterless branches, reaching out for help in grotesque, deathly poses. The brush and plants were all but gray skeletons of withered twigs, colorless and wretched. The sight was nearly unimaginable. A feeling of empathy grabbed his heart and squeezed hard.

Sinking to his knees, a tear ran down Sarghon's cheek. "How

could this be?" he whispered to himself. "Why would anyone do such a blasphemous deed?"

As he looked out over the desolation, immense anger sparked and grew from deep within his core. His fists clinched tightly and his temples bulged with the pressure of his blood. His eyes grew larger and larger, as he grasped the handle of Gladanteus with increasing strength – more than he had ever done before.

In a deliberate motion, he released the sword from its sheath, raising it high above his head. Sarghon let out a blood-curdling scream that echoed far across the land in a roaring war cry coming from deep within his bowels.

Swinging the sword around his head with both hands, he yelled as he fell on one knee. Sparks flew from the blade as Gladanteus struck the Earth deeply. A huge surge of energy vibrated from underground, trembling out in all directions beneath the sword.

Suddenly, from the place where the sword had pierced the Earth, a river of greenery and life erupted, expanding out into the distance across the barren landscape. A plethora of plant life appeared in a multitude of green shades, shapes, and sizes. Bushes and vines shot out of the ground, unfolding like a blanket in a wide track, reaching across the scorched Earth, bringing it to life once again. Large, broken trees filled their branches with new leaves, as fresh trees burst up from the ground in streams of pointy peaks, surrounded by flora blooming in every color of the rainbow.

A flock of birds exploded from one area of trees, fluttering into the air. Butterflies and insects began to appear all around. It was a truly magical sight.

As wonderful as it was to witness the Earatheen powers at work, Sarghon knew it would take much more than this one attempt to make up for the loss of life still reaching for hundreds of miles all around.

Kara and Aidan ran up from behind. "Are you well?" Kara asked with concern.

"By the Gods of the Earth and sky!" Aidan shouted, gazing out over the new strip of life in front of him. "Did you create that?"

"Me and my earthen sword, Gladanteus. She is mighty, indeed. I apologize for waking you in this manner. I was overcome when I saw the devastation. My emotions are heightened and more intimately connected to nature now. I was distraught with anger."

"If this is what you do when you get angry, then I choose to stay on your agreeable side," Kara said, tilting her brow to him. "But I do not think even you and your mighty sword can repair so much loss of life," she said, looking out over the barren landscape beyond. "I have not flown this far north in some time. When I was last here, the mountain forest reached for many more leagues. It is almost too shocking to comprehend."

Kara bowed her head in sadness, placing her hand on the Earth. "I represent the Valkyrie," she said, glancing back at Sarghon with determination, "and our laws state that any act of high treason must be punished. This is beyond any crime ever committed. I consider this an act of war. If Malock has an army, three of us are no match for him. If we are to defeat such an enemy, we must find the weakness in his armor, tactically. No one is imperishable, so we must seek out a flaw."

"Agreed," Sarghon said sternly. "Since I am not yet ready to fight him, perhaps we can enter his fortress undetected or in disguise? We must determine his plan."

"And rescue our people and Atasha," Aidan added.

"I hope that will be possible," Sarghon replied, placing his hand on Aidan's shoulder. "We will save anyone we can, but we must be smart and diligent, as your people have taught me."

They collected their things from their makeshift camp, before walking back to the forest's edge. "Where is the road to Malock's fortress?" Sarghon asked Aidan.

"It lies to the north, winding between the two rising hills, just there," Aidan said, pointing north. "They are called The Twin Sentinels. The fortress is another two hours beyond them at a rapid pace."

"Good, then we're closer than I thought," Sarghon said. "After we have our fill of fruit, nuts, and berries from the new flora, we will be on our way. Now that it's daylight, we can travel by air."

"We?" asked Aidan, surprised.

"I have been thinking," Sarghon continued, "I should be able to tie a strong vine around your waist and carry you, dangling below me in the air. You may spin around a bit, but we would all be together."

"I would carry you," Kara said, "but you are heavy and I may not get very far before having to stop and rest.

"Then let me make it simple," Aidan said, candidly, "I am fastest on foot. I do not fancy being towed through the air by a tether high above the ground. Besides, I am not fond of heights. I may know the fire dance, but I have no intention of ever flying a horse, or otherwise."

"Then we will look for you once we arrive."

"I will run as fast as I can, which means I may arrive before you," Aidan said with a wink. "I will meet you at the stables. It will be where they are keeping Atasha. Gods be with you!"

Aidan shot off with lightning speed, as Sarghon and Kara walked into the newly grown greenery to pick the fruit they desired for breakfast.

As they ate, Kara spoke softly, "What do you think of our new friend? He is determined, brave, and certainly pleasant to look at." Sarghon knew she was inquiring about more than his physical attributes.

"Yes, but he is afraid to fly and that makes him unworthy of a Valkyrie," Sarghon answered, biting into a ripe, red piece of fruit.

"I was not inquiring as to his worthiness of me. I have no interest in seeking him out as a mate; but as a man, he is a fine specimen," she said, swallowing a hand full of berries. "You are correct, however. My mate would need to be able to fly... and much more."

"As it should be. And he must be a warrior, one worthy of a warrior princess," Sarghon said, taking another juicy bite of fruit.

Kara watched the juice drip all the way down Sarghon's chin and on to his shirt. "Are you quite finished?" she said with a wily grin. "I am eager to know exactly why Malock feels it necessary to destroy everything in sight," she said, spreading her wings, before taking flight in a gust of wind that blew Sarghon hard onto his backside. "It is time for warriors to take action!" she shouted, shooting up into the sky like a soaring spear.

Sarghon took one last bite of fruit, wiping his hands on his leather vest, before positioning his arms and legs for flight. Concentrating on where to place the air, he lifted himself steadily off the ground, following Kara into the open sky.

Flying felt easier than before – more controlled and steady. He was able to catch up with her in no time. They flew in the direction instructed by Aidan, quickly finding the path leading between the Twin Sentinel mountain peaks.

The higher they flew, the more devastation was visible across the horizon. The dead trees and scorched land stretched for leagues in every direction. Where once a beautiful, lush forest grew, now remained only barren wasteland. Sarghon felt a pit growing in his stomach as the sight became increasingly ominous.

After flying another twenty minutes, they spotted Aidan running like a wild animal on the road far below. In the distance, the sky turned a deeper shade of gray, darkening toward a circular cloud that resembled the ashen smoke from a large fire – but no flames were visible.

"The fortress must lie in the center of that black cloud beyond The Twin Sentinels!" Sarghon shouted to Kara.

"We should land soon!" she shouted back. Once we enter the cloud, our visibility will be greatly diminished and my wings will weaken, as I mentioned! The gates to the fortress lie beyond a stone ..." Kara stopped talking. In the distance, three black spots approached them in the sky.

"Look!" Kara shouted, pointing toward the oncoming visitors.

"What do you think they are?" Sarghon asked, seeing them for himself.

"As I had feared ... Wyverns!"

As their distinct features came into view, Sarghon counted three of them. He had read about Wyverns with Ambroas in his training sessions, but never saw one in action. He knew they were related to dragons, but had only two legs and were smaller and more nimble in the air. They could be vicious when provoked, with nasty tempers if not tamed. Their talons could easily tear off armor and flesh, and their razor sharp, spiked tail could shear off a man's head with one stroke.

"They will be under the Dark Lord's spell," Kara shouted. "Like the Qilin! Be prepared to use whatever force necessary to defeat them. They are aggressive and very agile in the air!"

*In the air,* Sarghon thought. *I can fight them with wind, but if I release one arm to do so, my balance will be compromised and I will fall.* He realized that the same would happen if he used his sword arm and blade. "Kara, I have not yet battled in the air. I need both hands to stay afloat!"

"We are high up. Can you not steady yourself with your feet while using your hands for battle? If you fall, you will have ample time to correct yourself. You must get your head in the game quickly!"

*My feet? I hadn't thought of that,* Sarghon pondered. *Can I use the Air element with my feet, alone?* It seemed a physical gesture was needed to create the flow of air from his body, along with focused concentration. Discipline of thought was key, *the lightness of the mind,* and Sarghon knew he needed to focus clearly to manage these new aerial tactics.

"They approach!" Kara shouted. "Be ready!"

The Wyverns swooped in like flying daggers, gnashing their razor sharp teeth. Their speed and agility was impressive for being slightly larger than a horse and having a wingspan of seven meters or more.

With Kara in the lead, the first one went directly for her shoulder. She ducked to her right, missing the scaled beast by only inches, as some of her feathers flew off.

The second one went for Sarghon. "Beware the spiked tail, Sarghon. It bears a deadly stinger!" she warned.

*Right!* he thought. *I had forgotten that detail.*

As the Wyvern came at Sarghon, a violent look inhabited the beast's orange eyes and he knew they were being controlled and manipulated. It swung its spiked tail back in preparation for strike, but Sarghon released a sharp jolt of air from his feet, shooting him up and over the creature. Once above the animal, he circled his arms over his shoulders, catching his balance. With one arm, he shot a blast of air at the Wyvern's body, but it tucked its wings in, spiraling to one side. The air strike had missed its mark.

Having been pushed to one side by his one handed attack, Sarghon lost his balance as the creature came back around with its gaping mouth and jagged teeth. Steadying his flight with his legs and feet, this time he used both hands as he shot the beast with a strong, sharp blast of air, snapping one of its wings and sending it spiraling down to the ground below.

"One down," he said to himself.

The first one quickly came back around, heading for Kara again. Sarghon, still finding his balance, was too slow to assist her. Holding her sword to the sky, he watched the elegant, veteran warrior in her element as she summoned lightening from the heavens above.

Sarghon's heart pounded with excitement as he watched her swing her blade around, pointing it at the flying beast. As soon as her arm was fully extended, a discharge of lightning pulsed from the blade shooting out toward her attacker, exploding all over the creature and searing its wings and scaly body in a spectacle of flying sparks and crackling rivulets of electricity. The beast went numb, falling straight to the ground.

The third Wyvern was already swooping down upon Sarghon in a spinning dive from above. Looking up at a fierce mouth of razor sharp, serrated teeth ascending on top of him, Sarghon paused. He didn't have enough time to raise a hand and concentrate. He was in trouble.

Sarghon sent his focus to his feet as fast as he could, shooting air from below and sending him barreling into the animal's left wing with a hard hit to his shoulder. After seeing stars for a moment of stunned pain, his body curled up into a ball, limp and vulnerable. He was falling out of control, disorientated from the blow.

He heard Kara's voice yell, "Steady yourself! Concentrate! I'm coming!" He realized he was falling backward toward the Earth, as he saw the last Wyvern swooping in for the kill. His head throbbed as wind rustled loudly past his ears. Still disoriented, Sarghon was unable to reestablish flight. The beast was almost upon him.

Positioning its tail above like a scorpion about to sting, the Wyvern sent its wings out wide to each side, creating the momentum for its tail to swing under and attack. Sarghon realized he must do something fast, but what?

Just as the beast swung its tail in for the strike, Kara's blade came down from above, slicing its spiked tail clean off. The creature let out a horrific screech of pain as it fumbled in the air, blood shooting out its back end like a geyser. It fluttered agonizingly down to the ground, hitting a large shriveled bush in a cloud of dirt and dust.

Before Sarghon knew what had happened, he opened his eyes to a shiny, metallic orb in his face. It was the breastplate of Kara's armor. She had caught him and was carrying him just above the dead, withered tree line. With his face pressed against her breast, and her arms around his body, Sarghon opened his eyes in a surprisingly comfortable daze.

"That was exhilarating!" he said to Kara.

"Indeed. Now if you would return yourself to flight, I can put my sword away," she replied, floating mid-air in a momentary embrace.

"Right," Sarghon said, flush faced, as he once again placed air in the proper areas, giving him flight on his own. Kara returned her bloody sword back into its sheath.

"Thank you, Kara," Sarghon said, slightly embarrassed. "I owe you one. It seems I have much to learn about combat in the air. Will you teach me?" he asked with a subtle smile.

"I am certain I could teach you a great many things," she said, staring at the sweat dripping down his brow. "At this moment, however, you are a liability if we need to battle while in flight. I believe you may be better off on the ground."

"Indeed," he replied.

They continued in the air toward the dark cloud and when the air became too thick with darkness to see through, they landed. "I have a feeling Wyverns are not the worst of our troubles on this day," Kara mumbled. "This dark fog surrounds the hills above. We must be close to the fortress."

"There is no doubt."

They ventured further into the dense fog, unable to see more than several feet ahead at any given moment, when through the gray mist emerged a massive fortress castle. The dark cloud layer dissipated around the castle, like being in the eye of a great storm. Once again, they could see clearly.

The fortress was taller than any Sarghon had ever seen, with its stone walls standing like an armada of angry soldiers after a fight. Dead bushes with black, withered branches surrounded the foot of the wall all the way around. Beyond the wall could be seen the peaks of a large, stately castle with five turrets pointing toward the dark sky. The atmosphere was eerily quiet.

"This place is ominous," Sarghon said in a breathy voice. "I do not sense any life at all; no birds, no insects – nothing."

"We must find a way inside. If all the gates are closed, we will need to fly over the outer wall," Kara suggested.

They circumnavigated the outer wall, locating one main gate and two smaller gates, but none were open. If people were there, they were all inside the gates or not at all. "I could blow open the gates," Sarghon said, "but it would give away our position, and any chance of a stealthy entry."

"If I fly over the wall, my large wings and shiny armor would surely be noticed," Kara said.

"No doubt, Princess. My simple way of flying will draw much less attention," Sarghon suggested.

Very quietly, Sarghon gently lifted himself with pockets of air under his arms, landing on the top of the wall without incident. Surveying the courtyard, he spotted several guards stationed around the castle entrance. In the distance, he witnessed groups of men and women training in a variety of fighting styles and techniques.

Delicately floating down the interior side of the great wall without being noticed, Sarghon saw two guards stationed at the gate as he landed. Quietly creeping up on them, he placed the tip of Gladanteus to the ground while concentrating on his earthly desire.

Two vines violently erupted from the dirt next to the guards, growing quickly up their legs, wrapping, and twisting around their bodies before they knew what was happening. Dropping their weapons, the guards mumbled in confusion before the vines covered and bound their eyes and mouths. They were immobilized.

Sarghon carefully opened the gate and let Kara inside. They made their way to the main castle entrance, where they found more guards stationed. Kara's keen eye noticed something unusual. "Those guards," she whispered, "can you see their eyes? They are orange in color, like the Qilin and Wyverns.

"My vision is not as keen as yours, Princess, but I do notice something peculiar as well – a sensation I felt before and… an odd smell. It's as if they are not themselves – none of them. This will make things difficult. They may all be under a spell. They could all be innocent in this."

"It would be easier to just kill them," she said, nonchalantly, "but alas, you are correct in your assessment."

"As soon as we move through the courtyard we will be noticed. I don't want to kill anyone today, but we must act quickly. Stand back," Sarghon said, raising his hands in front of him, summoning the air element. A moment later, a steady flow of air shot from his hands, across the courtyard toward the main entrance. The four guards in front of the door were no longer standing. They had been blown aside by the gust of wind. Two were unconscious and two got up, staring befuddled into the sky.

Sarghon directed more air at the remaining two guards, sending them both flying in opposite directions across the courtyard. Now all four men were out of commission. No one else was in view.

"We should locate the stable before entering the main castle," Kara said looking around, as the light reflected from her gleaming, amethyst eyes. "Aidan will be here shortly and we may need his assistance with the horse. We will stand a better chance when outnumbered once you acquire the fire element."

"You're beautiful when you are apprehensive," Sarghon said boldly, staring at Kara without looking away. Kara responded with only a raised eyebrow.

Someone approached from behind. Kara instinctively raised her wings and sword simultaneously. It was Aidan. "You two are easy to spot, what with the strewn guards and Kara's grand wings." "Follow me, I have found Atasha!"

Aidan led them to the stables around the east side of the fortress and past the serving quarters, where a lifeless Spider Oak grove lined the walkway. Shriveled and dead, the trees looked more like spiders than trees. In every direction they saw only devastation. Sarghon vowed to soon make it right.

At the end of the path stood a large row of stables guarded by eight strong men. Several of the men looked in their direction. "They have spotted us," Kara said.

The men all started toward them with weapons drawn. "Stand back. Don't approach them," Sarghon cautioned as he grasped the handle of Gladanteus and struck the blade to the Earth. The ground began to quake, but the men continued their approach. The Earth in front of the guards split open with a furious crack! The ground rumbled and widened, creating a ten-foot deep crevice. Four of the men went tumbling, while the other four came to a halt.

"We cannot let them escape," Kara indicated. Sarghon gave her a glance of concurrence. With the blade still penetrating the Earth, Sarghon concentrated on the crevice. The soil behind the men suddenly gave way, sinking around them on both sides, creating a small island of land surrounded by an empty mote.

The men were trapped.

"Clever thinking," Kara said, "but their calls will alarm others. Shall I blast them with lightning?"

"As much as I love watching you in action, Princess, you know the answer to that question," Sarghon said, sheathing his sword and walking around the mote toward the stables. The men who were still standing called profanities at Sarghon.

"You cannot defeat the mighty King Malock!" one man yelled. "He will tear your head off and feed it back to you on a ..."

Sarghon flicked his wrist, sending a swift burst of air at the four remaining men, tossing them head-over-heels into the dirt pit below. "I'm not hungry," Sarghon said, ignoring them and walking toward the stables.

"Astonishing!" Aidan said, admiring Sarghon's handiwork. "Follow me. Atasha is over here."

They followed Aidan into the stables. At the far end was a large, interior feed storage area surrounded by wooden spikes set inwardly at a forty-five degree angle. Atasha was chained up in the center of the spikes. A metallic collar had been fastened to her neck, chaining her to two bolts attached to the ground on both her right and left.

She was breathtaking. Her mane glistened in the filtered sunlight, giving off reflections of red and yellow hues. Her pale brown eyes flickered with beautiful intensity, anxious, yet wise. Even while held captive, she was majestic to behold.

Aidan approached her. "She recognizes me as Basai, but will not let me near her mane to detach the collar. She is scared and, if she desires, she could burn me to a crisp. I hope you will have better luck."

"We need to get her free from the bindings," said Sarghon. "Kara, if we both cut the chains, perhaps the collar can be released after. Take the far side and we will strike together."

Following his suggestion, she readied her sword. "OK," Sarghon said, "on the count of three … One, two, three!"

They simultaneously struck the chains with their swords, breaking both chains with ease. Atasha kicked up on her hind legs, letting out a cry of freedom. Still, she was surrounded by the wood stakes and burdened by the collar and heavy hanging chains. Sarghon decided to approach her. "Stay back," he cautioned Kara and Aidan. "I don't want to spook her." Atasha backed away from Sarghon at first, but then allowed him to come forward. Without touching her, he found a small latch on the collar behind her ear and turned it. The collar released and fell to the ground. "She obviously trusts you, Santeen Sarghon," Aidan said.

Sarghon cleared his mind, calming his energy and recalling Elda's instruction of the "first movement" before the dance. He approached Atasha slowly, while reaching out his hand. "Atasha, great fire horse," he said, "I am Sarghon, bearer of the Diaglyphen Prophesy. I come to you in need. I offer you my touch so you may determine my worth."

Atasha didn't back away. She allowed him to place one hand over her eyes, placing his other hand on his cheek. Sarghon then closed his eyes, allowing her into his thoughts. Images from his life flashed euphorically before his closed eyelids. His body felt light, yet he stood perfectly still as she filtered through his memories and emotions, taking them in, assessing their value and truth. At the same time, Sarghon connected to Atasha's spirit, feeling her pain and knowing her thoughts.

After a moment, he opened his eyes and stepped back. "What did she convey to you?" Kara asked softly, with great interest.

"Stand back," he answered. "She trusts me now."

Atasha began trotting in a circle around Sarghon, who remained in the middle like a circus ringleader. Surrounded by the large wooden stakes pointed inward at them, there was no exit, only a roof and four walls beyond the steaks. Atasha started to gallop. Kara and Aidan stepped as far away as they could, nestling between the stakes so not to get trampled. Sarghon, recalled the movements of the dance as he ran along side Atasha, picking up speed. He then began the dance.

He followed each movement in sequence getting faster and faster, until he was moving as fast as she was. Like before, his speed became supernatural, whipping through the movements in a blur of dazzling motion. He appeared to be channeling an inherent energy from deep within.

Atasha's mane burst into brilliant flames. It was a spectacular site. The flames bounced off her neck like continuous ropes of bright orange and yellow fire. Her hoofs caught fire as well.

As he circled in close to her, Sarghon wasn't alarmed at all or distracted by the great display of majesty. When the dance sequence started over with the first movement of reaching out and clinching a fist, he reached out and grabbed hold of her burning mane.

He then stepped in for the second and third movement, shuffling and hopping on his feet. With a high jump up into the barrel roll, he landed right onto Atasha's back. Reaching his other arm back, Sarghon balanced his posture with the next movement, leaning down with his legs and forearms to complete the sequence.

He was riding her. His legs were warm against her skin and his hands were hot, but he did not burn. A feeling grew from deep inside his core – wonderful, exhilarating, and tingling out in all directions.

Atasha continued to run in a circle within the confines of the ring of stakes. Sarghon felt the fire energy building up inside his body. He felt as if he was going to explode. He felt the fire energy flowing through him, igniting his passion from within. The heat mixed with his fervent energy was creating a symbiotic relationship with the element.

Just then, his back arched and his hands burst into flames. Sarghon let out a guttural scream from deep within. His legs and torso remained perfectly balanced on her back, as she continued her blazing circle.

They finished a final lap, ending up in the center. Sarghon's hands returned to normal, with the still fiery mane in front of him.

Atasha reared up on her back legs, shooting flames into the air from her nostrils, landing with a strong thump. Sarghon looked victorious on her regal, muscular frame, as Kara and Aidan slowly approached.

"It is done," Sarghon said. "And I must say, I feel amazing!"

"Are you not burned?" Kara asked with concern.

"No, and as long as I have this gift, I can never be burned. Atasha showed me how to control it with her thoughts. She's a marvelous creature, sentient, intuitive and strong. As you may have noticed, I have acquired the fire element from her. It's a wondrous feeling. More exhilarating even then when I acquired the air element. Magnificent, I tell you! Meet me in front of the stables. I am going to set her free."

Kara and Aidan ran outside toward the front of the stables, as Sarghon patted Atasha's neck and said, "Thank you, great one. You have given me a wonderful gift."

Lifting his right arm above his head, while holding tight to the flaming mane with his left hand, Sarghon focused his energy toward the roof, sending a strong blast of air up toward the ceiling. A large section of the roof blew out, scattering in a vortex of wind. Gripping tightly to her mane with both hands, he whispered, "You are free now."

She began her circular gallop once again. Sarghon leaned in close to her neck, holding tight with his legs, as she kicked up and into the air above the sharpened stakes. They were flying. Atasha hastened her fiery hoofs gracefully through the air, as if running on an invisible surface. They rose up and out through the hole in the stable roof.

High above the stable barn, they circled several times in a blazing streak of light, before coming down with an impressive landing. Kara and Aidan stood waiting. "You have done well, young warrior," Kara said.

"I never thought I would live to see the day a new rider took flight," Aidan said with delight. "We are blessed by this courageous deed, Santeen."

They turned to see a large assemblage of armored soldiers approaching from the fortress. Sarghon jumped down from Atasha's back and turned to face her. "You must go now, great one," he said with admiration and caution. "I hope to unite with you again soon. With all the uncertainty in our world, thank you for trusting in us."

Sarghon tenderly touched her cheek one last time before looking deeply into her sparkling, fiery eyes. She then leapt into the air like a majestic god and flew over the outer wall like a shooting star.

# MALOCK

The soldiers approached quickly as Kara unsheathed her sword, ready for another battle. There were dozens of men encroaching on them, each with the same light orange eyes as the next. "Kara, we cannot hurt these people," Sarghon said. "This may be an opportunity to find out what King Malock is up to."

"You are not yet ready to fight him," she warned.

"I don't want to fight him, I just want to talk to him."

The soldiers were upon them with lances and swords drawn. Kara stepped forward, igniting her sword with lightning to intimidate the on-comers. Her sword crackled with electricity and the soldiers stopped. Kara stood firm, but did not attack. "As you wish," she said, lowering her intimidating blade.

Sarghon stepped forward to address the men. Speaking with authority, he raised his arm. "I wish to speak with King Malock. If you do not do as I command, I will wipe you all away with a sweep of my hand!"

The leader of the soldiers stepped forward while looking the three of them up and down. "Then we are here to escort you," he said with a vacant smile. "Good King Malock awaits. Follow me."

"Good?" Kara asked sarcastically.

"Stay close to me. Both of you," Sarghon murmured under his breath as they followed the lead soldier back in the direction of the main building. Kara was not foolish enough to drop her guard; she kept her sword poised ready to strike at any moment.

They were escorted across what was once a beautiful topiary herb garden with animal and spiral shaped hedges, but where now existed only withered and shriveled twigs. The animal shapes looked as if they had been parched to death by an everlasting waterless summer as they stood moaning and reaching for their last drop of water.

As Sarghon walked past the foreboding shapes, he wondered what Malock would be like. *I have never seen the King before,* he thought. *He must be repulsive and vile. How old is he? Will he be guarded by more orange-eyed followers who do not see the havoc he has*

181

*wrought?*

They approached a large double door entrance with lions carved into the wood on either side. Once escorted inside, they were led across a long foyer, then through a spacious mass dining area and into an ornately decorated receiving room. The walls were covered with gold-gilded frames holding lavish paintings, the floors covered with carpets imported from lands far away, and the furniture was definitely suited for a king. A decanter of wine and a plate of fresh fruit sat on a table. The guards left the room.

"Why do you suppose they are treating us like guests?" Aidan asked with utter curiosity.

"After breaking in, freeing his trophy, and attacking his guards, I am wondering the same question," Kara replied. "I am better equipped for battle than conversation."

"So far we have done half of what we set out to do," Sarghon said lowering his voice. "If we're to find out his plans, shouldn't we just ask him? If I have to, I will fight."

"There's no need for threats in my Kingdom," Malock said, entering the room. "Besides, you are my guests. Please have some wine and fruit. You undoubtedly had a long journey, so eat, drink."

Malock was not at all what they expected. He stood tall and regal, with shoulder length chestnut colored hair, handsome features, and the same orange eyes as all the others. His eyes seemed to be even more brilliant, shimmering in the light as he looked around at each of them. He wore a stately black and red velvet tunic brocaded with gold thread. The design on his chest depicted an ascending phoenix, the same design as Sarghon's dagger. He held no weapon or sword of any kind, but wore a large, leather embossed belt which was embellished with gemstones in ornate twisting patterns.

"I'm sure you have many questions, my friends. I am here to answer them all."

"We are not your friends!" Kara snapped. "And I do not drink or eat with callous, malicious vermin who surreptitiously declare themselves ruler of all the land. I was born into royalty and one day I will be a true Queen of my people."

Sarghon's eyes widened as he stared at Kara, admiring her courageous manner, yet stunned by her audacity.

"King Malock," Sarghon said, "my name is Sarghon. We come to you requesting answers. You have destroyed our land and the land of many people. You have captured thousands of helpless souls against their will. These are not the actions of a king. These are the actions of a tyrannical and ruthless dictator. Why do you do this? Why destroy your own world?"

"My young friend, soon you will understand everything," Malock said calmly. All that I have done is for the better. Do you see anyone fighting to be released? Do you see malcontent of any soul whatsoever in the Kingdom? My subjects are at ease and comfortable in their life here. It is natural to resist change, but they have come to a new understanding and all is well."

"You abducted hundreds of my people from the great forest!" Aidan spoke out. "Where are they now? Why have you not allowed them to return home to their people? What do you want with us?"

"Your people helped me find the fire horse. They now serve me happily. As I said before, all will be understood soon. Please have a drink."

"What magic have you used to blind them?" Kara asked heatedly. "Why can't they see the devastation around them?"

Walking over to the wine decanter, Malock poured four glasses of wine. "Soon everything will be crystal clear, my dear. But first and foremost, you are my guests – and esteemed guests you are. It's not every day I entertain the bearer of a prophecy."

The group stiffened and grew silent. "You know who I am?" Sarghon asked.

"I know a great many things, my boy. And soon I hope to share them all with you. I have never seen the great Diaglyphen stone myself. It is masked by magic – a magic I'm not privy to, I'm afraid. Our friend Ambroas saw to that. I know the essence of it though. And I know you are the one of whom it speaks. But, it is incorrect."

"Our friend? How do you know Ambroas?"

Malock looked Sarghon straight in the eye, "As I said, I know many things. You do not have any desire to hurt me now do you young, valiant Sarghon?" Malock said, more like an order than a question, before turning around and sitting in an ornately carved wooden chair incrusted with gemstones. "No doubt, you have come for answers to your questions," he said, looking back at Sarghon with glittering, orange eyes and taking a dramatic, deep breath. "It's regrettable that menial life forms must parish to gain the influence that I need to fulfill my goals, but that is my power. I lay it all on the table for you to see. I have the ability to absorb energy – to transform it. I take energy and absorb it into myself. Then I can do with it what I see fit in order to create a better life for us all."

"And you, alone know what is better for us all?" Kara asked curtly.

"Do you remember your father?" Malock continued with Sarghon, ignoring her question.

Sarghon had grown up with his aunt and uncle, having little memory of his mother, and nothing about his true father, who he was told had left his life when he was very young. Sarghon wanted to find out exactly what Malock knew, so he decided to appease him by taking a glass of wine. He handed another to Aidan.

"No, I don't remember him. And how would you know of this? What could you possibly know of my childhood? We have never met."

"Must I repeat myself yet again?" Malock continued. "Did you know your father was a very powerful wizard? He could read other's minds and influence their thoughts. He must have left you for a good reason, no? Otherwise you would have grown up at his side, learning the craft. But I assume you came into your powers recently, or we would have met sooner."

Malock reached over the table, taking one of the remaining glasses of wine. He handed it to Kara, but she refused. He nodded politely, drinking from the glass himself with an overindulgent quiver of satisfaction, as the wine went down his throat.

"What you don't know is … he was our last King."

Everyone turned to Malock in disbelief. "Which makes you my brother. Well, half brother, to be exact. We share power, as well as royal blood."

Sarghon stood dumfounded, unable to voice any response. "Our father was shrewd," Malock continued, "but insensibly unconscious. He ruled the land like a chessboard, moving influential people around in a mindless, cataleptic strategy to seek an ideal balance. But he was never satisfied with his efforts. You and I were considered mere pawns in his grand scheme. I used to revere him – even fear him. People worshipped him. But he was a fool. What he miscalculated was the future."

Malock looked Sarghon straight in the eye with a fierce sneer. "He forgot that a pawn can take a King!"

Kara placed her hand on Sarghon's shoulder to steady him, silently warning him to be cautious and discerning of what he was hearing.

"I was immune to his powers," Malock went on, "and I knew one day I would take his place to create a better world, one in which my decisions would be heard and obeyed! And now, you have the opportunity to be a part of that future, dear brother."

*Could this be true?* Sarghon thought. *Did Ambroas lie to me? Could I be the son of a King, or is Malock completely mad?*

"If what you say is true, Ambroas would have told me," Sarghon said, "or my family members! Don't you think they knew who my father was? It can't be!"

"Your mother was a whore. She knew on the day you were born that your path was to take another direction. She also knew you were a bastard and I was the legitimate, older son who would be crowned King. So in essence, you were superfluous at the time. But I knew one day we would meet. And that day is finally here, dear brother. You have come home to join me in creating a pure world regime. Our destiny has brought us together, and *together* we can rule the land as the most powerful brothers in the world. It will be glorious!"

Sarghon was still silent and numb. The information he was hearing overwhelmed his ears and psyche. So much had changed in the adolescence of his adult life. This was more than the icing on the cake, it was the cherry on top of the icing. He didn't know quite how to process what he was hearing. He went to take a sip from his glass, when Kara screamed.

"Stop! Do not drink that! Look at Aidan's eyes."

Sarghon whipped his head around toward Aidan. The young man was standing still with a wide, blank stare. His eyes were bright orange.

"What is this?" Sarghon demanded. "What have you done to him?"

"He has not been harmed, my friends," Malock said. "He is in *the awareness*; a state when things can be perceived more clearly, cleanly, and fully. I assure you, he is better off."

"Who are you to determine that?!" Kara demanded, running to Aidan's side. "Aidan, can you hear me? Are you OK?"

"I am perfectly fine," he answered with the same blank stare.

"Do you know why you are here?" Kara went on, "Atasha, your people; we must find them."

Malock intervened, looking Aidan straight in the eye. "Your

people are fine, young man. And you will also be taken care of," he said in a soothing, seductive voice.

"I am fine," Aidan answered. "I see no cause for such alarm, Kara. I believe the good King's words. He would never hurt anyone."

Sarghon sniffed his wine glass before throwing it to the ground with a crash, as Kara brought forth her sword. "It was in the wine!" he shouted. "Aidan was the only one who drank. What is this poisonous magic?" Sarghon demanded, sensing the same odd smell as before, now knowing what it was. "You have tricked us."

Sarghon gripped the handle of Gladanteus.

"If you drink, you will understand. If not, you are no match for me young brother," Malock said in a deeper tone. "But if you wish to fight me, know that your cause is futile. I will be triumphant in the end and you will have wasted your efforts."

"You should leave," Malock said to Aidan, "and join your people on the training ground located around the west wing." Aidan did as he was told, turning around and walking out of the room obsequiously.

"We will return for you Aidan and make this right!" Sarghon shouted, as Aidan left the room. Malock pulled up the shirtsleeves on his regal garment, taking a step back. "Now to test your powers," he said, raising his hand and filling it with pulsating blue-green energy.

A barely visible, rippling energy wave shot from Malock's hand directly at Sarghon, pushing him harshly against a wall. Fixed in place by the energy coming from Malock's arm, Sarghon struggled to free his arms and legs.

Kara acted quickly, taking a warrior stance. She instinctively lit her sword with electricity, considering whether it was a smart move to do so knowing that Malock could readily absorb energy.

Moving in for a strike, she released the full power of her blade at Malock's feet. Sparks and shards of stone burst out as the blast hit the ground, breaking a small hole in the floor inches from Malock's foot. "Release him!" She ordered.

Glaring up at Kara, Malock flashed a cunning grin, not at all doing as she requested. Sarghon still struggled in vain against the wall, as Kara went in for another sword strike attack, hoping to cut off Malock's outstretched arm holding Sarghon at bay.

Stepping forward with astounding speed she reared back her sword arm, but Malock quickly raised his other arm catching the blade in mid-stroke with his bare hand. The electricity surrounding the blade ran

186

up his arm and into his body. It electrified his mouth, ears, nose, and eyes.

It was a hideous sight, as Malock's veins and skin pulsed up and down with the intake of energy, like a viper swallowing its prey.

He then shot the electricity back at Kara, singeing her wings and knocking her backward over a gaudy decorated couch. She fell unconscious.

"No!" Sarghon shouted. With Malock's focus on his attack toward Kara, Sarghon was able to free his hands. Although his arms were pinned to the wall, Sarghon was able to bend his wrists forward and shoot a powerful burst of wind at Malock.

Caught unaware, Malock was blown backward hard against his chair.

His hold on Sarghon was released.

Sarghon quickly drew Gladanteus from her sheath and with a heaving breath, he swung the sword across his chest, striking it into the ground.

Instantly robust, thorny vines burst from the stone floor, writhing upward toward Malock, who stood undaunted, laughing at Sarghon's derisory attempt. The vines wrapped around Malock's legs but before they reached his waist, he grabbed each vine by its growing neck and drained them of all life in an instant.

Their life force could be seen flowing into Malock, like little streams of pulsing light energy being absorbed through his hands and arms. The shriveled vines turned into dust at Malock's feet. Sarghon was aghast!

"As I said before, your attempts are futile," Malock said laughing at Sarghon with a frenzied, indulgent look. "Earthen energy holds with it the most pleasurable and potent energy of all! Just one drop is all it takes."

He walked over to the table of wine glasses and made a fist with his hand, squeezing it over one of the wine-filled glasses. A single drop of opalescent, silvery liquid dripped into the glass like blood being squeezed from a cut.

"See," he said looking up at his audience with eager pleasure, "*you* can provide what I use to gain the influence I need over my subjects so they see my truth: A world of one vision and one people who all understand each other completely. If you just drink this, you will see things as I do. You and your sword can help provide all the energy we

187

will ever need."

He took a step toward Sarghon, reaching out his arm and offering the glass of wine to him. "Come take your place at my side where you belong. Power like this is the way of the future, dear brother. It is how the new change will happen!"

"Not if I can help it!" Sarghon became livid with the idea of being stripped of his free will and his wits. "I don't need you or anyone else to tell me how and what to think!"

With the intensity of his emotions taking control over his body, Sarghon's hands suddenly lit furiously with fire. He felt the fire element racing through him as it did when he rode Atasha. *Let's see how you deal with fire,* Sarghon thought, reaching out daringly with his arms and sending two explosive burning streams of flames at Malock.

In that split second, Sarghon realized that fire was just another form of energy and that, most likely, Malock would be able to absorb fire as well. But it was too late. The flames hit Malock dead on, leaping up and surrounding him, swirling over his body with heat and fury.

Malock stood stoically firm, raising one hand as the flames entered his body, spiraling up and twisting through his skin in another ghastly display of power. When he was done, his garments smoked from the heat he had just absorbed.

Groggily, Kara sat up. "Sarghon, we must leave," she said, gaining consciousness.

"I think not," Malock said, turning to Kara. "You two have done enough damage for one day. If you do not drink my wine, the winged beauty will be grounded, taking the place of my fire horse. A princess of the Valkyrie will make a fine trophy!"

Raising his arms, Malock took a step toward Kara as he filled his hands with blue-green energy.

"No!" Sarghon shouted, summoning all the power he could muster before Malock could attack. He reached his arm out creating a vortex of wind between them, blocking Malock from reaching Kara. Malock placed one arm into the wind tunnel, absorbing the energy, as Sarghon continued his air attack.

"Kara run!" Sarghon shouted, knowing his energy was being drained with every precious moment. He continued his efforts by raising his other arm and shooting a stream of fire at the couch, which burst into a wall of flames between Malock and Kara.

In desperation Kara tried one last attempt with her sword, filling it with electricity.

"No Kara, he will use it against you! You must escape!"

"I will not leave you!" she replied with deep concern, ducking below the burning couch. "I would never leave you like this. We are together as one!"

Malock raised his free arm. "You cannot win!" he shouted. "You know this to be true!"

With one arm still absorbing the slowing vortex of air energy coming from Sarghon, Malock directed his arduous gaze back at Kara. He reached his free arm through the burning flames coming from the couch in an attempt to touch her and drain her of energy as well.

She caught sight of his advance and quickly launched up into the air, becoming a moving target. With her sword still lit, she released multiple streams of electricity throughout the room creating an erratic distraction. Lightning shot everywhere. Sparks bounced against surfaces all around and Malock lost his target.

With his focus back on Malock, Sarghon lifted his free hand once again in an attempt to disrupt the assault on Kara, sending a stream of fire at Malock's turned head. It was a risky move. Malock whipped his head around, catching the fire in his hand mid-stream before it could strike him. Now Malock was absorbing both air and fire energy from Sarghon, taking in both elements simultaneously, one from each arm.

He faced Sarghon with deliberation, as if to teach him a lesson. "Ha! Keep it up, brother. Give me all your power!" he said, eyes burning with glints of orange and red.

Malock's face grew into a maniacal smile. They were connected in a deathly embrace, arm and arm, locked to each other by power as Malock slowly sucked away everything Sarghon had to give.

Becoming too weak to continue, Sarghon couldn't hold on any longer. Just as his last bit of energy left him, Kara came swooping in from above, scooping him up by the waist and carrying him across the room in a flurry of feathers and steel.

The elemental bond was broken.

She flew toward the main doors, as Malock stumbled backward into his chair in a state of euphoric elation. The energy absorbed from Sarghon was overwhelmingly intoxicating, rendering him immobile. Malock sat slumped in the chair, breathing hard with bulging, bright, orange eyes as sweat dripped down his trembling brow.

With Sarghon dangling in her arms, Kara flew through the massive dining room and out the entry corridor toward the front entrance. She noticed the doors were shut tight. "Hang on, dear one," she whispered in Sarghon's ear, gripping him tight as she wafted her powerful wings backward in strong strokes, readying herself.

Kara wore a metal helmet with a single jewel in the center representing unbreakable strength. She hoped it would be enough protection as she ducked her head down, holding Sarghon close. She then flew straight at the massive stained glass window above the large, arched wooden entrance doors. With a spectacular burst of colored glass and feathers, they came crashing through the window and were free.

Shaking off shards of glass stuck in her wings, she headed east, holding Sarghon's unconscious body tight against her breast. Kara flew straight up as high as she could, trying to avoid the dark cloud surrounding the castle fortress. Her wings burned as they touched the edge of the dark cloud, feathers withering at the tips. Finally clearing the deathly magic, she flew over the dead landscape and back toward the protection of the living forest.

When she could no longer carry the burden of his added weight, Kara landed in a dense area of trees and foliage. Completely exhausted, her body ached from the long journey, the battle with Malock, and the varied cuts and bruises she sustained breaking through the window. Kara gently placed Sarghon down on a bed of grass and loof moss and he slowly came to.

"Where are we?" he whispered with drowsy breath.

"Somewhere safe, I hope," she replied breathing heavily and looking around.

"You saved me again, Kara. I owe you my life," he said, reaching out to take her hand.

"And you saved mine," Kara replied, leaning into him, placing her head on his shoulder. "If anything had happened to you, I would not have been able to forgive myself." Sarghon cupped her head in his arm, then bent over her face and kissed her gently on the lips. She didn't stop him.

The kiss was sincere and tender – a juxtaposition from the fierce and worrisome tension the past several days had been. Looking up at him with alluring, fatigued eyes she said, "That was only a test, you know."

"The kiss, or the fight?" he asked, arching his eyebrow.

"Both," she said, with a subtle expression he had never before

190

seen on her face.

They sat breathing in unison, holding each other in silence for a while before Sarghon laboriously stood up. He stumbled as the blood rushed back into his head. "Are you well?" Kara asked.

"I'll recover. But I feel very weak. Malock must have drained me more than I thought. I felt an emptiness overtaking me while we were connected. It was unnerving and intimidating. He absorbed nearly everything I had to give. How can I possibly fight a power that can take away everything with a wave of one hand? I am useless against him. And to find out that we are brothers! It's all too much to take." A tear ran down his cheek, as Sarghon fell to his knees in exhaustion. "I don't think I can do this."

"You are one of the bravest men I have ever known," Kara said. "I do not speak these words superfluously. You have heroism in you. You must know that."

"But how can I defeat that which is undefeatable?"

"You just need nourishment. Strike your mighty sword to the ground and grow us some fruitful dinner. You will feel better afterward."

Sarghon wearily drew his sword as she suggested, striking the Earth at his feet, but nothing happened. He tried again concentrating harder, but alas, nothing.

"What is this?" he said. "Have I lost my power?"

"Try again. Just relax and focus. You have been through much. I am sure it will come back to you."

Sarghon stood back, taking several deep breaths before his next attempt. He closed his eyes while drawing the sword over his right shoulder. With a swift, concise movement, he struck the blade to the Earth cleanly, focusing on his hunger and need for sustenance. When he opened his eyes, there was only stillness.

Once again, he fell to his knees letting out a brutal cry of defeat. "Ahhhh!! What has Malock done to me?" Sarghon moaned, reaching his arm out trying to summon fire in his hand. None came.

He attempted wind with his other hand and still no elemental powers came to him. "What is this?" he said in a panic. "He got inside my head somehow. He has taken my power!"

Sarghon slumped over with utter exhaustion. "It's over. The Earth has deemed me unworthy of this task. I have failed you, Ambroas. And all the land."

"You must take hold of yourself. We will find a way. This Dark Lord is as crafty as he is manipulative and he has you exactly where he wants you. Do not let him believe he has won. You possess magics that are beyond belief. I have seen what you can do and *I* believe in you."

"But if he has taken away my power, how can I possibly face him? I may as well be dead. And he wants me to join him and rule at his side? I would have to be insane to take on his offer!"

He looked at Kara and then to the ground. "I'm so tired. I feel an impossible emptiness inside me, something I have never experienced before. It's as if he reached inside my heart and squeezed it dry and now I am worthless. I'm a fool with no direction at all."

"As Valkyrie, we believe our armor is a symbol of our strength. If it is damaged, if our metal skin is broken, pierced or torn, then we replace it with a stronger piece. We make sure the same area will never fail us again – and with that, we become stronger. It is through our greatest weakness that we find the way to our greatest strength."

Sarghon sat exhausted staring hopelessly into space, wondering if the stars may offer some insight or guidance, but nothing came to him. He just hung his head in defeat, as Kara knelt behind him, placing her hands on his shoulders.

"All is not lost, dear one. I think I know of someone who can help."

# Chapter XIII

## THE LAGOON

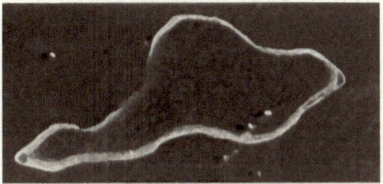

"Rise and shine!" Christian yelled from the mouth of the tent. "Breakfast is almost ready. By the way, who's Kara? You talk in your sleep. Kept mumbling something about losing your power or whatever. Sounded pretty wild."

Thane sat up rubbing his eyes, still bewildered. "What? I said what?" he said, taking a quick inventory of his surroundings, surmising he was on the atoll island in Tahiti just where he was the night before. "Oh, man! I had one of my reoccurring dreams again. They're incredible. I'll have to tell you about them some time."

Thane slapped his cheek a few times, collecting his thoughts before mustering the energy to get dressed. Feeling hung-over and disorientated, Thane went straight for the coffee. Malock was still on his mind and Thane wondered who or what Malock might represent in the real world.

Christian and Thane spent all morning collecting a variety of items from their immediate surroundings to run tests on. Thane took lots of photos with his new camera, trying to document everything they saw and found, including the tropical island surroundings.

They began with surface sand and soil samples, then moved to rock, coral, plants and shells, separating each into its biological category. Next, they collected a variety of organic marine life including: seaweed, sea snails, small fish, sea urchins, sand crabs, and living corals. Each item was numbered, categorized, and checked for radiation. The Geiger counter detected a steady amount of radiation, with levels between 200 and 400 millirems. All levels were higher than anything the French government published publicly, but were not considered to be dangerous to touch.

"So how bad is it, professor?" Thane asked with a quizzical smile.

"Well, put it this way – I wouldn't want to build a vacation home here. The levels are pretty steady for nuclear activity, but the ion levels fluctuate between a hydrogen headache and 'get me the hell outta here!' There's beta activity in the air, with cesium and strontium still remaining in the atmosphere, ground, and water. We're safe for the time being but like I said, long exposure to this area could result in serious problems."

For the next several days, Christian and Thane continued their tests and sample taking without being detected by French military or coast guard. Every hour, Thane would take a slow, secretive walk in each direction along the beach where they worked, scoping out the surroundings for any prying eyes or boats on the horizon. So far they hadn't come into direct contact with any other people. Using binoculars, they determined the broken down buildings across the lagoon were uninhabited with no apparent movement on the military grounds. At night, several lights came on in the buildings, but Christian suggested they might be outdoor lights with sensors left on for the French Navy or the Maritime Gendarmeriecoast (French coast guard) when they came.

"No one in sight in either direction," Thane said, returning from a quick scout.

"Good. Tomorrow I want to collect some core samples from several feet underground and test items from the floor of the Lagoon."

"How do you plan on getting us out in the Lagoon without being noticed?" Thane asked. "Wouldn't we be a moving target, taking the boat out there?"

"Yeah, but they may not spot a single swimmer at night," Christian said, with a crafty grin.

Thane's eyebrows shot straight up. "You want me to swim to the bottom of the lagoon at night?"

"Well, since it's your first mission and I have the bod for it, I guess I'll let you off the hook and do the daring deed myself."

Christian was athletic and muscular. He routinely worked out and ran track. Whenever he was on a mission, he was known to map out the surrounding area by taking a ten-mile jog. Enjoying the personal challenge, Christian was always the first to volunteer for any physically demanding jobs.

"Well if you say so," Thane replied, "I'll keep watch. But, it would fully freak me out to swim underwater in the dark."

"Me too, but it sounds exciting, doesn't it?" Christian said, while cleaning the equipment and finishing up for the day.

After a late lunch of bologna sandwiches, Christian took off his shirt, grabbed the football he brought along, and tossed it to Thane when he wasn't looking. "Think Fast!" Christian shouted.

Thane turned around just in time, barely catching the ball before it hit him square in the chest. Christian lightly tackled Thane to the ground, grabbing the ball. "Go out long for a catch!"

Thane obliged with a smile, running across the sandy stretch of beach between the lagoon and the ocean. Christian threw a clean, thirty-meter pass and Thane caught it before tumbling to the ground. "Good one!" Christian shouted, "Now just stay on your feet and you're golden!"

"Hey, I'm lucky I even caught it at all! I'm sporty, but football was never my thing,"    Thane said, throwing it back with a slight wobble.

"No worries, I won't judge. Everyone has his or her own special qualities about 'em. Mine are in biochemistry and sports. Cut left!"

He threw another long pass to Thane, who ran as fast as he could trying to impress Christian. Reaching up to catch the ball with his left hand, Thane's fingertips touched it, but the ball slipped away as he fell to his knees in the sand. Thane just smiled with some reluctance, truly enjoying the leisure time with Christian.

They continued their game of catch for another twenty minutes, before retiring to their camp. After quenching their thirst with water and snacking on fruit roll-ups, Christian laid out a picnic blanket. "Come on over here. I want to give you a reading."

Christian placed a set of Tarot cards on the blanket in front of him. "Have you ever had a Tarot card reading?" Christian asked.

"Cool. Yeah, I had one years ago, but I think the lady was a bit of a quack," Thane said, sitting down in front of Christian, legs crossed. "She said my spirit guide was standing there watching and that he looked like a little grey alien. But I can't really recall what else she said."

"Well, I know Tarot isn't very scientific and should go against all my schooling, but I like how it can interpret what's not calculable by science or mathematics. I do the *past, present, future* reading. It's simple and to the point."

"Here, shuffle the deck," he said, handing Thane the cards. "I only use the Major Arcana." Thane did as instructed, handing the cards back to Christian. "OK, before we start, I need a little guidance." Christian reached into his small fanny pack and pulled out a joint and lighter. He sparked it up and took a drag before handing it to Thane.

"You're just full of surprises, aren't you," Thane said with a mischievous grin.

After sharing a few tokes from the joint, Christian began the reading. "Alright now, the top card represents your present." He flipped it over, placing it on the blanket in front of them as Thane examined the image. The card pictured a carefree fellow with his foot in the air, carrying a satchel hanging from a walking stick, standing on a precipice with his little dog at his feet.

"Ahh yes, *The Fool*," Christian said, "I like this card. It's a good one for you, my young friend. It represents new beginnings and a carefree attitude toward life. But be careful – see this cliff here in front of him?" Christian asked, taking another drag from the joint, pointing to the depiction on the card, "he stands on a ledge looking away, dreaming. If he's not careful, he could walk carelessly off the rock and fall."

"What did you say?" Thane said, eyes locked with Christian's.

"I said, be careful you don't fall off a rock when you're daydreaming. But don't worry, I'll be there to catch you while were here on this island. And there aren't many high rocks, so you should be fine."

Christian took another drag, before handing the joint to Thane, who took a long puff. "What's this all supposed to mean?" Thane asked, more intrigued.

"It refers to your current path, or your current journey – one that's solitary and internal or personal. And keep a friend close – that's represented by the dog at his feet. It's warning you to be cautious of distractions so you don't lose touch with your path and your purpose. But for the moment, this card tells me that you have an open, creative mind and a free spirit."

"You don't know the half of it," Thane said, looking up at Christian.

Christian placed the second card face up on the left of the first card. "This is your past. It represents what you experienced in order to get where you're …"

"What the hell?" Thane said with concern. "That doesn't look good at all, man!"

The card was the number thirteen, *Death*. It pictured a cloaked, skeletal reaper carrying a black flag on a white horse. The king lies dead as a bishop prays.

"Don't freak out on me now. It's not all that bad," Christian explained. "Obviously you aren't dead and since this represents the past, it's about something or someone that died and evolved into something else. This card is all about transformation and a new cycle of life. See the horizon," he continued, pointing to the card, "the sun is dawning on a new day. It shows the end of one thing and the rebirth of something else. It's also about intuition and transition into a new state. Tell me, have you been transforming lately?"

"I have," Thane said, with a befuddled stare, "You know it's the new thing – all the rave these days."

Christian let out another chuckle before taking a drag from the joint.

"This is just too weird," Thane said, fascinated. "I don't know if it's the pot or what, but everything you're saying is clueing in with freaky precision. I've been feeling things, seeing things, and experiencing things I don't completely understand, but I think they're all connected somehow." Thane exhaled a deep breath through his teeth. "This is really a long conversation for another time, but yeah, you're tripping me out right about now."

"Cool, well let's see what your future holds," Christian said, flipping over the third card, placing it on the right side of the spread. It was the number one, *The Magician*. "Figures," Christian said.

"What figures?" Thane retorted.

Christian finished the joint, putting it out in the sand. "That your future would be filled with magic, or an earthly sense of magic. This card represents many things: eternity, spiritual awakening, the connection between Heaven and Earth, personal power or talents, manifestation, the elements of Earth, air, fire, and water."

"Are you kidding me?" Thane's eyes opened wide.

"Your future card is always the one people want to know about the most. It's like a prediction, but I don't like to think the cards predict anything at all – rather they can be used as a guide to your ultimate potential. You may become a teacher of something very special or acquire sacred knowledge of some kind. You mentioned that you're experiencing certain things you don't completely understand, right? Well, this card represents a launching point. It's the number one, the first of the Major Arcana. You have something extraordinary and unique about you. You were chosen for something special, man. It's right here in the cards."

Thane sat back, staring in wonderment at the fantastical images on the cards unsure of what it all meant, but knowing it somehow connected his life with his dreams.

"Here, let's look at it all together." Christian studied the spread intently as he pointed to the cards from left to right. "So, this tells me that in the past you had a significant loss that knocked you to the ground, filling you with insight and the capacity for transformation. You are currently on a personal mission of some kind, not knowing if you may step off a precipice, but willing to take a chance, nonetheless, because your dreams guide your way. And your courage may pay off because you will use intuitive gifts to teach something of great importance to people using your mind – some would say magical knowledge, talent, and ability."

Thane looked up at Christian, unable to speak, as a single tear ran down his face. Christian placed his hands on Thane's knees to steady him. "Are you alright? Did I say something that upset you?"

"No, no. I'm OK – it's just … I wasn't expecting that in a matter of minutes, someone would be able to explain my life to me better than I ever could myself. I've been trying to put into words what I've been feeling for years, not making much sense to my friends and family. But everything you just said spelled it out more clearly than ever. It actually made complete sense to me. Thank you."

Christian leaned over and gave Thane a heartfelt hug. "And thank you for indulging me," he said. "Who knows where we're headed, my friend. Life works in mysterious ways. But for the moment we have each other to lean on, alright? Like the cards just said, you're on a journey and us being here in this incredible place at this moment in time proves it."

"Ok, but once you hear my stories, you may get more than you bargained for," Thane said, with a crooked smile.

That night, they set their plan in motion to gather the samples they needed from the bottom of the lagoon. After taking core samples from the shallows, Thane was to keep watch while Christian prepared to swim out toward the center of the inner atoll pool, dive down to the bottom, and collect underwater samples for them to test.

The stars were spectacularly bright, yet the moon was only a sliver – perfect for their surreptitious escapade. Christian stripped down to black trunks. He put on his fins before adjusting his mask and snorkel, then he slowly stepped into the water. A shiver ran down his spine. "This is spookier than I had imagined earlier," Christian said, with hesitation in his voice. "The water looks so dark. Hand me the flashlight, will ya? Don't worry, I won't turn it on until I'm at least fifteen or twenty feet down."

"How will you know how deep you are in the pitch dark?" Thane asked.

"The lagoon drops off to about twenty five feet after a hundred yards out, or so. I'll be careful, don't worry. OK, hand me the mesh bag."

"Christian... be careful, OK?" Thane said, doing as instructed.

He gave Thane a wink and a tentative smile before quietly swimming out into the lagoon. As he calmly swam into the dark nighttime water, he was nearly blind, with the only light coming from the glittering stars above. It took him about ten minutes to swim out far enough for the specimens he wanted, and even though he knew there were no sharks in the lagoon, it was impossible not to envision one lurking around by chance.

Everyone had seen the movie Jaws, with the famous opening 'nighttime shark attack scene.' Images from the horrifying film flashed like still frames in his mind. Christian blocked it out as much as he could, focusing on his task.

The flashlight was waterproof, yet cumbersome to hold while swimming. He decided he would have to bite down on the handle, carrying it in his mouth when he dove down, in order to use both of his hands to swim.

Looking up at the brilliant, starry sky, Christian took three deep breaths before heading into the darkness of the water. He swam down, completely blind to anything in his mask's vision. Once he was deep enough, he grabbed the flashlight from his teeth and turned it on. Instantly, underwater images came into focus like a spotlight on a pitch-black stage. He saw thousands of slow-moving particles caught by the light of the beam. Eight feet below him lay the coral reef.

At first, following the beam of light across coral shapes and the lagoon floor was disorienting. He noticed only one fish that seemed intrigued by the light. His breath was running out, so he grabbed a dead chunk of coral and a broken shell from the bottom sand, placed them in the mesh bag tied to his waist, and headed for the surface switching off the light on his way up.

Breaching the surface as quietly as he could manage, he took a long, deep breath. The lagoon floor was deeper than he had originally expected, but he needed more items.

After resting for a moment and relaxing his lungs, Christian gazed up at the stars above once again, noticing that the Milky Way appeared brighter than he had ever seen it before. He took three more deep breaths and headed down again. At about fifteen feet, he switched on the light once again. The second time didn't seem as ominous as the first, as he followed the turquoise beam of light toward the bottom.

He went straight for items easily accessible. He found a rock, a living sea cucumber, and another piece of coral. That was all he could grab and place in the bag before he needed to resurface.

Quietly breaching the surface, Christian gasped a breath of fresh air while realizing the coral he saw on the bottom wasn't alive. Everything on the floor of the lagoon seemed to exist on dead coral – not a good sign for the procreation of future animal and plant life.

His bag had become heavy, so he started swimming back toward the beach. After a few strokes, he heard an unwelcome noise.


On the beach Thane scouted the areas on either side of their location, keeping an eye out for any suspicious movement and unwanted visitors. He tried to keep an eye on Christian, but in the dark, Christian had become only a tiny blip in the water. Once he'd gone under, Thane lost his location all together, unable to spot him out in the darkness. He worried about Christian, wondering what it must be like to swim out into the dark lagoon, diving deep into the black silence, suddenly flashing on the light underwater. It was an unnerving thought and it made Thane anxious.

While sitting on the sand looking at the horizon wondering if Christian was OK, Thane heard something unnatural in the distance. Ducking next to a mangrove tree, he realized it was the sound of a motorboat out in the Lagoon. Whipping his head in the direction of the sound, Thane could barely make out the shape of a small Boston Whaler outboard coming toward him. He tried to spot Christian, but he was too far out and it was too dark.

The small motor craft approached fifty yards out from Thane's location on the beach. He could hear distant shouting in French before the boat circled, coming to a stop. *Don't swim back yet,* he said in his head to Christian, like a short, sweet prayer.

Suddenly, a bright torch light shot out from the boat across the shore toward Thane. He ducked deeper into the mangrove, scraping his knee as he maneuvered under the intertwining root-like branches of the thick ground covering.

Looking away, not wanting the retinas of his eyes to reflect back, Thane felt the light pass over his body. It flashed by several more times, crossing Thane's hidden torso, before shooting off into the lagoon.

Treading water as silently as possible, Christian watched the boat approach and stop near his position. He realized if their bright light passed over him, he was close enough to be discovered.

He positioned himself with just his eyes and snorkel tip above the surface, as the torchlight from the boat came sweeping across the water in his direction.

Taking a deep breath, he went under. *Shit,* he thought, *I can't stay under very long holding this bag.* Fifty seconds went by and he had to surface soon. The snorkel had filled with water and needed to be cleared. This meant he would have to empty it somehow and the normal way of clearing the snorkel by blowing the water out into the air wasn't an option.

While under water, he decided to blow the water out slowly while covering the top of the snorkel with his thumb, allowing for air to fill while water escaped. *Only a few bubbles would disturb the surface,* he thought. As he did this, he was soon out of air and needed to get the top of the snorkel above the surface.

From underwater, he could see the bright torchlight scanning the water above. He waited until the last second before bringing the snorkel above the surface for the vital air he needed.

As he breathed in, there was still some water in the bottom portion of the snorkel that went into Christian's lungs. Ripping the mask and snorkel from his head, he coughed under water, hoping the bubbles wouldn't be noticeable in the calm lagoon. Surfacing again, he took a quiet breath, watching the light sweep back toward the shore. He cleared the snorkel carefully, breathing once again with only his eyes and snorkel tip above the water.

The boat's motor started up and the scout vessel headed back across the lagoon toward the lit buildings in the distance. They were leaving the area.

Christian gathered his wits and belongings before thankfully swimming back toward the beach. Still hiding under the mangrove tree, Thane saw Christian swim up onto the beach.

"Are you OK? That was really close," Thane said in an anxious whisper.

"Actually, I nearly drowned," he replied with a slight laugh, while taking off his gear. "But it was exciting as shit! Did you see those guys? Must have passed that light over me three times. I was slipperier than a frog, if you get my drift."

"Damn it, that was close. Too close! Did you at least find anything down there?"

Christian reached for the mesh bag, emptying its contents on the ground. "What the hell is that?" Thane said, referring to the foot long slimy turd-shaped item.

"It's a sea cucumber, one of the echinoderm or marine invertebrates, class: holothuroidea. Basically it's a very slow, fat sea worm. It won't last too long above the water, so let's hope those scouts are gone so we can get to our tests!"


After they brought the snorkel gear and items back to their camp, Christian and Thane recorded data from their Geiger counter and nuclear chemical testing equipment. Thane watched closely as Christian conducted test after test, humming, grunting, and making unusual sounds after each result came in.

A true scientist, Christian conducted each test three times with the results coming through exactly the same each time. "Just what I thought," Christian finally said, with concerned excitement. "These readings are higher than the ones taken from articles outside the lagoon. The levels are hundreds of times higher than they should be. The rock fragment is the highest, measuring an iodine 131 concentration of 22,000 picocuries per kilogram. By far the strongest radioactivity we have measured."

"That sounds bad," Thane said, not knowing what those abstract measurements meant.

"Other material from the lagoon contains an estimated 20 kilograms of plutonium, as well as cesium and strontium. And yesterday

I found tritium levels of 500 Becquerels per liter of material from the surface and air."

He shook his head, placing both palms on his cheeks. "That's not in safe parameters. These radioisotopes are indicative of more than recent bomb testing. There's a leak somewhere and I believe it's from stored nuclear waste under the surface. It's the only viable explanation. This place is essentially a huge nuclear waste dump! There's more plutonium-239 here than I can count."

Thane could tell the findings were disheartening, as Christian went on. "The underground coral and rock is the real danger. As it erodes, it'll expose more and more of the highly radiated rock and could be a future disaster waiting to happen. I was just on the surface of the lagoon floor, what lies beneath is the real question. Fissuring in the destroyed coral can alter land plates and release excessive amounts of iodine 131, a chemical that causes thyroid disease, cancer, and more."

"Man, you really know what you're talking about. You sound so scientific. Are we safe then?" Thane asked tentatively.

"We eat only the food we brought and what we test, OK? I think we'll be fine though. I've been keeping up on my history of this place. The French government keeps a very low profile, but we found out that radioactive material was deposited on Mururoa to be stored as waste. Scrap metal, wood, plastic bags, and clothing were placed in a huge heap on the north coast of the atoll, which covers 30,000 square meters. In addition, on July 21, 1966, a bomb broke apart on the surface, dispersing plutonium 239. Then, five years ago, a storm washed radioactive waste from the coral rim into the lagoon and out to sea."

"So, this trip was worth it?"

"Damn straight, Thaney boy!"

"Ha, Sharla, my best gal-pal calls me that. Did you see any glowing fish or two headed octopuses?"

"That would be octopi, and no – but I did notice something interesting. The coral in the lagoon wasn't living – at least not where I was. There'll need to be more tests in the future, but from what I saw, every bit of coral was dead. Coral exists in a very delicate balance of water temperature and sunlight, as well as salinity and symbiotic relationships to other marine life. If one of these things is upset or altered, coral will die and then the other animals that normally live on and around the reef disappear."

"If more people knew about all the harm that's been caused by these bomb tests, surely they'd stop, right?" Thane asked. "I guess they figure way out here in the middle of the ocean, no one's here to see it."

"We are! And now we have more proof."


The next morning, Christian got up early for a long jog, both for exercise and to scout out the area for onlookers who might be too close to their camp. He ran a mile in each direction, but didn't find anything suspicious or locate any more boats on the horizon. He came back to find Thane finishing up breakfast.

"What's the word, Hercules?" Thane said, as Christian stood in the tent entrance panting. Christian looked like a Roman warrior with a headband, white shirt wrapped around his waist like a tunic, and sweat glistening from his muscular chest.

"I went for a run and scouted the perimeter – didn't see another human being in sight."

"Good for us then. Those guys last night freaked me out. I thought for sure we'd be discovered."

"Not a chance! Hey, let's go for a swim. Race you to the top of that rock. OK, go!"

Christian took off like a wide receiver toward a rock on the shoreline shaped like a balancing loaf of bread. Thane admired Christian's tenacity for life as well as the fun he put into everything, even the dangerous stuff. He could go from scientific nerd to Olympic athlete in a split second.

Knowing he could never keep up with Christian's stamina, Thane played along, chasing him out to the rock outcropping along the lagoon side of their campsite.

Several round boulders lined the beach, with another large rock perched on top. Christian climbed half way up before Thane was even close.

"I just ate my breakfast!" Thane shouted. "If I run much faster I'm gonna puke it up all over the sand!" Thane slowed to a walk, noticing Christian had already climbed to the top of the rock mound. "OK, you win Herc."

"And the crowd goes wild!" Christian shouted from the top.

Thane stood winded in the sand below, with no intention of climbing the rocks. He just smiled up at Christian, admiring his antics.

Christian began teetering on top. "Whoa, I'm falling!" he yelled, losing his balance. With his arms held out spread eagle to each side, Christian fell backward, disappearing off the rock.

"NO!!!" Thane yelled, "Christian! Christian, no!"

Thane ran toward the rock in a complete panic. Shaking with fear, he slowly stepped around the rocks to see Christian swimming in a pool of crystal blue water.

"Got ya!" Christian said with a devious grin, splashing around in the water.

Still shaking, Thane was unable to speak. He fell to his knees grabbing his face as he let out a sustained, emotive moan that continued until his eyes were filled with tears.

"What is it?" Christian said, running over to him. "It was just a joke, a prank. Thane, I'm sorry if I scared you. I'm so sorry."

He put his arms around Thane in an attempt to comfort him. Thane was crying uncontrollably, still shaking. He looked up at Christian with a mixture of utter relief and shock in his eyes. "How could you have done that?" Thane said in a broken whimper. "You have no idea what you ..."

He broke down again, falling on to Christian's shoulder, crying into his neck, gripping his arms so tightly his fingers dug into Christian's skin. Thane had lost control, experiencing an emotional breakdown. Images of Aaron and their fall off the rock at camp flashed through his mind. He was reliving the nightmare all over again.

Thane's body shivered as he recalled the sensation of falling and hitting the ground, bones shattering, feeling disorientated, and seeing Aaron's broken body. The pictures flashed in his mind like a sickening, psychedelic drug trip.

"I'm so sorry," Christian said, trying to steady him. "It's OK, I'm OK. I'm here for ya. Just settle down."

Christian tenderly held Thane's head with one hand, hugging him close and trying to calm him as Thane gripped tightly to Christian's shoulders.

Finally Thane stopped shaking, his body going limp in Christian's arms as tears still streamed down his face. Thane's blue-green eyes were red and wet as he caught his breath, trying to form a complete sentence.

"You … you said before in the reading that I must have lost something or someone close to me in the past. My best friend and I fell off a huge rock. I watched him go over the side and then followed him down. We landed together and we both… died."

A single tear ran down his face. "The thing is, after a while, I came back and survived, but he didn't. When you fell back off the rock, I thought you …" Thane began to cry again, covering his eyes.

"Oh, God. Thane, I'm so sorry. If I'd known, I would never have done that. Please forgive me. I'm so stupid."

"I don't think I could go through that again. I can't lose another friend, not like that."

Christian held Thane in his arms. "I'm sorry, Thaney. You feel like a brother to me and I would never want to hurt you – ever. I mean that. I hope you believe me. There's a lot going on behind those pretty eyes of yours. I hate to think my pranks caused you any pain. Please forgive me."

They walked back to their camp in silence. Thane decided to clean up the campsite in order to take his mind off things, straightening up the equipment, washing dishes and meticulously folding each piece of clothing.

Christian took his blanket out to the ocean side of the atoll, making a comfortable spot in the sand to meditate quietly under a tree. After a time, Thane figured he had cleaned enough, so he decided to sit down and write a poem in his journal.

### *Contemplation*

*I often look across the sea,*

*Into a stone, or into space,*

*To find an answer to a thought,*

*Or clear the fog where questions trace.*

*A rose can make one bleed in more ways than one,*

*And skies can pour with rain in the middle of the sun.*

*A mind full of questions, a world full of need*

*A heart full of desire and life.*

*Reality shows us that everyone can bleed,*

*Like a cut with the back of a knife.*

*Fire holds passion with mystery and flare,*

*A sign of renewal and bravery to bare.*

*But where does the search for the answers begin?*

*It stems from a spark that's ignited from within.*

*By: Thane Winstrom*

The morning became afternoon, as a light breeze blew from the northwest. Thane walked over to Christian and sat next to him. "It's not your fault," Thane said quietly. "You didn't know what happened to me in my past and I haven't spoken about it in years. When I saw you fall ... I'm sorry I reacted like that. I'm rather embarrassed."

"Never be sorry for having feelings. They're a gift. It's what reminds us that we're alive, ya know? I envy you that you care so much – that you have it within you to love deeply and feel with the core of your being. Your emotions are what make you unique and special, Thane. I tend to hide mine away through my work, keeping my true self sheltered behind a façade of happiness."

Thane lay down on the blanket, placing his head on Christian's lap, staring up to the sky. "That's just it. I want to be more like you," Thane said honestly. "You're so confident, so strong and sure of yourself. You take life in your hands and shape it as you please, molding it into your current whim. You're smart, brave, funny and kind. How can I help but admire you? I lost a part of me when I lost my best friend. That emptiness feels like there's a missing piece, disconnected, floating somewhere out in the heavens."

"Human interaction is a mystery we continually analyze and try to explain," Christian said, placing his hand on Thane's forehead and gently brushing the hair away from his eyes. "Psychologists have a variety of answers as to why we're so complicated, with infinite room for discussion. The question more people should be asking is: 'Why aren't more people truly happy with who they are?' Now, *that* would be a real question worth answering."

Christian looked down into Thane's eyes. "My friend, I wish *I* were more like you. You have feelings, emotions, and the kind of empathy I long for. Your soul is alive. You're a true dreamer."

"I sometimes wish I were more like the person I become in my dreams," Thane said glumly. "He's powerful and creative. He has a purpose. In my dreams, I'm happy. I understand that world and I feel things there profoundly. And... I can love." Thane sat halfway up, "You know, I've often felt like the dream world was my real life, and this life is the dream. Sometimes I feel more alive in my dreams than I am in reality. Maybe that's why I don't really know who I am."

Thane looked out at the serene ocean, noticing the various shades of blue stretching out onto the horizon. "But you know exactly who you are, don't you," Thane continued, "You inspire me to want to understand my life and see what's out there – to take the chances I never could or even wanted to before."

Thane closed his eyes, as Christian placed his hand on Thane's shoulder. "You can be anything you want to," Christian said, "even the person you become in your subconscious. Don't ever stop dreaming. That would be my best advice to you. Be yourself, no matter what anyone says. Be true to your feelings and never be afraid of them. If I could follow my own advice, I would," he chuckled. "Ya know, there are moments in life when we feel completely connected, like you described before. It's in those special moments that everything feels worthwhile. Like this one right now – it's sincere, real, and unexpected. Humanity needs more moments of random, creative spontaneity. Then, maybe everything wouldn't always seem so serious."

Thane wrapped an arm around Christian's knee and yawned. "Random, creative spontaneity – nice. I totally get it," Thane said. "You make me feel safe – like a brother I never had and a friend that's been missing."

Christian sat leaning back on the coconut palm with his eyes closed, listening to the lulling sound of the shallow waves crashing lightly ashore, as Thane rested peacefully in his lap. The island breeze was an ideal temperature and the moment was as perfect as a moment could be – utterly relaxing and tranquil.

After a short time Thane began to snore very lightly, having drifted off into a deep, thoughtful sleep.

# Chapter XIV

## NAYUBU

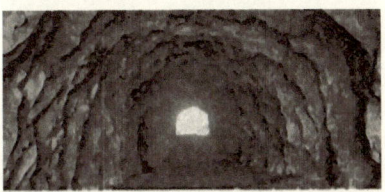

The cool night breeze whistled through Sarghon's ears, as his eyes slowly fluttered open to a view of blue mist swirling along steep mountain tops covered with massive pine trees. His neck ached from hanging forward to one side. *I must have been asleep*, Sarghon thought, clinching and straining his eyes into focus.

He and Kara were several hundred feet above the treetops, soaring through the air. Kara had been carrying Sarghon for a long distance. Her great wings and strong arms were fatigued and near exhaustion – she had to land.

Coming down hard, she lost grip of Sarghon's shoulder as they hit the ground abruptly on a grassy knoll near the top of the Great Shadow Mountains. Kara reached her destination, landing in a very precise location near a high peak on the eastern slope. She hadn't been to this mystical forest in many years and remembered how different the light, shadows, and sounds were so high in this unusual place.

As Kara sat catching her breath, Sarghon felt uneasy. The light reflected duotone shades of deep blue and silver. Only this spectrum of color was visible under the giant umbrella pines, giving everything a preternatural quality. Glowing fireflies covered the forest floor moving in trance-like unison, making the ground appear to swirl like liquid.

"Where are we?" Sarghon asked, brushing his hand through the fireflies. "This is a strange part of the forest."

Kara, still catching her breath, didn't answer.

"Forgive me my princess, "Sarghon said, "You have obviously carried my weight once again, tantamount to a lifeless boulder. You must be exhausted. If I could summon you a sumptuous feast, you know I would do so at your very command; but alas, I am impotent."

Kara gave him a shrewd smile. "We are in the Great Shadow Mountains, where I believe someone still lives who may be of help. He is a wise soothsayer. Come this way," she indicated, standing up slowly. "If I recall correctly, his dwelling is near that rock outcropping just ahead. I must warn you, though, Nayubu is eccentric. He has lived up here in the Shadows for more than one hundred years and my mother believes he has gone mad. I met him once when I was a child. He was odd even then. He made me laugh – the only male to ever do such a thing."

"Eccentric … how, exactly?" Sarghon asked tentatively.

"If we find him, you will see for yourself."

They walked for several minutes, fireflies dancing all around their feet. Still very weak from his battle with Malock, Sarghon felt unsure of this mysterious forest, not knowing if what he felt was apprehension or the foreign thoughts of the ancient trees playing tricks on his mind.

Stopping in front of a large rock wall, Kara looked around with a sense of familiarity. "I will need to make our presence known. Stand back," she warned.

Holding her sword above her head, she summoned lightning, which burst upon her sword like a beacon. Enjoying the spectacle, Sarghon watched as she released a thunderous bolt from her blade, exploding on the rock face. Shards of granite shot off in all directions.

"Great Nayubu, seer of truth," she said, "grant us your audience! It is I, Kara, daughter of Freja, Queen of the Valkyrie. I come with the Spirit King, bearer of the *Diaglyphen Prophesy*. We seek your most needed assistance."

A moment passed, but there was only silence.

"Is this how people normally knock upon his door?" Sarghon asked.

"If he still lives, he heard my … knocking," she replied.

The Earth below their feet began to vibrate and rumble as the rock wall split apart like a titanic curtain opening from either side. When it finally stopped and the dust settled, a deep triangular cave entrance appeared. "It seems he remembers you after all," Sarghon said. "I am curious to see if he can still make you laugh."

Entering the magical dwelling, they walked the length of the triangular corridor until they came to a large domed room lit with fire burning wall sconces. Filled with books, tapestries, statuary, and ancient bric-a-brac of every kind, the room of odd treasures felt like a museum exploded in all directions.

Across the room, the sound of a rattling teakettle came from a narrow hallway. "Confound these impossible contraptions!" a voice screeched.

Kara and Sarghon both turned their heads at the same time. "Tea should be a simple pleasure after all," Nayubu said, entering the room while shaking his wrist from the weight of an antique kettle shaped like a dragon. In his other hand, he held a tray with three etched, metallic glasses. "It's my little, laughing harpy then, is it? And you brought a young friend with you I see. Imagine that," he said, peering over small, round spectacles that hung off the end of his pointed nose.

Dressed in long, tattered robes once regal in stature, Nayubu's tall, thin frame made him appear ghostlike. He had an olive complexion with an angular jaw and he hunched over slightly at his shoulders. His head was completely bald, except for a semi-circle of gray hair that wrapped around the base of his skull from ear to ear, hanging straight down his back.

"We come to you out of great importance, old friend," Kara explained. "You see, Sarghon here has …"

"Do you think I don't know why you have come, my wondrous, witty, winged child?" Nayubu said, his bony fingers shaking whenever he gestured. "Do you forget that I know … things? Why else would I be called a soothsayer, huh? Bah! Any half-witted erudite with any sagacity at all could deduce your quandary."

He looked Sarghon up and down as if inspecting a vegetable before biting into it. "You lost your wits, now have you? Well, I know a thing or two about that. Ha!" he yelped out in a loud cackle. "They say I lost mine many moons ago!"

Nayubu sat in a large chair as he poured tea into the three ornate goblets. "Your eminence, I … ahh …" Sarghon was taken aback. Slightly flustered, he began again. "Sir, I had great powers of the Earth given to me by a Tarpin, as well as elemental powers of wind and fire. And now …"

"They have vanished," Nayubu said, waving his hands in the air as if fanning away a pesky mosquito. "Where did they go?"

"We hoped *you* might be able to tell us the answer to that question," Kara said.

"This, I cannot say," Nayubu replied. "One never knows why things come and go the way they do. One day you have a cup of soup and the next day it's gone. Where did it go? In my belly, I would gather."

Sarghon glared at Kara with a look of confusion and concern. "A Tarpin you say? Nayubu continued, offering Kara a cup of tea. "Clever little trolls. Haven't seen one in ages. Last time I encountered a Tarpin, the thing stole my favorite shoes."

"You see sir," Sarghon said, attempting to get back on point, "we believe King Malock found a way to take my powers from me – steal them somehow. It happened during our first encounter. He is seductive and shrewdly devious. His dominance is beyond anything I have ever … well, what I'm trying to say is, that he is unbelievably strong and powerful. He must have absorbed my energy somehow and I don't think …" Sarghon once again sounded defeated, "how could I possibly defeat him?"

"Ahh, you admire this man then, do you?"

"What?! Are you mad?"

"Quite, I assume," Nayubu said frankly, taking a sip of tea.

"The reality is," Sarghon said, getting slightly agitated, "my powers are gone and unless I find a way to get them back, this world as we know it will soon be lost!"

"You are the prophesized child then, yes." Nayubu asked, cleaning his glasses with a piece of his tattered garb. Sarghon opened his mouth. "That was a rhetorical question," Nayubu said, before Sarghon could speak. "So tell me this – why is a prophecy even a prophecy at all?" he asked, shaking his teacup in his hand. "Well, because it *is*. Malock did not steal your powers. Elementals can only be given, not taken. There is another reason then."

As he continued his wacky explanation, Nayubu paced in a figure-eight pattern in the center of the room on his faded, red-fringed carpet. "How are we to *know* something if we do not know it at all?" he asked, puffing out his cheeks. "If a star explodes in the sky, and we cannot hear it, does it make a sound? To be or not to be … Yes, the tint-antithesis of the universal dichotomy, my boy. Do we even exist at all? Do you exist, do I exist?"

He scratched his head with the same hand holding the half finished cup of tea. "Hmm, maybe I'm just dreaming that you are standing here in front of me? Or maybe you are dreaming that you are the bearer of the Diaglyphen Prophesy, but in reality you are a normal, young lad asleep in your bed in some far off, wondrous land at this very moment? Who's to say what reality really is, huh?"

Sarghon wandered over to a tattered, over-stuffed chair and sat down. He then stood up with a quizzical look on his face about to say something, but sat down again, obviously confused and frustrated with the nonsensical logic coming from Nayubu. Leaning into Kara's ear, he whispered, "This is a waste of time. What does this loon have to tell us that may be of any help at all?"

"I warned you that he is eccentric, but his babbling often covers a deeper meaning."

"Now, that's all well and good," Sarghon said, turning to Nayubu, "but, is there anything you can tell us that might be of assistance in our dire quest?"

"Lo! There is where your problem lies!" Nayubu said, looking up from his cup, eyes ablaze with excitement. "Ha, I have found it. Yes!"

He jumped up waving his cup in the air, splashing the remainder of his tea across the floor in front of him, stopping suddenly before pointed a long, bony finger at Sarghon. "I just now remembered something," Nayubu said with a curious grin. "*I* am the cousin of the last great King Zavior, the wizard King, and father to Malock. It's been so long, I nearly forgot my own family ancestry. What am I like?"

Looking from side to side like a chicken following a kernel of seed as it bounced across the ground, he went on. "King Zavior had a similar power to my own. He was an empath. He could see the truth of one's intent by merely gazing into one's eyes. He would then sway your decisions using your own emotions. He knew exactly whom he could trust, who would lie, as well as one's deepest desires. He also felt their sorrow and pain, which was a constant hindrance to him – as one can imagine. His jealous son, however, was immune to his power and thus a vacant page, never to be read or understood. Malock must have assumed his father's ability to influence the mind."

Sarghon and Kara came to the same conclusion simultaneously, but Sarghon spoke first. "Then you are my distant great cousin? Malock revealed to me that we were half-brothers. King Zavior was my father as well."

"Hmmm, a curious finding indeed. If what you say is true, then the deductions you surmise are intriguing. I wonder why I didn't know that fact until just now? But alas, it would appear that you are correct, my boy. Such prophecies, magical talents, fate and destiny seem to run in our lineage. Welcome to the family!" he said, raising his teacup over his head, splashing the last drops of tea on the floor.

Feeling completely dumbstruck, Sarghon didn't know whether to laugh or cry. "So you see," Nayubu said, "your power was not taken from you – *you* were taken from your power! Yes, that's it. I am certain! What was lost when you faced Malock, huh?"

"My strength," Sarghon retorted.

"NO!" Nayubu snapped. "Kara, care to make a conjecture?" She glanced around the room like a bird watching a moth. "Could it be that simple?" Kara answered.

"What are you two talking about?" Sarghon insisted, with annoyed confusion.

"My dear, befuddled boy," Nayubu said, "it seems the *reality* of your current state of affairs is that you have lost your audacity."

"Lost my what?" he replied.

"*Bravery* is a key ingredient in the heroic ongoings of a prophesier. Your adversary must have depleted your confidence, not your earthen energy – and this in turn, disrupted your power. You have an acute lack of courage, my boy!"

"Are you saying I still have the power I need to face Malock?"

"Indeed, I am. No need to search hither and yon for potions and pragmatists. There is no other reasonable explanation for your circumstances. And also, because I am rarely wrong, reason dictates that you have it within yourself to regain the strength you desire. I am ninety-nine point nine percent certain of it! The mind is a tricky device, my boy. Perception is the key to transformation. Reality, remember, is both subjective and malleable. Do not allow your thoughts to betray you, believing you are as weak as your enemy believes – otherwise he will be able to take advantage of you in these unexpected and dare I say, *gifted* ways."

Sarghon stood for a moment with a blank expression before speaking. "So he manipulated me while I was weak. He made me believe I would never be able to stop him, no matter how powerful I was. And you are right – I believed him. I remember now. He sent a repeating thought through my mind while we were connected in battle. 'YOU WILL FAIL', is all I could think!"

"And do you believe him now?" Nayubu asked.

"Now that I understand his vulgar tactic, NO. I do not!"

"Then, once you have realized completely and for certain that within you lies the ability to face your opponent equally, your powers should return."

Sarghon squinted in disgust, but Kara seemed relived. "This is good news," she said. "The battle has not been lost."

"Now don't try growing a forest in my house just to see if your gifts have returned!" Nayubu barked. "If I know my prophecies correctly, and I most certainly do, you could demolish my home with a wave of your untamed hand. Take heed when using such power, young cousin. Vast power can also destroy or corrupt vastly."

Sarghon began to appreciate Kara's instinct and reasoning for bringing him here. "Kara," Nayubu said in conclusion, "you must tell your mother that I foresee a change in the political hierarchy of magical beings within the next two conjunct moon cycles." He shot a look at Sarghon. "And that goes for Ambroas as well, prophesier! He may not have the power of foresight that I have, but he will certainly be affected – yes he will."

Sarghon recalled his world had two moons that lined up side by side every several months, creating the lunar conjunction cycles.

"I will relay your message to the Valkyrie and to my mother," Kara replied. "Sarghon, we must go. Our host has been most helpful." She turned to Nayubu and bowed her head in gratitude. "Your insight has once again proven worthy to a great cause, old friend."

"You are brave to call me old!" he snapped. "Now your work begins. Encourage the boy to believe in himself or we all may end up slaves to a tyrant!"

Still lost in thought, Sarghon wasn't listening to them anymore. He felt violated in a fetid way, raped by Malock in body as well as mind, energy, and spirit. He realized how the animals and trees must have felt before perishing to Malock's will, being transformed into the pure, liquid energy essence he coveted. It made Sarghon sick to his stomach.

"Thank you for your words of wisdom," Sarghon said, nodding to Nayubu. "I have much to consider. You have opened my eyes."

"One more thing, my boy... before you attempt another confrontation with the dark King," Nayubu said with a feisty look in his eye, "beware your half-brother's fate. His hubris is linked to you, bound by blood. Consider why your first attack failed. You, along with your sword, possess the power of *all* the Earth, not just the trees and plants you see above ground. You must think as a wizard, seeing every facet, as I do – or as I see... however that makes sense to you. If Malock has the ability to absorb energy, then prudently you should attack with something that has no energy, yes? Ambroas is a good teacher, but only you can find it within yourself to utilize the power you were given, balancing out the elemental gifts to their highest potential."

Nayubu's eyes opened very wide, his long, wispy eyebrows arching high on his forehead as he stared scrupulously at Sarghon, pointing a boney finger at him. "The Aurora is strong with you. Indeed you *are* the bearer of The Prophesy – yet, there is more …"

Nayubu grabbed Sarghon's arm, peering intently into his eyes while attempting to read him more deeply. "I see a great battle on the Field of Kings. There is confusion, bravery, death, and power – *great* power. It's magnificent!"

Still pointing at Sarghon, his finger began to tremble. The shaking moved into his arm. "But there is something else … What does it mean?" He concentrated even harder, using his power as a seer, staring wide-eyed at Sarghon. Then, his eyes went completely white. "I don't understand, I can't see …"

Suddenly, a strong gust of energy blew Nayubu backward, off his feet into the tattered chair. As he sat up in confusion, his eyes returned to normal. "Never before has my vision been blocked. There must be something where the nothingness is – and yet, how can there be anything if nothing is seen. Alas, if I see nothing, then nothing becomes something, which is an all-together different quandary. Now, be off and leave me to my tea. You have a world to save, do you not?"

With Nayubu muttering to himself, Kara and Sarghon left the cavern dwelling and returned to the shadowy duotone forest outside. Enraged, Sarghon stomped the ground, kicking up gravel with each step as he walked. "You must allow your powers to return," Kara said. "We may face a battle at any time."

"I can't believe how easily I was seduced by Malock's influence. He moves in shady measure. I will not be so susceptible in the future, I promise you that! I'm sickened by the thought of him manipulating my mind and stealing my life force, mettling with the very core of my strength and faith – the root of my essence! How dare he!"

Sarghon raised his hands in the air. "It infuriates me!" he shouted.

His hands began to tingle. "I was given a responsibility. Failure, defeat, surrender – these are not an option for me!"

In his rage, he straightened his fingers out in front of him with a coarse gesture, as a violent stream of fire exploded from Sarghon's hands out across the dark blue forest floor, burning and scattering fireflies, leaves, and loose brush in all directions.

"It seems the old babbling soothsayer was right to kick us out when he did," Sarghon said with a smirk. "I think with a night's rest and a proper meal, I will be ready to leave this place of my own accord." Kara gave him a look of relief.

Grasping the handle of Gladanteus, he released the sword from her sheath. With a very particular purpose in mind, Sarghon stabbed it to the ground near a thick, umbrella pine tree, concentrating as he had before.

At first nothing happened, but after a moment the ground began to stir and rumble. Sprouts of roots shot up from of the soil, twisting and writhing like an organic machine, growing moving parts that worked together to create the next. Branches emerged from the root stalks, growing out like a dancer's arms swaying back and forth, interweaving like a basket until it formed a cave-like protective enclosure large enough for them both to sleep in.

The movement ceased after the enclosure solidified itself with a light layer of strong bark. With a heavy sigh, Sarghon put away his sword. "Finally, it's good to feel like myself again. Please sleep," he said, gesturing toward the newly formed earthen structure. "I owe you my life, dear battle princess. You deserve rest after carrying my heavy weight up to this far-off place. We have much more work ahead of us, as you well know."

Stepping toward Kara, he tenderly ran his hand through her golden hair. "I am truly grateful to you in so many ways, my dear Kara. Thank you."

She looked at him with unblinking eyes, not taking any notice of the implication that she would ever belong to another. "I am glad your vigor has returned, as well as your senses," she said. "I was worried for you and for our future. I can say that now, but I never lost faith in you."

Cupping his face with one hand, she kissed his cheek gently, then neatly folded her wings behind her back and crawled into the wooded enclosure.

Sarghon remained outside for a time, taking in the serenity of the firefly's fluidic movement across the forest floor as he leaned against the large tree whose roots had grown to create their wooden grotto. Pondering Nayubu's words of wisdom, as well as his blindness to Sarghon's ultimate future, he realized his destiny was yet unwritten.

Once again, the forest surroundings felt peaceful all around. Sarghon understood why a hermit like Nayubu would conceal himself away in such a remote place. There was a sense of calm and serenity that

217

permeated from the colorless forest, despite its austere and uninviting nature.

He was glad Kara was with him. She made him feel safe, cared for, and loved. Their growing affection for each other was clear, although he had never courted a princess before; especially one with wings who controlled the electricity of the sky. His mind had to stay in the battle for the time being and he knew that.

Before calling it a night, he sat a moment longer meditating to the sound of the billowing wind and night crickets, wondering where his travels would take him next in search of the last element, *Water*.


Time seemed to pass like magic, as the orange sun rose on the misty blue horizon beckoning the next day. The moisture in the air and over the flora sparkled like tiny gem stones floating along the forest floor.

As Sarghon crawled out from their protective wooden grotto, he stretched his arms out wide, feeling revitalized, knowing that his strength was returning as well as his resolve. After taking a large sip from his leather water sac, he sat against a tree meditating on a true path as Ambroas had instructed him so many times before.

Focusing on the element of water, Sarghon reached into his mind, visualizing where his search should take him. In his mind's eye, he could see tops of mountains surrounded by an ocean on all sides, followed by a vision of a land with hundreds of lakes of various sizes and shapes. The scenery then faded as his mind focused on wild dogs running across a shallow river toward a cave opening covered by a sheer waterfall drawing him in with intrigue, closer and closer, until …

Sarghon's eyes snapped opened wide. Kara was standing next to him in silence, having witnessed Sarghon's meditation. "Have you discovered something of use to your quest?" she said with interest.

"Good morning to you as well, my winged beauty. I have had a vision. A land with hundreds of lakes, large wolves running fast, and a waterfall covering a cave. The waterfall was like a mirror. I saw my face reflected in it as clear as I see you now. There was something in the water – something alluring."

"Then we shall go there. The only place I know of with so many lakes can be found is in the southern plains and swamps."

"This is not a place with swamps or plains. It is a land of mountains surrounded by water – an island perhaps, with the lakes inside. It's like no place I have ever been or envisioned before. But I am certain that it is in that direction." Sarghon pointed toward the west.

"There is fabled to be an island off the Gallandrean Coast that is hidden in the mist," she said, contemplating his vision. "Ships avoid it for fear of crashing on its jagged rocks. No one has ever lived to return with a true account of its existence. Valkyrie fear flying over the open ocean – for once we land in water, we cannot take off again. We must have land in order to take to the sky. None of my kin have dared fly so far across the water."

"Then I will have to go without you."

"No," Kara said, insistently. "I will not leave you. If indeed you saw this place in your vision, then that is reason enough for me to brave the journey."

"If I insist on doing this alone in order to keep you safe, would it do any good?" Sarghon said with a half-smile.

"I am Princess of the mighty Valkyrian Empire and have no desire to be kept safe!" she barked. "You could insist all you like, but I freely do as I see fit for the interest of all. Besides, you may still need me," Kara said, crossing her arms while looking him straight in the eye.

"Of that I am certain," Sarghon replied with another smile. "Believe me, I do not wish you to leave my side. You are the bravest of all I have encountered in my short lifetime and I do need you – of that there is no doubt. But you were not in my vision on the island of lakes."

"Who was with you?" Kara asked, with an envious glare.

Just then, from high above the trees, a flash of color unlike anything in the nearly colorless forest soared across the sky in a bright, blazing stream of red and yellow. As it got closer, Kara raised her eyes to block the glare before realizing what she was seeing.

In a magnificent display, Atasha came in for a grand entrance with fire ablaze from her mane and hoofs. Once on the ground, she shook her head and the flames from her neck and hoofs receded, vanishing into waves of heat emanating out from her body.

Sarghon bowed in the customary fashion and waited.

Atasha approached him.

Reaching his arm out and placing his hands over Atasha's eyes, he waited. She then stepped back, bowing with acceptance. "This is the only other female I would trust to accompany you on your task at hand," Kara said, with a raise of her eyebrow.

"I thought you would understand," Sarghon replied. "If I were responsible for drowning the Princess of the Valkyrie, I could not live with myself. You are too precious to me. If the island is as far as you say, I will not risk it. Atasha has made it known to me that she can fly for days without rest if need be."

"Then she is the correct choice," Kara conceded. "I will return to my people and prepare them for battle. Once we receive notice from you, we will be at Malock's fortress within a day's time."

"I will return to you, dear one," he said, looking deeply into her eyes.

Without hesitation, Sarghon kissed her passionately on the lips, not knowing if she would resist. She didn't, returning the kiss with passion rarely displayed by her kind.

Their lips separated slowly as their eyes met with intensity. "I will hold you to that," Kara said with certainty. She then leapt into the air, spreading her wings wide before taking to the sky and flying off like a vision over the misty mountains and out of sight.

Sarghon gathered his few things but before departing, he jabbed his sword into the Earth while focusing his energy. A sapling tree sprouted, growing up several meters, before bursting with large ripe red apples. He picked several and put them in his satchel. He then picked three of the largest apples and gave them to Atasha, who gobbled them up in a few bites.

"OK, Atasha, it's time to go," he said, smiling at her with excitement.

She acknowledged his request, rearing up on her hind feet. She circled back around and came at Sarghon, who was recalling the fire dance in his head from the Basai village, counting the steps as he steadied his hands and feet. Atasha galloped at him with strength and speed.

As she approached, he reached out one arm, beginning the sequence of steps. With lightning movement, Sarghon jumped to one side, reaching out his left arm and taking hold of Atasha's mane. Shuffling his feet in the double quickstep movement, he jumped into the barrel roll up and on to her back, bending down into her weight and speed before adjusting himself by balancing his right arm behind him to complete the full movement series.

He was now riding her freely on the ground with power and strength that was magnified by the open terrain – something he had not been able to experience in the confines of the stable when he last rode her.

Her mane and hoofs burst ablaze with fire. It was a brilliant sight and once again he wasn't burned. Easily holding the flaming main of hair with his bare hand, Sarghon felt the vigorous and fervent energy coursing through his body.

In an instant, they were in the air, shooting into the sky above the giant trees of the colorless forest. The mist disappeared behind them, as they flew like a streaming comet westward across the sky.


# WATER


The coast came upon them quickly, the ocean appearing like a vast blue-green carpet stretching out across the infinite horizon. The land disappeared as they rode across the sky like a steady shooting star.

Sarghon and Atasha were linked in a knowing, psychic bond – she able to understand his wishes and intentions, and he able to read her thoughts and desires. They communicated intuitively, with or without words.

He closed his eyes, the breeze cooling his face as he focused on the image of the island from his meditation. "That way," Sarghon spoke out loud, pointing slightly to the right of their current course. She understood him completely, adjusting their heading.

After several hours, a low hanging cloud appeared on the horizon sitting alone in an otherwise clear, blue sky. *Could that be large enough to be an island?* he thought.

They headed for the isolated cloud mass, approaching its perimeter before realizing it was much larger than it appeared from a distance. Like an optical illusion, the cloud seemed to expand out as if floating on the water itself.

"We must go into it," Sarghon said.

Atasha retorted with thoughts of reluctance, but agreed there must be something inside. "Hold steady, girl," Sarghon said, stroking her glistening, black neck. "I'm going to make us an entrance. Do not be alarmed."

Sarghon steadied himself on Atasha's back, grasping her fiery mane with his left hand for support while raising his right hand in the air.

Focusing deliberately on a precise area of the cloud, he slowly rotated his fingers, creating a wind funnel.

It grew larger and stronger into a swirling tunnel through the clouds, like a straw piercing through the foam of a milkshake.

"Fly in!" he shouted. "We have our path."

The mist was heavy and wet on their skin, but Atasha's flames held steady as they entered the cloud tunnel. The tubular walls turned grey as the light faded behind them. In the distance a round blue opening appeared, growing lighter as they continued forward. "This must be it, we've made it!" he shouted with excitement and relief.

They emerged through the thick cloud into a spectacular, island paradise. The sun shone from above through a giant hole in the top of the cloud, creating a perfect ring of blue sky streaking down in misty beams of light. Surrounded by crystal blue water, stood verdant mountain peaks reaching high into the sky like bulbous, organic fingers. Cascading waterfalls poured and misted from the crevices of each mountain, flowing into countless, winding rivers and streams. The lush mountains surrounded an inner basin sanctuary where the rivers lead to a network of lakes, creating a wondrous landscape.

"This place is truly a sight to behold," he said out loud, as a tear ran down his cheek. "It is a shame more cannot enjoy its glory." Atasha agreed.

The natural untold beauty permeating all around was indeed overwhelming, provoking an emotional response. Atasha felt his emotion, nodding her neck several times, acknowledging the honesty of his reaction.

They flew down a crater-like basin over several small lakes, their reflection following underneath like a mirror across the serene, watery landscape. Colorful birds fluttered out from the trees as they soared by.

"There," he said, pointing across one of the lakes in front of them. "Land in the meadow near that winding stream."

Atasha altered course to the place he suggested, landing softly on the grass and baby wild flowers. "This is an island sanctuary," Sarghon said, stretching his limbs as he dismounted. "I have never seen anything so beautiful in all my life. Good thing Malock doesn't know about this place."

Placing his cupped hands in the stream, Sarghon drank from the crystal blue water. Atasha followed suit, taking her well-deserved fill. He handed her several of the apples from his sack, before eating one himself.

The atmosphere felt inviting: bubbling rivers, the faint whispers of waterfalls in the background, the occasional chirp of a bird. It was as perfectly beautiful a picture as nature could create.

Sarghon sat on a patch of long grass admiring the surrounding flora. Touching his fingers to the Earth, he became aware of each plant's name as before, some of which were foreign to him. He detected tropical species such as: Hyatian Tree Ferns, the fantastically shaped Pyruvian Orchids, and Babakan Lilies, which grow in a very fastidious climate, as well as a wide variety of extra large butterflies. The environment felt euphoric.

Atasha suddenly became anxious, indicating to Sarghon they were not alone. *Be on guard,* her thoughts said to him.

Looking around, he saw nothing. "Steady, brave one. I will protect you. There is no need for alarm."

Several silent moments passed, when Atasha identified something watching from behind the trees. Two enormous wolves walked into view. They were calm and silent in their movement, observing with large, pale blue eyes. Their size was intimidating, but their demeanor soft and subtle.

Atasha reared. "It's OK, girl," Sarghon said, steadying her. "I do not believe they mean us harm."

The two wolves walked toward them in perfect unison, both stopping together as if being instructed. Sitting down at the same time, they both looked to their left, then back to Sarghon. After a moment, they took off running.

"I believe that was an indication to follow them. Quickly, Atasha!"

Lurching back, Atasha ignited her hoofs before galloping toward Sarghon. He grabbed her mane, leaping on her back like before and they were off.

The wolves' speed was impressive, hurdling across streams and riverbanks with agility and grace. As the wolves were nearly her size, Atasha was barely able to stay with them as they lead through lush paths and over muddy terrain, emerging next to a stunning waterfall flowing over a beautiful, tropical grotto.

The water fell over the top of the grotto opening in a solid, clear slice like a sheet of curved glass empting tranquilly into the pool at its base. The two wolves stood like statues on either side of the falls, staring straight ahead with their piercing, pale blue eyes. Like stoic sentinels, their masculinity and beauty added to the grotto, as if they were stone sculptures. Sarghon couldn't help but venerate their idyllic stature.

"I saw this in my vision," he said to Atasha. "We are in the right place."

A hauntingly beautiful female voice echoed in song from within the cavernous grotto behind the waterfall.

Drawn toward the sound, like the singing sirens luring in a ship of pirates, Sarghon dismounted Atasha. His body felt weightless and numb, his ears yearning to hear more of the enchanting music. He became caught in a trance, unable to control his limbs as he walked drunkenly toward the waterfall.

The wolves turned and ran through the middle of the waterfall, disappearing into the cavern opening behind the glassy falls. Enchanted by the euphoria, Sarghon helplessly continued as he stumbled toward the grotto, stepping knee deep into the water. The lure was overpowering, guiding him where the music told him to go.

He walked directly into the glassy falls, disappearing behind the water, not caring that he became drenched. When he emerged, he found himself inside the cavernous, watery grotto. Shimmering crystals protruded from the walls all around and the water glowed with brilliant radiance from deep within, lighting up the entire cavern.

Walking deeper into the grotto, still mesmerized by the music and beauty, Sarghon closed his eyes unable to think for himself. The deeper he walked into the cavern, the louder the music grew.

Swaying fluidly with the melodic rhythm of the music, he finally stopped. Drowsily opening his eyes, smiling in his euphoria, Sarghon beheld a beautiful woman singing the enchanting, ethereal melody.

As she approached, she stopped singing. Still paralyzed, Sarghon stared at her in fascination.

Tall, slender, and statuesque, her skin shimmered in the reflecting water. Her eyes glowed cerulean blue and her black hair fell straight down her shoulders, spilling like liquid over her upper chest and back. She wore only a sleek skintight aquamarine chemise, disappearing into the water at her feet.

"You are not what I expected," she said, tilting her head as she stared into Sarghon's eyes. "Yet, brave and worthy enough to find your way here to my sanctuary. It has been a very long time since a man has come to visit me. What do you seek, young warrior?"

Sarghon stared for a moment longer, before snapping out of his euphoric state. "I, um …" He shook his head, trying to clear his mind. "I am Sarghon, bearer of the Diaglyphen Prophesy, mistress. I come in search of …"

"I am not a mistress. I am Malhara, an elemental guardian," she replied sharply.

"Then, it is you I seek."

"I am sought by many. What makes you so special?"

The two large wolves moved to her right and left, placing themselves under her palms. "My wolves tell me you came here on a fire horse. Very clever, to be sure. But do you possess what it takes to command the power you seek? Can you control your emotions?"

Sarghon stood silently listening to her. *It must be a test*, he thought.

"I am willing to do what it takes," he replied.

"Water is connected to our emotions," she said, staring at him without blinking. "We make it with our feelings. We can release it when we cry or allow it to surge through us when we are passionate, enraged, or … in love. It's wild and free, like a raging river or a fervent storm. No one can truly control it. Emotions are held like a bubble within us waiting to burst."

Moving closer to Sarghon, she undressed him with her shimmering, blue eyes. "You must realize, there is no path to finding love; love simply is the path. But, if you want to try, you must prove yourself worthy!"

Grabbing hold of Sarghon with extraordinary strength, Malhara pulled him in close before diving head first into the glowing pool of water, taking him with her.

They sank deep under the water before she released him. The crystal blue water glimmered like sunlit satin, billowing in a light breeze. Beams of light shot toward him from giant underwater crystals, refracting colors in all directions. He felt like the focal point of a brilliant diamond.

Floating merely feet away, her hair reaching out like a web, Malhara faced Sarghon and spoke with words understood clearly under the water. "If you are who you say you are, then I must know for sure. Do exactly as I say, or you will drown. Kiss me."

At first Sarghon was confused, but remembering what she had told him about the water element being attached to his emotions, he swam up to her and kissed her mouth tenderly.

Keeping his lips pressed against hers with his eyes open, Sarghon waited for something to happen.

"NO!" she yelled, violently pulling away while water pulsed, bubbled, and rippled out from her in all directions. "You must feel me, use me; let me flow through your body as if I were part of you, inside you. Give in to me!"

Sarghon needed air, but there wasn't enough underwater for him to manipulate and none to breathe.

Sarghon literally had to sink or swim. In this case, he needed to trust his feelings. With only seconds left, he reached out his arms grabbing hold of Malhara pulling her close. Thinking about his feelings for Kara and what he desired from her body, Sarghon locked lips and kissed her with rigorous passion. Their bodies rubbed together as her arms wrapped around him, cradling Sarghon in an intimate embrace.

Her lips locked, becoming one with his while he surrendered his body over to her. Lightheaded, he continued the kiss with vigor, pressing his body into hers, while giving in to his emotions.

His blood flowed faster and faster. Then, like an explosion, Malhara blew a hard burst of air mixed with water into his mouth.

His body shuddered, as his muscles filled with adrenalin. He felt as though a strong psychedelic drug had just hit, transferring through her lips to his core. It felt both terrifying and fantastic at the same time. At first he began to choke, gasping at the last bits of air, but then his body calmed as he took in a full breath of water. Calm and clean, it felt like breathing in a heavy whiff from a bunch of freshly cut mint leaves.

He was breathing underwater.

"You seem to have what it takes, my young, passionate warrior," Malhara said, releasing him. "The element of water is now yours to manipulate. Use it wisely and protect our land and seas."

"I thank you for this great gift," Sarghon said, speaking as she had with complete clarity under the water. "I will use it to the best of my ability and fight for our world with all my might."

Malhara slowly spread her arms, as the water swirled below Sarghon's feet. He was rising to the surface. Malhara remained underwater as the swirling water bubbled, lifting him above the surface until he was standing on top of the water itself.

"The elements are truly fascinating," he said, walking across the water's surface like a dragonfly, peering down at the giant underwater crystals.

Making his way back onto solid land, he noticed the majestic wolves had gone. Sarghon walked back through the glassy waterfall, exiting the grotto cavern. He found Atasha waiting patiently for him outside. "It is done," he said, dripping wet.

Atasha articulated her head in a gesture of acceptance.

"But before we go, I should see for certain that what I feel within me is true."

Walking back to the stream leading out from the grotto, Sarghon looked into the shallow, flowing water. Focusing on the element, he thought of Kara as he allowed himself to feel the energy of the water flow through his body. A tingle moved across his skin and into his muscles and his bones. He felt exhilarated!

Moving his hand in a sweeping motion, Sarghon made the water flow backward in the stream. He raised his arm and the water followed suit, rising up in a large sheet, like a mirror reflecting back at them.

His body still tingling with energy, he remembered Malhara's account of how his emotions were attached to this element. He also felt a wave of lustful passion running through his veins. *It's just the power taking over,* he told himself, *control it!*

Atasha and Sarghon saw their warped and rippled reflection staring back at them as it rose higher and higher, accumulating more and more water from the stream. Once it reached over thirty feet high, Sarghon stood back.

"Stop!" he yelled. But nothing happened. It was getting bigger and bigger, like a cobra rising up and flaring out its cowl. The water in the stream had become but a trickle, with most of it in the air above. "What now?" he said, "It's not obeying my command. Malhara mentioned that no one can truly control it. But I must do something!"

Taking another step back, they watched the sheet of water arching and bowing in the air. Atasha became agitated, shaking her head and neighing. She reared back and shot a direct stream of fire at the water from her nostrils, bursting a hole through the center of the wave. A cloud of steam misted out, before the wave returned to its previous shape.

"A good effort!" Sarghon shouted, "but the power behind the water is now attached to me and *I* must be the one to stop it."

He felt the connection to the element deep inside – within his loins. Sarghon had been thinking of Kara when he summoned the water, so he knew he must think of something else.

He shifted his thoughts to his childhood. But what childhood was that? He couldn't remember his childhood or his family life. It was a blur. What then should he recall?

A vision of his mother began coming into focus, a woman he hardly recognized, but it quickly vanished. Then, a vision of King Zavior, his … father.

Instantly, the wave burst like a bubble, exploding water in all directions. Hit by the splash, both he and Atasha were now drenched. Atasha shook the water off of her body, beginning with her head and rolling down her entire body. "Well, I guess we both needed a bath then," Sarghon said with a chuckle. "This is certainly the most mysterious element yet. That makes all four elements. We can go now."

Comfortable with the learned movement from the dance, Sarghon mounted Atasha with agility and ease before shooting off in a blaze of fire. Once again, he summoned the funnel of air to create another tunnel for them to fly through, returning to the outside ocean. Sarghon's sodden clothing quickly dried in the warm air and heat generated from Atasha, as they set course back for the mainland.

As they flew, he thought of Malock. *How must I use these abilities to fight the Dark King – my brother?* The last time, Sarghon nearly escaped with his life and he put Kara at great risk. With the newly acquired water element, came heightened emotion in return.

*Kara, where are you now?* he thought. *Do you feel the same way I feel for you when we are together? What does our future hold? Where is Ambroas? Why did he lie to me?*

Sarghon's mind was a torrent of questions, as he looked out toward the vast, azure horizon reflecting in the sunlight. Becoming sleepy, he closed his eyes, feeling the ocean breeze blowing through his hair. His head fell to one side and with the sweet, salty air in his nose, his mind drifted with the whispering wind, as it filled with thoughts of passionate love and fierce battle.

# Chapter XV

## PERCEPTION AND REALITY

As the sun shifted in the sky, the morning turned to afternoon, casting shadows of palm branches across their bodies. The breeze had picked up, and light flurries of sand occasionally swept across Thane's face gently stinging his skin.

He opened his eyes to find his head still in Christian's lap, his vision slowly coming back into focus. He was back in his real body surrounded by Tahitian blue waves crashing on a perfectly serene beach, but his mind was still in another world of flying horses and water goddesses.

"We must have dozed off for a while," Christian said, yawning and stretching his arms. "Looks like the afternoon breeze is picking up too. Man, this place is beautiful."

Seemingly out of nowhere, a hummingbird flew directly between them hovering only feet from their heads, while peered back and forth between their faces. As if defying gravity, the tiny bird floated mid-air; its wings only a blur of motion, its body shimmering like metallic gold and cobalt blue paintbrush strokes.

For a brief, awe-inspiring moment, the world was moving in slow motion with the bird's eyes seemingly saying: *I am here, take deep notice of me, understand me, protect me.*

After one last look directly into Thane's eyes, the bird flew away as fast as it had arrived. "Incredible," Christian said, "he was looking right at us! Did you see that? And where on Earth did he come from? The odds of a hummingbird surviving here are like: a million to one. Man, nature truly is magnificent."

"I love it when those things happen. That was awesome. Hummingbirds seem to follow me wherever I go," Thane smiled. "I think it's connected to what we were talking about the other day."

"I'm all ears."

"Well, I just had another one of my reoccurring dreams," Thane said, sitting back against the coconut palm. "I'm still in a surreal blur of imagery. My dreams are incredibly intense – so detailed and realistic. It takes me a while to acclimate back into this world."

"What was it about?"

"It's a long story. Are you sure you want to ask that question?" Thane chuckled, uneasily. "OK, so remember what we were talking about before, when I told you there was more to my dreams? Well, they say our dreams are connected to what's happening in our lives at that time, resulting in our subconscious trying to make sense of it all, right? When I was sixteen, I began sensing energy around certain things in nature. After my near death accident, it happened more regularly and the energy became personified in my dreams."

Thane looked quizzically at Christian. "I've tried to describe this to a few other people, but not everyone believes me. Words never do it justice. You see, when I fell off that rock a few years ago, I went somewhere."

Christian looked intently at Thane.

"I went to the light," Thane went on, "like so many people talk about when they flat line or have a near death accident. It wasn't one of my crazy dreams or anything like that. When you wake up from a dream, you know you were dreaming. This was real. When I woke up, I knew I had been awake somewhere else."

Thane reached his hand out in front of him with stretched fingers. "I drifted toward this beautiful, soft glowing light. I didn't have a body or anything, just my... my soul, I guess. Not very scientific, I know."

Christian rubbed his eyes. "There's no way to quantify a soul. Sounds pretty wild."

"Right, but there's more," Thane went on. "There's no other way to say this – but recently Aaron, my best friend who died, visited me. He came to me with a message during a lucid dream. It was as real as our conversation is right now. Everything in the dream just froze and he was the only thing in complete focus. In that moment of absolute clarity, I knew I was dreaming. I even asked him, *'Am I dreaming right now, Aaron?'* He answered me, *'Yes, you're dreaming, and I'm real. It's really me, and I'm fine.'*

"Wherever he was, he wanted me to know that he was OK. He also said everything I'm feeling is real – that it's all part of something bigger! He described it as an energy made of love, light and emotion – or something to that effect."

Placing his palm on the trunk of the coconut tree, Thane looked up at the billowing fronds in the breeze.

"I'll never lose all the pain from his death, but when I woke up it felt like the burden had been lifted. I was more at peace with everything. He did that! And I know it was real, because I experienced the same exact feeling of love and light energy when I went to the light – exactly the same. It was like a confirmation."

He paused. "I hope I'm not freaking you out. Sometimes I think I'm brain damaged," Thane said, looking pensively at Christian. "You must think I'm really odd."

"No," Christian said, sincerely, "I think you're lucky. Your experience allowed you to open your mind to something special, scientific or not. If more people could feel as deeply and honestly as you, appreciating all the incredible beauty out there, the world would be a better place."

"Ha! My friend, Angelica said something like that too."

"You aren't damaged; you're an inspiration."

Thane slouched back down against the tree. "Thank you for listening to me Christian. I know there are others who have these feelings. I'm not so special. There's all kinds of people who have unexplained spiritual awakenings."

"I'm sure of it," Christian said. "Spirituality is subjective, based on personal experience not scientific proof. I believe there's more to our lives than meets the eye."

Thane's eyes opened wide. "What about that hummingbird! Why did it come to us like that? Was there really a higher meaning to it or was it random?"

"Scientifically speaking," Christian said, "something attracted it to us, something tangible."

Thane stood up, trying to focus his thoughts. "And energy is tangible. Attraction is tangible, even though it's invisible – the 'Law of Attraction,' right? OK, so then physically and maybe scientifically speaking, interconnectedness to nature must be tangible energy!"

Thane felt a sense of relief. "In my dreams, it's the same way. I connect to the energy of the Earth in all its amazing and incredible beauty. In my dream world, they call it the *Aurora*."

"I think I'm beginning to understand your reaction during our Tarot card reading," Christian said with a smirk. "Human nature is a complicated series of questions, my friend. We're a diverse race for sure. No one person's perception is exactly like another's, and as they say: *your perception is your reality*. It's so very true. That's why we have wars, differing beliefs, religions, morality and immorality. It's all how you look at things. We were born with free will, but human beings can be easily influenced to believe whatever they're taught, whether it's true or not. That's why science and deductive logic are so important.

Christian drew a line in the sand with his finger. "Our mutual global perception of protecting the Earth for the future isn't a reality yet. Earth and humanity are constantly at war, but we don't need to be. One side of human nature makes a case about why we should utilize all our resources, taking what we want from the world in case we need it for ourselves or for power over others. Nuclear bomb testing on his beautiful Polynesian island is a perfect example of that. It's a dog-eat-dog view of the world. But, we could alternatively *choose* the other side, a more peaceful way with environmental protection and mutual respect for the Earth's vast treasures. Which opinion is right? Who is wrong? It's all how you *perceive* the issues by how you were taught to think, behave, and respond."

"It seems clear in my mind which one to choose," Thane said.

"Not always. Remember – perception and reality. If a child is taught by parents to hate a particular race, have certain political opinions or religious beliefs then, most likely, he or she will follow those rules and behaviors into adulthood. On the other hand, if a child is brought up to think for oneself and search for his or her own set of beliefs and truths through free will, then logic and scientific reasoning should play into his or her decisions."

"Free will," Thane said.

"Exactly," Christian replied, "and a desire to find out the truth! The problem is, too many people are *told* what to think – void of our natural human thought process. Fear and hate is a learned behavior after all. It's one of our worst flaws. The result is, humanity not only is the aggressor, but becomes the victim as well."

Smiling at Thane, Christian kicked the sand around with his foot. "But what's amazing about *your* experiences is that no one's imposing them on you. You're experiencing great emotion, connection, and enlightened thoughts without anyone telling you how, when, and why to feel them. They're just part of your life and your natural evolution, spiritual or not."

"I believe they are spiritual," Thane said, "or Godly, or whatever word best describe something indescribable. I know I didn't just create them in my head or imagine them, no matter how imaginative my dreams are. I don't tell the energy when or how to happen, it just happens on its own. But whatever is happening, it's amazing and it's beautiful and … it's important. Angelica had a brilliantly crazy theory that I've been considering as well."

"Have I turned you into a true scientist then?" Christian said with a wink. "What's your theory?"

"Well, remember when we were talking about the energy that surrounds the Earth?

"Yeah."

"So, what if these experiences and other's like mine could be a stepping stone toward the next phase of human evolution? We could be tapping into unused parts of our brain without knowing it. They say we only use a small percentage of our brain, so what if the energy is like a trigger or conduit helping us evolve. That could be what's happening every time people experience super-connectedness like the *Aurora* from my dreams? Could that be possible? Like a fifth element? There must be a scientific explanation, right? Could we actually be tapping into an energy that's been here all the time just waiting for us to evolve to its level?"

"Wow, you're a scientist and a philosopher all in one," Christian said. "I admire your mind. I suppose anything is possible, really. There would need to be extensive tests and studies to validate your theory, as well as concrete scientific evidence. But, I like where you're going here with this. The other day I tested the radiation levels of a coconut tree, and wouldn't you know, the milk of the coconut was less polluted than the bark and leaves of the tree. It was a perfect example of nature fighting back against chaos. It was healing itself, filtering out the radiation, evolving past the turmoil of pollutants."

"I wish we could communicate with the Earth," Thane said. "It would make things so much easier."

"Maybe the energy you're talking about IS nature's way of communicating," Christian said. "That would be something. Miraculous things happen in nature all by themselves, without added chemicals, influences, or biases. Nature is my miracle – my God. When I'm out in the majesty of nature looking up at the giant redwoods, hiking a tropical waterfall, or at the top of a crisp, clean, snow covered mountain – that's *my* church."

"Amen to that."


Approaching the end of their week on Mururoa, with only one day left before their scheduled pick up at the rendezvous spot, Thane spotted two boats anchored on the far side of the atoll near the military buildings.

"Well, I don't think there's more than two boats out there beyond the barracks," Thane said, looking through his binoculars. "They look like Coast Guard or something similar."

"Military commandos, most likely," Christian replied, grabbing another set of binoculars. "I can make out a few numbers on the side of the ships, but we're too far away to see any names. My guess would be military scouts. But they aren't like any I've seen around here before. These are bigger. Looks like they're about ninety-footers. We need to take a closer look!"

"My camera has a nice zoom lens on it. I'll take some pics," Thane said, getting excited.

The light from the stars and moon created enough light to see at night without a flashlight. They would be able to scope things out covertly while still being dark enough to stay out of sight.

Having collected more than enough samples, measurements, and readings, Christian was certain Captain Parker would be pleased with the scientific intel. They packed up most of the gear, equipment, and samples, then discussed their evening plan over a dinner of Top Ramen noodles with celery, carrots, and sliced hotdogs seasoned with Christian's own blend of seasoning from the ship.

"Alright," Thane mumbled, mouth full of noodles, "we need to find out what these guys are up to – get the low-down on their next move. I took two years of French in high school, but I'm not sure what I remember. I was too busy staring at my crush in the front row."

"Well, my French isn't much better. If we can get close enough to hear them, one of us should be able to pick up some info. If they're planning a test soon, we need to know about it, get the word back to Greenpeace and hopefully do something about it before it happens. We need to be careful Thane," Christian said earnestly. "We can't be found out. It'll be a risky move creeping up on these guys at night. Our readings and samples need to reach the *Black Pig*. The Captain's depending on it."

"I can do it," Thane said with bravado.

"We'll do it together. I'm responsible for you, remember?"

Dressed in dark clothing, they packed one small backpack with water, binoculars, gloves, pencil, paper, and a small med kit before hiking along the rim of the tropical crater, keeping as quiet as possible. Stepping in rhythmic pace, the two moved quickly and quietly for several miles.

With the boats only three miles down the atoll rim, Thane's blood rushed faster with each step, his body filling with adrenalin. "What if they're planning to set off another bomb test while we're here?" Thane asked in a hushed whisper. "How would we get away?"

"Tomorrow's our last day here," Christian said. *"The MV Greenpeace,* along with her convoy, will arrive across the no-sail barrier to the lagoon rendezvous location at twelve noon. No doubt they'll cause some commotion. But if there *is* a test scheduled for tomorrow, we need to know about it, pronto. As a last precaution we have flares to let them know someone's here on the island, but I'd really love to keep our covert business to ourselves. The two military boats make me nervous enough. They usually don't come here unless something's about to happen."

"Then let's get a move on."

Thane picked up the pace as they traveled silently for the next mile careful not to make any obvious signs to their movement. With less than a quarter of a mile from the buildings and boats, they stopped to take a breath. "We're nearly there," Thane said impatiently, before taking a sip of water.

"Keep your voice down, eager beaver," Christian said, catching his breath. "We don't know how many of them are around and we have to keep ourselves … ahhhh."

Christian's voice trailed off over Thane's shoulder before he had time to whip his head around to find Christian no longer behind him. Christian had slipped off the ridge of the trail into a ravine. "Where are you?" Thane yelled in a soft whisper.

"Down here," Christian replied laboriously, before Thane found him in a ditch grasping his ankle.

"Are you OK? What happened?"

"The ridge gave way and I slipped. I think I may have screwed

235

up my ankle pretty bad."

"Here, give me your hand," Thane said, reaching for Christian, pulling him out of a ravine carved into the hillside by rainwater.

Sitting on the trail together, Christian gave Thane a regretful look. "I'm sorry 'bout that. I guess Hercules isn't all-powerful."

"Do you think it's broken?" Thane asked with concern.

"No, but I can't put weight on it. Hurts like a motherfucker. You'll have to go on without me. Don't be a hero though," Christian said, massaging his ankle. "Do you hear me? Just get whatever intel you can, and get your ass back here. You know exactly where I'll be. Take the gloves and large binoculars; you'll need 'em. I'll wrap my ankle and stay here, but I'll be watching you with the other pair, so don't do anything stupid like I just did."

"You sound like my mother," Thane said with a crooked smile. "Don't worry, just take care of that ankle."

Reaching into his pack, Thane placed his camera around his neck. "I'll take some pictures. I want my family and friends to know I wasn't just on a tropical holiday. Plus, the captain will want to see this shit!"

"Be smart."

"I'll be back," Thane whispered while putting on the gloves. Dressed in dark colors with his camera and binoculars dangling around his neck, he looked like a Peeping Tom as he scurried off.


As he approached the compound, Thane saw two main buildings, both of which had lights on inside. The military boats were anchored just off the coast along with two motor skiffs beached on the shore. Thane noticed smoke burning from a lagoon- side campfire behind the buildings. Surveying the surroundings with his binoculars, he assessed no motion in his immediate vicinity. Gingerly approaching the compound, he kept low to the ground and out of sight.

When he came around the barracks, Thane discovered six men sitting around the campfire as well as shadows from others inside one of the buildings. Still too far away to hear what they were saying, he crept in closer.

Flames from the campfire flickered against the building casting shadows across the beach, as Thane quietly crawled along the brush. Creeping up to the barracks, Thane took some photos of the buildings and men. Out of sight from the men sitting around the fire, he scurried along a wall and hid between the two buildings.

Seven steps led to the door of the building on the right. He went up six steps before hearing several voices inside. Deciding that was a bad idea, Thane quietly went back down toward the front. Moving in even closer, he could see the men around the campfire smoking cigarettes and chatting. Opening the backpack, he took out the paper and pencil.

"Tu devrais respire profondement," *("You should breathe in hard,")* one Frenchman said. La fumée provenant de votre cigarette est meilleur pour vous que la fumée de l'incendie." *("The smoke from your cigarette is better for you than that of the fire.")*

The men chuckled. "Demain, nous allons être loin. Je ne sais pas ce que le lieutenant veut nous sauver de ce naufrage rock, mais si les tests sont de continuer, ils peuvent les effectuer lorsque nous sommes rentrés," *("Tomorrow, we'll be far away. I don't know what the Lieutenant wants us to salvage from this sinking rock, but if the tests are to continue, they can do them when we are back home,")* a man on the right said.

"Je vais prendre la maison un noix de coco radioactifs. C'est la seule chose qui reste ici," *("I'll take home a radioactive coconut. It's the only thing left here,")* another man on the left said, before they chuckled again.

"Trop dommage que cette ile ne sera jamais un resort de vacances. Ce serait beau, tu sais?" *("Too bad this island will never be a vacation resort. It could be nice, you know?")*

"Bien, je ne veux pas être n'importe où près d'ici, lorsque le prochain test a lieu. Ne devrions-nous pas être quitter maintenant?" *("Well, I don't want to be anywhere near here when the next test takes place. Shouldn't we be leaving now?")* another commented.

With Thane's two years of mentally aloof French classes, he was only able to pick up a list of random words from their conversation. He made out: *smoke, cigarette, fire, tomorrow, Lieutenant, salvage, tests, continue, radioactive, coconut, bad, island, vacation, I don't want, here, leaving,* and *now.* All were words that didn't sound good.

The men from the building came outside joining the group around the fire pit. When the coast was clear, Thane quietly slipped into the building where the men had just been. It was a small room with random, antiquated radio receiving equipment. A desk sat in the corner with a single chair. He rifled through the drawers, but only found old pencils, a roll of tape, and a rusty stapler. A modest bathroom sat off the left side of the room with the door slightly ajar.

Thane walked toward the bathroom before carefully opening the door. It was dirty inside, with a rusty toilet and a broken window. Debris had been scattered on the floor. He picked up a few pieces of wilted paper and stuffed them in his pocket before hearing one of the men approach.

Catching his breath, Thane quietly closed the door to the bathroom just as the man entered. He went straight for the bathroom door and opened it. Standing frozen behind the door, Thane held his breath as the man stared at the dirty toilet shouting back to his comrades, "Je retiendrai ma pisse jus qu'au retour sur le bateau. Cette merde de toilette, ne vaut pas ma proper merde. C'est degoutant." *("I'm going to hold it until I get back on the boat. This piece of shit toilet isn't worth my own shit. It's disgusting!")*

He turned around and exited the building. Thane had been holding his breath the entire time, finally letting it out with a relieved huff. With his heart pounding hard, he crawled through the broken bathroom window and up to the roof, having understood what the Frenchman said without knowing every word.

From his new vantage point, he took a few more photos as he watched the men gather the two skiffs before heading back to their ships. With a sense of relief, Thane crawled to the edge of the roof and jumped down to the ground, his heart still pounding hard in his chest. "That was close," he said softly to himself, before stealthily making his way back to Christian.


Following back the way he came, Thane found Christian sitting on a fallen palm tree near where Thane left him. "What's the word good buddy?" Christian said.

"Not exactly sure, but it didn't sound good," Thane said, pulling a folded piece of paper from his pocket. "I wrote down these words: *smoke, fire, tomorrow, Lieutenant, salvage, tests, continue, radioactive, coconut, bad, island, vacation, I don't want, here, leaving, and now.* Oh, and *cigarette.* Sorry my French isn't up to par, but when you put those all together it sounds bad."

"Well, all I heard just now from your lips was: 'tests continue, radioactive, bad, leaving now.' That's all I need to know. We need to get outta here – soon!"

Thane gathered the contents of the pack together before helping Christian to his feet. "Put your arm around my shoulder," Thane ordered. Christian obliged, hobbling in pain as he grabbed hold of Thane for support. "I found something else," Thane said, "a few pieces of paper from the bathroom."

"You went into the building?"

"I thought I would find more. It was pretty empty – just an old desk with an old radio. The bathroom had some papers on the floor, so I grabbed these."

Thane produced two dirty, crumpled pieces of paper from his pocket. "Not sure exactly what they say, but I can make out some dates," Thane said.

"Hmm, if I'm correct," Christian said, "you've discovered an old laundry list and let's see – this one looks like an invoice for provisions. Good work Watson, but not what you had hoped, I gather."

"Not exactly. Guess that doesn't help us at all, then. Damn it!"

"It's OK. You did good. You heard enough to make me sufficiently nervous. Alright, help me back to camp and let's get stoned. This ankle hurts like hell and I need to think."

With Thane's help, after several hours and thousands of arduous, painful steps on Christian's injured foot, they made it safely back to their camp. Thane finished packing up the rest of their belongings while Christian sparking up a joint, hoping to relax his ankle.

Exhausted, Thane finally laid down. "I had an incredible time with you here," Thane said, sliding into his comfy sleeping bag. "It's something I'll never forget – ever."

"Me either, Thaney. This was truly awesome, man. You're really a great guy; you know that? You feel like a little brother to me. I have this crazy urge to protect you – like family."

Thane leaned over and gave him a hug. "Me too, like family."

"I think we've done something good here buddy," Christian said, passing Thane the joint. "The world needs to know what's happening way out here in the middle of the ocean – the truth, ya know? The information we gathered will shock some folks; but more than that, it'll shed more light on what the reality of nuclear testing is doing to this eco system and why it should be stopped. People need to open their damn eyes."

"Yeah, they do. Just leave that flare gun in plane sight. If we suddenly wake up to sirens, one of us can let them know we're here before getting blown to smithereens."

"We'll be on our way by then, for sure. The convoy flotilla will arrive like an international freedom parade. It'll be 'glorious', as the Captain said. The Frenchmen won't know what to think," Christian said with pride. "Oh, and I'll leave it up to you to spread out the Greenpeace flag before we leave. It's a huge one! It's in that black pack over there against the tent wall. Just place it in a visible spot on the sandy beach so aircraft can see it clearly. Put heavy rocks all around the border so it doesn't blow away. It's really big, so once we've gone, the world will know we've been here."

"It's too bad, ya know," Thane said, solemnly. "I don't think those guys on the beach even knew what was about to happen or why they were sent out here. They were just enjoying themselves like any normal guys, laughing and sitting around a campfire on the beach. If people knew all the facts, I don't think everyone in France would agree with what's going on out here."

"Not all of them do. That's why we're here, my boy," Christian said, unzipping the top portion of the tent so they could view the breathtaking spectacle of stars splayed out before them on their last night together on the island.

They both laid back staring up at the magnificent expanse of the brilliant Milky Way, as the stars looked back with millions of sparkling eyes. The warm Tahitian night air made for a perfect temperature, as soft waves crashed in the distance. Mesmerized by the stars and exhausted from the day's activities, they both silently drifted into the unconscious.

# Chapter XVI

## THE UNVEILED TRUTH

The crisp morning air swelled across mountain reeds that peeked over the hillside, billowing in rippling waves along the precipitous landscape. The deep red-orange sky beckoned with beams of sunlight, casting long, translucent fingers through the outstretched ethereal clouds.

With Sarghon on her strong, muscular back, Atasha walked cautiously across the tall grass. Ambroas had sent a message through the trees asking him to meet atop a particular hill.

"There, just ahead," Sarghon said, pointing in front of him. That's the meeting place Ambroas informed us of."

The tall blades of grass bent away on either side, forming a path through the bending reeds leading to the top of a grassy knoll. Atasha reared back suspiciously. "It's OK girl. The flora is on our side. The path is being shown to us." Patting and stroking her neck lovingly, they walked up the newly formed pathway toward the hilltop. *Ambroas has some explaining to do,* he thought as he approached the peak.

It only took a few minutes to reach the hilltop overlooking a vast rock garden surrounded by a large, lush forest. The monolithic stones peered up from the trees like tall, narrow eggs; some of which held spherical stones balancing on top of oblong shapes, teasing the eye that they would fall. A great meadow lay in the far-off distance.

Surveying the surroundings, Sarghon watched a small flock of blue and yellow birds fly out from the woods as a man approached wearing a long, brown, hooded cloak.

It was Ambroas. "Ahh, Sarghon, my long lost friend. I see you have had many adventures since last we spoke young master. I hope you fare well. And what a gallant steed you ride."

Stopping ten paces from them, Ambroas bowed toward Atasha. She then bowed in return before he approached. "Atasha, it is indeed a rare and privileged honor to make your acquaintance. I am Ambroas."

"She agrees with you," Sarghon said curtly, speaking for Atasha.

"Ahh yes – as well she would," he replied, somewhat awkwardly. "And I am happy to see you looking so well after your foolish maneuver to seek out Malock face to face. Yes, dear lad, the trees talk! It was a risk you should not have taken until you were ready. Have you forgotten our lessons?" he said with a flamboyant hand gesture.

"Time is of the essence!" Ambroas went on, "The Dark King approaches from the north destroying everything in his path. I have gathered able villagers from over a hundred leagues in all directions to help us fight the impending battle. They only await our arrival. Have you acquired and learned to control all four elemental powers?"

Sarghon was silent for a moment before responding. "Such an all knowing wizard as yourself should know the answer to that."

"As I do," Ambroas replied. "And I am very proud of you for your accomplishments and bravery. I knew you had it within you. You have grown in more ways than one. Come, we must talk."


Ambroas led Thane and Atasha to a wooded area protected from view where he had been camping for several days awaiting their arrival. A small campfire smoldered under a teakettle hanging from a wooden stick. A pot of Ambroas's famous rabbit stew sat on a rock near a splayed blanket with a jug of wine, hand carved utensils, and a satchel with bread and cheese.

"Please, come join me lad," Ambroas asked, sitting cross-legged on the blanket. "I made a lovely rabbit and wild mushroom stew for your arrival. You must be hungry. Please, please eat."

After dismounting Atasha, Sarghon sat next to Ambroas in silence. An awkward tension filled the air between them. Taking a deep breath, Sarghon finally spoke. "I am glad to see you well. I know I shouldn't have faced Malock so soon, but I wanted to know what I was up against. *Know your enemy* – one of your many lessons. Besides, I had Kara with me."

Frustrated, Sarghon paused before asking what was really on his mind. "Why did you lie to me? Why didn't you tell me Malock was my brother? Does he speak the truth; do we really share a father? Why in all these years would you not reveal this to me? Help me to understand!"

"Your questions are all valid and I will do my best to answer them all; however, you must understand that I had little choice in the

242

matter. You were to be protected at all cost. That is what was *most* important."

Handing Sarghon a mug of stew, Ambroas continued. "You have grown in this short time, young man. I can see it in your eyes. I knew you would find the elementals. Others doubted me, but I had complete faith in you. Now, please let me explain fully before you judge my actions."

Ambroas pulled his S-shaped pipe from his cloak sleeve and filled it with a wad of herb before lighting it with a magical wave of his hand. "I will answer your most immediate question first: yes, you share a father with Malock, but I did not lie when I told you he was no brother of yours. You may share the blood of our previous King, but family is much more than a mere bloodline. A brother is someone you can trust, someone you know intrinsically without doubt, who would do anything for you because of your bond. A brother is made from a union of knowledge and integrity. Malock does not know you – nor you him. He's a stranger as well as an opponent. He harbors a darkness within him that you were not born with. He set out to destroy you from the time he knew of your existence. A true brother would never want to harm his brother. Malock is manipulative, cunning, and dangerous. So, I did not lie entirely."

Ambroas sat down on a rock near the campfire. "Malock was not always evil," he said, taking a puff from his pipe. "I was his teacher when he was a child. I was Personal Magical Advisor to the King and mentor to his son. The boy grew up in the kingdom like most normal privileged children – nothing too unusual. As you may know, King Zavior and his wife, Queen Mariel were good people ruling over a stable and prosperous land. The King was an empath, able to know when people told the truth or were dishonest. He also felt their joy and pain as well as a variety of other emotions. He used his ability to keep the kingdom in check. With me as his senior advisor, there was peace and prosperity in our land."

"What of Malock? Sarghon asked.

"Malock inherited a special aptitude from his father. He had the ability to heal. He would heal wounded animals as well as cuts and injuries sustained by his family and friends. It took his own energy to do so, leaving him weak after each healing. I showed him ways to harness energy from the wilderness to employ instead of his own energy. After many lessons, he learned how to gently absorb energy from trees, shrubs, and other various plants, utilizing it for his healings. He never took too much. The plant or tree would recover after only a few days. I was his mentor and his friend. He was a fast and smart learner, apt and clever. But that all changed."

"What happened?" Sarghon asked eagerly.

"Your mother happened. She was the King's nurse. Her name was Aubrey. She was a pretty little thing with auburn hair and green eyes. She had a kindness about her that people are only born with. Naturally, she drew the King's affection and since he was extremely charismatic, she came to love him as well. They would meet in private or while the Queen was away from the palace on weekend hunting and nature trips. It didn't take long for their affection to become intimate. I tried to sway his behavior, warning him of the precarious consequences, but Aubrey was with child before The King could stop himself. I advised King Zavior to let her return to her village where she could have the child unawares, but he kept her near to him. When she began to show, I insisted she be taken out of the kingdom for her own safety. He finally yielded to reason and I took her back to the country village where she grew up. At that point, no one knew the truth about the affair and she had the child, you – born in her village on the morning of the third day of the third month of the third millennium. You are quite aware of the details of that moment. When I found out the aspects of your birth, I placed protection spells around you, keeping a keen eye on your upbringing."

"What happened to my mother? And why can't I remember any of this?"

"I'm getting to that. Patience is a virtue," Ambroas said, with another puff from his s-shaped pipe. "I wanted you to have a normal childhood growing up in a quaint village with amiable people around you. Of course, no one could know who your true father was. I insisted Aubrey keep that secret to her grave. Not a soul could know of your circumstance or your prophetic station. It would have placed you in danger and Aubrey knew that as well. She was a good girl, doing as I commanded. The King wanted to visit her, but I would not allow it, never revealing where she was living or any information about you. He was extremely cross with me, and as his powers did not work on my mind, he threatened to use his empathic ability to go from village to village looking for the truth. But, he knew it would have looked suspicious to the Queen and to his son. As it was, he suffered in silent longing.

"The years passed and Malock grew into a man and you into an active boy. I became your teacher and advisor. Then, the moment I most

244

feared happened – the King could no longer live with his secret. It had eaten away at him inside, like a cankerous, burrowing sore. Being the inherently honest man that he was, he decided to tell the Queen and Malock about Aubrey and his bastard son. The Queen's reaction was extreme and she flew into a hysterical rage. She went mad with anger and jealousy, shocking her into frantic insanity. Malock had just turned twenty. He didn't know what to think about the King's imprudence at the time, so he distanced himself from his father. The Queen sent her soldiers to find Aubrey, but they were unsuccessful. She doubled her efforts each week, still coming up empty handed. The King was useless to stop her, retreating to his chambers in shame. Having nothing to go on and without any results, Queen Mariel went completely mad, ripping out her hair and scratching at her skin. Malock healed her of course, trying to bring her back to sanity, but his efforts were futile."

"So, Malock was caring."

"At that time, yes. But a dark anger grew inside him and he changed. He witnessed his family being crushed by betrayal and sadness. I tried to console him, but my presence was not welcome. After two years, the Queen's men finally found your mother. She had Aubrey taken from your village and publicly executed – stoned to death. You were there, you saw everything."

"But, I can't ..."

"I am getting to that now! You were fourteen. You didn't understand what was happening or why soldiers murdered your mother. I needed to keep you safe and that was my first priority. You could not be told of your true heritage, your birthright, or of the prophesy at that time. You were not ready and it would have devastated you. I decided to cast a memory spell in order to protect you. I took away the thoughts of your mother's murder, your childhood, and most of your early years, replacing them with memories of growing up the nephew of a carpenter and his wife. I brought you to my home village where dear friends raised you these past few years, as I continued on as your teacher. Your only memories are of growing up in the woods with your aunt and uncle in the village where we live."

"Then, they are not my real relatives, only a magical recollection of them being so?"

"Yes, I am afraid that is the truth. I devised an elegant solution to a not so elegant situation. For that, I am truly sorry. But I saw no alternative."

Sarghon sat silently staring into space for several moments before responding. "I wish I remembered the years you took from me – my mother – but I understand why you did what you did. If you hadn't, I may not be alive now and we would be at the mercy of a twisted, rampant madman."

"If there had been another way I would have considered it, but there was no time, and as I have said so many times already, your safety was my most important task. Perhaps one day there may be a way to restore your memory, but now is not that time."

Staring through the forest of maroobi pines, Sarghon noticed the silhouette of Atasha backlit by the stone garden as he pondered all that had occurred in his life, grateful he had such capable friends looking out for him.

"Thank you, old friend," Sarghon said. "I know now that you were only protecting me. I never asked for this position or life path, but who ever does? We are like ships sailing into uncharted waters, not knowing where we will venture or what we will find next on our journey."

"Fate is a dispassionate beast, my boy," Ambroas said shrewdly, "unfettered, detached and unbiased toward consequence, yet steadfast in her constitution. You will find that no path is the incorrect one, for they all lead to the next place you happen to find yourself. And in so saying, forgive me for hastily accusing you of being a fool to face Malock, for it is exactly where fate placed you at that moment in time. And who am I but a foolish old man to say what fate and time have in store? I leave that to those who prophesize. But never forget, although we cannot control our fate, we *are* in control of the decisions we make. So, I can at least say that it was a foolish decision, yes?"

Sarghon nodded with a guilty grin. "Yes, my wise and wily friend, it was. But, I now know what I am up against. Malock is as crafty as you say and very powerful. It will take everything I have to defeat him."

"You will need to think differently than he, using your new gifts in ways he may not be prepared to defend. You control the Earth, air, water and fire. They can be combined to enhance each other."

"We have another powerful weapon on our side – the Valkyrie. Kara, daughter of the Valkyrian Queen, has an army of mighty flying soldiers awaiting my signal to attack. She and I have become friends – good friends."

"Indeed," Ambroas said, looking at Atasha. "Powerful magical females seem to be drawn to you. That is fortunate for us both," he said, with another grin, "and not too soon. We must sleep tonight, eat, and rest. Malock is on the move and will reach our bordering lands in three days time. We must be prepared to meet him. My civilian army is stationed two leagues from here at the base of Maderian Field, ready to fight for their land and people. Our problem, however, is a tricky one. Most of Malock's army consists of our own brainwashed brethren; thus, we will be fighting our own people. We cannot harm them, Sarghon. We must find a way to diffuse their onslaught without hurting any of them too coarsely. Once Malock is powerless, his influence over them should be released. As I mentioned, we are up against a precarious quandary. Tonight we will discuss several options, sparing as many lives as we can. My army knows of whom they fight and will attempt to subdue them without deadly force. Malock will be left to you, and as the prophecy states, *you, and you alone will face him*. But all in good time. Eat now, young prince. My stew is simply delectable!"

For the remainder of the night, Ambroas and Sarghon discussed strategies for battle, interrupted by stories of Sarghon's past several months of adventures. By the end of the evening before settling down to sleep, Sarghon informed Atasha of the plan. She agreed to help as best she could. Their bond had grown and his attachment to the beautiful and magnificent beast had become psychic in nature. Most of the time he was able to read her temperament and disposition. She, in turn, would predict his actions by measuring his mood and behavior. Their connection was most keen while in flight, due to the fire-bond's symbiotic nature, allowing them to mentally speak with one another.

Sarghon walked up to an old and wise tree, hoping magical tree sprites might inhabit the treetops or live in the bark. He needed their help in delivering the information to Kara.

Placing his hand on the knotted bark, Sarghon reached out to the ancient tree and spoke, *"Caranath, to shonosh vaarashta. Weneth-toeyna Sargonath ey Ambrosenath, ko toeyney Valkyrenath Karanath aat shevnesha slothenethta. Dotan ey shootesh whorethesta, aat Miderianath. Sprethnana Scyllianathta vas toeneth, ra. Warana ssleneth to spiriteneth. Earanath shantana toranth shoonashtua."* (Great wise one, I ask your humble assistance. A message must be sent from Sarghon and Ambroas to the Valkyrian Princess, Kara, to meet us for battle at the great Maderian Field at the border of the Scyllian Mountains at dawn in two days time. Send the tree sprites quickly to this task. Thank you my friends, and may the earthen spirits be with us all.)

The tree acknowledged the request and answered: *"Aray senoteth. Earanath shantana toranth shoonashta."* (As you wish, chosen one. May the earthen spirits be with you.)

Ambroas walked up to Sarghon, placing his hand on his shoulder. "I am proud of you," Ambroas said sincerely. "All these years I have kept you hidden from sight and from your destiny. I want you to know it has been with a heavy heart that I have done so. I never meant to deceive you or lie to you. You came to me out of destiny and I think of you as a son."

Sarghon's eyes welled up with tears as he leaned over to Ambroas and gave him a heartfelt hug. "All is forgiven. It seems you also had a destiny… watching over me."

"Indeed."

The light suddenly changed as wind and leaves swept around Sarghon's feet in gentle, whirling patterns. Ambroas turned in the direction of the old tree. "I sense something peculiar coming from the wood," he said walking away.

Staring frozen in his tracks, Sarghon watched the colors of the forest shift as if the contrast had been suddenly turned up. The whirling leaves began to move in slow motion, spinning more and more slowly until they were floating inches above the ground, barely moving at all. The trees and surrounding background became but a blur – all except the one old tree he had been talking to.

He watched a figure step out from behind the tree. She was a middle-aged woman wearing a beautiful flowing dress. She appeared like a watercolor painting coming to life, stepping forward and focusing her attention on Sarghon. With flawless, mocha skin and clear, beautiful, brown eyes, there was something very familiar about her.

Sarghon stood mesmerized. *I know you,* he thought. *But you are … could it be?* "Angelica? How are you here?" he said, glancing around at the blurred surroundings, then back at Angelica. "I'm dreaming, aren't I?"

"Yes you are," she replied. "I wanted to check up on you – to see how you're fairing on your quest."

"Sarghon's or Thane's?" he said with a smile. "I miss you."

He embraced her. She appeared healthy and strong, filled with natural beauty and life. "I'm so proud of you, my boy," she said. "You have such a passion and drive in you. You will go far. You've been so special to me. Know that, always."

"And you know you're special to me. Wait ..."

He came to a sudden realization. "If you're here, then you must be ... are you ...?" His heart sank for a beat.

"You are such a wise one, honey. I had to come and see you. You knew I would when the time was right. I'll be there whenever you want to talk. Just talk away and I'll be listening."

She gave him a hug. Thane felt her kindness, love, and sincerity. "I know you will be," he replied, looking back at her with only love in his eyes.

"I can't stay long. Just long enough for you to know that I'm OK. I'm good with my life and you'll be OK as well. Live in the love that's all around you. That's the message, my dear. Be at peace with this in your life and with the emotions inside you. Always treat yourself with the respect you deserve."

She hugged him again.

"Please, can you stay longer? I want more time," he begged.

"I have to go now, darl'in. But you were right about the things we discussed. There's more to it all than most people know. Follow your feelings and instincts. You're guided by your ability to love. That's the key. Follow your heart, child. You're on the right road."

"I love you," he said, as she began fading away.

"And I love you, always and forever."

With a last little wave, Angelica gave him a loving nod. As her image gently faded into the background, the forest slowly came back into view. The leaves started to twirl again, floating silently to the ground. Ambroas was only a shadow, as the forest slowly disappeared into a ghostly blur. Then, it all vanished.

# Chapter XVII

## THE CHASE

Thane lay paralyzed, unable to move his arms or legs. His body felt as though it were floating six inches above the ground. Although his eyes were still closed, they were filled with warm tears dripping down his face.

Thane was in the *Aurora*. His visit with Angelica filled him with powerful emotion and love, mixed with that indescribable sense of understanding. The energy still permeated throughout his entire body as he realized in the moment that, once again, these were the very same overwhelming emotions and feelings he experienced during his near death experience years before. It was happening again right here and now in full force.

Slowly his body responded, gradually coming back into his skin – back to the reality of where he was and what had just occurred. Tears of joy and sadness still streamed down his face, realizing that Angelica's visit from beyond meant she had passed away. Now he knew without a doubt that Aaron's visit had been real as well.

Reaching to wipe his eyes, Thane heard a voice in the distance. It was speaking French. Snapping out of his euphoric state, he gingerly sat up in his sleeping bag. Christian was still asleep next to him as Thane sat frozen, listening. The only word he could make out was: *American football*.

Thane grabbed Christian's arm. "Christian, Christian," he said in an urgent whisper, placing his hand over Christian's mouth. "Don't say a word. They've discovered us."

Christian stirred into semi-consciousness. "Huh?" he said, slowly opening his eyes.

"The football. We must have left it out on the lagoon beach," Thane said quietly. "They found it. From what I gather, they haven't made our location yet, but it's only a matter of time."

Their tent had been camouflaged with brush and palm leaves, as was their skiff parked on the ocean side two hundred meters away.

Sitting up in his sleeping bag, Christian grabbed his binoculars. He slowly crept outside the tent's entrance, looking in the direction of the voices. Through the binoculars he located the sandy beach where he and Thane had been throwing the ball on the lagoon side of the atoll. Christian saw three men on the beach throwing the football to each other.

One pointed, saying, "*Empreintes de pieds*" (footprints). They stopped playing and began looking around.

"We're in trouble," Christian said, re-entering the tent. "We need to get outta here – pronto. There's two dinghies on the beach and they've begun looking around. They know someone's here."

"I have an idea," Thane said, eagerly putting on his clothes before quickly gathered up the rest of his belongings, stuffing them into his pack. "How long until our Greenpeace convoy arrives?"

"Two hours or so," Christian said, looking down at his watch.

"OK, can you get all this stuff to our boat by yourself? How's your ankle?"

"Not without being discovered," Christian said. "I'm still limping pretty bad. What are ya think'in Thaney boy?"

Thane glanced over at the large equipment box. "I can carry the heavy box with all the samples to our boat before they discover us. If you can gather the rest of this stuff and get the skiff out on the ocean side, I'll create a diversion. I'll steal one of their boats and drive it out into the lagoon. They'll follow me in the other one. Then you can escape on the ocean side to meet the convoy. They'll be too busy chasing me around the lagoon to notice you."

Christian looked at Thane with a blank stare, assessing whether his insane plan could actually work or not. "You're either out of your mind or brilliant … or both," Christian said, with a wary smile.

"I'll still take the flag," Thane said, "I have an idea of what I want to do with it."

Thane grabbed the backpack with the flag, stuffed in a bottle of water, binoculars, and some snacks, before packing up the remainder of their belongings. Christian kept guard, peeking out from time to time, judging how far away the French scouts had come to their camp.

"OK, is the coast clear?" Thane said, hurriedly chewing on a fruit roll-up. "Can I take the equipment and samples box out to our skiff?"

"I have two guys in view and they're getting closer," Christian said, "maybe a couple hundred yards or so. You better go now. Just stay out of sight and be back ASAP."

"Righty-O," Thane responded, making an OK sign with his fingers.

He dragged the heavy box out from the tent, across the backside of the small hill toward the ocean beach area where their skiff was parked under a camouflage of branches and palm fronds. So far the coast was clear.

He brushed branches off one side of the boat before lifting the box inside. Running back to the tent, Thane heard mumbled voices getting closer.

"OK, step one complete," Thane said, diving into the tent. "Are you sure you're gonna be alright with the rest of this stuff?"

"I'm a gimp, but I'm not completely useless," Christian replied. "If you can lure them away, I'm good to go with the rest of this stuff. I give your crazy plan a fifty/fifty chance of succeeding – but it's pretty awesome. Not sure if I would've thought it up on my own."

Christian flashed a smile as he limped over to Thane. "Listen, be careful will you? I don't want anything bad happening to my little buddy. You mean a lot to me. I'll never forget this adventure with you," Christian said, giving Thane a hug. "When this is all over, you and I are gonna take a vacation together. Somewhere where there's no canned soup, global economic warfare, or radioactive coconuts."

"You're the best, man. Thanks for being such a great guy," Thane replied with another hug. "You're *my* brother. Now get back to the Greenpeace and have them pick me up from the oilrig. I'll be waiting there. Later alligator."

Grabbing the black backpack and Frisbee, Thane ran toward the lagoon.


On one side of the atoll lagoon stood a tall rusty oilrig, not used for drilling oil, but used to drill holes into the mantle of coral for underground tests and possibly for depositing radioactive materials. It stood approximately one hundred and fifty feet into the air, sticking out of the lagoon like a giant rusty erector set. It would serve as the beacon and final destination point for the MV Greenpeace and its convoy of international protest ships. It also played a part in Thane's audacious plan.

Making his way down the beach toward the lagoon, Thane found two outboard motor dinghies with pull-start Evinrude motors, a kind that he had started and driven before.

The scouts were roughly a hundred yards away, headed directly for Christian and their camp. Thane had only moments to create his diversion.

Crawling along the bushes and rocks toward the beach, Thane gauged the wind was blowing easterly in the direction of the lagoon coast. He figured if he threw the Frisbee at the right angle, it would catch the wind and soar back down the beach, away from the dinghies.

This, however, all depended on Thane's ability to throw a Frisbee properly. He wasn't the finest Frisbee player in the world, but he believed his tactic could work – at least in theory.

Watching the scouts heading up the sandy slope toward their camp, Thane had to act fast. Testing the air once again with his finger, all seemed good to go. "Here goes nothing," he whispered to himself. With that bit of confirmation, Thane knelt down, wound his arm around the Frisbee, and with all his might released it at a sharp angle high into the sky.

The plastic disk caught the wind, taking flight high above his head.

*What if they don't see it?* he suddenly thought to himself. *I hadn't taken that into account.* Watching with baited breath, Thane saw the Frisbee soar over the Frenchmen's heads, landing back on the beach.

"Please, please," he whispered in prayer.

Just then, he heard the men shout, "Il n'y a, regardez là-bas. Qu'est-ce que c'est? Rapidement, nous devons voir," *("There, look over there. What is that? Quickly, we must see,")* as they ran in the direction of the Frisbee.

*It worked,* he thought.

Thane sprinted down the beach toward the two French outboards running as fast as he could, while the men ran in the opposite direction toward the Frisbee. Once he reached the first dinghy, he tossed his bag in the boat, pushed it straight into the water, and hopped in.

Within moments, the men realized the scheme, running back in Thane's direction. He pushed the choke in and out a few times on the engine before pulling the starter chord on the motor. On the third pull it started. He was off!

He shot full throttle into the lagoon along the inner rim. It took the men a full minute to run across the beach, hop in, and start the second boat. Thane was half a mile away before they were after him.

They followed his boat path around the inner edge of the lagoon for some time. His plan was working.

Meanwhile, Christian made trips back and forth to their skiff with the rest of their gear and bags, completely undetected. He broke down the tent as fast as he could, stuffed it into its polyester bag and hobbled to their skiff before tossing everything in with a hurried rush. Still in a good amount of pain, Christian focused diligently on his mission while looking down at his watch. It was approaching eleven AM. With a last look toward the lagoon, he mumbled, "Thaney Boy, I hope you know what the hell you're doing. You better get out of this in one piece."

Painstakingly, he pushed the skiff into the small, lapping waves while hopping on one foot, before starting up the motor and heading out into the open ocean.


Jetting along the inner lagoon coastline, Thane gunned the motor at its top speed. The three Frenchmen weren't far behind. Being the only person in his boat, Thane was rear heavy, not planing well in the water – thus, allowing the chasing boat to catch up quickly.

Having led the other boat along the shoreline, he approached a sharp turn toward the inner, narrow end of the lagoon. Thane turned hard along the curvature of the beach, heading off toward the opposite end. The scout boat turned at the same time, narrowing the gap between the two boats, gaining at lease one hundred meters on him. Thane realized that within a circular loop, he could only keep this up for so long. He tried maneuvering left and right, but couldn't outsmart the men.

Thane had another idea. While the motor was still at full speed, he found some rope and tied it around the motor's handle, keeping it cranked full speed. Carefully maneuvering his way toward the front of the boat, he leveled out his hydroplane, allowing him to go faster, but unable to steer. With his new weight distribution, Thane was now flying on the water faster than his pursuers, but had to jump back to the rear every time he needed to turn.

In their game of cat and mouse, Thane had a higher speed on the long stretches, with the perusing boat gaining leverage on the turns.

After 20 more minutes, Thane realized he would eventually run out of fuel. He had to change his tactic. Coming up on the next go around, the scout boat suddenly turned, shooting across the middle of the lagoon. *They're trying to cut me off,* he thought.

He grabbed the motor, slowing his boat. "What now," he said to himself out loud.

*Failure, defeat, surrender,* these are the words that started circulating in Thane's mind. Failure, defeat, and surrender were not an option for Sarghon in the battle to save his world. The only logical course of action was to think like Sarghon.

"Well, it's now or never!" he said, changing direction. He noticed the scout boat heading for the opposite end of the lagoon to cut him off, so Thane steered toward the oilrig. At top speed, he aimed directly for the rusting tower as the scout boat headed off in the opposite direction. The Frenchmen didn't notice what Thane was up to at first, but once he reached the rig, they turned and came back around.

Approaching the oilrig tower, Thane noticed it was rusty but sturdy, with a ladder up one side leading to the base of the scaffolding.

He turned the skiff around before turning the motor off. He had another plan! With the rope, Thane tied a makeshift knot with one end, securing it to the rear, port side cleat. He hurriedly wrapped the middle of the rope around the steering handle, turning it to its full throttle position while tightening the knot. He tied the rest of the rope to the starboard side cleat, holding the steering handle in place, before reaching back and tugging hard on the starter chord.

It didn't start.

The Frenchmen were getting very close. As they approached, he could hear them yelling obscenities in French.

He pulled the chord three more times with no success. They were only feet away when, on the fourth pull, the motor came to life. The empty boat shot away from the oilrig like a floating missile.

The scouts were stunned for a split-second, staring at the unmanned boat motoring off on its own, before one crewman finally shouted, "Allez, allez!!" They were off after their pilotless boat, leaving Thane alone on the rig.

*These guys must think I'm completely insane,* he thought. Thane wondered what else the Frenchmen must be thinking: Some random guy runs off the deserted beach, distracts them with a Frisbee, steals their boat making them chase him around the radioactive atoll lagoon, then strands himself on an abandoned, decaying oilrig in the middle of the pacific ocean with no one else in sight.

Thane made his way up to the base of the tower, climbing the rusty metal girders with his backpack securely on his back. After several more meters, he became uneasy. "This frigg'in thing better not collapse," he mumbled to himself.

So far, so good. The metal hadn't deteriorated to the point of bending under his weight, so he continued to climb higher and higher up the rusty carcass of what used to be a fully working pumping rig. What it pumped from the middle of the atoll was anyone's guess, but Thane didn't waste any time worrying about it as he climbed higher and higher up the metallic ladder.

The unmanned skiff took the three French scouts on an escapade. Thane's antic jaunt sent them haphazardly chasing their unmanned boat across the lagoon, while they attempted to catch it before it hit land. On their first attempt, their boat sped alongside the unmanned skiff, bumping it and sending it off to the left. Now, it was racing off in a large counterclockwise circle, spitting up water from its engine onto the pursuers. They chased it around and around several more times before abandoning that idea.

Half way up the length of the rusted steel monster, Thane found a sitting spot before having a laugh, watching the three men chase the wild, speeding boat around the lagoon. He grabbed his pack and pulled out a granola bar and the flag. Chewing on the granola bar, he realized the flag was heavy, having been folded up tightly into the backpack. Balancing his weight, he opened one end noticing it was the front-left side. He tied the upper corner to a beam above his head before tying the lower corner to a beam below his feet, stretching it out to its full side length.

"Here goes nothing!" he said, tossing the rest of the flag down the length of the rusty scaffolding.

It unfurled with the sound of a spinnaker sail in the wind, revealing a long, green flag with the famous "GREENPEACE" logo on it. The flag bellowed in the wind as Thane sat completely satisfied that his dicey plan had actually worked.

Hearing lots of screaming, Thane looked back at the men in the lagoon, as they made one last ditch attempt to commandeer their out-of-control vessel. Chasing alongside, trying to match its speed and circumference, one guy leveraged himself on the edge of their speeding boat, while the unmanned boat continued to soar across the water in its counterclockwise circle.

When they seemed to get close enough to the boat, the guy dove head first into the moving boat, flying across to the other side. He knocked his face into the rubber seat before bouncing out of the boat – ass first into the water, creating a grand splash.

The unmanned boat changed direction, heading for land. At first they went after it, but soon realized they were out of time. Stopping their boat, the men watched their speeding, unmanned companion head ashore toward a shallow, dead coral reef that pierced the top of the water.

Helplessly they watched as their boat bounced off the rocks and reef, before beaching itself with a loud roar and rough grind. The motor cranked recklessly on the rocks and sand like a giant beached tuna, flopping its fins in the throws of death.

Picking up their floater, the men headed to the beach to rescue what was left of their wrecked boat and motor.

Thane could only laugh louder as he watched the whole thing from his towering vantage point. His strategy had worked better than expected. Watching the scouts in the chase was worth every moment of risk – but before he could think of what he would do next, the answer came around the open mouth of the lagoon.

Two ninety-foot French Navy vessels were headed directly for him.


Christian headed out to sea in the direction he knew the MV Greenpeace and convoy of ships would be coming from. If the Captain was on time, which he usually was, and if Thane's diversion worked, then he may be in the clear.

Christian looked back to see if any boats were in pursuit. So far no scouts or French military seemed to have noticed him leave the island.

He spotted something on the horizon. Grabbing his binoculars, he made out a distant ship, and then another, and another. The convoy was there, as promised. "Thank God they're on time," Christian said, heaving a sigh of relief.

Looking at the fuel gauge, he realizing he may not have enough fuel to reach them. He grabbed the walky-talky and clicked it on. "Calling the Black Pig, calling the Black Pig! This is Night Shark. Do you read? – over."

He waited for a response. After a moment, he repeated his call, but there was no answer. He was out of range. Hoping and praying, Christian continued his course toward the convoy, "Please, God, let them see me before I run out of gas."

He chuckled to himself, looking up to the sky, "Even if I'm a scientist who believes in fact over fiction," he whispered, "I can still pray."

Getting closer to the convoy, Christian made out several other ships as well. He saw the outline of the *Mary Weather*, a British ship known to support Greenpeace from time to time, as well as the *Grand Mal*, a luxury yacht owned by a brain scientist and large contributor to Greenpeace.

Christian also recognized the *West Wind*, a large tri-mast sailboat owned by a French millionaire who was against the testing of nuclear warfare in French Polynesia. He counted sixteen ships in all.

"Calling Captain Parker of the Black Pig. Come in, – over! This is Night Shark. I'm heading for your coordinates. Do you see me? – over!"

Christian held his breath. A moment went by, then his walky-talky crackled. "Roger, Night Shark. We see you on our ten o'clock. Why are you in the open water, Night Shark? Are you OK? – over."

"Slight change of plans. Coming in for a landing with you. Precious cargo in hand and running low on fuel, so keep me in visual range, – over."

"Roger that. Coming to get you now, – over."

"Good to see you guys! May have military in pursuit, so be on the lookout. More ships around the far side of the island. Fill you in soon, – over."

"Roger that, Night Shark. Be there in a jiffy. Over and out."

Christian was relieved, but suddenly very concerned for Thane. *What was the kid up to?* he thought. Hoping Thane was safe, Christian held on to only positive thoughts as the convoy approached.


Thane sat half way up the tower of the oilrig, when one of the military commando ships approached. It was much larger up close, looking very official with its military gray and black numbers painted on the side.

A second ship approached following the first one. These were the same two military ships he'd seen the night before anchored off the coast from the military compound.

The two ships circled the tower like sharks sizing up prey. Thane watched as a man holding a megaphone stepped out on the deck of one of the ships. "You are trezpassing on private property. You must come down and zurrender yourself immediately! Zere is no one to elp you escape," he said, with a strong French accent.

Thane sat silently for a moment. He had been mainly concerned with getting Christian to safety and hanging the flag on to the tower. What to do at this point hadn't been calculated into his dynamic plan.

Thane sat in silence.

"You must come down eer. We are zee French Coast Guard and you are inside zee exclusion zone. Eet's very dangerooos!" the man continued on his megaphone.

"If you're the Coast Guard, why aren't you guarding this coast from nuclear bombs and radioactive pollution?" Thane yelled down to the man. "I have as much right to be here as you do. This world isn't a test site for reckless humanity! You'll have to come up and get me!"

*Well, that solved the issue of what he would do next*, Thane thought. He would wait up on the scaffolding of the tower until they sent a team up to get him.

"Mon dieu!" he heard the man say as they argued in French back and forth among themselves.

Thane knew he would most likely get captured, but he also knew it was a necessary risk in order for Christian to return safely to Greenpeace with the gear and data.

His heart raced with a sense of satisfaction mixed with adrenalin. He was enraptured by the moment of being the focal point of a global controversy, while making a grand statement of peace. Even if it was just to this small group of people, much of the world would know what happened here today at this moment in time.

Filled with a sense of joy, his body felt light, as a huge smile unfolded across his face. It was a smile of knowing that whatever happened, he would always remember this exact moment in his life as one of great importance and fulfillment. His body tingled, sensing warm, magnetic energy around him – penetrating, yet calming.

Clinching his fists, he sat stoically looking out over the exquisite tropical landscape, feeling an instinctive sense of purpose toward the Earth. In that moment, he fully understood why Greenpeace and organizations that fight to save the environment, do what they do diligently and selfishly year after year. He *got* it.

Turning his head toward the ocean, something caught his eye. It was the flotilla of ships heading toward the opening of the lagoon. Still several miles out from his vantage point atop the oilrig tower, he could see the whole convoy spreading across the distant horizon, with the MV Greenpeace leading them all.

Thane knew the commando ships didn't see the convoy, nor did the men on the beach rescuing the damaged outboard skiff. They had attached a rope to the damaged boat and were towing it behind them as they headed back to the larger Military vessels.

Thane had to stall the French vessels until the convoy arrived. He needed to keep the flag up long enough for the convoy to get there, photograph it, and make history. He didn't know what else he could do, so he began to sing: "Let it be, let it be, let it be, ohh, let it be. There will be an answer, let it be!"

The men stopped arguing and looked up at the tower. For a few moments they just stared at him, as he sang loudly. He couldn't remember all the verses, so he repeated himself several times.

*This isn't going to work*, he thought. I need a different kind of diversion. Any moment, they would come up and take him off of his perch, along with the flag. One of the boats turned, heading toward the ladder that hung off the side of the rig's platform.

*They're coming up*, he realized.

Dropping two rubber bumpers off the starboard side of their ship, crewmembers reached for the ladder. Thane had to do something fast. Taking the backpack off his shoulder, he yelled, "Hey you guys!" before heaving it as hard as he could toward the opposite side of the rig. The crewmember let go of the ladder, pointing to where the pack landed in the water. Both boats backed off the platform and went to explore the area where the bag had splashed down.

Several minutes went by, as they carefully collected the wet bag and inspected it. Once they realized it wasn't a threat, they proceeded back to the opposite side of the platform with the ladder.

Thane could see the convoy getting closer to the entrance of the lagoon, but still not close enough to see him. *It would be at least another ten minutes,* he thought. *What else can I do?*

The men began climbing up the ladder again.

A crazy idea came into Thane's mind. *Am I too high up? Could I? No, that's just insane,* he thought to himself. *OK, I will!*

Thane stood up, leaning as far as he could with one arm off the rusty rafter. The men below were running along the base toward the tower. Contemplating his next maneuver, Thane said a quick prayer, before yelling down at the men again. "Bonjour mes amis! Je suis Superman!"

Once he was sure they were all looking in his direction, Thane stepped off the tower, as the Tarot card of *The Fool* stepping off the precipice, flashed through his mind. It was a leap of faith into the unknown.

"Ahhhhhh!!!" he yelled, bicycling his legs and arms, flying out past the platform through the air like a unicyclist balancing on a tightrope. It seemed to take forever, as the water got closer and closer. With a thunderous crash, he hit the surface. It was like being punched by twenty grown men all at the same time.

Suspended motionless underwater, stunned by the impact, Thane saw only stars. At first he couldn't move, his body tingling all over with pain and shock, but he opened his eyes and swam up to the surface, gasping for air. Choking in a breath of air, he coughed out the water he had swallowed during the impact.

Taking a few more gasping breaths, Thane regained his bearings. When his eyes focused, he could see the two ships on the opposite side of the rig. The men were scurrying back down the ladder into their vessel.

Turning his head around, Thane saw a very welcome sight. The Black Pig was in view. *It worked,* he thought. *They're more concerned with me than with the flag.*

One of the ships came around the rig tower to gather Thane from the water. When they got to Thane's location, both ships spotted the convoy heading their way. Shouting warnings to each other, they pointed at the approaching vessels. The closer ship tossed a rope ladder over the side, slowly maneuvering into position next to Thane. He had no choice in the matter and having done everything he could think of to distract and stall them, Thane finally surrendered.

Thane complied, as the commander of the French ship ordered him onboard. Climbing up the rope ladder, the other men mumbled to each other in French. Thane could only make out the word, "stupid."

The captain of the vessel approached Thane, throwing a towel at him. "Now zat you realized zat you cannot fly, you are under arrest. Who are you, and what do you sink you are doing eer?"

261

"I'm Fernando Pereira," Thane responded. He didn't want to give his real name, and since he had no identification on him, he figured he would stay the point by giving the name of the photographer who had died during the attack on the Rainbow Warrior.

"Ahh, a comedian," The captain replied. "Emmener" *(Take him)*, he ordered to his men, as they grabbed Thane.

The convoy of sixteen vessels headed directly for the oilrig. Gazing at the Greenpeace flag hanging down the tower, Christian now knew what Thane had planned. Christian felt a sense of pride, knowing his best buddy had accomplished the task so well, but where was he?

"Thane was supposed to stay on the oilrig with the flag, but I don't see him anywhere," Christian said to Captain Parker, peered through binoculars at the tower. "Man, the flag is perfect! Did my boy do good, or what? We should get some photos and give him a medal!"

"Green Leader to convoy team," the Captain said on his CB radio, "Spread out and surround the rig. Take photos and video. Ready horns and megaphones. No aggressive maneuvers; I repeat, no aggressive maneuvers, – over."

Each boat in the convoy responded with acknowledgment, surrounding the oilrig and French Military vessels. They snapped dozens of photos as they circled the giant, towering flag that waved in the wind like a beckoning arm.

Before the Black Pig could make a full revolution around the rig, they heard a megaphone. "You are trezpassing in a secured exclusion zone. We are zee French Coast Guard. You are not allowed eere! You must leave zees place immediately!"

Captain Parker knew the French ships most likely weren't from the Coast Guard, as he responded on his Megaphone. "We have joined in this effort to protest what you are doing here. We speak on behalf of the rest of the world, as well as your own country of France. We speak for the environmental right to protect our oceans and lands from nuclear pollutants!"

"Zees eez not your ocean. Zeez islands belongs to French Polynesia!"

"They belong to the Earth, and the Earth belongs to us all!"

A roar of cheers and beeps exploded from the megaphones of each ship, followed by a cacophony of triumphant horn blasts from each boat in the convoy, echoing like an orchestra of bass brass instruments warming up before a concert.

Thane heard everything from inside the commando ship, thinking it was magnificent. Throwing down the towel he had been given to dry himself, Thane ran out onto the deck waving his arms and shouting, "We did it! We did it!"

He was quickly apprehended and taken back inside but Christian, Captain Parker, and many others saw Thane on the French ship. As happy as Christian was to see Thane alive and well, he was concerned about his capture, wishing he'd made his way to the beach, hiding in the brush waiting to be rescued. Christian knew the French wouldn't just hand him over – not after the stunt he just pulled on them. He stood proud, however, knowing Thane would get most of the glory for this day's work. They would have to find another way to retrieve him from the authorities back in Papeete, on the main island.

A French ship sent two men to climb the oilrig to untie the flag. Every member of each convoy ship began to cheer together: "Greenpeace, Greenpeace, Greenpeace, Greenpeace," occasionally blasting their horn as they chanted in unison.

When the two men reached the top section of the flag, they untied the knots, letting it fall to the base of the platform. The ruse was over, as the roar of cheering and horn blasting began again throughout the convoy. It went on for more than five solid minutes.

Once the enthusiasm had settled down, the French captain spoke loudly into his megaphone, "I understand why you are eere. You have made your point. Now you must go away! We have captured your colleague, and ee must be arrested and eld accountable for your nonsense."

"What you call nonsense," Parker shouted through his megaphone, "we call freedom of speech and our right to protest your country's actions. We will retrieve our comrade and he will be praised for his actions. Do what you must, but know that we will never stop fighting for the protection of the Earth and for the wildlife living in it!"

The military ships didn't care to respond. Anything they could say would only fall short in the present company. The French Captain gave the order to turn on their sirens in a weak attempt to encourage the convoy to leave.

After making a last full loop around the oilrig, horns blasting, the convoy headed back toward the lagoon entrance and the open ocean. Before they left the lagoon, Christian picked up the megaphone and shouted, "Be strong, little buddy. You made us all very proud today. We'll find you and bring you home! Promise! You're a hero!"

Holding his towel and smiling, Thane heard every word as he sat quietly on the hard molded fiberglass seat of the military vessel. The remaining men on the rig bunched up the flag and hopped back aboard their ship. They waited for the full convoy to leave the lagoon before following them out, wondering if there was anything else the group of vessels had planned for the day.

As Thane's ship headed back to the mainland, the other vessel stayed behind to pick up the stranded skiff and patrol the circumference of the atoll. While being escorted to a small cabin, Thane heard the captain shouting in French on the CB radio. They brought him some water and bread with cheese, ordering him to remain there for the duration of the voyage back to Papeete, Tahiti.

After finishing several bites of food and water, Thane settled his body on the small corner bed. Bouncing off the waves, he shifted to-and-fro on the small, hard mattress. The repetitive movement lulled him back and forth and his tired, sore body finally began to relax.

Closing his eyes, Thane gently began to cry. It wasn't because he was alone in the middle of the Pacific Ocean, captured by French commandos, heading for a foreign country to be arrested and locked up in who-knows-where. Nor was it because he had lost connection with his Greenpeace team and his new best friend. Thane wasn't shedding tears because of his current circumstances at all. It was because of his dream.

That morning, Thane woke up in a powerfully spiritual and emotional state. Too much had happened way too fast and he hadn't had time to process what he already knew – that Angelica had died while he was away. He knew it as certain as if the message had come in the form of a phone call from Sharla. Now that he had a moment to himself undistracted, it sank in with the heaviness of a lead weight on his heart.

His sobs only lasted a few minutes before he realized something profound. She had given him a message. She told him that she was OK and that he was on the right track. She gave him that message lucidly, reassuring him that it was genuine and valid.

Feeling slightly better, Thane now understood the message, knowing beyond a shadow of a doubt that she was somewhere safe. A weight had lifted from his soul. She also gave him the wonderful gift of saying goodbye.

Drying his eyes, Thane reached over to the wall and turned off the light. The room became pitch black, with no porthole or ambient light at all. It felt calm and pleasant as he lay there in the darkness, eyes wide shut, mentally and physically depleted.

It was now late afternoon and knowing they were still hours away from land, Thane finally relaxed on the bed. Clutching the pillow close to his face, a final tear ran down his cheek as the lulling of the boat helped him slowly drift off to sleep.

# Chapter XVIII

## BATTLE AT MADERIAN FIELD

The dawn came like a slow receding tide over a sandy, barren beach before a tsunami, silent and ominous. It was the calm before the storm.

Ambroas's army was stationed at the base of the giant meadowland known as Maderian Field, where he put Gannon Direfoot in charge. Direfoot was a general of the late King Zavior's army, who defected once the Queen had gone mad on her murderous rampage searching for the King's mistress, Aubrey and bastard child. He was a trusted member of the past kingdom and friend to Ambroas.

Hearing voices, Sarghon yawned as he poked his head through the entrance of Ambroas's tent. "We've arrived then?" he said drowsily, in a somnambulistic fog.

"Yes, we have been here all night if you recall," Ambroas said, greeting Sarghon with a bowl of his famous forest-berry porridge. "You took my advice and got a full night's rest. Good boy, you will need it. Now you must eat a full portion, or even two, of my delectable berry porridge. Your belly needs to be filled before we march. General Direfoot is awaiting our signal."

Sarghon sat cross-legged in the entrance of Ambroas's tent, watching Kara. She stood tall with her graceful wings halfway open, sizing up the battlefield as she tested the airflow and temperature.

In her full battle armor, she was a majestic creature, blond hair flowing in the breeze from under her shimmering, silver and gold embellished helmet. To most, Kara would be recognized as a God and if Sarghon didn't have his powers, he too would have felt like a mere pawn under her beauty and magnificence.

Atasha was near, letting out an eager neigh, gaining Sarghon's attention. He walked over to her and stroked her neck. Since the fire bond connected them, there was no need for formalities. Their trust was now intimately inherent.

"Malock is near," Ambroas said, keeping a slight distance from Atasha, "The trees whisper his approach upon Maderian Field within several hours time."

An ancient battleground from centuries past, Maderian Field was a place kings were made and killed. Located in a large clearing of the Scyllian Forest three miles in diameter, the field was covered in short, ankle to knee-high grasses and wildflowers, surrounded by a circle of tall trees. A shallow river ran along the northeast corner.

Apparently it was spring and Sarghon was keenly aware of each flower species blooming in yellow, purple, and orange patches, with blood-red poppies scattered in rows along the riverbank.

A monument with a wide set of stairs chiseled from white marble faced the battlefield at the west entrance, with the tallest of trees as a backdrop. Standing twenty meters high, the grand white stage had been the place where conquering kings would announce victory to their troops.

Bordering the four corners of the large, stone platform, stood giant, black obsidian urns, carved with battle scenes of years past. At the rear of the platform, a small enclosure with a pointed roof pierced the sky. This notorious building was where slain kings would be taken and placed on an altar to be stripped of their armor and sword by the conquering king. It was called *The Red Room* for the blood that covered the ground, staining the stone floor.

The entire altar resembled an empty burial tomb with writing carved on the interior walls, telling of great battles fought there over the years.

"Sarghon, you will have to focus your mind, as I have taught you so often in our lessons and training," Ambroas said. "Your powers can be overwhelming, I am sure, but you also know I believe in you and in your destiny. After all this time and all these years, the prophesized battle is finally upon us. The Earth herself supports our cause. It is indeed a special day!"

"Let us hope we remember it in victory and not defeat," Sarghon said.

"General Direfoot and the civilian army are stationed just outside the south end of the field awaiting word. I must go to him now. Stick to our plan, yes? We will make the first wave of attacks focusing on Malock's hypnotized army of plain folk. Remember, the people we fight are our brothers and sisters under his spell. Do your best to protect them. Be vigilant with your powers; you wouldn't want to blow over our entire army whilst gesticulating hither and thither."

"I have come to realize that the elements do not always follow my exact requests," Sarghon responded. "Elements in nature are untamed. I am only the conduit for which their energy can be focused. I will do everything I can, old friend. My vantage point will be from the sky with Atasha. When the time comes, Malock will be my sole focus, as you and the prophecy request."

"You have grown, my boy. I can see that you are now a man."

Walking up to Sarghon, Ambroas placed his hand on Sarghon's shoulder. "Do not let that manipulating malefactor get the best of you," he whispered, so only Sarghon could hear. "Find his weakness and use it against him. Kill him if you must. Can you do that?"

Sarghon hadn't actually imagined killing Malock. Somehow, he thought he would be defeated and imprisoned. Now, with the eminent battle upon them, death had become a reality.

"Yes," Sarghon said. "I will do what must be done to save our world and our people from the tyranny of Malock and his twisted mind. I have one last question, though." Sarghon looked toward the meadowland battlefield. "Malock mentioned that the Diaglyphen Prophecy was incorrect about his desire to conquer. He told us he wanted peace – '*a world of one vision, one people, who all understand each other completely.*' Those were his exact words. Do we not have a similar intention in mind?"

"Do not presume to know his true meaning," Ambroas stressed. "He is a master of manipulation, charismatic in his delivery, yet toxic in his objective. Make no mistake, the world he means to create is one where we are all enslaved to his whims and desires. His fanciful tongue is as sharp and venomous as a dragon's, no matter how he charms and twists the language."

"I witnessed his magic control the mind of Aidan, a friend of the Fire People. He did whatever Malock asked of him, blindly and submissively. It was disgusting."

"I will not be a blind servant to a tyrannical King. Nor should anyone!" Ambroas said, sternly.

He grabbed Sarghon by both shoulders, giving him a sturdy hug. "Be ready and be focused. Do what you must. Malock is as scared of you as you are of him. You are also the son of King Zavior, giving *you* a true right to his throne and land. You are the Spirit King!"

Nodding to Sarghon, Ambroas whisked off toward the southern end of Maderian Field, where General Direfoot and his civilian army were stationed.

Grabbing Gladanteus from inside the tent, Sarghon returned to Atasha, stroking her shiny black mane. "Are you hungry, girl? We have a big day ahead of us. How about a nice big breakfast for you as well?"

Walking away from the tent, Sarghon led Atasha to a small grassy area. Gripping the handle of his sword with both hands, he pierced the Earth while concentrating on Atasha's desires. A variety of scrumptious grasses emerged from the ground, popping up in tall, thin, green stalks of all sizes, creating a round mound ten feet in diameter. In the center, the ground trembled as a single plant grew up above the rest. It writhed and twisted, growing taller and taller as branches reached out from the main stock.

It became a tree bursting with long, oval leaves and lush, green fuzzy tufts of foliage. Then, beautiful soft pink flowers blossomed into round fruit that grew larger and larger – ripening from green to yellow, then orange, then red with orange stripes running down the top. They were Sulkanian Apples, Atasha's favorite.

He had been able to read her mind, knowing she fancied this particular variety of apple. Trotting over to the tree, Atasha gave Sargon a look of satisfaction before digging in to her feast.

Walking back to the tent, he found Kara waiting for him near the entrance. "She appears pleased," Kara said.

"I do sense her satisfaction. Will you come inside?" Sarghon said with a gesture.

The tent was large enough to sleep several people. Animal furs covered the floor where Sarghon and Ambroas slept, along with two feather pillows. "It is good to see you," he said, approaching her.

As Kara took off her helmet, Sarghon looked into her penetrating, amethyst eyes. "I have missed you," she said, taking a step closer to Sarghon.

"And I, you," he said, letting Gladanteus fall to the ground.

Sarghon grabbed her arms, kissing her passionately while reaching around her metal-clad waist. Taking his head in her hands, she guided his lips powerfully on to hers, taking his mouth, like quenching long awaited desert thirst.

They parted lips, catching their breath. "Your armor is quite impressive," Sarghon said, without taking his eyes off hers. "The curves and artistry shape to your body immaculately. How long does it take to put it on?"

"With assistance, it can be donned in only a matter of minutes," she answered honestly, "but it takes even less time to take it off."

Sarghon felt a tingle run through his body and down to his loins. Jumping into action, he unbuckled the side panel of her breastplate, as she worked on the straps of her shin plates. Then, he tore off his belt, pants and tunic, standing in his sheer loincloth, as Kara removed the last of her armor.

Mesmerized by the sight of her, Sarghon watched as she loosened the leather strapped skirt she always wore. It fell to the ground. Wearing only her undergarments of ultra-soft leather, she stepped toward Sarghon. This was the first time he had seen Kara partially nude. Sarghon was even more impressed with her stunning body than with her magnificent armor. Her wings tucked neatly behind her back, outlining her curves with a powder white glow.

Sarghon approached, cupping her bosom in one hand. "I see now what your armor truly protects."

Reaching behind her neck, she unclasped her top garment and it fell into his hand, revealing her bare breasts. He pressed himself into her with another impassioned kiss, grabbing her unclad waist of real flesh, reaching up her back, finding the area where her skin met her wings. It felt as soft as a duckling's down, as he slowly caressed his fingers into the small of her back, where he found the indentation between her wings. Her body shivered as he stroked the soft untouched body part. She let out a slight moan as he continued to stroke her back, pressing his chest into hers.

Reaching down, she pulled off Sarghon's loincloth, before picking him up from under his arms and vehemently laying him down on the animal fur with her body on top of his. Sarghon lay captivated under her naked body, staring into her piercing eyes.

"I have never been with a human male," she said. "Valkyrian men are strong, intelligent, and good for building and farming. They are not known for their passion or lovemaking. I have heard stories about human men and their accomplishments with their women. But, as I mentioned long ago, it is forbidden to mate with a human. Is it alright that I am on top? Women are dominant in our species."

Sarghon let out a slight gasp, feeling himself growing ever

harder against her body. "Yes, you are perfect where you are," he said, grabbing her shoulders, pulling her face down to his lips. They kissed passionately, as he caressed her muscular body, feeling every ripple of her smooth skin undulate with fervor. She was strong, yet supple, and he became increasingly excited by every new inch of her body.

Sarghon reached down, placing his hands on her hips, taking control of the action. Kara allowed him to do so, grabbing hold of his firm buttocks, running her fingers over his athletic legs. "I know for certain that your love is real," Kara whispered. "Your body reveals the truth."

Maneuvering himself closer between her legs, Sarghon grabbed her hips and slid his firm manhood inside her. Letting out a moan of pleasure, she allowed him to continue. They moved in pace together, kissing even more passionately.

Sarghon then rolled Kara onto her back, being careful to cradle her wings under their bodies. He was now on top, and with impulsive desire, he went deeper into action, kissing her neck as he pressed himself further into her. Her folded wings acted like a spring, as he pulsed down on her in a steady, flowing rhythm.

As they continued their passionate lovemaking, Kara fell into an ecstatic trance. "You are mine, my warrior Princess, now and forever," Sarghon said, with anticipation.

"I am yours, my love," she replied, before kissing him deeply, allowing him to go faster.

In his excitement and ecstasy Sarghon couldn't help himself and with an inescapable moan, he came to a climax. Kara pulled him close, wrapping her giant wings around them both, like a cocoon. They stayed like that in silence, breathing together as one, in their own unique and intimate bond.

Once they had taken enough time to catch their breath, Kara opened her wings and sat up. "I had not believed the rumors about human men, but I am obliged to change my mind. You, my darling, have surprised even me – not something easily accomplished."

"I have never known much about Valkyrian men, but I am glad I am able to surprise even you, great one," Sarghon said, with a sly grin. "You continue to surprise me with each passing second."

"Our men do not have wings, nor an imaginative perspective in life. They are passive and serve the female Valkyrie with pleasure. Think of them as dedicated worker bees. They enjoy their simple lives and are content as such. You, on the other hand, are another breed of male all together – something I have become ever more intrigued by with each passing day." Sarghon smiled. "I am a Princess, and will become Queen one day. I will change the rules regarding human and Valkyrie. You and I will make positive change together. Does that sound appealing to you, my love?"

"Without doubt; I want to open the eyes of people of all races in many ways. I have accepted the fate handed me and today we must prove victorious."

"Be careful," Kara said sincerely, placing her palm on his cheek. "I have never spoken those words to another in my entire life, Valkyrie or human. Before a battle, I would usually say, 'Be victorious', but Malock is a formidable opponent and, as strong and magnificent as you are, he is the strongest force of evil this land has ever known. I now have more to lose than my freedom."

"You know I have no choice in the matter, but I will think of you with every strike of my sword and power. I can think of no stronger weapon than my feelings for you, my love."

Sarghon reached around her neck, pulling her close for one last passionate kiss. He lightly dressed himself before helping Kara on with her clothes and armor. Kara helped him with his new chest plate and shoulder guards, a gift from Ambroas set aside for this day.

"My army will strike from the east," Kara said, pulling his shoulder strap tight. "Malock is traveling with an army of Wyvern as well as human. We will be ready to do battle in the air while you focus on Malock, as Ambroas suggested. Leave the wretched beasts to us."

"I look forward to fighting once again at your side, my beauty," Sarghon replied, gazing at her shining, statuesque silhouette in the sunlight as they exited the tent. "Return to me unscathed, or I will pulverize the beast who dares harm you."

"And you, to me," she said, spreading her giant white wings, flapping them in a whirlwind of dust and leaves, before rising straight up into the sky. "To victory, my love, my King!"

As Kara flew off toward the eastern forest surrounding the battlefield where her Valkyrian army awaited, Sarghon closed his eyes. A new man had emerged on this day, one that valued the individualism and passion that grew in his heart, as well as in the essence and glory of the land he so loved. He would fight for his people, their freedom, and now, for love.

Using his sensing technique, Sarghon stood with his legs together, palms open to the sky, as he reached out into the distance for Atasha. In doing so, he also sensed the strange and ominous energy of Malock's army approaching from beyond the battlefield.

Atasha eagerly came to his side in a gallant canter. Poised for action in his shimmering new armor, Sarghon took a double step to the right with arm and hand outstretched, ceremoniously mounting the fire horse in the traditional way, before taking off in a blaze of flaming brilliance.

Sarghon and Atasha flew high in the sky toward Maderian Field, as the bright red-orange sun rose in the east like a giant unblinking, beholding eye. In the distance, the three-mile wide circular field appeared, with a dark gray cloud of dust moving toward it.

Recalling the battle plan in his mind, Sarghon felt ready for action. *Don't rush in too fast,* he told himself. *Stay in the air. Watch, listen, and study the enemy before engaging.*

Sarghon was never one to sit back and do nothing, learning the hard way during his last encounter with Malock, that patience is often a virtue. This time, however, he had a few new tricks up his sleeve.

The cloud of darkness broke through the far side barrier of Maderian Field, revealing a military style army of men and women fashioned in black, leather battle gear. As they emerged, the trees along their path shriveled from lush green towers, to brittle twigs, some falling to the ground. Behind the army lay a track of dead Earth, like a river of burnt ash – the smoky dirt littered with dead birds and forest animals.

Malock had absorbed the energy of the forest as he traveled, searing a path of death and destruction toward the field.

*I will fix that,* Sarghon promised himself, gripping the handle of Gladanteus.

The black army filtered out like pawns on a chessboard, inching their way forward toward the beige armor clad rivals. It was hard to believe they were all just innocent townsfolk, captured and manipulated into the biddings of the Dark King, unaware of what they were really doing.

"We must stay back, girl," Sarghon reminded Atasha. "Leave them to Ambroas, as planned. We will announce ourselves when the time is right."

Ambroas and his civilian army emerged from the opposite end of the field, heading toward the opposition. They were outnumbered nearly two to one.

"Remember, no matter how hard they fight, do NOT kill anyone!" Ambroas yelled to his troops, "These are your brethren, your family members, and your friends. Do anything you must to keep them subdued and unharmed. As you all know, they are under a spell and will not recognize you, so be mentally prepared for this! We fight together, as one, to reunite our people and our land under a new king, a new law, and the promise of a better future!"

The members of his army all yelled a loud, triumphant "Hurrah!"

Both sides marched through the knee-high grass and wildflowers toward each other, shortening the gap with every step. As Ambroas held up his wooden staff, his civilian army halted. He walked out alone toward the oncoming enemy, breathing in a slow, concentrated breath before muttering the words, "Bara tarana, cooicoth selamara," as he waved his staff over the ground several times.

He was casting a spell on the wild blood-red poppies in the field in front of them. The poppies began shooting black spores into the air in little puffs all around. As the rival army approached, many stumbled and fell to the ground. Every third member or so would roll his or her eyes back, passing out cold. Some avoided the magic, walking around the flowers.

"Do not be alarmed," Ambroas called back to his troops, "they are only passing out due to the sleeping magic I placed in the poppies. Stay away from the red flowers!"

The numbers were now evened out with a nearly one-to-one ratio, as the armies finally met sword on sword, staff on mace, shield against shield.

The eyes of the black, leather-clad army glowed orange as they marched forward like automatons under Malock's control. Ambroas had cast a protection spell on his army, keeping them as safe as he could, but the onslaught was fierce. If there were a non-lethal blow, the sword or spear would jet to one side causing only a scratch, if anything at all. The spell, however, was unable stop a direct and deadly blow.

The sound of battle was now in full force with the clashing of steel, as well as the groaning and grunts of the fight.

"Do you not see you are being manipulated into attacking us by a tyrant king?" one female from the civilian army said, her attacker coming at her with a blow to her shield.

"We fight to protect the wellbeing of our people and our land!" the woman shouted back, lurching forward with another strike.

"The wellbeing of your land? Are you kidding me? Your leader is destroying the land everywhere he goes! Can you not even open your eyes to see the truth?" she shouted, butting the woman in the black armor, shield to shoulder.

"The land is a resource, and resources were given to us by God to utilize for our people. My King is providing us the life we all want and deserve. You are in our way!"

The woman in black armor came in for a hard strike with her sword, grazing the arm of the civilian woman.

"But we are of the same land and heritage, the same people! You dare say that God gave your King our land to destroy and use as he sees fit?" She struck back hard with her sword. "You are hypocrites to your own land and people. How can you not break free of this spell? Use your reason, woman!"

"If we do not follow the structure of life shown to us by our King, we will be taken over by rampant nomads seeking to influence us with their alien and exotic ways. They will destroy our children," she said, raising her arms into the air. "Our King follows the one truth that will guide us all to salvation."

The civilian woman finally took the hilt of her sword with both hands, jamming it down hard into the back of the other woman's head. She fell down hard, knocked unconscious.

"There's more than one truth in this world, buttercup!" the civilian woman said, looking down on her rival with a look of disgust. "I sincerely hope you don't remember any of this. I know it is not your fault."

The second wave of attack came bursting through the dark cloud onto the field with fury, as dozens of Wyverns shot across the sky from high above. This was expected, and Kara and her Valkyrian sisters were ready for an air attack.

The Wyvern's assault came like shooting arrows from all directions. Kara led her winged army in from the west, flying toward the center of the field. With a motion of her sword, they spread out in a circle, surrounding the Wyvern beasts in an attempt to herd the dragon relatives into the center of the field's airspace.

The battle swiftly became a thrashing of jagged teeth, slashing of swords, and a thunderous cacophony of violent lightning strikes. Each Valkyrian warrior took on her own dragon, maneuvering with superior training against each attack.

One of the larger beasts chased Kara. Its speed and agility was impressive. She couldn't out-fly the creature, so she turned to face it head-on. She swung her sword, but the dragon was too fast; Kara only sliced a small gash into its wing as it knocked her sideways. Its barbed tail swung around catching Kara in the leg.

Pain shot through her thigh, as blood trickled from the wound. As the beast came around for another strike, Kara threw her wings out wide. "Enough playing around," she said in a huff. As the creature flew toward her, she dove directly at him. Gaining speed, she stared the beast in its reptilian eye. Milliseconds before they met, she flipped over, tucking her wings in and twisting as she flew upside-down toward its underside.

With a precise curve of her wrist, she swung her sword around, slicing open the length of the Wyvern's belly as she passed below him.

Blood and entrails splattered all around as she performed a reverse loop, then hovered in the air watching the creature fall from the sky, moaning and spitting blood on its way down to impending death.


On the ground something unusual emerged onto the battlefield. Through the dark haze and dust came a creature only spoken of in horror stories or imagined in nightmares. Standing fifteen feet tall with the lean, muscular body of a lion, two heads, and a serpent for a tail, the dreaded Chimera came into view. One of its heads was a vicious goat-like creature with twisting horns – the other, a ferocious lion with extra huge teeth.

The Lion roared with its giant mouth gaping open, shooting out a stream of fire as it burned the last tree standing in its way. Sarghon witnessed both armies scattering to get out of its way for fear of being scorched or trampled.

The serpent head on the end of its tail swung around, spitting acidic venom in large droplets toward the civilian army. "Shields!" Ambroas called out in the loudest voice he could muster. The army dropped to their knees behind their shields, as the oncoming splatter seared burning acid into the metal.

When the venom came in contact with skin, it burned and melted the skin away within seconds. Painful moans were heard all around.

"Retreat, retreat!" Ambroas called. "We are not prepared for such a monster!"

Kara watched the Chimera from above, scorching the Earth wherever it went. She momentarily flew toward it, veering from her aerial battlefield. Holding out her glimmering sword, she summoned bolts of lightening from the clouds above, directing the lightening down at the monster.

The lightening crashed down with a thunderous echo onto its back and all around, but the Chimera shook it off as simply as if the electricity were rain droplets on a coat. "You are going to have to wait, vile creature," she said, before choosing another Wyvern from the flurry above, soaring into pursuit.

From out of the dark cloud emerged a larger winged beast, with a man saddled atop its back. It was Malock, riding the largest of all the Wyvern dragons. Sarghon couldn't hold back any longer. People were getting hurt and he needed to take action.

Instructing Atasha to fly toward the field, he finally joined the battle. *Malock must not want me near the Earth, knowing I can summon its energy,"* he thought.

"If Malock wants a battle in the sky, I will oblige!" he shouted, turning in Malock's direction.

Sarghon and Atasha flew around the battling Valkyrie and Wyverns, toward the east end of Maderian Field. *Remember, he will absorb your energy any time he has the chance. Be smart!* Sarghon could hear Ambroas's voice in his head as clearly as his own.

Atasha's stream of blazing fire was easily recognizable and Malock spotted them quickly. He sat upon a custom made saddle fashioned to the giant beast, riding with reins like a horse. Its eyes glowed orange, like Malock's, and Sarghon knew it was also under Malock's influence, doing his every bidding.

As they flew closer, Sarghon prepared for an attack, holding one hand out to utilize whatever element he desired to summon.

Atasha nervously shot both nostrils full of fire at the Wyvern's feet. The fire bounced of its coiled claws as the dragon reared back, almost knocking Malock from his seat.

"Your steed appears eager for battle, brother," Malock said with a smile. "It is not too late to join forces and rule together. We would be unstoppable, you and I. Think of what we could do together!"

Looking him dead in the eye, Sarghon slowly raised his right arm. "I only have one thing in mind, dear brother." With that statement, he released a blast of wind in front of him, sending Malock and his beast hurling backward, tumbling in a whirlwind.

The giant animal recovered, with Malock sliding back upon the saddle, gripping hard to stay on. The smile on his face had vanished. "So be it, brother," he said, flying into the air above Sarghon and Atasha.

"Quickly, Atasha, don't let them get too high above us. We need a clear vantage point to fight."

Malock flew down from above. "Up, Atasha! Straight up!" he yelled. But she wasn't fast enough. Malock gained the height, coming at them before they could reposition themselves. He shot an energy wave directly at Sarghon's chest, knocking him backwards off Atasha.

Thrown back through the air, Sarghon began to fall toward the ground, his chest heaving with pain. Summoning the wind with his hands and feet to steady his fall and regain altitude, he recovered his composure.

Sarghon flew back up quickly, wondering how he would get Malock on the ground where he would have more power at his disposal. In the meantime, he mentally called to Atasha for a joint attack. Reaching out his arm, being sure to keep the wind energy balancing him from his other limbs, Sarghon shot a stream of fire at one of the wings of Malock's Wyvern as Atasha shot fire blasts from her nostrils at the legs of the beast.

The fire was too far away for Malock to reach and absorb. Sarghon's stream hit the beast in the thin membrane of its wing, scorching the skin and leaving a large, black smoldering mark as Atasha's blast hit the creature's thigh.

The animal let out a wretched screech, as Malock whipped his head around while raising his arm toward the fire horse. *Find safety,* Sarghon mentally told Atasha. *I must do this alone and you could get hurt.*

Atasha shot off like a soaring flare before Malock could strike.

"We don't have to do this, Malock!" Sarghon called out, forcing Malock's attention back on him. "I know you blame me for many things, brother. Ambroas told me everything. It's not your fault what happened to your family."

"Everything, you say? You never had the illustrious opportunity to watch your mother slowly grow insane, or live for years while your father and your closest advisor lied to you day in and day out."

Malock sent a blue-green electrically charged energy ball at Sarghon. "No, I had my memory erased," Sarghon said, deflecting the energy to one side with a burst of air, "so I don't much remember my real childhood at all. We are both victims of the poor choices of our dear father."

Sarghon shot a sharp burst of air at Malock, but Malock also deflected it with a wave of energy. "Your devious mother seduced my father away from the Queen," Malock said. "She wanted the throne for herself! And then you came along, the bastard child. My life was never the same again. If not for you, things would be very different."

"You have chosen to believe in these lies to suit your anger. Sometimes people just fall in love. It's what makes us human. Ambroas told me something changed in you when your father died. You weren't always like this. You must find a way to come to terms with how things are and release your pain."

"Oh, I have come to terms, dear brother. And this is how I release my pain!"  Reaching out his arm, hand and fingers extended toward Sarghon, Malock shot blue-green electricity out from his fingertips toward Sarghon. The electricity caught Sarghon before he could escape, wrapping around his torso and arms like glowing ropes, shocking and holding him in place.

Malock kept the energy flow, constricting the electric rope-like coils, tightening them more and more as he spoke. "Did Ambroas tell you how my father died or what he told me on his deathbed?" Sarghon could only groan in pain. "When the great King Zavior came to me with his final wishes, he made me promise not to make the mistakes he made. Oh yes, I promised, alright," Malock said with distain, "and then I absorbed his power, sucking out the last bit of energy he had!"

Clinching his fingertips, Malock tightened the electric ropes harder against Sarghon's body, as Sarghon let out a blood-curdling moan. "Ahhhhhhhh!!!!!"

Just then, Kara came swooping in from behind Malock like a gleaming falcon from the heavens. With a precise stroke of her battle sword, she sliced off the entire tip of the spiked tail from his great Wyvern. It jolted back flapping its wings to steady itself, the bloody, spiked appendage falling toward the ground.

Malock instantly lost balance, as well as his energy grip on Sarghon, as he slipped off his saddle – barely able to hold on to the reins.

The beast cried out in pain, flapping its wings erratically.

Sarghon, still in immense pain, was now falling to the Earth, barely conscious. The wind rushed through his hair whistling sharply in his ears, his body still unable to react, still numb from the attack.

He opened his eyes to find Kara catching him in a mid-air embrace. "My love," Sarghon whispered, "take me to the ground where I can regain my strength. He will be after us promptly."

"He will not be able to fly very well on a maimed beast," she said, with a slight air of pride.

"Once again, you have helped me when I needed you the most," Sarghon said, holding her body close, as they descended toward the ground near the stone altar.

When they landed, Sarghon caught his breath, before taking a long drink from his leather water pouch. Shaking off the last feelings of the electricity from his body, he unsheathed Gladanteus. "He will have a harder time with me on the ground."

"First, we need your assistance with the three-headed beast," she said. "It is burning our troops, and too strong and fast for our lightening strikes. We must hurry, before Malock finds you."

Kara led him to the Chimera, where they found the creature shooting fire in the air at hovering Valkyrie. It moved surprisingly fast for its large size. Sarghon needed to find a simple way to slow it down without causing more casualties.

"Never before have I seen such a strange and extraordinary being. It is vicious beyond belief," Sarghon said, peering in awe at the fascinating combination of animals.

The goat head of the Chimera shot a stream of fire from its mouth fifty meters, singeing the back of an army man. "Malock surely went out of his way to acquire such a monster. I will need the help of our great mother Earth to stop it in its tracks."

Sarghon raised his sword in the air, before plunging it into the Earth at his feet. The ground trembled out from the sword toward the creature's feet, as giant twisting roots shot from the ground near each of the Chimera's legs. The roots grew larger, wrapping around each of its legs like thick rope.

The beast fought the sudden immobilizing grasp from the Earth: the goat head snorting puffs of smoke, the lion head letting out a fearsome roar, and the snake head on its tail spitting venom in all directions. The creature pulled and tore against the earthen bindings as Sarghon concentrated, growing the roots even thicker.

The beast was now stuck in one place, unable to take a step.

A striking, mature Valkyrie dressed in ornately sculpted battle gear, landed next to Kara.

"Your stories of the prophesized one seem to be true, Kara," she said, eyeing Sarghon up and down. "Thank you, Prince Sarghon for your assistance with the Chimera. We can destroy it now without further incident."

"Sarghon, may I introduce my mother, Queen Freja," Kara said.

As Sarghon bowed his head to Queen Freja, another beautiful, young Valkyrie landed at Freja's side. "And this is my sister, Tyri," Kara continued. "She is young, but as much a Battle Princess as I was at her age."

"It is an honor to meet you, Prince Sarghon," Tyri said, with a coy smile.

"And I, you, Princess," Sarghon replied.

"I see you have immobilized the Chimera. All the better. Now we can fight!"

"Don't be so eager to do battle, young Princess, there is much else in life more important," Sarghon retorted.

"The sooner you can stop this madness from the Dark King and take his place on the throne, the sooner we can all return to our customary lives," Freja said, with an imperturbable tone.

"I leave this in your capable hands then," Sarghon said, heading back toward the altar. Looking over his shoulder, he glanced at Kara, giving her a loving nod and smile. Freja couldn't help noticing the sincerity.

"You are correct, Kara," Freja said, "He is different from other humans. I am sure we will be seeing more of him in the future. Now to our task at hand. Ready your swords!"

Freja unfurled her giant wings, before shooting skyward, pointing her battle sword to the heavens. Kara and Tyri following closely behind.

They flew above the Chimera, circling it, preparing for a strike. "Kara, opposite me. Tyri, at the point!" Freja shouted to her able warrior daughters, as they followed her command, creating a triangle in the air above the struggling beast.

Trying to lift its front leg, the furious beast roared, but the thick, entwined roots held fast. In its frustration, the goat head shot a stream of fire at Tyri, who lurched back just out of range of the flames.

"Ready your swords!" Freja shouted, "By Odin's lightening bolt, we summon thee!"

The skies above shook and crackled with thunder, as lightening began to ignite all three of their swords. The lightening filled the air all around, connecting their triangle in a fantastic display of energy and electricity. Like a synchronized routine, they each aimed their swords at the Chimera, blasting huge bolts of lightening at the beast. When it hit, the sound crackled all around as the electricity enveloped the Chimera. It cried out in pain, shooting streams of fire up at the Valkyrie.

The beast was unable to run, suffering the bombardment of lightening bolts on its torso. Strike after strike it endured, held in place by the roots of the Earth, until it could take no more. The singed and burned beast collapsed, unconscious, in a foul pile of smoking flesh.

Freja and her two daughters landed, making sure it was dead. The lion's head lay with its mouth open, its tongue sprawled on the ground. The eyes of the goat head had rolled back into its skull and the creature wasn't breathing.

"This abomination of an animal is no more," Freja said. "There are still several Wyvern hiding in the tall trees that must be …"

Just then, the snake head at the end of the Chimera's tail whipped around in a last throe of death, spraying acidic venom in their direction. Kara was the first to react.

"Mother, duck away!" she shouted, extending her wings to protect the Queen from the deadly spray.

The venom hit Kara on her right wing as well as on the backside of her breastplate armor, burning into the flesh of her wing and through the metal protection.

Tryi jumped aside, catching only a small splatter of the venom on her leg, before blasting a bolt of lightening at the snake's mouth, sending its scaly, scorched face and forked tongue to a dead thump on the ground.

Falling to her knees, Kara moaned with pain. The acidic venom continued to burn through her wings like smoldering lava. Freja unclasped Kara's breastplate as quickly as possible, but the venom was too hasty. Her skin blistered and singed to the bone, Kara fell unconscious.

Malock had been waiting for Sarghon near the altar steps. On one side of the altar grew an ancient Scillian Mountain Oak, standing over four hundred feet tall and seventy feet around – the largest and oldest tree in the meadow.

Stepping out from behind the tree, Malock confronted Sarghon. "You have ambitious friends," he said with a grin. "But how does your earthen blade stand up to a true fight against steel?"

Brandishing his own shimmering sword, Malock took a combative stance. "We will see who the more worthy opponent is."

"That we shall," Sarghon said, unsheathing Gladanteus as he stepped forward. "I am not the same boy you met before, brother. I am now the man who will stop you!" Sarghon lurched forward with a strike to Malock's chest, but it was easily blocked. Malock came around with a swing to the left, as Sarghon parried the blow, coming back with a riposte. Malock dodged the return attack, swinging around with experienced poise and grace. Sword-to-sword, steel clashed on steel, sparks bursting with each blow.

This went on for several more minutes, non-stop. Occasionally each would sustain a scratch or bruise, but the fight remained level and equally matched. Malock surged forward in an impressive display of attack-and-dodge movements, but Sarghon kept his stamina, returning each attack fiercely with skill of his own.

Finally Malock began to tire. Making another advance forward with his blade in one hand, he filled his other hand with a ball of blue-green energy. Malock struck hard with his blade, while forcing out an energy blast at Sarghon's chest, sending him tumbling through the air and landing hard on his backside.

In a daze of floating stars, Sarghon sat up. "So, gentlemanly conduct is off the table then," Sarghon said, gaining his composure.

"Mmmmm," was all Malock could muster, in a low, daunting growl.

"So be it!" Sarghon shouted, throwing his free hand out in front of him, creating a swirling funnel of wind. He released it potently at Malock with a fast, determined twist of his wrist. Malock was lifted off his feet, tumbling head-over-foot, suspended in a continuous mid-air cartwheel. Sarghon held his concentration, spinning Malock around and around.

Dropping his sword, Malock thrust forward an energy wave with his hands like a giant shield, dispersing Sarghon's advance. Falling to the ground with a thump, stunned and obviously dizzy from the spinning, Malock could only sneer in anger.

Purely livid, leaving his sword on the ground, Malock walked up to the gigantic, ancient oak tree beside the altar. With a look of utter malevolence, he placed one hand on the trunk and began sucking the life from the great tree.

Malock's golden eyes grew vibrant with color. Sarghon fell to his knees, feeling the pain from within the core of the old tree. His inherent connection to the nature of the land had grown more sensitive. As tears welled up in Sarghon's eyes, he heard the tree cry out – *Paratath garoshanasta vo Eratheeneth! Shrasta ess cashereneeth!* "Forever glory to our Earth! Destroy the blasphemer!"

Suddenly, a voice cried out from behind Sarghon, "Stop Malock! You have gone too far!" It was Ambroas. He also felt the despair of the ancient tree. "Why do you destroy what you once held so dear?"

"Ahh, my old advisor, Ambroas," Malock said, taking his hand away from the tree. "It has been many years, old man. The child you recall is no more. He died with the rest of my family. You should know that. You had a hand in it, after all."

"I tried to avoid the catastrophe! I warned your father of the consequences. But I never taught you to do anything like this."

"Alas, dear teacher, I have become what I am. So, what do you make of that?"

Ambroas looked into Malock's golden eyes with disgust. He knew whatever he said would be futile and that Malock had corrupted his own mind with greed, dark magic, and a thirst for power created by the behavior and tragedy of his family. Ambroas could only beg at this point.

"Please, Malock. I beg your forgiveness for keeping secrets from you. I was only looking out for your best interest and the interest of your brother."

Sarghon, still on his knees, sat listening in silence.

"It was you who encouraged this bastard's mother to poison the King's mind from his family," Malock said, "and it was *you* who tore my family apart! My mother knew you were the mastermind behind it even before she went mad!"

Malock's golden eyes glowed even deeper orange with his rage, as one of his hands filled with electricity. "It's time I properly thanked you for your services."

"You are wrong, Malock!" Ambroas replied, passionately. "You only believe what you choose to believe. Your father foolishly fell in love with another, plain and simple. You have poisoned your mind into believing the lies you created in your own twisted head and it has turned you into a rampant beast!"

Malock vehemently released the electric voltage blast at Ambroas, who quickly held out his staff in front of him, deflecting the energy blast to one side. "You've been a thorn in my side for too long now, old man and it is time you are plucked out!" Malock yelled harshly, as he shot several more electric blasts at Ambroas, who feebly deflected each one, being pushed back harder and harder with each blow. "Besides, my plans for a new and better future do not include you!"

"You disingenuous scoundrel!" Ambroas shouted through each pummel.

Sarghon stood up, rearing his hand back in an attempt to summon water from the surrounding brook, but Malock anticipated the move. With lightening speed, he caught Sarghon in another energy coil, paralyzing him like before.

Ambroas aimed his staff toward Malock, releasing a magical blast of smoke, but Malock absorbed the energy easily.

"It's time we end this!" Malock shouted, filling his empty hand with a growing ball of blue and white electricity.

With an ostentatious grin, he swung the energy ball over his head and around like a bowling ball, releasing it straight at Ambroas. It hit him dead in the torso, sending him tumbling head-over-heels thirty meters high and more than a hundred meters back.

"Nooooooo!" Sarghon cried out. But it was too late. Ambroas landed with a hard thud against the dirt and grass, his body bouncing like a rag doll. "You animal! You murderer!" Sarghon cried out, still trapped by Malock's squeezing energy ropes.

Sarghon froze, his eyes dancing in his head, as a fog began to lift over his memories. Images swarmed back into his recollection as Sarghon instantly remembered the years when he lived with his mother in the village Ambroas found to hide and protect them. He recalled his friends, his childhood, and all the experiences that had been magically blocked from his mind. They came to him like a whirlwind of vivid pictures and emotions.

He also remembered how devastated and heartbroken he had felt during his mother's brutal murder, watching her being stoned to death by the Queen's soldiers. He recalled Ambroas had been like a father to him, a protector and teacher throughout his entire life.

As Sarghon slowly opened his eyes, now with all his memories back intact, he knew Ambroas's memory spell was gone – and with it, Ambroas.

An anger rose within him he had never felt before. Sarghon's pain came back so profoundly, he couldn't control himself. It welled up inside, causing the element of water to take over.

A violent storm formed in the sky above, swirling and howling with intensity. Still trapped in Malock's energy coil, Sarghon clinched his fists as he looked up to the turbulent sky. The rain came pouring down in sheets of water, as the hurricane thundered all around.

Fearful of his power, Malock arduously reached back to the giant tree, continuing to suck energy from it. The leaves shriveled crisp and brown, as the branches curled up and broke off. Everyone for miles, even those who did not speak or understand the Eratheen language, heard a long and agonizing ethereal moan from the ancient tree, as Malock sucked the last bit of life completely dry. It was now dead.

"Ahhhhhhhhhhh!!" Sarghon cried, the storm swelling even more. Hard rain droplets pelted against Malock's face as he opened his long coat. With his fist clinched tightly, Malock squeezed the silvery liquid absorbed from the great tree as pure energy, into his water pouch.

Seeing this disgusted Sarghon to a point where he relinquished his battle tactics. Dropping his sword to the ground and clinching both fists, Sarghon created a funnel of wind around his body, dispersing the energy coil and setting him free from Malock's grasp.

Still in a fit of rage, Sarghon sent a large stream of fire at Malock, forgetting he could manipulate its energy. Malock took in the fire with one hand, shooting it out with the other right back at Sarghon.

In a split-second reaction, Sarghon doused the on-coming fire stream with a jet of water, creating a scolding cloud of steam between them. Enraged, Sarghon went after him with his bare hands, grabbing Malock's arms. Punch after punch, both men made impact blows.

With their bodies entwined, Malock threw Sarghon over his back, sending him to the ground as both of their water pouches caught together before falling to the grass. The pouches were very similar looking: one holding water, the other filled with the highly concentrated energy tincture.

Both men sat on the ground catching their breath, battered from the fight and soaked from the rain. The storm shortly died down, dissipating as fast as it had arrived, as each contemplated his next move.

Malock then jumped forward into a summersault roll, grabbing his pouch off the ground, as well as Gladanteus in the process. Leaping back, he smiled. "You have lost your most precious weapon, brother. How careless of you. Now its power is mine!"

Jamming it into the Earth, Malock waited but nothing happened. He repeated the gesture over and over with no avail. With both hands, he shoved the sword deeply into the ground and it stuck. Malock tried to pull it out, but it held fast, immovable.

"It seems you are impotent, brother. Did you think the Earatheen powers would be yours after how you have treated the land? Nature is not foolish; in fact, it is much wiser than you know."

Sarghon reached his hand down, brushing the tips of the grass with his fingers. As Malock reached for the handle of the sword, it leaned away from him just before he could grab it. The Earth released it flat onto the ground and before Malock could reach it, the grass lifted the sword, passing it along from blade to blade, like an ocean ripple toward Sarghon.

"No!" Malock shouted, falling on one knee. Placing his hands on the ground, Malock soaked up the life of the grass all around. Instantly, the grass turned brown and died from the area where Malock placed his hands and outward toward the sword. Sarghon jumped forward to catch Gladanteus from the wave of green, just as the grass fell dead and barren.

Sarghon ran over to Ambroas, who lay slumped awkwardly to one side. He picked up Ambroas's head from behind his neck, embracing him before laying him back down. "Thank you for all you have given me," Sarghon said, brushing the hair from Ambroas's face. "I will not let him win, old friend. I make you that promise here and now."

"Even your great powers cannot bring back the dead!" Malock shouted with arrogance.

Sarghon squeezed Ambroas's hand without looking up in reaction to the hurtful statement. He then closed Ambroas's eyes with one hand, silently saying goodbye.     Standing up, Sarghon brought Gladanteus over his head with one hand. "But I can, brother! I can!" he said, striking the Earth with the mighty sword in the direction of the giant shriveled tree. The ground trembled as the tree filled out, becoming erect again. New branches burst from its trunk and fresh leaves grew from every branch.

It was returned to its full glory.

Sarghon then struck the ground in the direction from where Malock's army had marched. The dark gray cloud vanished to show only the dead trees and shrubs, like a massive, black stained road. With the earthen power surging through Sarghon's blade, the path of death and destruction burst with wild flowers. Concentrating even more, all the dead and broken trees grew forth with new life. A flock of birds shot out from several of the new trees. Where the land had been decimated, trampled, and sucked dry, now grew a lush grove of new trees and ground cover.

The look in Malock's eye was tense and uneasy. "You know I can merely take the life essence back whenever I choose, yes?"

Sarghon didn't answer. *To defeat him, you must use the elemental powers together,* Sarghon thought, remembering Ambroas's words. *Think as other's may not. What power do I control that he cannot manipulate?*

Lifting his sword again, Sarghon looked Malock straight in the eye. "Try sucking power from stone!" he shouted, shoving his blade into the Earth while concentrating on the rock beneath the ground.

Malock stepped back, filling his hands with blue-green electricity. But before he could attack, stone shot up from the ground all around, encasing his legs in solid rock. Malock moaned in aggravation, trying to electrify the stone encircling his legs. It grew from the ground like clay molding around a wire structure, encapsulating his legs and torso.

His hands were still free, sending energy pulses at the stone covering his body – but the rock held. "You think this will hold me? I have tumbled far stronger stone than this!" Malock yelled, shooting another strong energy pulse at the ground around his feet, cracking it open.

Still grasping the hilt of his trusty blade, Sarghon focused his thoughts again on the Earth. The cracks in the stone closed, as more rock formed on top of the rest, growing up and covering Malock's arms and hands.

Malock burst one hand free with an energy pulse. "OK, OK! If I surrender, what will you do with me?" he pleaded.

"You will be imprisoned and tried for your crimes," Sarghon replied.

"Never!" he shouted, shooting a burst of energy at Sarghon, who easily deflected it with a wave of wind.

Malock did this several more times, each less effective than the last, lacking force.

"Your power is weakening," Sarghon said. "No trees or animals in reach to replenish yourself?"

"So you think this is the prophesy finally coming true, then? You think you can rule in my stead? You took my family and now you take my Kingdom? Who is the true tyrant?!"

Malock tried reaching out to the grass on the ground, but it was too far away. His demeanor then changed, taking on a dramatic, benevolent personality. "All I want is a world free of conflict, a land where we all understand one another. I can bring that to the people. With my influence they are subdued, calm, and orderly. I can create a new world where people don't have to live in fear. Can't you see what I am trying to accomplish here? You can be my conscience. You can replenish the land I need with your great power. Join me, it's not too late."

Repulsed at the notion of ruling by his side, Sarghon stayed silent, knowing this was another manipulative tactic.

Reaching down to his belt to grab his sword, Sarghon accidentally grabbed something else instead. It was the small glass vessel hanging in a pouch at his side holding the venom from the Turquoise Spider. *Nepenthe*, he thought, with a new approach to the situation. *I know what I must do.*

Taking a step away from Malock, Sarghon held Gladanteus to the Earth with both hands. The ground once again began to tremble as the Earth around Malock sunk in, like a circular, empty mote. Malock was left in the center.

Sheathing the blade and reaching out with his arms, he thought of Ambroas and Kara. He also recalled an image of his mother, as his eyes welled up with tears. Drawing forth an emotional response, the empty mote filled to the rim with groundwater. Malock stood trapped in stone, like a monument in the middle of a pond.

"No one will survive the coming on-slot of carnage!" Malock yelled, like a false street prophet. "Woe is he who strays from my path. He will be damned... damned for eternity!"

Sarghon ignored the rambling, as he called out to Atasha with his mind, beckoning her assistance. Standing back while looking at the water, Sarghon reached out his hands again, focusing on the fire element.

Streams of fire shot from his hands against the surface of the water creating a wall of steam. The steam grew thick all around, bubbling up from the water everywhere the fire touched down. Before long, the cloud of steam surrounded the entire area.

"I am glad to see that you are well, dear friend," Sarghon said as Atasha landed at his side. "I need you to focus your fire on the water as I am doing, keeping the steam heavy and thick." She obeyed, shooting streams of fire from her nostrils on the water's surface.

Continuing to create steam, Sargon walked around the mote behind Malock, who was forcing out energy blasts in small waves, trying to knock Sarghon down through the steam. They had no affect.

Sarghon unsheathed Gladanteus, placing the blade to the ground between his legs with both hands on the grip. Clay and stone rose from the ground, covering Malock with another layer of rock, immobilizing him completely.

"Ahaaaay!!" Malock shouted, as the steam cloud grew so thick and hot that nothing could be seen through it. Focusing his thoughts once again while holding Gladanteus to the ground, Sarghon fashioned an earthen bridge across the water behind Malock.

As Atasha continued to make steam all around, he quietly made his way across the short bridge toward Malock, stealthily approaching him from behind. Reaching down to his belt, he found the pouch with the glass vessel of Nepenthe. Unlatching it from his belt, Sarghon held it very close to his face so he could see it through the steam. Standing very close to Malock, unable to see him, Sarghon felt his presence, as sweat dripped from his skin and hot steam filled his lungs.

*Keep the steam heavy,* he reminded Atasha, telepathically.

Still ranting and raving about the coming doom, Malock's mumbles became a whisper as Sarghon crept silently up to his encased body from behind. Inching his way around to Malock's face, still in a blinding cloud of steam and only feet from his lips, Sarghon raised the glass vessel up to his eyes while thinking of all the time he had lost with his family – all the years he would never be able to reclaim.

A tear ran down his sweaty face as he cupped his hand under the glass orb. Touching the top with one finger, he heated a section so hot that it melted a small hole through the glass. He then called upon his feelings of love for Kara, controlling the liquid with his emotions as he poured it into the space above his cupped hand, making sure not to let the Nepenthe liquid actually touch his hand, but rather hover in the air, like a globule, just above his hand.

His emotional state enhanced his control of the liquid, flowing through him like the blood pulsing in his veins. Another tear ran down his cheek as images of his mother flashed in his mind. She was crying out to him while being pelted with stones.

He stood transfixed, staring at the swirling, blue liquid Nepenthe, recalling Malhara's warning: that his emotions were instrumental in controlling and manipulating the precarious element of water.

Moving ever so quietly forward, Sarghon lifted the Nepenthe through the air toward Malock's face. When he was barely able to see his mouth, Sarghon waited for Malock to say something. *Only a drop needs to enter his mouth,* he thought to himself.

"All will be reconstructed in my name," Malock said, "All will be undone. We who sacrifice our way of life to aaahhhhh …" Sarghon suddenly shot the Nepenthe forward, directing the splash into Malock's open mouth. He licked his lips and spit.

It was more than enough.

Malock froze, staring blankly forward. Sweat dripping down his face and arms, Sarghon waved the steam away with a burst of wind, revealing himself to Malock, who appeared dazed and confused.

Tilting his head slightly to the left, Malock looked at Sarghon with a curious expression. The golden-orange color in his eyes began to fade as he blinked, squinting and shaking his head, and then looked around with his former brown eyes. "Oh, God. What have I done?" he said, dropping his jaw.

The steam dissipated, as Sarghon indicated to Atasha to stop heating the water with her flame. Covered in sweat, Malock and Sarghon stood eye to eye gauging the next move.

It was Malock who finally spoke, "I remember everything. You are Sarghon, my half-brother. I know you should not believe me, but whatever you did has given me clarity I have never known. I've done atrocious things and I must be held accountable. I abused my power in unspeakable ways. I remember it all, but… how? I thank you, brother – so much more than you will ever know."

Sarghon was hesitant, wondering if this was another rouse constructed by Malock's deviancy.

A group of black leather-clad soldiers approached Sarghon, dropping their shields and swords, their eyes no longer orange. "Please help us," they said, confused and disorientated. "What are we fighting for? Why are we here? Where is my family?" The questions became a rumble of noise and confusion.

Standing before the confused gathering, Sarghon gently drew Gladanteus. "I am Sarghon, son of King Zavior and Aubrey. I am here to help." Looking back at Malock, Sarghon touched the sword to the Earth as the stone around his body crumbled to the ground, releasing him from his earthen captivity.

Malock fell to his knees, covered with dust and dirt, tears running down his face. "I am so sorry. All of you, I am so very sorry."

More and more people from around Maderian Field began to gather. Many were awestruck by Atasha, bowing to her and whispering blessings as they passed. The fighting had ceased and the remaining Wyverns flew away.

"Take this man to the Red Room," Sarghon said, indicating to several of Direfoot's men. "And keep him under heavy guard." As Malock was dragged away, there was a buzz from above. Tyri landed near Sarghon in a panic, followed by Freja, who carried Kara in her arms. Kara was unconscious, barely alive. Her burns were deep and severe.

"Kara! Dear God, what is this?" Sarghon shouted, running over to them.

"She was hit by the beast's poisonous acid while protecting us. Is there anything you can do, Sarghon?"

His heart sank as he thought frantically. "I do not have that kind of magic. I can bring back life taken from the Earth or grow a tree, but I cannot heal flesh." He placed his hand on her still face. "Kara, my dear Kara."

Pulling away from the guards, Malock ran back. "Sir, you must come with us, or we will use force!" one guard shouted.

"Beware, he is coming to attack you!" another shouted.

"No!" Malock replied, "I can help."

"Let him come," Sarghon ordered, grabbing Malock's arm forcefully. "Ambroas told me you once had the power to heal. Is this true? Can you help her?"

"I have not used that power in a very long time, but yes, what he told you is true. I will do my best to help her."

"Don't touch my sister, you demon!" Tyri shouted, holding her sword to his throat.

"Wait," Freja said. "Look into his eyes. The fury has gone." She looked around at the black-clad soldiers. "And from the soldiers as well. How is this?"

"I used Nepenthe," Sarghon replied.

Freja took a short moment of comprehension and then understood. "Your foresight is wise indeed, young Majesty," she said. "Let him approach. It's OK, Tyri. His pain has been lifted."

After gently laying Kara on the ground, Malock approached, placing his hands on her skin. Closing his eyes, Malock gradually and steadily swayed back and forth as the palms of his hands glowed with a light golden color. Kara awoke with a torturous moan.

"Keep her still," Malock said, continuing his trance-like movements. Placing his hands over the areas of her body that were burned and seared by the acidic venom, the skin slowly reformed and healed.

He then moved to her wings, where bloody holes had burned all the way through. As he brushed his glowing hands over her injured wings, they rippled in the glow, growing back together and mending like fabric. He focused his energy over and over the damaged areas until they were completely healed and whole again.

Freja turned Kara onto her side, exposing her burned back. Once again, Malock placed his hands on the bloody, scorched skin, repairing it with his magic, as he swayed even more. Finally he finished, falling to the ground in exhaustion. "It is done," he said, nearly out of breath. Now weak and dizzy, it was clear the process of healing took much of his energy.

Weary and confused, Kara sat up and looked around, surprised to see so many people gathered from both armies, as well as a smattering of Valkyrie throughout the crowd. *And was it really Malock who lay out of breath next to her?* she thought.

"You have done it!" Sarghon said, rushing up to her. "Kara, you are alive. A moment ago, I thought I had lost you."

"What has happened here?" she asked, as Freja and Sarghon helped her up. "The last thing I remember was being burned by the Chimera."

Malock, still on the ground, arduously regained his composure. "We have Malock to thank for your injury as well as your healing," Sarghon said.

"It is the very least I can do," Malock said in a labored whisper. "When I have replenished my strength, I can begin healing minor injuries from the soldiers."

"Escort him to the temple," Sarghon directed, gesturing to the guards. The crowd was treating Sarghon as their leader, many bowing to him in reverence when he walked near. "Kara, are you well enough to walk?"

"I am," she said, walking up to Sarghon, cupping his head in both hands, a show of affection completely uncustomary for a Valkyrie – Princess or not. "And I am most grateful to you." She was publicly showing her affection for Sarghon, a move he did not expect.

Relieved that she was safe, a single tear ran down his cheek. "It was about time I returned the favor, my love," he said quietly, so that only she could hear. "These people need answers and guidance," Sarghon said, turning to the Valkyrie and Captain Direfoot. "Freja, Tyri, if you will, meet me on the temple stairs in a moment's time. Kara, please come with me."

Before going to the temple, Sarghon led Kara to Ambroas. Standing over his still and lifeless body, Kara felt deeply saddened that he did not survive the battle. "He was a great and wise man," she said. "He cared for you very much – of that I am certain."

"If not for Ambroas," Sarghon said sincerely, "there would have been no resistance, I would have been killed, and all would have been lost. He is my hero and will be remembered as such."

Leading Kara back to the temple, they found an increasingly growing crowd. People bowed, making room for them to pass as they made their way to the top of the temple stairs. With its wide stone platform, framed by the giant obsidian urns, it was the perfect place to address the people.

Once all the key players stood on the top platform, Freja and Tyri moved behind Sarghon, with Atasha claiming her own space on his other side. The bewildered crowd gathered and grew at the bottom of the stairs as they mumbled in astonishment, eager to hear his announcement. With Kara by his side, looking as vigorous and magnificent as ever, Sargon began...

"People of the Kingdom, hear me! I am Sarghon, second son of King Zavior and bearer of the Diaglyphen Prophesy. You were captured and placed under a spell, which has now been broken. And as you can see, we have triumphed on this day!"

The crowd cheered. "You are brothers and sisters, mothers and fathers, cousins and friends. We are all one and the Kingdom will be restored to its former majesty!"

Louder and louder, the crowd cheered. "King Malock no longer has control of your minds or your lands. He has been defeated and his wrath has been subdued. His control over you is no more! You are free to return to your villages, to your families, and to your lives. Your property will be restored, and I will see to it personally that your land is more fertile and fruitful than it ever was before!"

The crowd roared with jubilant celebration as Sarghon unsheathed Gladanteus, placing the tip of the sword on the marble stone at his feet.

The stones began to shake and people gasped. Fruit trees sprung up all around, growing instantly throughout the meadow, bursting with flowers and leaves, before maturing into fresh fruit of all kinds. The people cheered and applauded with excitement. "Eat and replenish yourselves as you like!" Sarghon shouted. "You deserve this and so much more!"

In keeping with the triumphant mood, Sarghon uncorked his water pouch, holding it into the air. "Drink with me; drink to victory!"

The crowd began to chant: "King Sarghon, King Sarghon, King Sarghon …" Then it began to slowly change to, "King Spirit, King Spirit King, Spirit King, Spirit King, Spirit King!"

Lifting his water pouch to his lips, he shouted, "To our new future!"

A shriek was heard from behind. "NOOOOOOO!!!! Stop!!"

It was Malock running toward him from the temple. Sarghon had already taken a gulp from his water pouch, before dropping it to the ground.

He stood spellbound staring straight ahead, his eyes swirling in bright colors. "He mustn't drink that!" Malock screamed. But it was too late.

Kara grabbed the water pouch, pouring some of the liquid into her hand. Shimmering and thick like blood, it was the concentrated silvery energy elixir Malock had been collecting from the forest and using to manipulate the people. Their water pouches had been accidentally switched during their battle and Malock had only realized it now.

"What's happening to him?!" Kara shouted toward Malock, who stumbled as he pushed past Tyri onto the platform.

"Quickly, look into his eyes!" he shouted. "What do you see?"

Malock noticed the canteen on the ground. "Good God, he drank enough for a hundred people or more. I don't know what that kind of power will do to someone who already has so much within him."

Kara took Sarghon by the shoulders and shook him. "Sarghon, Sarghon, can you hear me? It's Kara!"

Gazing into his eyes, she saw swirling colors fill his eyeballs. Fluttering his eyelids for a moment, Sarghon shook his head before opening his eyes fully at Kara. They were glowing bright orange, brighter than Malock's had ever been.

"No, No!" Kara shouted, standing back in horror, knowing what the implications could be. "What have you done?"

Sarghon glanced around with his new vision, as if seeing everything for the first time. "Of course," Sarghon said, looking curiously into people's eyes. "I understand now. It's alright Kara," he said turning back to her, expressionless.

His demeanor had changed to one of controlled confidence, speaking directly and softly in a poised, light monotone. "I understand everything that is – past, present, and future. It all seems so perfectly clear now. I finally see what I have desired to see my whole life, and now I know what I must do."

Sarghon dropped his arms to his sides with his palms facing up. Energy emanated from him as he lifted into the air, floating without the use of the air element. He just quietly rose above the crowd as they gasped and applauded.

Stopping in mid-air, Sarghon looked around at his audience, before raising his arms in a priestly fashion, speaking in a quiet, magical voice that each and every soul could hear…

"You are flawed, but imperative. The time has come. Soon you will be perfect. I now know why the prophesy called me the Spirit King, but until this moment, I did not fully grasp its true meaning. I must leave you now, but when I return, I will usher forth a future of magnificence and glory."

"You cannot leave now, " Kara gasped, calling up to him. "Please Sarghon, I must stay by your side."

Sarghon ignored her, as victory horns blasted consecutively in triumph from throughout the audience. "Where do you plan on going?" Kara pleaded. "I am with you whatever your endeavor. I will stay by your side, I insist! My love!"

Unfurling her magnificent wings, Kara wafted into the air toward him, but before she could reach him, Sarghon shot off in a stream of orange light across the sky, over the Scillian Mountains and out of sight.

# Chapter XIX

## THE AURORA

Thane's eyes bolted open. He lay absolutely still, staring at the ceiling of the room as he heard the ship's horn blast several more times. The French militia patrol ship had arrived at a military harbor in Papeete and was approaching the dock.

Once the ship landed, Thane was escorted to a holding room with a small bed, a lamp, and a modest desk. He was given a change of clothes and a meal, and told he was under guard, not to leave until the authorities arranged a proper arraignment.

Thane knew it would take time for Greenpeace to gather enough political momentum to get him out, but that didn't matter to him now. With his duel-life fresh in his mind, he didn't even care. He felt rejuvenated by his dream epiphany, calm and collected, unlike the Thane that began this journey.

He ate the dinner that was given him, then decided to check out the desk. There was a pen in the drawer, as well as some paper. He figured it was there for a reason and with so much on his mind, Thane began to write:

### *Thanes Memoirs*

*"I awake today a new person. I see more clearly than ever before what I have to do. We are all tiny pieces of a much larger picture. Humanity is more diverse than we had imagined and the brain holds untapped answers to unfathomable questions.*

*We have profound possibility as a race, but we need to become aware of that fact. As Rod Serling so aptly quoted: 'There is a fifth dimension, beyond that which is known to man. It is a dimension as vast as space and as timeless as infinity. It is the middle ground between light and shadow, between science and superstition.'*

*I have touched this place, beyond my body and this life. Could I be a conduit to another plane of existence? I know it exists. I've seen it, I've felt it – if only for short moments of time. We are moving toward a higher consciousness – of this I am certain.*

*I am free to think and believe outside the constraints of conformity and systemized belief structures. God and the energy that we call God, is ubiquitous, everywhere, for everyone – not just for those who follow the rules of religious organizations or self-proclaimed prophets.*

*As we grow more intuitive and enlightened, we also grow more fearful and foolish – the Yin and Yang of opposition. The balance of life always has immense pleasure and ecstasy mixed with vast pain and dread. Our nations are fractured and in need of repair.*

*Why must our views lead us to hateful opposition? We are ONE humanity after all. Are we not all one race? Should we not come together to solve the world's problems? Republicans, Democrats, Christians, Muslims, and Jews – why should it make any difference? Ahh yes – perception and reality, I almost forgot.*

*Throughout my personal experiences as well as those in my dreams, I know something profound lies beyond this life. Sarghon, my dream alter ego, has helped shape my thoughts and desires toward a life filled with imagination and purpose.*

*But if we represent everyone in our dreams, I must also be Malock, darkness transformed – a new destiny. I must strive to shape the thoughts of the many and open their eyes to the possibility of an evolution toward our next state of existence. I must show them a reason.*

*We are changing. We are growing. I feel the power and the impulse surging in my veins. I want more, I know there is more.*

*What would my high school biology teacher, Mr. McBraggen think of my theory of evolution now? Would he cringe at the unscientific method in which I have come to my realizations, calling me a mystic, a spiritual dreamer who should be searching for evidence of the 'energy' of which I speak? Or would he encourage me to follow my path set forth by my personal and interpersonal experiences, examining where they lead?*

*One thing I do know for certain – the eyes of the soul are beginning to open for our kind, cracking the veil ever so slightly, enabling us to glimpse a fraction of what is yet to come. We are moving into a higher level of consciousness and have been for years.*

*Be not afraid of humanity's future, but of humanity's ignorance. For that is what causes hate, war, and fear. If we do not allow ourselves the room to adapt and grow into our natural state of continuation, we will destroy ourselves instead. Breathe, feel, and see all the hummingbirds before you. They will show you the path.*

*I am on a mission of awareness, calling forth those who have felt The Aurora and know of its existence. My path is toward those who have glimpsed the light of the future. I will find you. I know I am not alone. Others will come. I strive to find the more that exists in the now – in this life and beyond. We will grow strong together and show the world that we are ready to evolve!*

*There is so much more – much, much more…"*

Thane put the pen down, staring at the paper. It seemed to be looking back at him with curiosity and awareness. The words were like orders being given by an authority of all knowing omnipotence.

His compulsion grew from deep within and his mind felt clear and clean, like a flawless crystal being held up to the light, refracting and focusing in perfect rainbows.

This was not the same young man who set off on an adventure to help activists make a statement about nuclear testing. This was an entirely new man altogether.

Glancing around the room, he realized there were no windows and only one door. He tried to turn the handle on the door, but it was locked. "Excuse me, hello!" Thane yelled, knocking on the door, "I need to use the bathroom!"

A guard opened the door and pointed down the hall. Thane walked past another guard sitting half asleep in a chair, smoking a cigarette falling out of his mouth.

He turned one corner, then another, before finding the bathroom. There was no lock on the door, the stall open to anyone who entered. He noticed a small handle-crank window in the upper corner of the room for ventilation.

Quietly climbing onto the top of the toilet, Thane grabbed the edge of the window frame. As fate would have it, the crank on the window was broken and the window could be pushed further open. It wasn't apparent that a body may fit through, but this wasn't a high security facility, only a Coast Guard holding area.

*There's a reason why I'm compelled to do what I'm about to do,* he thought.

Thane wedged his foot against the corner of the wall, while reaching up to a pipe along the ceiling. It held his weight. Thane wasn't surprised. He knew his destiny wasn't to be locked up like a caged rat for weeks until the US government was able to release him. No, he had a different future – one that allowed a focused mind to silently scale a bathroom wall to a window that hardly anyone even knew existed.

Maneuvering his body like a contortionist, he reached his head and shoulder through the window. With just a few more inches, he was able to squeeze both shoulders through, finding half of his body outside on the ground level surrounded by weeds and dirt.

*The holding room must have been one floor below ground,* he thought, exhaling nearly all the air from his lungs, allowing him to inch his chest and torso through the opening. Like a snake, he wiggled his legs through before quietly shutting the window.

Thane was now outside the building on a hillside near an air conditioning unit and parking lot. It was nighttime and the warm Tahitian breeze wafted through his nose. It was the same sweet scent of tropical flowers he had smelled when he first arrived in Tahiti, but this time it smelled different. To Thane, it was the smell of a new life.

He saw guards stationed in a booth at the lot entrance gate, as well as along the opposite side of the facility near another building. He noticed no one was patrolling the tropical hillside past the air conditioning units. He needed to move quickly before the guards realized he had escaped.

Jumping behind the air conditioning units, a feeling of awareness rippled through his body as the warm wind blew through his hair. Thane stood up, casually walking toward the hillside. He didn't run; he just walked with purpose toward the darkness, realizing fate had placed him there at this exact moment in time. He understood that life was about the connections of love we make. Whether it be family, a friend, a lover, with a tree or a bird, or those who have moved on in death to the next place, there is always a connection to be made through love. He didn't know how, but he knew everything was connected – if not physically, then once again through the unseen energy of compassion, wisdom, and love.

After several moments, Thane found himself in the tropical brush. He continued past a grove of coconut and banana trees to an exterior fence bordering the property, not too tall and easily climbable.

As he started to climb, he heard the siren go off on the base, but didn't look back. At the top of the fence, he stopped for a moment to look around. It was dark, lush, and mysterious. The sweet scent of tropical foliage was alluring and over the sound of the sirens, he heard the chirping songs of the night crickets and frogs.

Just then, he saw a small shadow pass in front of his eyes. Looking up, he noticed the dim, blue and red shimmering of a hummingbird floating in front of him. It sat in mid-air for several more moments, buzzing and fluttering its wings before heading off into the trees beyond the fence.

Thane climbed down the other side of the fence, landing softly on the moist Earth. Stepping forward, Thane knew he was taking another leap of faith – the first step toward a future he only recently envision with the help of his dreams, as he set off in the direction of the hummingbird.

## THE END

# ABOUT THE AUTHOR

Paul Bradley Sterman has been writing creatively since he was a child. While mostly a writer of music, poetry, and short stories; his dreams, wild imagination, and near death experience has led to this novel. Being an LA native, Paul is first and foremost a creative spirit, continually striving to be innovative and artistic. As a writer, he has been published in *IN-LA Magazine*, as well as a published international pop-music composer/lyricist. Paul's writing also includes musical theater: book, lyrics and music of the musical, *CHASING DREAMS*, an original pop/rock/Broadway style musical.

**The Spirit King – *A Destiny Awakens*,** is Book One of a series planned for the future, as the story unfolds with more excitement and adventure. Stay tuned!

(*You can also find **The Spirit King** as an e-book on Amazon.com)

www.ingramcontent.com/pod-product-compliance
Lightning Source LLC
Chambersburg PA
CBHW031556240626
47153CB00002B/524